ANYTHING GOES

PANTHEON BOOKS

60 YEARS OF PUBLISHING

ALSO BY

MADISON SMARTT BELL

ANYTHING GOES

Madison Smartt Bell

Pantheon Books
New York

Copyright © 2002 by Madison Smartt Bell

All rights reserved under International and Pan-American
Copyright Conventions. Published in the United States by
Pantheon Books, a division of Random House, Inc., New
York, and simultaneously in Canada by Random House of
Canada Limited, Toronto.

Permissions acknowledgments are on page 307.

Pantheon Books and colophon are registered trademarks
of Random House, Inc.

Library of Congress Cataloging-in-Publication Data

Bell, Madison Smartt.
    Anything goes / Madison Smartt Bell.
      p. cm.
    ISBN 0-375-42125-4
      1. Young men—Fiction.   2. Fathers and sons—
Fiction.   3. Southern States—Fiction.   4. Blues
musicians—Fiction.   5. Rock musicians—Fiction.
6. Bands (Music)—Fiction.   7. Guitarists—Fiction.
I. Title.

    PS3552.E517 A59 2002   813'.54—DC   2001055449

www.pantheonbooks.com

Book design by Johanna S. Roebas

Printed in the United States of America
First Edition
9 8 7 6 5 4 3 2 1

For the boys in the band
including but not limited to
Pete Ramos, Steve Ramos
and James Alonso
with special thanks to Bill U'Ren
for improving my time

and for Wyn and Shawna

Do you
know how I got this scar? Is its shape familiar?
Come on, come on please talk to me, tell me
you bit me, say you're the one who left a
mark on my arm, a little scar to remember you by,
I'm asking you, I'm begging, good God I'm pleading,
you're the only one who knows if it's a scar in
the shape of what you would say if you would talk.

From "Talk," by Wyn Cooper

CONTENTS

ACKNOWLEDGMENTS

This novel incorporates lyrics to six original, co-authored songs with words by Wyn Cooper and music by Madison Smartt Bell: "Secret Heart," "On Eight Mile," "Now I Lay Me," "Too Late," "Room Full of Tears," and "Anything Goes." All lyrics are by Wyn Cooper © 2001 by Wyn Cooper Music (ASCAP). "On Eight Mile" is a pre-existing poem by Wyn Cooper, which appears in his collection The Way Back (Buffalo, N.Y.: White Pine Press, 2000). To hear these songs and others co-authored by Bell and Cooper, visit http://faculty.goucher.edu/mbell/AnythingGoes/anythinggoesportal.htm

Special thanks to Molly Melloan, Clem Johnson, Matt Hebert, Peter Kim, Stuart Wright, Dave Rountree, Lou Trombley, and Ed Lopata for their fine work on the demo tracks. And very special thanks to Robert and Glenda Holmes for making the 2002 session a success.

ANYTHING GOES

1. NEVER MIND

Kurt Cobain was teaching me how to play "Lithium." One of two songs off that record I ever liked well enough to care to learn it. How the changes were just so brutally stupid, like they went out of their way to pick the exact wrong chords. The funny thing was I was playing guitar. Kurt was explaining to me—you got to keep it rough. Which it seems like rough was built into the chord progression anyway but maybe it wasn't quite so simple as I thought. So he was reaching for the guitar to show me what he meant but somehow the guitar sort of went tilting away from both of us and that's how I woke up.

The girl was up. That's what it was. She was so pretty. Getting her clothes. Kind of a sack dress with some discreet little flower print on it, she was just now diving into. When her arms came out of the sleeves, I touched her on the elbow, to slow her down—I didn't necessarily want her to come back to me but she didn't need to feel so rushed. She shied away from my hand, eyes spinning white like the eyes of a spooked horse, and I wanted to call her name, like you might with a horse to quieten it, bring it back to itself, only I couldn't just then think what it was. She'd turned her face away from me, toward the other bed, and when she saw the smear of snarled hair and snoring across the pillows there she snapped her head back in the other direction, dropping it so her hair swung in her face. Straight black hair as glossy as a grackle's wing, just long enough to graze her collarbones where they showed out of the V of that thin cotton dress. Long enough it hid her face. She turned around toward the door, stuffing something in her purse, her bra. I saw our faces swimming together in the mirror for a second, in the dim green water light that came through the curtain from outside.

What time was it? Daylight slapped my head when she snatched the door open, a red hot hammer opening my headache up a little wider. I was still hearing the "Lithium" run in my head, that awkward shift over G-flat, D-flat to A. And at some point I must have jumped into my jeans because there I was blinking in the motel parking lot, barefoot and bare-chested but at least with my pants on. What motel was it, anyway? This bright daylight was just messing me up even more.

"Hey," I said to her, "hold up—" And she did stop to face me for a second, barefoot too, holding her Doc Martens in the other hand from the purse. The clunky shoes looked cute because they were so little.

"Let me take you to breakfast anyway," I said. Smile felt dry and cracking on my face. "Something . . ."

"I gotta go." She dropped her head again so the black hair swung, such a sweet movement, but I knew I shouldn't touch her. She would be thinking that people might be watching us from behind the curtains on all three sides of the motel courtyard. I was looking down on the part in her hair, which was kind of unusual because I'm pretty small myself. Then following her as she stalked across the asphalt, which was soft and hot already—must be pretty late.

"Let me give you a ride somewhere?" The name, Karen, Sharon . . . Damn it. She glanced back.

"I got my car I gotta go." Without a pause. Now she was in it too, red VW Rabbit, shying away from her own face in the rearview mirror and then adjusting it to drive. I was moving up to tap on the window but she just flashed me a quick unhappy smile through the glass and almost ran my bare toes over, peeling out of there.

I waved at her tailpipe, kind of limp. Oh well.

Ocean City, that's where we were. Been there for a three-week run so it ought not to been such a trick to remember. Older motel of the type Perry favored. *They got more character,* he would say, then Chris would go, sarcastic, *Yeah, and a whole lot cheaper too.*

In a way they both were right. Somebody'd planted roses around to pretty it up and there was a fresh-painted metal spring rocker by the door of every room. But when you got inside, the bathroom was mildewed and the beds all sagged in the middle— matter of fact, we had kept rolling together in the swag of my bed, which I really thought was kind of nice, and we even woke up and did it once again before morning. So what was her hurry? Unless that had been a dream too.

Daylight changes your mind about it all, maybe. I don't know.

The motel was a couple blocks off the beach, but you could smell the salt from there, and I even thought I could hear the ocean except maybe it was just traffic. I went shambling over toward the restaurant, concrete cracked and stubbled with weeds under my bare feet, till I remembered they wouldn't want to serve me without a shirt, maybe not without shoes either. There was quarters enough in my jeans pocket to buy a Coke out of the machine so I did that. Thought I might carry it over to the beach, but when I got to the roadside of the motel the traffic started slicing into my head like a saw blade and I knew on the boardwalk, Saturday morning, it would be like I was trapped in a pinball machine.

So I went back in the motel courtyard and sat on the back bumper of the van, drinking my Coke and partly wishing for a cigarette, partly knowing it would just make me feel worse if I had one. I did wish I had my sunglasses, for sure. And "Lithium" still slamming in time to my hangover. Cobain was right, I thought then, I'd been trying to pretty it up, soften it and sweeten up a melody, when what it really needed to do was just pound.

I crumpled up the empty can and headed back toward the room, thinking I'd like to actually try playing the song. Trick was I didn't have a guitar along this whole trip, because I joined Perry's band as a bass player, but I figured I could borrow one of Chris's. I didn't have my key when I felt my pocket but as it happened the door wasn't locked. I might have been in there as long as a minute before it registered that Chris and his girl had woke up and were going at it again. Maybe they didn't know I was in there or maybe they did and didn't care or maybe they did and they liked the idea. I felt a kind of weight drop down from under the waist button of my jeans, and that sick anticipation in the back of my throat, and in one way I wanted to sit down and watch or join in or whatever—do the absolute worst that was in me. Then I caught sight of myself in the mirror again so I just grabbed my sunglasses and a shirt and went back out.

Chris had snagged his usual big-blond-hair babe, looked like she had just stepped out of a *Playboy* centerfold or at least would be willing to step into one. Last night I remembered her in this tiny white leather miniskirt and a fringy top that showed off her belly button and at the same time more or less jammed her tits in your face. The fringe had colored beads that whipped around while she danced. My girl, meanwhile, her little friend, had been a good deal more subdued. The granny dress with the Docs clashing against it—and socks with a little pom-pom if I remembered right. Not so much makeup. She wore black lipstick and black nail polish—on her toes too. But that was all. And she danced the Deadhead way, like something swinging from a hook. Eyes mostly closed in that slow dreamy sway like she was high on something or more likely wanted you to think so. Definitely she was dancing by herself, not like Big Blondie, whose dance routine was just as plainly meant to catch the eye of everybody in the room. They'd been coming in every couple nights for about ten days, with a gang of some other women and a few guys too, but nobody really paired off or anything.

Sunglasses helped, but I wished I'd took the time to hook some aspirins out of the bottle in the bathroom back there. I crossed the soft asphalt of the parking lot again, still barefoot, buttoning up my shirt and letting the tails swing loose. Ought to be enough to get me into the motel restaurant, where I could charge, because I still hadn't picked up any money either.

I caught sight of my face again in the glass of the door as I pulled it toward me, heavy on its pressure hinge. That was the face she would have seen, without the sunglasses obviously. Black hair like hers with a little wave, slicked back with the natural oil to frame big long-lashed eyes, Bambi eyes, like the girls would say. Small gold circle through the right ear and the eyes molten in my olive face. The dark skin would have made her take me for some kind of Latino like a lot of people did. It was the soft eyes and long lashes that made the face too pretty for a man. *Pretty boy,* like my father used to say, leading up to another beat-down or coming off of one or maybe sometimes in the middle. I known it without him telling me, since my first teens. Same for me as for a good-looking woman, I thought sometimes—it would get you attention all right only half the time it was attention you didn't want. And the Big Blondie types always wanted to mother me, press me into the space between their Playmate breasts, but I didn't want that. Fact of it was, I never met my mother.

Inside, I went toward where Perry was sitting at a table by himself, hearing the door puff shut on the pressure hinge behind me. I was at that point on the hangover curve where everything was just too loud, that door hinge and crockery banging and the waitress hollering to the cook and people clanging their knives and forks together—even though it really was quiet enough in there, midmorning lull and only a couple tables full besides the one where Perry was at.

He looked up at me as I pulled back a chair, his eyes pale green under the faded yellow brows. Perry had started out as a redhead, they say, but now all his hair was that washed-out yellow, yellow sprigs of hair covering the freckles on his arms. He had the local paper folded to the funnies beside his plate and he was eating sausage and eggs and grits. Breakfast was Perry's favorite meal, he always said—he'd hunt the places where you can get it twenty-four hours a day. I sat down and pushed back the sunglasses to rub my eyes a minute.

"Having too much fun," Perry said.

"Shut up and give me some aspirin." I pulled the shades back down like a visor—can't say I really liked the light. All of a sudden the waitress was at my elbow.

"Just coffee," I said. "And a large orange juice." She wrote on her pad and went off.

"Didn't work up no appetite last night?" Perry said. Grumbling because he went home by himself, I guess. I waved him off like you would a fly, but Perry wasn't flyweight. He was a solid ten years older than the rest of us and he'd always been the leader of the band.

Coffee hot on my mouth and burning in my throat. I was looking over Perry's shoulder at the traffic going silent on the street beyond the plate-glass window . . . whatever. And when I blinked, I'd see flashes of Chris and Big Blondie working, half under the sheet and half coming out. Was that just now, this morning, or last night? I remembered the time with my girl in the middle of the night when it was quiet and dark but the rest was foggy and I couldn't recall anything at all about when we first had got back to the room.

A click against my saucer and I saw Perry had flipped me his little plastic box of Bayer. He wasn't looking at me now, just folded his paper a new way and started studying Ann Landers. I took three and chased it with the orange juice. Then flicked the box back over to him, pinwheeling over the red flecks in the formica.

"Thanks," I said.

"Anything else?" Perry goes, mock-servile.

"I'd take a cigarette if you got one," I said. Perry shot me over his pack of Camel straights. But it was too early for a smoke, and I was too slung. Almost gagged on the thing when I lit it. Perry forked a link sausage into his mouth and then pushed it partway back out and gave the end a greasy wiggle of his lips.

"Now what does that remind you of?"

I closed my eyes behind the sunglasses, sucking on my cotton mouth, and here came the eyelid movies again, Blondie with Chris and flashes of my girl too. Didn't quite know how to put it all together, if it had been anything weirder or nastier than just the four of us using the same room. I'd always draw the one that didn't usually do that sort of thing, maybe because I didn't either . . . not usually, I mean.

Chris was working on Big Blondie every time we took a break, laying out the flash pickup lines he of course had to go with the loud bright lead lines he laid out on guitar. But you'd be surprised how often Big Blondie turns out to have this little-bit-mousier friend. And some pause in the conversation where she'll turn to me and go, *Oh, so you must be the quiet one* . . . that's where it usually starts. Karen, Sharon . . . Susan, that was it. There'd been a point, some time at the after-hours place we went with them after our last set, when I started calling her Brown-Eyed Sue. Then she smiled and ducked and swung her hair and maybe even blushed a little. That ice-white skin, not dark like mine. But our eyes were the same color.

The cigarette Perry'd give me was smoking itself in the ashtray. I held my left hand against the coffee for the heat, and rubbed along the joint of my thumb where it would hurt from reaching for the bass notes, because my hands are small. I had just started feeling that, waiting for the aspirin to kick in. Perry was stirring egg yolk with his fork, which I didn't want to look at but it seemed like too much work to look away.

"When you once get above Virginia they can't make grits no more," Perry was beefing. "Don't know why they bother trying. Just look at it running around on my plate."

"Thanks anyway." I drained off the orange juice and somehow I stood up. Perry kind of glared at me. He was peeved for real, I saw, not at me but something about the set last night.

"Just sign the check, okay, boss man?" I said, and I went out.

Sunlight was still stabbing down into my face when I came out, and I was starting to feel that bitter crumble of the aspirins in my belly. Allston was up on the berm that divided the motel from the highway, doing one of his nunchuck patterns, just wearing his ninja pants and bare-chested to show off his drummer muscle, or just for the heat. He quit when he saw me and waved me to come up. I shook my head, only then I thought maybe it still wasn't a good time to go back to the room.

"Oughta move around a little," Allston said. "You know you'll feel better."

I climbed the last few feet of the berm on all fours, it was that steep, scrabbling in the stubble of the grass. Felt queasy and light-headed when I straightened at the top, and my head was still thumping me too. I told Allston to keep on what he was doing while I sat down to stretch a little, fanning my knees on the warm grass and watching him whip the chucks around his head, fast or faster than he would his drumsticks. Working out or beating the drums, his time was rock-solid, muscles rolling smooth under his chocolate skin. Being a regular black dude, he was darker than me, enough that the scar over his belly showed up white across the ridges. I didn't know what it came from though—you didn't ask Allston that kind of a personal question. It wasn't the first time I sort of wished I was bunking in with him instead of Chris. We depended on each other, bass and drums, so it would have made sense that way. Allston was a clean-living character. He would drink maybe one beer for every set we played and at the end of the night he'd have himself a glass of soda water and go back to his room and eat carrots out of his cooler, I think. Didn't run with no girls on the road—never happen. He always took a room by himself on the idea he'd fill it up with drums and all, except half the time the drums were just left set up wherever we were playing.

He finished and stuck the chucks in his waistband, came over and gave me a hand to lift me out of my split. We did some karate-type kicks and punches together, then a monkey-style form he'd been teaching me while he learned it himself. After that we played push-hands for a while, trying to unbalance each other off the top of the berm. I'd never be a real match for Allston, partly because of natural talent I guess and partly because he gave a lot more time to it, hunting out different hotshot instructors and different styles and things. When Allston was going good, you just couldn't hit him—I'd rather stick my hand in a meat grinder. But push-hands is softer, gentle-feeling, or at least it seems that way till Allston's got you and down you go streaking grass stains all over your shirt while you slide down the berm. It was just about a yard wide at the top, so that kind of added some interest. On the highway side there was a metal barrier at the bottom before the pavement so we didn't have to worry about rolling right out in the roadbed to get mashed by the cars streaming by. It was a Saturday, end of the season, and people were pouring out of the cities for a last day at the beach.

Allston took me down a few times, though it took him a while to do it, and I'd laugh while I skidded through the grass and dandelions, every time I took a fall. It was true, I did start to feel better once I broke a sweat. Allston and me had a pretty good feel for each other from doing this together off and on since high school times, when he first talked me into training with him. It didn't interest me like it did him, I wasn't cut out for a fighter, but he had guessed it out somehow that it would be worth my while to teach myself how to not get hit. Like the teachers would sometimes guess at it too, even though Daddy didn't mark up my face—he would cuss it but not hit it. I guess you can know if a dog's getting whipped even if dog skin don't show bruises. But that was a kindness from Allston to me, even though we never talked about the reasons. I never told nobody none of it in those days or since. And Allston trained me well enough that now, up on the berm, when he thought he was pushing me, he was leaning on air instead and I gave him a little help on the way so down he went sliding through the grass himself, laughing and shouting *whoa* while he traveled.

"Done," I huffed, when Allston stood up. "Quit while I'm ahead, I think."

"Cool," says Allston. "Guess I'll take a shower."

He went on off to his room and I started for mine. I did feel better for the exercise—stomach was steadier and my head had quit hurting. The room looked empty when I opened the door, only there wasn't no evidence anybody had put on their clothes. Then the water started in the bathroom along with some giggling, then some grunts. Big fun was still going on, it looked like. I found my swimming suit and put my pants back on over it. It took a few minutes to figure out where I hid my wallet the night before, when it seemed like maybe a good idea, you know, with strangers.

So I walked on over to the beach and did a turn on the boardwalk, which was jumping by this time, all bells and whistles and buzzers, the barkers calling and the smell of beer and old fry oil and mallets thumping from people playing Whack-a-Mole. I was watching the girls from behind my sunglasses, half-wondering would I run into Brown-Eyed Sue, but not really thinking about it or thinking I would. I still felt a little woozy but it was pleasant now, more like a high, and it felt like I was invisible to the people I was watching, not just my eyes behind the shades but all of me. Maybe so. Half my head was somewhere else, back in the workout with Allston or further than that, but I didn't want to make that next connection. I went down the next stairs and walked across the burning sand, through the people laid out on towels or lounge chairs all shining with oil, kids digging or running and kicking up sand. Just above the high-water line I laid down my shoes and my shirt and my pants, rolled up around my wallet and the room key. People were jumping and shouting in the low surf and the gulls were calling while they dived for scraps and trash.

The water was warm where I waded in, foam sizzling around my ankles, then my knees. I walked out through the kids with their balls and floats in the shallows, letting the low breakers slap across my waist and ribs. Then came a good-size wave curling up and over me like a wall of rolling green glass, and I dived through it. It was colder, deep under the wave, then I came through it, up among the easy rollers, sucking air. I swam for a while parallel to the beach, but far enough out a lifeguard stood and shaded his eyes to study me a minute before he sat back down. For a couple hundred yards I swam against the northways drag, then rolled onto my back and floated, letting the current carry me back, my eyes closed and glowing red with the sun shining on the lids.

Push-hands is something like waves, says Allston, finding the current in yourself and the other guy and how they mix together. I was feeling pleased to have caught him the way I had earlier, which was rare enough it counted for something, and I liked re-playing it in my head. The wave lifted me under the shoulders and let me down easy in the next trough and on the red screen of my eyelids appeared the figure of my father, that first time he couldn't connect his punch . . . he swung through the place he thought I was so hard he damn near threw his own self on the kitchen floor. I knew right then it was all over, he'd never get a hand on me again—I just wasn't gonna be there where his fist was, not no more. And of course I could have nailed him then and there, he was wide open to any one of Allston's hits or kicks. Payback time—I could have put it all back in his hide, everything he'd ever taken out of mine. That would have pleased him in a way, confirmed his notion of the way things were—it might of made him almost happy. Maybe it hurt him more I didn't do it than if I had, but that wasn't why I didn't. I known all along he beat on me for other reasons, didn't have a lot to do with me myself, and if I was to wail on him it wouldn't of solved my problems either. So after a minute I just walked on out the kitchen . . . then, a year or so later, out of the house altogether.

I had this other dream, a few months after I first got in my own place, where Daddy was himself but not, like for instance he had a beard and one of those stupid hats you see in movies about England. Our house was ours but it wasn't either, and everything was like that. In the dream he was holding us prisoner and doing all kinds of bad stuff he never really did in real life, us because I dreamed there was another one, like my brother or my twin or something, anyway it looked enough like me, what Daddy told me in the beat-downs, like a goddamn Melungeon, goddamn Melungeon is what you are. Then I thought, well, I don't have to keep putting up with this. I dreamed Daddy was asleep on the couch so of course we could kill him that way and the only question was should we cut his throat like a hog with a knife or stave in his head with the fireplace poker (in real life there wasn't no poker or fireplace either one). Me and this twin person were arguing about it when I woke up, spitting salt water because I must have got crossways to a wave, and realizing then that the other one wasn't my twin this time at all, it was that brown-eyed girl. It was because of her I'd been thinking this old stuff I usually never thought about, because of love.

I swam in closer to the beach and started body-surfing, catching a wave to ride up on the sand and then running back to catch another one. That song was running in my head in time with the waves, and I could feel my hand holding down the power chords:

E, G-flat, D-flat, A . . . it was almost my voice, singing the words, and nothing else to think about because the guitar *brang* was washing it all away. But when I sat up in the sand from my last ride, I thought, *Daddy must have loved me too, because he taught me how to swim.*

I rinsed off from a shower head there by the boardwalk steps, then walked on the beach carrying my clothes, splashing ankle-deep till the sun dried the rest of me. Not a thought in my head and that was just fine. The light was changing as the sun tilted to the west, and out over the deep part of the ocean the water changed from green to darker blue. Fresh wind was raising white-caps out there, among the little pale triangles of the boat sails. A flight of pelicans came along and dumped in the water one-two-three, then sat there rocking on the waves, like I had. Getting fish, I thought, and then I knew I was hungry.

I sat on the steps to brush the sand off my feet before I put on my shoes, then strolled the boardwalk looking in the booths, be-ginning to figure what I wanted. Pretty soon here was Perry and Chris standing at a chest-high table in a stand by the Whack-a-Mole game, eating shrimp and drinking draft beer out of tall clear plastic cups. What they had looked good to me, so I swung in be-side them before I realized they were having a fight.

Too late to book without being obvious, so I got myself a beer and some boiled shrimp, and turned off my ears so I wouldn't have to listen. I could sit there peeling shrimp and eating and sip-ping, thinking my way through that chord progression again so as to be doing something worthwhile. This argument of Perry and Chris was same-o same-o anyway—even Chris didn't have to listen too close because he already knew the script. I could shut down to where I could watch Perry's mouth moving but not hardly hear anything coming out but the chords of "Lithium," with the Whack-a-Mole mallets next door keeping time and a carney bell at the end of each line, like a cymbal. I knew all the same what Perry was telling him, *When you showboat like that you wreck the whole act*, because last night Chris had been soloing too loud and too long, and splicing lines of his originals into the standards which was all we ever played, so Perry would have to be telling him now, *Don't nobody want to hear some shit you made up, they want to hear the stuff they already know they like it*. Chris wasn't saying much. He looked like he'd been through the wars and swallowed the canary at the same time, if that was possible. Big Blondie was nowhere in sight, although the trouble was probably mostly over her if you boiled it down.

It wasn't that Perry chased a lot of tail himself. He just didn't like to watch Chris do it. I went and got some more shrimp and beer because it was good and besides I hadn't had anything all day. Time I got back Perry was coming to the part about *if you want to use that guitar just to talk to the slot between some chick's legs then save it till you get back in your room—you're up there to play for everybody not just for whoever you want to get down with* . . .

I thought I could face up to a cigarette by this time, and one more beer. When I got back from getting it, Chris was gone.

Perry was drumming his fingers on the table, the two picking nails on his right hand making clicks on the wood.

"Lord, Lord," he said. "Lord have mercy." On Chris, he meant, for making Perry be disgusted with him . . . that was what I supposed. People turned their heads at the counter when Perry dropped his voice deep. He used to preach the revival circuit when he was younger and his voice would get your attention that way. It was all bogus, Perry said, his preaching, just another hustle he'd done right well at for a few years—but now it had all gone on the TV, so Perry said, the religion business was shot for a guy like him.

I lit my smoke and watched Perry suck his lips in tight and

chew at the insides of his mouth. "What do you do with a feller like that?" Like he was asking the whole boardwalk, but I didn't answer him—I knew he wasn't talking to me. I just put my mind to blowing one smoke ring inside of another, a skill I'd developed in front of the bathroom mirror back when Daddy would be out at work when I came home from school. Perry was talking to himself, had really been talking to himself the whole time he was jawing at Chris as well. His opinions about how the lead guitar ought to do was the same kind of thing as how he thought his grits ought to be cooked, you couldn't quite figure where he got them from but they were wrote in stone. It was Perry's notions that held the band together, but he could drive you crazy sometimes, and I didn't really blame Chris for walking. I finished my smoke and told Perry, "Dig you later," and I walked on back to the motel.

Chris wasn't in the room when I got there. The motel people had been to make up the beds and straighten up so there wasn't no evidence of last night except for about one finger of Southern Comfort in a pint bottle there on the glass-top dresser. Made my stomach do a flip-flop to see it. Big Blondie had come up with that out of her purse when we left the after-hours place, and we had all been passing it around in the car. Lucky not to get arrested. I could sort of chain from that memory to the four of us tumbling back into the room, and after that there still were some blank patches but it didn't seem like there had been any swapping or group stuff or anything that would specially horrify somebody who didn't usually do that kind of thing, when they woke up next day.

I took off my shoes and laid down on the neat tight coverlet of my bed and slept for almost four hours without dreaming. Rap on the door woke me up finally, and a voice calling, "Twenty minutes." I couldn't make out if it was Allston or Perry because it was through the door and I was asleep anyway. My hair was stiff and my skin crackling with salt in spite of the rinse I had under the boardwalk shower head, so I took another fast shower and then shaved and stood soaking my hand in the sink, to loosen the stiff tendon of my thumb, watching my face come clear in the mirror as the shower steam melted off of it. The Melungeon face, whatever that meant. It had something to do with why my mother split the minute I was born almost, but I didn't really know if it was her or Daddy that was one or if maybe they were both renegade Melungeons. They must have been renegades because we sure didn't associate with any other ones and Daddy seemed to hate them anyhow. Or maybe my mother went back to them, that's where she went. I didn't know, I never even knew if it was something you just were like being black or something you had to do along with it, like being a Jew. The first time some kid in school started talking how I had nigger blood I didn't know whether to get mad and fight or not, because it was plain I didn't look like the black kids either, plain enough to them at least. But none of that seemed to matter now.

Perry and Allston were in the van when I came into the dark parking lot, dim lights on the motel eaves and a crescent moon shining down. I slung my bass in the side door and climbed in after it. Perry gunned the motor.

"Where's Chris at?" he said.

"Dunno," I said. "He took his guitars wherever he went." Because I had noticed they were gone from the room.

Allston looked around the parking lot from the shotgun seat he was buckled into—big believer in seatbelts, Allston. "His car's gone too."

Chris had decided to drive his own car this trip, a bright yellow Trans Am he claimed matched his hair. You wouldn't have missed it if it had been there.

"So I guess he'll meet us at the place," I said, not knowing if I believed it or not. I didn't know if Perry did either, but he didn't say nothing one way or the other, just dropped the van in gear and steered it onto the road.

The place was on a strip toward the edge of town, a few miles out the four-lane highway. The name of it was something like Rebel's Roost but Perry called it the Black Cat. We played road-houses like that one all up and down the East Coast, following the weather, and Perry called all of them the Black Cat, it was one of his notions. He said you didn't have to remember the name as long as you knew how to find the place. The original Black Cat was down in South Carolina, a cinder-block biker joint without any windows, but this one in Ocean City was a big old wooden barn. A poster for Anything Goes was peeling off the door, with a way-back promo picture from when Melissa was still singing with the band. Anything Goes was Perry's name for us—he said it would put people in the mind to party. *Ought to call it Anything Don't Go,* Chris would bitch when his mood was sour, *Anything Goes if Perry Says It Does.*

Inside there were a few people at the pool tables in the front bar area and maybe twenty more in the big back room where the stage was. The place felt empty (it would hold a hundred or so), and you could smell the old smoke and stale beer. Later on when it filled up you wouldn't notice that smell anymore, it would be people, sweat, perfume, fresh cigarettes. I saw right off, walking to the stage, that Chris's guitars were set up there, the Strat and Les Paul too, which was a big relief because there'd been no sign of his car out front. There was more parking, though, around the back.

I climbed on the stage after Allston and plugged in my bass and switched on the amp, then slapped it around a little just to show I knew how. Perry was fussing around with the P.A. I put the bass on a stand and slung on the Les Paul, but goddamn it was heavy, so I sat down on a stool to shed the weight. They were playing a Clapton album of old blues stuff, and I followed a little bit of his lead, leaving Chris's amp turned low. The fretboard felt nice and natural to me—it was no-frets like the one I had before I sold it when I switched to bass.

Allston was sitting at his drum set—he gave everything a sort of pat and tightened the spring on his snare. The Clapton tape had run out, so I turned up a little and hit the low E hard, letting it throb till the snare talked back to it from behind me. Then E, G-flat, D-flat, A, and louder, C, D, hold on B and back to the top except Cobain, the dead guy, was shaking his head—*uh-uh, it turns around on D before it repeats*—and that was it, you could hear it in the lyrics too because even they were sort of mismatched with the chords, slip-sliding around on top of the progression. I stood up, not noticing the guitar weight so much anymore. In the verse it was all power chords, you only had to hold down the major triads, vamp it just a little. I had the rhythm now, damping a little with the heel of my hand, but the tone needed a little sand in it or something. Chris had this effects thing on the floor that looked like he might have pried it off the dashboard of an intergalactic spaceship, and I kicked the foot switches till I found something that sounded like the flanger. A little shimmer, a little crunch, and now that was more like it. . . . Cobain, the dead guy, would be nodding his head except in reality he didn't have a head since he blown it off with that shotgun. Then in the chorus you want to open it up and play more of the full chord without damping, and all of a sudden Allston was backing me on the drums and we didn't sound half bad, I thought *I like it I'm not gonna*—

Perry swung around from the mixing board and killed my amp.

"The hell you think you're doing?" he snarled. "Nobody wants to hear that Seattle crap."

So he was still in his same tricky mood, I could tell. But all right, we didn't play Nirvana, we didn't play punk and we didn't play grunge, we definitely didn't play any originals and we also (praise the Lord!) didn't play Top 40. We did play Chicago blues standards, and white boy blues like Clapton and Allmans and Stevie Ray Vaughan, plus rock warhorses from Hendrix and the Stones and Neil Young, or we might even take it a little bit country too if that's what people seemed to want. Which was in fact the way I liked it—I never was a Nirvana fancier, it was just this one odd thing.

I unslung the Les Paul, but Perry was going, "I didn't *say* put it down."

I looked at him.

"He ain't here, Jesse," Perry told me. "So guess what?"

"Don't tell me that," I said, and I went on and set the guitar on the stand.

"Hey," Perry said, "Wasn't *my* idea to play fruit-basket turn-over."

My hand was twinging me already. I jumped off the stage and headed for the front bar, taking a long look at everybody. Some more people had been coming in, mostly guys so far but none of them was Chris. Mike poured me a double shot of bourbon and I sat there nursing it and looking at my hand—it didn't seem to be shaking at least, though I could feel butterflies in my stomach. The pain wasn't *there* there, but I could just feel it waiting. When I did use to be on guitar it would get so bad sometimes I couldn't even pick up a coffee cup with my left hand, much less hold down a bar chord. Tendonitis, the doctor said, from repetitive motion. I could rest it and soak and eat aspirins on it. But what really helped was playing bass instead, which meant it had to be partly a head thing because I had to work my hand harder on bass anyway, because of the longer reaches. The good thing about bass was I could hang back with Allston and keep my head down and be the quiet one, nobody paying me much mind—except tonight it wasn't gonna be that way.

"Jesse," Perry was calling me over the mike. Ten minutes or so had gone by somehow, and I saw I had drank up my whiskey. I got a beer to have on the stand, and I went back to the other room.

" 'One Way Out,' " Perry told me when I got up on the stage. He had my bass strapped on him already. Our usual lineup was Perry on an acoustic/electric Gibson, singing and strumming or Travis-picking while Chris did the major guitar work. But Perry could play passable bass and sing over it if he had to, and it was do-what-you-have-to time.

I flipped the Les Paul to the front pickup and stomped the floor controller for clean. The basic riff was simple enough— Perry would usually play it himself on the L-5. *Bap Bap Badda da DOT dot da dadda dadda*. . . . I went through it a few times for an intro, long enough to start turning people toward the stage. Next should have been Chris coming in on the Strat with slide but this wasn't available so Allston just landed hard on the drums and then Perry stepped to the mike for the first verse . . . He had a decent voice, Perry, sounded something like Greg Allman, on a good day. Then the verse was done and I didn't quite know what to do next being that I was out there all by myself, so I just kept on with the riff over the I chord, vamped the IV, riff over I, vamp the V and back. Perry was giving me a look that said *That's pretty lame* which it was, and me shooting one back that wanted to say *Yeah, but this is supposed to be a two-guitar project* and quite a few other things as well.

I hit the turnaround, so Perry had to start singing. At the end of the second verse I thought I'd better try the solo, since Perry looked like he was fixing to kick me or something if I didn't. I could of handled it if there'd been the other guitar to keep the riff going behind it or better yet, me doing that while Chris took the lead, but it was too thin with one guitar, plus I was trying to come back and quote the basic riff fairly often so people would remember what it was they were supposed to be listening to. Two things at once was too many for me, and I got lost, couldn't hear the progression, dropped out the bottom on the wrong note and then I couldn't hit the riff again, just could not play it. I had a handful of broken matchsticks where my fingers had been, and there was sweat breaking out all over my body. I thought the weight of the Les Paul was going to bring me right down. I had stopped playing, just stopped cold, and Perry wouldn't even look at me. He was having to sing the third verse over just bass and cymbals while I stood there frozen, wondering if I was going to puke or pass out first. I was thinking I should have borrowed Cobain's shotgun instead of his song. Then my ears started working again and I realized it didn't sound bad that way, kind of cool actually. My hands came back and I started throwing in some fills. At the end of the verse Perry mouthed something at me and I knew he meant to try and pull it out by doing the first verse one more time, so we did that, and Allston smashed it out and we were done.

I looked over the room and what do you know? The people in front were stamping and hooting and the usual turkey was hollering " 'Whipping Post!' " (which we probably would get around to sooner or later). Everybody that was listening was already drunk and the people that weren't drunk weren't really listening. Same as every other Black Cat from Key West to Alaska.

Meanwhile, Perry was leaning across and kind of bellering in my ear. "Why? Why does he have to do this to me?"

This was a question that might have a long answer—wasn't the first time Chris had dusted off that way. Always after Perry had come down a little too hard on his case. If he really wanted to leave us screwed and tattooed, he would have taken his guitars along with him when he cut out, but what he wanted to prove instead was that we needed him. Which was a fact. He'd come back once he made this point, usually by the second or third set but sometimes not till the next night. The catch this time was it was the last night of this entire trip. Sometimes we stopped out at the Black Cats of Virginia on the way down, but tomorrow we were just headed straight home.

"You maybe were ragging on him too hard," I told Perry. "Could be it makes him think you don't love him."

"Jesus Christ on a cracker," Perry said. "Ain't enough I carry the son of a bitch?" His voice went down to the preaching register, gloomy and dour like he'd just had to shoulder the whole entire burden of God. "Ain't enough I carry him—he wants me to love him too."

Then Perry appeared to think this was funny because he all of a sudden bust out laughing.

"What the hell," Perry said. "Let's try and make'm happy."

So we played "Sweet Home Alabama." This went over well enough that the usual turkey started hollering for "Free Bird." We did "Cajun Moon," and the turkey hollered for "Cocaine," which made him a smarter turkey than I'd have suspected. But Perry seemed like he really wanted to mess with the guy, take it out on him more or less, so we did "After Midnight"—not Clapton-style but the J.J. way, which is right and true but also a little narcotized for the first set at a Black Cat on a Saturday night. People were drifting when we got done with that one, and the turkey didn't holler for anything at all.

Then we did "Wicked Game," to throw a curve—the girls seemed to like that one. There were more of them there by this time; the place was filling up. Almost an even-steven mix of blue-collar and college types, with the turkey and his friends sort of on the fence in between, over-the-hill underemployed frat boys with their livers starting to go bad. Chris Isaak didn't seem to say anything to that sector, so we did "Sympathy for the Devil," "Jumping Jack Flash." This started up some dancing. The turkey hollered for "Brown Sugar" but we did "Midnight Rambler," which seemed to put Perry in a straight blues mood, so we did "Gypsy Woman," "I'm a Man," "Red House," "Statesboro Blues." The turkey hollered for "Whipping Post" again, naturally, after "Statesboro."

" 'Blue Sky,' " Perry said to me off-mike, and threw a wink.

"Duane's dead," I told him. "I ain't trying that one with just one guitar." I had been holding my own up to then, was even beginning to somewhat enjoy myself, so I felt like I had a right to refuse one.

Perry shrugged. " 'Cinnamon Girl.' "

When we got done with that, the turkey hollered for "Down by the River," of course, but Perry called "Tonight's the Night." Actually what he did first was yell for tequila, then stood there waiting till it came—a water glass about half-full of something that looked like old fry oil. Perry killed half of it and showed it to Allston, who of course shook his head. Perry passed the glass to me.

"Just do it," he said. I took a sniff. I didn't know what he had in mind but we'd been up there an hour or so, so what the. . . . *Aaargh.* Never wished for a lemon so bad.

"Tonight's the niiiight," Perry sang, and hit the signature bass line. For a second I thought I was playing it myself—the tequila had smashed between my eyes like a bullet and I almost forgot I had the guitar. Then I recovered, partly, and hit the foot controller for max distortion. Perry was singing over the slow bass walk-down. *Tonight's the ni-i-i-i-ight*—*waaarrgghhh-aauuwmpp*—that last part was me. By now I was feeling no pain whatsoever, but luckily this song only has about one and a half chords in it so I could get away with almost anything. By the end I was doing knee bends behind the amp and turning the Les Paul belly-up to scoop huge bowlfuls of black feedback and dump them out over the crowd while Perry muttered and groaned the words and I wondered how much of this it would take to french-fry the P.A. altogether . . . was thinking I better pull back a little when I came up halfway out of a crouch and *there she was*. The stage was only about a foot high so we were almost nose to nose. She was dressed different, cigarette jeans and a loose white shirt, hair pulled back tight instead of swinging like the night before. It was her. Her look was clear and unintelligible (I don't know what mine would have said to her either) but still I could see well enough that whatever had happened between us hadn't harmed her, which was, I guess, what I'd been hoping to learn somehow all day. She wasn't skulking under some rock. She was out and showing her face, and looked proud of it.

I wanted to play something just for her, something to show I got that message, but Perry was going to take us on break, I knew, once this one ended. I straightened up, holding the feedback crescendo still, while Perry stared at me wondering when I'd ever let it drop. They had opened the second bar in the band room and I saw Chris was standing there with of course Big Blondie. I felt relieved, a little disappointed too. This would be my last one. "Brown-Eyed Girl"—Perry wouldn't sing it; "Beautiful Brown Eyes"—too country for tonight; "Brown Eyes Blue"—not without Meredith. Then I found it, or my hand did; I could just swing over on the same note into A minor. I was already playing the hook and Perry was giving me the hairy eyeball, but he was stuck, he had to sing it now or else look stupid.

Didn't matter it wasn't my voice singing, I was talking with the guitar, my fingers humming on the strings and my eyes connected straight to hers. I took the middle solo close to the sound barrier as it would go, hand running deep in the cutout. I saw the sound wave lifting her wings, billowing the white cloth of her shirt, like she was standing in a wind tunnel or a cyclone. *Like a hurricane . . .* Perry was belting it out. She twirled, a maple seed in a windstorm, and I lost her in the crowd. I held that last note hanging in the air like a sheet of hammered foil, till Allston shattered it with a cymbal smash and the shreds came glittering down on everything like snow.

"We'll be back," Perry was saying. The Les Paul was on the stand and I was down, pushing through the people toward the back bar. A couple of strangers said stuff to me—my ears were ringing and I couldn't hear, but they were smiling. A bartender stuck on a Little Feat tape, which sounded thin and far away. I had a cigarette stuck in my mouth and was feeling for a match, but at the bar Chris snapped his lighter and waved me over for a drink, which I was more than ready for. The girl was gone, but it didn't matter.

2. MY SOUL IS POOR

The guitar was still right where I'd last left it, hanging with the rest of the Gibson acoustics in the back room at Showbud. I circled it a while before I took it down, watching the other guys casing other guitars, watching George watch me from the cash desk with that *Oh yeah* look on his face. He'd seen me do the same thing before, too many times, I guess, by him. The guitar was an old Hummingbird, but a little scuffed-up to bring the vintage price: pale thumb track down the back of the neck and some scarring of the wood around the pick guard. The back side of the body was in better shape than you'd expect—no buckle scars to speak of and the inlay was all there. I always liked the inlay on a Hummingbird, thin double line like dashes on the highway; it repeated the path of the neck on the body in a way that seemed like it would almost lead your hand.

I slipped it down from the hook and sat down on one of those little wooden stools they always have handy. It was in good tune, or good enough. I played "Wayfaring Stranger," one verse, one chorus, a run on the fifth position and chimed out on the twelfth. George was drifting my way by that time.

"Hey, Jesse . . . back in town I see." Bored.

"It come with a case?" I said.

George jerked his eyebrows up. I reached in my shirt pocket and pulled out the fold—almost new money but not so new it stuck together. Hundred-dollar bills every last one of them.

"Well goddamn," said George. "Wait till I get that case for you right now."

The case was old as the guitar, I think, a solid black hardshell with the wood showing through in places. The top was marked with patches where stickers had been taken off and the handle was soft leather that felt easy on my hand when I carried it out onto the street. Still warmish weather, the first of October; I didn't need to zip my jacket. A little wind was blowing up Lower Broad from the river, and I walked down toward it, sidestepping a couple of panhandlers. Just a few tourists were wandering around on the usual circuit between the old Opry House and the Alamo, mostly dressed in that same old ridiculous western wear, plus a few regular suits coming off work from downtown Nashville and headed over to Merchant's for drinks. I was wondering a little about what stickers might have been on the guitar case, where the guitar had been its last time out and how it ended up back at Showbud. It wasn't a guitar you'd be glad to give up, but it was money if you had to cash it in. A lot of money—it took just about all what I'd made on the summer tour with Perry, though I kept back something to cover gas and food till we went out again. Held back just enough, I hoped.

There was music coming out the door of Tootsie's—fairly bad music but I went in anyway. Got a grunt from the the hundred-year-old barmaid when I went up to the counter. I took a long-neck Bud to a table in the back and sat down, guitar behind me, against the wall. The place was middling full already, and people were drunk though it was barely past five, stomping and shouting for the old chestnuts. I knew the guy on the stand a little bit, not well enough to call his name. He was playing old Johnny Cash stuff mostly, making a pretty bad job of it. Too loud—the place was so small you didn't hardly need an amp even, but they had one just the same. I couldn't think now what I'd come in there for.

What's-his-name finished off his set by limping through "Folsom Prison Blues," bass line dragging like a man with a broken leg. He stuck his guitar on the stand and came over to my table, collecting his bottle of free beer from the bar on the way.

"Jesse," he said, and swigged from the long-neck. He was looking at the guitar case behind my chair legs against the wall. "You buy something?" He was an old longhair, gray strings of it hanging out the back of this old beat-up cowboy hat down his back. I wished I could of said his name, even though the conversation didn't really require it.

"Hummingbird," I said.

What's-his-name made a silent whistle. "Musta had a good trip, hey?"

"Good enough . . . Hope so, anyway." I didn't much feel like talking about it, I was finding out, or the guitar, either one.

The chair across from me switched around so whoever'd been sitting there last could watch the bandstand up by the door, and What's-his-name threw a leg over the seat and sat down wrong way to, leaning toward me with his arms folded over the chair back.

"Sit in if you want to when I start back up," he said. "Try that sucker out."

I could feel my head shaking, even though I must have had it in the back of my mind when I went in there. But I was out of the mood now. A stitch of pain started up in the joint of my left

31

thumb and I laid my wrist against the cool wall of my beer bottle. "I can't stay," I said.

"Suit yourself," said What's-his-name. "Could I get a cigarette off you?"

I left before he started playing again, carried the guitar up to where I had parked on a coin lot about half a block behind the Ryman Auditorium. Perry's old beater truck was stone-dead when I turned the key, and I had to raise up the hood and diddle the battery cables before I could get it to crank. Perry had a bunch of these old wrecks out in the tall grass in front of his house and it was anybody's guess which one might decide to operate itself on any particular day. But once this one did turn over it ran smooth enough. I jumped on the interstate and headed south with the breeze coming in nice through the open windows, the guitar heeled over on the seat beside me. It wasn't but about twenty minutes to the get-off to Perry's place.

Twilight was settling in when I came rattling across the cattle gap and up the dirt drive toward Perry's house, and a few lightning bugs were winking in the seed tops of the grass, grown three foot high. It was about a hundred yards from the gate to where the house sat at the top of a low rise, and I pulled the truck over about halfway and parked beside a couple of other car hulks resting there in the weeds. A couple of dogs came out from under the porch when I cut the motor, but when they saw who I was they went back underneath without barking.

The house itself was a big two-story brick with Greek-looking columns out in the front. It must have been a grand house at one time, though now you could hardly tell by looking if anybody even lived there. Perry left old washers and stoves and mess like that laying on the porch and in the yard with the car hulks. It was security, he said, along with the dogs, for the stuff he had inside, which was instruments and sound equipment—Perry wouldn't have a TV. He didn't bother with an alarm system because he said by the time the cops could find the place somebody would have time to rip everything off and cook supper and eat and wash the dishes, except of course they wouldn't wash the dishes probably, Perry said. The dogs were mutts, a mean mix of Rottweiler and Airedale and Doberman; they were all right if they knew you but they could be rough with strangers.

Perry wouldn't mow the front—part of the same program, though he said it was just too much trouble to bush-hog around the hulks. I had took a swingblade when we got back and cut a path from where the drive played out to the porch steps so we could get through there without being eaten alive by the chiggers. I carried the guitar across that way now. Crickets were singing in the grass, but when I pushed the door open I heard canned music.

"Jesse," Perry said, slurring a little around a big fat joint he had stuck in his mouth. I said hello and put the guitar down by the door, sort of hoping Perry might not notice it. I checked around to see who else was attending the pot party, but the room was empty but for us two—just a bunch of rusty mismatched chairs scattered over the bare wooden floor. Perry wasn't much for furniture either; most of what he used looked like it could of come off a dump, and probably had. But the stereo was state-of-the-art and it was playing Emmylou Harris, *Wrecking Ball*.

I took a polite hit of the doobie when Perry offered, blew it out pretty quick and passed it back to him.

"Finally bought it, did you?" Perry looked at the guitar case. "Figured you'd been sniffing around it long enough?"

I opened the case and pulled out the Hummingbird to show it off—nothing else to do really.

"Pretty," Perry said.

I sat down on a three-leg stool with a pie wedge out of the top. Emmylou was moaning on the stereo and I found the scale and chimed in behind her. The guitar was in as good tune as I thought.

> When I die, don't cry for me,
> In my father's arms I'll be . . .
> Wounds the world laid on my soul
> Will all be healed and I'll be whole . . .

Old mountain hymn with some of the same feel as "Wayfaring Stranger," and I could use some of the same licks on it, though it was a different chord progression in a different key.

"Sweet," Perry said. Did he mean the guitar or my playing or something else altogether? He was listening close, and nodding his head. When the roach he was holding burned down to his fingers he flinched, and stubbed it out in the ashtray on the floor by his chair leg, alongside the matches and the dope sack.

"What a shame she's lost her voice," Perry said, and clucked his tongue.

Emmylou sang:

> So don't weep for me, my friend
> When my time below does end . . .
> For my life belongs to him
> Who will raise the dead again . . .

The voice was raw, true enough, but I might have put it down to the feeling—which was coming through good and strong, I'd of said. But now Perry had mentioned it I could hear how she was cracking a little, or dodging the high notes. I followed the chorus melody on the guitar.

> It don't matter . . .
> Where you bury me . . .
> I'll be home and I'll be free . . .
> It don't matter . . .
> Anywhere I lay . . .
> All my tears be washed away. . . .

The song was over and Perry clicked off the CD and started hunting through his vinyl albums, which he had a couple of thousand all alphabetical in milk crates going halfway to the ceiling, which was about as high as he could reach.

"If you heard her in her prime," he was muttering, and then he found what he was hunting and loaded the platter. The turntable was one of those high-tech jobs that stood on its edge so you could see the record going around like it was the face of a clock. Perry fussed with the EQ sliders to roll off that high-frequency vinyl crackle, and Emmylou's voice came up young and full and strong.

> I am a poor . . .
> Wayfaring stranger . . .
> Traveling through . . .
> This world of woe—
> There'll be no sadness . . .
> Toil or danger . . .
> In that bright land . . .
> To which I go—

Seemed like a sweet coincidence. I picked up the melody on the Hummingbird, hardly thinking about it.

"See what I mean?" Perry said. In fact I didn't, and didn't much want to—figured it was just dope talking anyway. Perry wouldn't smoke while we were on the road, at least not much and not frequent, but back at the ranch he could get pretty weird sometimes, with these long pothead lectures. Maybe he thought he was still preaching, I don't know. He shunted the album cover over the board floor toward my feet, so I could look down and see the picture of young Emmylou in jeans and white tooled boots and long straight hair parted in the middle, hippie-style. She was posed in front of a split-log house with smoke coming out the chimney, but she didn't look exactly natural there. The guitar solo came up on the record and I muted my strings with the heel of my hand so I could listen.

"Sounds like Tony Rice," I said finally.

Perry nodded. "That's 'cause it is Tony Rice," he said. And Emmylou took up singing again. I held the guitar still and just listened.

I'm going there . . .
To see my father . . .
I'm going there . . .
No more to roam—
I'm only going . . .
Over Jordan . . .
I'm only going . . .
Over home—

Sweet and pure, sure enough, but I thought there was something missing, compared to the other. She was hitting all the notes clean as you please, but she didn't seem to be hitting anything else. Something like that.

"Now Tony Rice," Perry said as he turned off the record and flipped open the box of a different CD, "has been going in the other direction." What came up this time was "Wayfaring Stranger" again. His singing job was no better than passable, but the guitar . . . I couldn't have followed his line in a thousand years. Screw it, I thought—I'd learned a good deal from Perry's little musical tours, over time, but I was out of the mood for where this one was headed. Listening to somebody as good as Tony Rice only makes you want to give your guitar away to somebody who could play it right, and here I had just bought a new one that day.

Hell, I was a bass player, anyhow. I put the guitar in the case and closed it. The pain stabbed at the root of my thumb when I snapped the catches. Perry was changing CDs again and we were back where we started from—"All My Tears."

"Break your heart," Perry said, nodding a little with the beat. "If she could get the voice she had then together with what she knows now . . ."

That got me almost annoyed enough to say what I thought— that *Wrecking Ball* was a great album, that Emmylou was singing truer now than she ever had and never mind if she'd lost a little something off her range, and that nothing anybody said could take any of that away from her. Almost but not quite. One great advantage of living with Perry was that I never had to bother polishing my own opinions. It was just as easy to use his.

He turned from the stereo and looked right at me. "Ain't that life for you, now? When you once gain the knowledge, come to find out you lost the wherewithal."

"The hell you think I need to hear that for?" I said. And I snatched up my beer and slammed out to the porch, surprising

myself a little, maybe. Perry would be watching my back with a
Wha'didIsay? look on his face—I didn't need to turn my head to
know it.

Must not of gone off the place for about two weeks or so after that.
There wasn't much of anywhere I really needed to go. It was more
than two hundred acres of land Perry had out there, though more
than half of it was in woods. He had rented out the cleared land to
a truck farmer who also ran some beef cows on the pasture. This
farmer lived in another house on the road front around the bend
from where Perry lived at himself, and he also looked after a couple of horses that belonged to Perry, big ponies really, so gentle
you could ride one with nothing but a halter.

We had picking rights on the truck garden and even in October there was still stuff coming in, late tomatoes and corn and
black-eyed peas. The turnip greens were starting to come in—
Abel, the farmer, would replant part of his garden in turnip greens
late in the season and sell them in North Nashville after the frost.
Perry would get a beef every year off this deal as well—he had a
couple of freezers out in this old falling-down barn, all full of
packaged-up meat. So you didn't hardly have to go to the store except for cigarettes and beer.

Trails went running back up in the woods if you want to ride
a pony back up that way. There was a little pond back up in there,
and Perry's land went on past that to the top of the ridge and clear
down the other side. If you went far enough in that direction you
would come to a place where a whole lot of pot plants were growing in amongst some patchy scrub cedars. These plants were a
little too regular and a little too many of them for me to really
credit they had got there by accident. I said something to Perry

when I first ran up on them, in case maybe he didn't know about it, but all he did was tell me to stay clear of there. We didn't have no picking privileges on the dope as far as I knew. I don't know if what Perry smoked came from out there—it would have been some mighty hard-hitting home-grown, but on the other hand I never knew Perry to use it unless he was on the farm. My best guess was that it was some kind of other-way-looking type of a deal—a bit more private than his arrangement with the farmer on the front end of the place. There was a dirt track that would take you out of that cedar patch to a whole nother road that didn't even connect to the one Perry's house was on, and if there was to have been a bust it would have been hard to prove that Perry knew anything about it, especially with how much he was out of town and all.

It was a big mystery how Perry had come by that place to begin with. I had heard other people ask him about it but I never heard him give out much in the way of an answer. Some people claimed to know that he had made a stack of money back when he was supposedly on the revival circuit and bought the place with that. Some claimed that he had inherited it someway or other. I didn't much think it mattered myself. I was happy to have the run of the place and that was all.

Every time we came in off of one of those road trips, it was like my ears would be ringing for at least a couple of weeks—it would take me that long to get used to not hearing either the P.A. or the highway sounds, about every minute I was awake. Allston and Chris would usually keep on like we had been doing—go out to hear somebody most every night, circle the bars and the clubs downtown. Whereas Perry and I would mostly just hole up for a while. I could have of course gone running the music spots with Allston or Chris or by myself even, raise some pin money playing pickup here and there. Free drinks and free women at the very least. But I was out of the mood for all that somehow—overdosed, I guess. Besides which I couldn't play anyway, because the day after I bought the Hummingbird my thumb locked up on me so bad I couldn't even lift a coffee cup with my left hand.

That morning, when I went to pull a carton of orange juice out of the fridge, the pain shot clear up to my shoulder and I almost dropped the thing on the floor. Managed to clutch it up with my other arm, halfway before it hit. Again. Tendonitis, the doctor had said. It would go away in time, he said. Trouble was, it also would come back.

The first two or three days I went at it head to head. I took the Hummingbird out or got down my bass and tried to play enough to prove I really couldn't play a lick. You can't do much on a fretted instrument without your thumb. I folded it under and tried to figure out a way to brace against the knuckle but it was useless—I could barely hold down a note, much less a chord. Then hot soaks with Epsom salts, and of course handfuls of ibuprofen. Every couple of hours from when I woke up in the morning I'd need to test it, try spanning a milk jug or a guitar neck just to prove to myself the pain was as bad, as crippling, as it had been an hour before.

This never had happened to me out on the road, but what if it did? You wouldn't have to be a genius to figure out the answer— I'd be out of my job as quick as that. Nothing to do but figure out some other way to make a living, that could be done with a hand and a half, I supposed. And if it got worse instead of better, if it spread to the other hand too? Didn't take much of that kind of thinking to put me in a fairly bad mood.

After a couple of days of doom and gloom I did what I knew I'd end up doing all along, which was tear off a piece of duct tape and bind the bad thumb up to the rest of my hand. Let it rest and heal itself. Don't do anything that hurts. The splint job left me about an inch of pinch-grip and as long as I didn't want to play music I could fumble my way through most other things.

With the tape on my hand I couldn't hide it from Perry. He wasn't the type to go slobbering sympathy all over you, though. He said he reckoned it would get better and then he didn't say anything more about it, which suited me fine.

Perry was in an iffy mood himself these days, it seemed. Restless. He got me riding into town with him nights, checking out the little music places—where he was even sitting in once in a while himself. This was unusual for Perry; when he was off he was off, he liked to say. We would run into Chris or Allston once in a way down there, but not on purpose. I got the idea that Perry was almost trying to avoid Chris. He was looking for something else, listening for something, and what it was he didn't know himself. There'd been a kind of dead spot in the band since Melissa dropped out, and I thought Perry must be groping around for something he could put there, before it came time for us to head south.

Of course I'd get asked to sit in too, some of these times, but there was no way I could do it. I didn't like saying the real reason why. Carrying that taped-up hand into the music spots was like trailing a limp through a rough neighborhood—bleeding in the water. I kept my left hand in my pocket and claimed I wasn't in the mood.

Back at the ranch, things were pretty slow. There wasn't a whole lot to do all day. I slept a good deal, I guess. I must have used to spend more time practicing than I gave myself credit for. Perry didn't keep a TV, and you could only read so many hours a day. I was nervous to ride the ponies, with the hand, but I would take long walks in the woods, or go fishing in that little pond. One weird day I started off in that direction without even a pole. My mind was running the way it would: What if the thumb didn't get no better? What was life gonna be like from now on, with one hand and a flipper?

I stopped off in that ramshackle barn partway up the hill and pulled myself a cold beer out of the extra fridge Perry kept there with the freezers. I drank it there in the shade of the loft, sitting on the edge of these square hardware-cloth cages that were raised up on four-by-four stilts to about waist-high. The story was that Perry used to catch rattlers and keep them in there, in between his preaching days and now. Never handled the snakes himself, he said, just furnished them to churches that did. I wasn't sure if I believed this part. Then again he could of been pulling my leg about the whole thing—those cages would have done just as well for rabbits, say. Still there might be some money in a snake business like what he described and he wouldn't have had to go too far to find a church that handled them.

The cages were half-full of dead cans now, waiting on a recycling haul. I tossed my empty in on top of the rest and walked up the hill through the pasture. Once, I turned back and looked down at the cows grazing, lower toward the road fence. It was cool enough you could climb the grade without breaking a sweat at all. I climbed over the woven-wire fence by a locust pole and went up through the woods, following an old rock-wall fence that straggled uphill with a trail beside it. Further up there was a three-strand barb-wire fence I could just duck through and soon after that I was at the pond.

I sat down with my back leaning on this big old oak on the high side of the water. There were acorns all over the ground around there and I scrabbled enough of them up to have a smooth place to sit, then flicked them one at a time into the pond and watched the ripples spread. The pond was all overgrown with weeping willows around the bank and so silted in there was not hardly anything in it but snapping turtles and frogs, probably. When the acorns gave out I sat still and let my mind go empty. The wind blew and the low hanging fronds of the willow moved trembling over their reflection in the water . . .

I came off the nod when I heard voices, one voice plain at least. It was rare to meet anybody you hadn't brought with you, up that way. I wondered if it could be the dope growers, but they wouldn't have much call to come on this side of the ridge. Or deer hunters, more likely, though Perry's land was posted. Either way, I thought I'd rather have the drop on them than them on me. I moved away from the pond into the thicker trees and circled down toward where the voice started and stopped and started again, moving slow and quiet as I could over the dry sticks and stuff fallen from the trees. It was hard to fix just where the voice was because it was coming across the water.

I couldn't make out what it was saying. It almost seemed to have a tune to it somehow. Then I came out from around this big old pin oak and jumped back like you will when you see a snake you're not expecting to. It's hard to get over that first reaction even if you are somebody who likes snakes, which I always like them well enough so long as they're not poison and don't take me by surprise. This thing must of been four or five feet long and it was up in the air all twisting around, balancing on Perry's arm. It wasn't a rattler, that much I could see right off. It had the red and black markings that are just about the same for a common water snake, which is harmless, or a copperhead, which will kill you graveyard dead. Only way to tell them apart except getting bit is that the pupil of the water snake's eye is round (Perry told me this, naturally), but the pupil of the copperhead's eye is slitty. Of course if you're close enough to see that difference you're liable to get bit anyhow. I was plenty too far off to know one way or the other and just as happy about that too, but Perry and this snake were eye-to-eye. They looked like they were trying to hypnotize each other. Perry didn't even have hold of the thing. It was just balancing there on the back of his wrist, snaking its diamond head around. If you lift up a snake around the midsection its natural idea is to try to balance itself, instead of coming after you. This was some more of Perry's snake information—from the look of things now, it appeared to be true.

Perry had his back to me, so I don't suppose he knew I was there. He spoke to the snake in his stadium voice.

"Son of Hell," Perry said. It would have woke you up in the back pew. "Who first allowed you into the garden?"

The snake didn't seem to have no answer to this. Perry had told me snakes were pretty well deaf anyway, meaning they could probably hear me playing the bass but they couldn't hear Emmy-lou Harris singing. But then Perry started singing himself, in a weird high quavery voice that was nothing like I'd ever heard him do onstage. I caught myself looking around to see if somebody else was there.

> Oh my Lord . . .
> Please don't forsake me . . .
> This is yore child . . .
> I'm tired and sore . . .
> Oh my Lord
> Can't you hear me?
> I need yore love . . .
> My soul is pore . . .

Some kind of spooky stuff like that. I guess I wouldn't have thought it was spooky if I had been listening to it in a bar. But it was nobody but me and Perry and the snake, and I felt like I made one too many. So I eased on out of there. Didn't quite know what to think. It was plain it was none of my business so I figured I didn't really have to think about it.

A few days after this, my hand did start to get better. I could go without the tape, most of the time. I could pick things up that were bigger around than a pencil. In four or five days I could play again. I got out the Hummingbird and ran my bag of tricks up and down the neck, but all of it sounded dull and distant. It wasn't the guitar's fault. I just couldn't think of anything I wanted to play.

If it was gonna be like that, why bother? I knew plenty of guys who played in bands that from the way they talked and acted had just as soon be swinging a nine-pound hammer. Easy enough for it to turn into any old kind of a job . . . Only I didn't have no other ideas either. Every tune I knew seemed dry.

I moped around for a couple of days, depressing myself with this kind of brooding. Then one night a strange car came over the cattle gap and nosed its way up toward Perry's house. We were both sitting out on the porch, me warming a beer in my hand and Perry with a drink of whiskey, and also blowing a doobie which he cupped in his hand when he saw the car coming, since we didn't know who it was. It wasn't quite good dark yet, just deep blue twilight with the first stars coming out in the sky, a straggle of cows grazing toward the hulks in the tall grass.

"Slick," Perry said, as the car parked to the left of the porch. I had to agree with him. It was a sixties Mustang, one of the nice ones, painted glossy black, like new. Someone had been loving all over the thing, that was clear. The driver door opened and a man got out and it was my father. The dogs came out and barked at him some, till Perry told them to shut up.

"Evening," he said, standing there below the porch steps. Not a big man, not much bigger than me, though we didn't favor each other much except for size. There was something different about him I couldn't quite figure—he almost looked younger than when I last saw him, or just in a little better shape. He wasn't much over forty anyway.

Perry glanced at me sidelong. He'd made that joint disappear somehow—I couldn't even smell it anymore.

"Well, come on up," Perry said. "You want a beer? Drink of whiskey?" He rattled his glass to give an example.

Daddy stood now at the top of the steps, one hand on the railing. He had come out here a time or two before but it never had felt real comfortable.

"I give it up," Daddy said. Like he had been assigned to say it just like that. "It wasn't doing me no favors."

It was real silent after that for a minute or so, except for a cow that started bellowing for a stray calf or something, back behind the house. Maybe we should have offered a Coke, but nobody seemed to think of it.

"Nice car," Perry said finally.

Daddy seemed to relax a bit. "Come take a look, why don't ye?"

We all clomped down off the porch and over to the Mustang. The dogs came back out from under the steps, not barking now, winding in between our legs and panting. Daddy pulled the car doors open and Perry slapped a dog back and stooped to look into the interior, which was all polished and perfect, even injected somehow with new-car smell, which was quite a trick considering the car was around thirty years old. He must have taken a long time, babying this thing for some special customer. We looked a minute more and then Daddy popped the hood and we all stood around admiring the engine. Perry whistled.

"Cherry," he said.

"Man," I said. "You been over this thing with a toothbrush, ain't you?"

"Try her out," Daddy said. I saw he was dangling a key tag, and I realized he was talking to me. Next thing I knew I was watching Perry shrink in the rearview mirror as I aimed the car back down toward the road.

Five minutes later we were flying up the interstate. This car had some muscle, not to show off but it was there if you wanted it. I let up on the gas a little, reached for the radio. When it came on it rocked me back in my seat. It looked like the radio original with the car but that sure wasn't what it sounded like.

"Loaded up the sound system, huh?"

"Got one of them big bass speakers in the trunk," Daddy said. He pointed under the dash. "I put in a cassette player too. It slides out if you don't want to leave it in the car."

I wondered a little over that—he'd never been much of a music lover that I knew of. Special order, must be. I cut the radio off and we rolled along listening to the nice even hum of the engine. It had been full dark for a while now, and the road felt smooth as black glass.

"There's this singer," my father said.

"Yeah?" I looked over, could only see the outline of his face in the dark, staring down the road ahead, into the pools of headlight.

"Over to East Nashville," he said, a little impatient, like we had already talked about this and I was being slow. "You want to go listen?"

I took another look at him and figured why not? See what other mysteries he had run up his sleeve.

He piloted me to the Woodland Street Bridge, and we crossed over the river. I had not hardly been over that way at all since I moved out from him, and when I looked down at the lights shining on the water, I started to feel kind of low. This sinking feeling got worse when I found out where we were going, which was a no-hoper roadhouse just a couple miles straight out Woodland Street from the bridge and downtown Nashville—no more than a long low shack with blacked-out windows, and straggling block letters in drippy white paint on the walls, telling about LIVE MUSIC and LADIES NIGHT and so on. I turned off the car and sat there listening to it tick and wondered what was giving me the weirds. The place wasn't that different from what you'd find downtown except it was too far off the beat to draw tourists. Aside from which it was a classic Black Cat, really. I'd played in a thousand places just like it.

I got out and made to pass the keys to Daddy across the roof of the car, but he waved them away.

"You hold them," he said.

We crossed the street toward the door of the bar, together but not too close, both of us feeling a little edgy I suppose. When we went inside I figured out what was bugging me. I had not been in there more than a time or two probably but I knew it as a place Daddy used to come home drunk from.

Inside was the usual Black Cat setup: bar with the beer signs and gag posters, a dozen or so wobbly tables and chairs, and toward the back two coin pool tables about the size of motel bathtubs. Place was about half-full of people from the neighborhood, even a couple I could recognize from what used to be my street. The bandstand was just a corner of the room with some amps and a drum kit and a dust-crusted P.A. that looked like it probably didn't work. Nobody was playing the drums but they had two longhairs with jail tatts on their stringy arms, knocking out an up-tempo blues on bass and guitar. In front of them was this woman with long dark halfway-matted hair, stone country-looking down to the floor-length gingham granny dress she had on. I sort of wanted to look at her feet to see if she was wearing shoes. But the first thing I noticed was she was so pregnant I figured she might have the baby when the band went on break. She wasn't singing anything yet; she was rocking on her heels and looking at the microphone in her hand like she expected it was gonna talk back to her. The way the mike cord waved around sort of reminded me of Perry with that snake.

Meanwhile Daddy was gladhanding his way through the room. Most people appeared to know him, including the bartender. I went over and took a long-neck Bud. The bartender looked at Daddy, who didn't say anything at first.

"Well, give me a goddamn O'Doul's," he said finally. The bartender chuckled at him as he paid.

We sat down at a free table; I crawled underneath and wedged a matchbook under one leg to stop it wobbling. When I came back up Daddy was pulling on his near-beer with kind of a sour expression on his face.

"You really quit drinking, huh?" I said.

"Yeah," Daddy said. "I been going to that AA."

I nodded. "You like it?"

"Hell no I don't like it," Daddy said. The edge on his voice made me want to take a long step back, maybe keep on stepping. But after a second he appeared to calm down.

"It's better'n nothing," he said.

I kind of wanted to know more, but I couldn't seem to think

of a question, much less whether I should ask it or not. It was uncomfortable there for about half a minute but then the mike popped and the country girl was singing.

> *Well I tole you purty babeh . . .*
> *Such a long time ago . . .*

I hitched my chair around pretty quick so I could see where that sound was coming from. She had a big voice, no mistake. If I closed my eyes I thought I could hear a little black in it. Whatever color, it was enough voice to fill the room, even without the mike, I thought. It even almost made you forget how lame the band was.

When she finished, somebody hollered out a request and she counted off and went into "You Ain't Woman Enough to Take My Man." I could hear more of a grit edge in her voice then, a mountain tone, with the longhair twanging on his beater Telecaster, but it was still a little bluesy along with that. Nice. She could have killed some of those old country tunes. I started to sort of wish that Perry was there to hear it. I leaned over to Daddy.

"What's her name?"

"Estelle," Daddy said into my ear, throwing the accent toward the front end of the name. "Estelle Cheatham."

Then for the next number she did this weird tune off the first Cowboy Junkies album—the one with "Blue Moon" spliced in for a bridge. And she came to that part of it, the moon came out of her mouth like a bubble blown in molten glass, shimmering all the colors of the rainbow, then breaking with a chime . . . I was broke out in gooseflesh all over, the hair on my arms standing straight up.

They closed out the set with that one. Estelle snapped the microphone back on this stand that was there and came over toward our table, lumbering 'cause she was so pregnant.

"Hidy, Wendell," she said to Daddy. "Thanks for coming out." She kind of cocked up her hip when she spoke to him, and I saw how she might be goodlooking if she fixed herself up. Supposing she got the baby delivered, and did a little something about her hair . . . She had snapping green eyes, and funny dark coloring that really didn't go with that country twang in her voice. She was missing a front tooth and her smile was a little twisted to try and cover it up.

"Sound good tonight." Daddy pulled a thumb at me. "This is Jesse."

Estelle gave the crooked smile. "Hidy." She sounded more country talking than she did singing. It seemed like the cat had got my tongue—anyway all I came up with was a nod. She was so pregnant I thought the baby was going to jump out on the table any minute. It was hard to know how she could draw the breath to sing like she'd been doing.

Estelle kind of sighed and sat down in a straight-back chair between our table and the next one over. She told me the names of the couple there. I realized the girl looked enough like Estelle to be her sister, and her last name was Cheatham too. Rose-Lee Cheatham. The guy was another longhair looked like he sucked eggs for a living or something like that, Greg, I think his name was. Estelle leaned back and crossed her legs, helping herself a little with a hand on an ankle. As a matter of fact she wasn't wearing shoes, just a pair of wooly red socks. She smiled around the missing tooth when she saw me looking.

"Feet swole up on me." She patted the baby through her gingham. "You know."

I looked at Rose-Lee to be looking somewhere else. She gave you an idea what Estelle might look like not pregnant—slender enough but still filling out her orange tanktop very nice, and without a bra, I couldn't help but notice. I'd have guessed her to be ten years younger than Estelle, at least—she wasn't much over twenty anyway. Then again it was hard to tell how old Estelle really was by looking.

I knew I'd been staring too hard at Rose-Lee now when she gave me her version of the bad-teeth smile and scraped her chair around so I was mostly looking at her back. I felt like maybe old Greg was giving me the evil eye too, so I looked off at the bandstand, which was empty now. The two longhairs had hit the door fast when the set was done. Anxious to shoot up, I wouldn't have been surprised.

Daddy went to the bar and bought a round for both tables. Estelle took a beer and smoked herself a Marlboro Red. I guessed she wasn't too heavy into any pregnancy health regimes or anything like that. There was country on the jukebox. About fifteen minutes went by and Estelle started looking jumpy. She leaned over and tapped old Greg.

"Kin you go see about'm?" she said. It was funny, the difference of her talking voice from her singing one. Like if you heard Mick Jagger talking you would think he was some kind of an Englishman, but once he tunes up to sing you know he's a black man from the Mississippi Delta.

There was a click of pool balls from the coin tables behind us, and I heard somebody cuss his shot. Estelle settled back in her chair and fired up another cigarette. In a couple minutes Greg came back in trailing the longhair bass player. Dude was still more or less breathing but he definitely looked a lot more relaxed than he had when he first went out.

"Whar's Tawmie?" Estelle wanted to know.

"Hanh?"

"Whar's Tawmie?" She stubbed out her cigarette so hard I

thought it was going to go through the ashtray and the table altogether. At the same time I sort of had the idea this problem probably came up pretty regular.

"Cain't wake him up," Bass Player said. He sat down on a chair, very loose-limbed, and showed us the whites of his eyes.

"You cain't wake him up," Estelle said. "Well shit on far."

"Have you got a set list?" I heard myself say.

Estelle rounded on me with her green eyes sparking so hot it was scary. I wouldn't of wanted to be old Tawmie, whenever he did come to.

"A song list, I mean," I said.

"Not really," she said. "We mostly just call'm out as we go. How come, kin you play guitar?"

"Sometimes I do," I said. I looked over at that Telecaster. Old Tawmie didn't have a stand for the thing, he had just wedged it up against the wall. I almost had the heebie-jeebies thinking about getting up there with her. "Why don't you just call me a few right now and we'll see which ones of them I know?"

Estelle stared at me for a second and then she nodded. Then she leaned across the other table with her arm swinging in this kind of slow lazy way and cracked the bass player on the jawbone with a slap you could have heard across the river.

"Hanh?" goes the bass player. He honestly didn't know she'd hit him.

"Git up thar," she told him. "You ain't done working yet."

We ended up turning out a decent couple of sets, in spite of some predictable problems with the rhythm section, which I solved by turning the dude's amp so low you couldn't hardly hear him. He didn't know the difference himself, but somehow he was able to keep up a kind of Quaalude walking bass—good enough, since I didn't feel required to solo much.

Estelle was long and strong on Bonnie Raitt covers, old stuff mostly—blues like "Kokomo" and "Women Be Wise" and "Everybody's Crying Mercy," plus also the ballads: "Louise," "Any Day Woman," "Love Has No Pride." She made the rafters ring on that last one; I was damn near crying myself. She wouldn't do a straight country song unless somebody asked for it, otherwise it was always something with a twist. She had a little Dylan ("I Shall Be Released"), some Stones ("Wild Horses," "Beast of Burden") and a fair amount of classic blues—damn if she didn't sing "Catfish," retooled for a woman's point of view.

When she was done she thanked me and offered me a piece of the tip jar, which I turned down. People had only been half-listening and there wasn't a lot in it anyway. She'd sung herself out and her eyes had gone dull. Long time to be on your feet, I guess, that pregnant. I gave Daddy the nod to get out of there, 'cause I wanted to miss the part where she sorted things out with the other guitar guy. After lushing on near-beer all night long, Daddy was probably more ready to leave than I was.

It had got to be one o'clock in the morning somehow by the time we hit the street. I started wondering what was the program now. Was Daddy going to drive me an hour out to Perry's and then himself an hour back to town? I wasn't planning on spending the night at his place no matter how pleasant the evening had been.

I offered him the car key but he wouldn't take it. He jumped into the passenger seat, which didn't leave me much to do but get behind the wheel.

"You can just drop me by the house if you want to," he said.

"Drop you. What?"

Daddy looked out his window, the other way from me, and started talking kind of fast for him.

"The car's for you, Jesse. I wanted to do something for you. It's nothing to do with anything else. I just wanted to give you something."

He looked at me for a second, kind of crossways. "I wish you'd take it." Then he was staring out his window again.

If it had been Perry or Allston or just about anybody I'd of reached across and touched him on the shoulder. But I didn't do that now.

"Well sure I'll take it," I said finally. "What kind of fool wouldn't?"

"That's all right, then." I heard him swallow. "It's late," he said. "I need to get home."

Ten minutes later I was pulling up the alley behind the house, a kind of crushed-looking old duplex. You couldn't tell anymore what color the paint on the back side used to be. The yard was all trashed up with car parts and stuff. The guy who lived in the other half had gathered around the bug light with some of his buddies. I cut the motor and sat for a minute.

"That's where Estelle and Rosie live at right over yonder." Daddy pointed across the alley to a house that was dark now. "Heard her singing in the kitchen one time. That's how I come to know'm."

"Worth the trip," I said.

Daddy nodded and got out of the car.

"Hey, Wendell." One of the guys around the bug light toasted him with a beer can.

"Title's in the glove box," Daddy told me. Then he was loping toward the back door and inside before I even said goodnight.

I cranked the car and drove back out to Perry's, not too fast, one eye out for the cops. Didn't hardly know what to think. Damn but it was a pretty car. I felt good about having it, that was simple enough, even if I didn't quite believe it yet. I thought I felt good about him giving it to me.

It was dark at Perry's when I got back. He was either asleep or had fired up one of the hulks and gone somewhere. The dogs came out to nose me, but they didn't bark. I wondered if Daddy showed up again would they bark at him. How many times would it take before they stopped? When I lay down it wasn't dogs I heard, but Estelle's voice ringing in my head.

3. THAT MAKES ONE OF US

It was cold in the house when I woke up. I stood by the window of the upstairs room where I stayed. The seed tops of the grass outside had just taken a dusting of frost; it would be gone by good light. I couldn't quite see my breath in the stone-bare room. Nothing in there but a mattress on the floor, heaped up with a couple of Army blankets, with a lamp and a lipping-full ashtray beside it, and then the Hummingbird case propped against the wall. That and a trunk of clothes with a half-bottle of flat beer sitting on the lid. The floor was splintered so I needed to be careful to pick up my bare feet. A campsite. I pulled on my yesterday's jeans and buckled the belt. My arms and chest were all broke out in gooseflesh from the cold, but I sort of liked this feeling so instead of putting on a shirt I fired up a cigarette, even though my mouth was dry, and went back to the window, blowing smoke against the pane and watching my breath fog the glass. We would be on the road again soon, one way or another. Perry's system: he wouldn't let a hard frost catch him here.

All that day I couldn't settle down to nothing. Tried to play a little guitar, practice on the bass against a drum machine, but I couldn't hit any kind of groove. I went for a walk out on the farm, thinking I'd snare up one of the ponies for a bareback ride, but come down to it, it seemed like too much trouble. Instead I fetched up against a fence, watching Abel run a manure spreader in the next pasture, driving it in tightening circles toward the center.

At Daddy's house, in a mood like this, I'd of most likely just set down and let the TV smother me for hours and hours and hours . . . which come to think was most likely the reason Perry wouldn't allow a television at his place. Only now what? Perry himself had gone off somewhere. These last couple of weeks he had been roaming like a dog that smelt something interesting he can't figure out what it is yet.

I loaded the Hummingbird into the trunk of the Mustang. There was just barely room to wedge it in beside that big bass speaker, but I didn't want to leave it in the back seat where it would show. I didn't exactly have a plan of where to go—just out, away from there, for a little while.

Albert King was kicking on that car stereo. "Born Under a Bad Sign." "Cross Cut Saw." That superwoofer in the trunk would really bring the bass back home. And the car was a sweet ride, that I could testify. I was humming up the highway, Nashville-bound, and there before I hardly knew it.

I dropped off the loop and drove down Eighth Avenue, south-ways again, turning down the sound considerably so people wouldn't stare as I passed by. Outside the shop where Daddy worked I pulled to the curb and watched, from the far side of the street, for fifteen or twenty minutes. I saw some of the guys I knew by sight, switching cars in and out of the bays, but I didn't see any sign of him. It might be he didn't work there no more—he had used to switch jobs pretty frequent, most often after some drinking tear. I hadn't been keeping up with that—had not laid eyes on him at all since the night he came out with the Mustang.

I cranked up the car again and drove over the bridge into East Nashville. Passed the same bar where I'd played with Estelle, then buttonhooked around to Daddy's block and pulled into the alley. Wasn't no car parked behind his house. In the next-door yard a couple of those guys were sitting with beers around a big cable spool turned flatways for a table; they gave me limp waves when I climbed out of the car. I went and peeped in the glass of the kitchen door, so grimy I couldn't hardly see through it. Still and dark on the other side. I still had a key if he hadn't changed the locks, only it must be somewhere out at Perry's—didn't even know if I could find it. I didn't bother knocking since it was plain nobody was home.

I had opened the car door to get back in, when the voice came from across the alley, dark and thick and tart:

> It's ohhh-ver . . .
> End of the line . . .
> It's ohhhh-ver . . .
> And you're doing fine. . . .

The kitchen window, Estelle's house, as Daddy'd pointed it out to me. All I could see was a pair of bare arms pistoning in and out of the sink, but even the splash of the dishwater sounded like it was keeping waltz time. I unlocked the trunk and hauled out the guitar. She was dead true to the key, I found out when I cracked the case and picked up the melody, and she was holding the note at the end of each line with an effortless sustain, like a brass-belling note from a saxophone.

Then she stopped singing all of a sudden, and the water in the sink shut off. The arms braced on the sink edge—maybe she was leaning down to squint at me through the window. Then *bam*, the kitchen window slapped shut, and I thought, had I done something to upset her or what? I quit playing and just sat there, guitar raised up across my knee, propped up on the rear fender of my car. But pretty soon around the corner of the house across the alley came a woman I hadn't seen before. She was like enough to Estelle and Rose-Lee to have been a third sister, maybe between the two of them in age. Looked more like Estelle in the face but she was slim and trim in blue jeans and a gingham shirt with the sleeves rolled up.

"Hidy," goes one of the men sitting at the cable spool. She looked at them enough to let them know she'd heard, didn't say anything back to them though. Crossing the alley, she drifted kind of sideways, turned her head to look at me out of one eye, like a bird. When she got near enough to hail me without raising her voice she goes, "Hey Jesse, why'nt ye come over and gitchee a drank?"

"Estelle?" says I.

"Who'd ye thank?" She grinned at me, black hole in the grin where the tooth was missing, and put her hands on her hips and twirled.

"You had the baby." I was still gawping at her, with my mouth hanging open probably.

"Had'm Sa'rdy," she said, walking back toward her own house now, but still smiling at me over her shoulder. "Well, air ye coming or not?"

In the front room of their house was a style of mess like you might have expected, clothes all heaped up on bursting stuffed furniture, a low table piled with old magazines and *TV Guides*. There was a loud racket from the television and the smell of stale milk and diapers. The baby itself was on the nod in one of those motorized swing gadgets.

"Thar he is," Estelle said. "James Culla Cheatham." Then she spoke to her sister. "Cut that down some, would ye?"

Rose-Lee was sprawled across a pile of clothes sprayed over a collapsing sofa, watching two televisions at once: a color set and a smaller black-and-white. They were both tuned to the same channel, I noticed.

"Sound don't come in good on that color set," she said when she saw me looking. Otherwise, she didn't stir. Estelle went over and cut down the volume on the black-and-white herself. Rose-Lee threw her a pout when she did it, but Estelle just walked on through the door at the other end of the living room, looking back at me once, so I followed her.

The kitchen was tidier than I'd have thought, wet dishes racked up neat in a plastic drainer, the torn linoleum floor swept bare. Estelle reached in the fridge for two cans of Stroh's, popped one open and passed it to me.

"Here's to ye."

I took a taste, then stooped down to peer out the kitchen window. Across the alley, I'd left the guitar case open by the car, but I figured probably nobody was going to bother it.

Estelle slugged a good one from her own beer, then swung her leg up over the seat of a straight-back wood chair and sat with her arms folded over the chair back, studying me like she was thinking about making a purchase. After a minute she fired up a cigarette.

"Well, set down, why don't ye?"

I sat down, across from her, put my beer can on the chipped enamel-top table between us.

"Ye know anythang else off that a'bum?"

I thought a minute. " 'That Makes One of Us'?"

Estelle gave the gap-toothed grin. "Take it away," she said. But she was the one that took it.

After about an hour the baby woke up and started in crying. Rose-Lee toted him into the kitchen, and Estelle switched her chair around and opened her shirt and fed the baby and kept right on singing the whole time—didn't seem to make no difference to her. I suppose she must have had more room for that voice now the baby wasn't taking up room in there—anyway there were times I thought it would blow the walls right off that little room. We were keeping in kind of a country vein and with that it didn't seem like such a big difference in the way she talked and the way she sang, except that power, and without even a mike. The voice kept coming out and out of her, standing up muscular and smooth.

After about two hours the kitchen door nudged open and a guy backed in, shouldering the door because his hands were tied up with a bucket of chicken and a six-pack of Coke. When he got turned around finally I saw it was my daddy.

"Hey," he said, and if he was surprised to see me sitting there he didn't show a bit of it. So I tried my best to do him the same way back.

"Don't let me stop you all," he said. But Estelle looked shy now, and I could claim that my fingers were sore.

Daddy shrugged and went over to the kitchen sink and spent a long time washing the grease off his hands. I remembered that slow thorough way he always would do that, orange soap frothing up to his elbows. Familiar ways. When he got done, Rose-Lee came in the kitchen (the baby had gone back to sleep by this time) and we all sat down at the table and ate chicken.

The weird thing I noticed was it didn't seem weird. It all felt normal and natural enough. When we got done eating and the plates rinsed off, Daddy proposed we should play some more. But Estelle didn't hardly seem to still be in the mood—don't suppose anybody feels much like singing that soon after supper. I let on that I was tired, which was true, and I packed up the guitar and left.

But I didn't stay gone for long. I was back within that week, in fact, just drifting in unannounced like before. Hell, I didn't even know their phone number. Estelle seemed happy enough to see me; I took it she didn't have a whole lot else on her schedule. It didn't appear she was working just then, other than a couple nights a week singing at that Woodland Street roadhouse. I suppose she might have been drawing welfare of some kind. Rose-Lee did have a job, it seemed, shuffling paper at some big warehouse on the north edge of town—she was pulling down a solid forty hours a week and would come home sour-faced and set for a session in front of those two TVs. Scroungy old Greg her boyfriend would be lurking around there waiting for her some days. If he had any type of a job it wasn't obvious. Drug dealer, maybe. No difference to me.

As for Estelle, she was generally free when I dropped by, un-less she was taken up with the baby, but old James Culla, small like he was, spent a good deal of his time sleeping. No sign at all that he had any daddy. Estelle didn't appear to have no man at all. I had gathered they hadn't been living in Nashville all that long, and if it was less than nine months or whatever, then she must've got knocked up wherever it was they'd come from.

I didn't ask her about that, of course. We didn't really talk much at all beyond *He'p ye-self to a beer* or *Do ye know this'n?* If I didn't know it I'd learn it by next time and if she didn't know it I'd bring her a tape. They didn't have any regular stereo in the house, but there was a tore-up little boom box that would only eat the tapes about a quarter of the time—it worked good enough for her to learn lyrics. I didn't go to that Woodland Street bar again, but I heard from Daddy she was beginning to drop some of the stuff she was doing with me into the sets she played over there with the two junkies.

Another thing was this worked out to be a way of me seeing Daddy from time to time, pretty often actually, but without having to set my foot inside his house, which tell the truth I didn't specially want to do. But he would be apt to turn up at Estelle's when I was there, coming by after the end of his shift at the shop, sometimes bringing a mess of takeout food, sometimes just his six-pack of Coke. For sure, if he saw the Mustang parked in the alley, he'd know he could find me over there. And once in a while he'd be there before me, sitting in the kitchen and sucking a Coke (I never seen him to touch liquor during this time).

It was a way of being in the same room with Daddy without having to talk much, because Estelle was singing. Or in between songs he might scratch his head and come up with an idea for some other old tune. He had more up his sleeve that way than I'd have expected, 'cause normally he didn't look like he cared much for music, would keep the radio off in the car, I remembered. But I remembered too one time finding a stack of old vinyl records back in a closet, with a flip-out mono player that seemed to go with them: Hank Williams and Patsy Cline and a scattering of old black blues guys too. I got him to play us some of this stuff, back when I was around eleven, and it wasn't too long after that he bought me my first guitar—a hundred-dollar Yamaha acoustic I played for a couple of years after that, till one day it got busted . . .

In Estelle's kitchen I didn't really have to think about how that guitar got busted or across what—because she was singing, or else we'd be talking only music, or if that baby needed something she would carry him in the kitchen and do for him there, between us, like she knew she oughtn't to leave me and Daddy too long by ourselves. He appeared to be a pretty agreeable baby, although I didn't really have the experience to know. Estelle seemed to have had a plenty though; she did all this baby stuff easy and natural and confident, like she'd had a dozen babies before, which maybe she had for all I knew about it. It started me wondering again just how old she really was—she was young-looking in the body as it showed through her clothes, but in the face it was hard to figure. She had lines around the corners of her eyes and mouth, but that gypsy-dark complexion made it near impossible to guess her age, and anyway it didn't matter. I was only there to hear that voice, spreading like honey, like red liquor in the little room, in the sunset hour when the light would come in slantwise through the window and pick up the gold wind on the Hummingbird's bass strings, would even make the dust floating off the furniture look gilded.

All of which kept me pretty well occupied, kept me from marking the passage of time, though it was definitely starting to get colder, even the days getting noticeably shorter. At Allston's I began to see that money was a little tight. He kept an apartment just by the I-40 overpass, in a building where he had the use of the basement too, fitted out with secondhand rubber mats and a heavy bag he'd made from an old green Army duffel. Allston had a little pack of neighborhood boys he'd train when he was in town, just to keep himself in tune, he said, and I was in the habit of stopping by there once a week or so, for more or less the same reason.

One day when we were done working out and all the young-bloods had scrambled back up to the street, I went up to Allston's to take a shower, 'cause we were planning to go get a beer afterward. I went first and got dressed while he was washing—cut myself a smoke standing close by the window and blowing it outside so as not to stink up his clean-living space. Somebody had a boom box pounding out rap, down there on the sidewalk.

Allston came out of the bedroom wearing a pair of khaki pants and the towel done up on his head like an Arab sheik or something.

"What do you hear from Perry?" he goes, scratching around the edges of that white scar on his stomach.

"What do I *hear* from him?" I said. "Snoring, I guess. Whatever, you know, like I live with the dude."

Allston pulled a black sweatshirt on over his head. The towel came loose and he wrapped it back on. "I was more thinking about the fall gigs."

"Yeah, I know." I took a quick look at my watch, though the point was more the calendar, of course.

"I got the feeling he's wanting to hire somebody."

"Well, he ain't gonna mess with the rhythm section."

"I didn't think that," Allston said. "No, but what I heard was he went down to the No-Name, to nose around Melissa."

"You're not serious," I said. "She'll never come back."

Allston shrugged. "Chuckee Dee saw him in there while he was tending bar," he said. "Perry was proposing her some kind of business, what he said it looked like, but she told him to stick it where the sun don't shine."

"That figures," I said. "Her part, I mean." It had ended bad with Melissa. Perry used to ride her the way he would Chris—he didn't seem to be able to help himself from doing it. Meanwhile

she had got in a quarrel with Chris about something else altogether. I reached through the window and stubbed out my cigarette on the bricks below the sill. Knowing Allston would fuss if I
dropped the butt, I stuck it in my pocket to get rid of later.

"All I know is we normally would have left out of here *last*
week," Allston said. "What it is, you want to drink a beer together,
we gonna have to go buy a six-pack and tote it back up here, 'cause
right now I can't pay bar prices."

"I hear you," I said. It affected me less since I ate off of Perry,
but otherwise I'd have been noticing the pinch.

"That's good," goes Allston. "In that case, why don't you see if
you can find out what Perry's waiting on . . . and when he's expecting it might get here."

So I drove back out to the countryside but Perry wasn't there.
In fact he hadn't seemed to be there much of late. All the dogs
came piling out when I parked my car, especially glad to see me
'cause they were hoping I might feed them, which I did. Then I
unfroze a hamburger and fed myself too, but Perry still hadn't
come back by the time I got done washing the dishes. I woke up
finally, hearing his boot heels smacking the porch floor, but it
must have been one in the morning by then and it didn't seem like
the time to be running down the schedule.

But Perry was out of there the next morning before I even got
up, though I was up early enough myself the frost was still cling-
ing to the grass, and it was getting to be a pretty heavy frost too.
I thought I'd hang around the fort that day maybe. Truth was,
my gas money was looking kind of slim. By noon it was warm
enough to be outside in shirtsleeves, so I took a walk for an hour
or so, up the hill and along the ridge. The leaves were just starting
to turn on the hills, and I thought how I hadn't been there to see
that last year or the year before. It was pretty, but it also let me

know that sure enough we were a good way off schedule, like Perry's system had broken down, or he had just abandoned it.

When I got back to the house, Perry was sitting up there on the porch, with his feet propped up on one of the dogs, and smoking a corncob pipe—just like a farmer, by God, except the pipe was loaded with dope, of course.

"Yo, Perry," I said right as I was coming up the steps. "Allston wants to know, what's up with the fall gigs?"

Perry looked at me for a minute, pale eyes under his yellow eyebrows. "Allston," he said. It seemed like it was taking him a long time to process this idea.

"Yeah, Allston," I said. "Seems like he's getting a little light in the pocketbook." I stuck my arms out to the sides. "Me, I believe in the Perry way to be—I don't even own a winter coat."

Perry stretched out his freckled arm, offering the pipe stem-first to me.

"Thanks," I said. "Too early."

"Allston," Perry said. His eyes scoped out the whole horizon in that slow dopey way. Finally he must have reached the conclusion that if Allston was asking that had to make it a legitimate question.

"You can call Allston," Perry said. "Tell him to be out here Saturday for a tune-up rehearsal. I'll be the one to call Chris."

"Oh yeah?" I said. This was a relief to me actually—I could even feel it in the backs of my knees. "So when're we leaving?"

"We're due in Myrtle Beach on November fifteenth," Perry said. He fished out a box of wooden matches and fired up his pipe again.

"Cool," I said. Actually I was a little bugged at this news, 'cause normally we hit the Black Cats of North Carolina on our way out to the coast. There had been girls in some of those towns I thought I might run into again this trip.

"How come you dropped the North Carolina dates?"

Perry pulled his feet off the dog and his soles slapped on the floor like he might mean to come out of that chair right quick.

"Who says it was me dropped them?" he goes. All of a sudden he didn't seem half so stoned as before, and his eyes were focused sharp and hard. So I just shrugged and sloped off somewhere, 'cause it didn't seem like that question needed me to answer it.

The tune-up get-together went off okay, I thought. We started in the afternoon, broke to eat some shrimp and beer, then played another set's worth after, sounding pretty good, to me. It was Perry's idea that we best all sort of avoid each other during the off times, so we'd be fresh when we did get back together, and from my point of view this did seem to work. I could hit the groove cleaner and sweeter and gladder just from having been away from it for a while. Clicking in with Allston was like a homecoming, that solid lockdown on the beat, and Chris was sounding all right too; he hadn't been letting his fingers rust. Perry might have been a little throaty on the vocals, but that was normal for this time of year. Once we hit the road he would lay off the dope, his lungs would clear out and he'd sing cleaner.

On all our old standards we sounded just fine. We would need to start out with maybe eight or ten new tunes in the rotation though—just to keep from boring our damn selves to death, as Perry would say. Perry had come up with three or four such, nothing too astonishing. A different oldie from the Allman Brothers, a different oldie from J.J. Cale . . . Chris, meanwhile, seemed to have taken special pains to think of stuff that would just irritate Perry. Dire Straits—you could see how this would draw a guitar player, but Perry was not going to sing those lyrics. Or some of your more unplayable Grateful Dead. Like that. Plus Chris managed to work it around to the old unpleasant question of shouldn't he, couldn't he, toss just one or two of his originals into every set?

Last year it had been my thing to cool this out with compromise suggestions, tunes that everybody somehow could connect with. This time all I could seem to produce was stuff I'd been playing in Estelle's kitchen. Alison Krauss, Bonnie Raitt, Emmylou Harris, even Rosanne Cash. When I proposed him "Seven-Year Ache," Perry give me a look that would have peeled paint.

Never mind a little bit of grousing here and there, I did think we were sounding better than decent, but still and all we knocked off early. And not with any big flourish either, more like people laying down instruments and drifting off toward the kitchen one at a time. There wasn't anything you could call tension really, everybody acted friendly enough, but at the same time Allston and Chris went home kind of early too. Last year we'd all hung out for half the night, spinning one disc after another and floating more ideas of stuff to play until it all got completely goofy and we were half-asleep in our chairs.

This year everything was cool, only at the same time it really wasn't. I went on the porch to wave Allston off. When I came back in the house, Perry was standing there staring at his five-thousand-record collection like he hated every last one of them there. The amps were still humming; I started turning them off.

"Well, I thought we sounded pretty good," I finally said, just to give him a target.

Perry kind of wheeled on me. "You did, hah? What did you

keep throwing me all that chick-singer stuff for, trying to get my goat? Goddamn."

"Take it easy," I said, straightening up pretty sharp. "I didn't mean nothing by it."

"All right." Perry let down a little. "I didn't mean nothing either." He turned back to the record shelf, still looking for something that wasn't there. Then glanced back at me, scratching his head. "You're right, we didn't sound half-bad, but I don't know, we still lack *something*."

I had just pulled my bass off the stand to put it in the case, when all of a sudden I put it together—felt stupid too, for not doing it sooner. Two years ago Melissa had been practically fronting the band about half the time—I mean Perry still was running the show, but she was covering half the lead vocals. Last year we'd made the same run without her and of course that had shuffled our repertory all around. Now this year we were starting to lose gigs.

"So that's what's eating you," I said. The bass was hanging in my hands like a maul or something. "Hang on—we still got two weeks."

"Two weeks for what?" Perry said.

"Listen," I told him. "There's somebody I want you to hear."

First I thought about just taking him by the Woodland Street Black Cat, only I hadn't been there myself but the one time, and there was no telling how it might turn out between her and her junky backup dudes. Not that I didn't trust her to pull it out, whatever, so far as putting on her own show—it was more like the sight of her busting her bass player in the chops might not lead Perry to think she'd be such a good person to add to the band. Then I decided it was best not to let her know anything was up in particular, but just fall by like I had been doing. Hell, I didn't ever even call over there before I showed up.

But the night before, I started worrying had I made the right choices. Then my thumb started to hurt, so I had to get up and take the ibuprofen, and about an hour later I got up and soaked my hand. I told myself finally it wasn't my thumb so much in the question, it was her lungs had something to prove, and after that I could go to sleep, and next day the hand didn't bother me.

We rolled up the alley between five and six, and just as I was parking the Mustang, the back door of Estelle's house shot open like dynamite just went off behind it—out came Greg with Rose-Lee right after him, cussing him six ways from Sunday and actually kicking him in the skinny seat of his jeans. He was laughing at her, trying to, but at the same time you could tell her toe was connecting up to the business. He limped off down the alley and she stood on the back steps cussing after him in a hog-calling voice until he turned the corner and then she stomped inside and banged the door, not quite hard enough to break the glass.

Perry looked at me. "She's got the volume, anyhow," he said.

"That ain't her," I said. I was just then pulling the guitar case out of the trunk. "It's her sister."

In the kitchen Estelle and my daddy were sitting there like they had been caught in the middle of some conversation they didn't want to have in front of nobody but the two of them—though maybe it was the scorch trail Rose-Lee had left when she passed through that accounted for that. Estelle was drinking a malt liquor, cigarette blazing, and Daddy was clutching his Coke can—there were times when I just wished he would break down and have a drink, maybe, though of course I understood why he didn't.

Perry and Daddy sort of nodded to each other. I introduced Perry to Estelle.

"Hi ye maken it?" Estelle said. Perry looked at me. That cracker accent. *Just you wait,* I thought to myself, unsnapping the catches on the guitar case. The two TVs were going loud in the next room, and you could hear Rose-Lee stewing, stomping up and down, still madder than hell. About the time I got the guitar swung up on my knee, old James Culla bust out crying in there too.

This was kind of unusual because normally he'd be asleep at this time of day. I could hear that Rose-Lee had picked him up and was trying to quiet him, though it didn't seem to be doing a lot of good, but anyway I started playing something I thought might warm up Estelle's tonsils—"Love Me Like a Man." I ran the intro and started vamping on the verse, waiting for her to kick in with that big barrelhouse voice, but she didn't. She just sat there watching the twin smoke trails come off the head of her cigarette where it was burning in the ashtray, listening to James Culla fussing louder and louder in the next room.

Finally she let out a sigh and got up and handed me and Perry two Colt 45s out of the fridge, handling them like they was heavy as bricks, and then she went off in the other room. I kept on playing that same song like I had been until it occurred to me that Perry wasn't going to be too thrilled by listening to me run acoustic guitar licks, so I quit and just took a pull on my beer. Perry lit up one of his short Camels and smoked the whole thing and she still hadn't come back.

Perry looked at me. Daddy nudged his chair back and started out of the room. In a minute the noise of the two TVs dropped off to almost nothing, and Daddy came back with Estelle following him. She looked bashful now, studying the floor—I figured Daddy

73

must have guessed what Perry was doing there and told her, god-dammit.

I started up "Love Me Like a Man" one more time, and this go-round she came in right where she should have, only it sounded like she was singing from some little small space right behind her teeth. She didn't sound *bad*, exactly, just nothing special. My fin-gers were brittle on the strings, like my first few times on stage. About halfway through, old James Culla tuned up again. I could make out that Rose-Lee had picked him up and that it still wasn't helping much.

This went on for half an hour, during which I broke into that kind of bad-smelling fear sweat that comes for instance in the midst of a car wreck. I could tell Rose-Lee was making an effort, walking that baby all over the house to try and calm him down, but the place was so small she couldn't really find nowhere to take him out of earshot. Meanwhile we tried barrelhouse blues, slow soulful minor blues, uptempo country, sweet sad country—Estelle couldn't hit a one of them. You would have thought a mouse was there singing the shit. Perry was dying. He was licking out the bot-tom of his beer can. Finally I gave up and laid the guitar away in the case like it was a corpse in a coffin.

Perry scraped his chair back. "Well, nice meeting you."

"Ayuh," Estelle grunted. I swear, now she sounded like she was being strangled even when she tried to talk. "Y'all come on back some time."

Lord help us. I was wishing I had taken Perry to the bar in-stead and wondering if I might *still* do that, except I thought once a jinx was on this hard it would take a lot to pry it off. Perry was desperate to get out of there—already had the back door open, when Rose-Lee came in, grim and drawn, to hand Estelle the baby. Old James Culla was red-faced and squalling but he seemed to settle a little bit as soon as his cheek came down on his mamma's shoulder. She stood up to take him, started swinging her hips in a slow rock.

I was bent over latching the guitar case shut when I heard air come out of Estelle like wind blowing over a bottleneck, and I froze where I was, didn't move a hair. Then the voice did come. When I dared look she had her own eyes shut and was swinging from the hips still, just singing to that baby and nobody else. At first you could hardly tell the words, just a big round bloom of sound like a horn solo. Then she sang,

> *When you wake . . .*
> *You shall have . . .*
> *All the pretty little horses . . .*

Perry was halfway out the door by this time, but when those deep notes rang in the room, his head whipped around so fast I could hear the bones popping in his neck.

4. LONELY AVENUE

Then we were ripping down the road at last—I-40 east toward Knoxville and the coast. We'd managed, due to Perry's whip-cracking, to get out of Nashville almost before daybreak, and now the sun was cracking on the horizon line, floods of light turning the interstate into a blazing silver river. I pulled down the visor and squinted across the wheel. Neil Young was jamming on the tape player, "Cortez the Killer," those long slow saurian guitar lines, good drive music, at least by me. South Carolina, here we come, though not for a good twelve hours yet.

On the passenger side Estelle clicked the lever to lay back her seat. From the rear, Rose-Lee crabbed at her not to crush the baby thataway—'cause old James Culla himself was riding back there in the regulation car seat Perry had made them buy so we wouldn't get stuck with a ticket. But Stell just yawned and pulled that black gaucho hat down to shade her eyes, to cover her whole face practically. Stella, Stell. . . . Perry bought her the hat the same day he let her know she had a new name, which he had cooked up that very first day he heard her sing, while I was driving him back to the country. *Cheatham just ain't gonna cut it*, was his words. *Estelle ain't so bad, maybe Stella? Yeah, we could live with that . . . but Stella what?* He might of been talking to me since I was right there only I knew he was mostly talking to himself, staring out the window. *Stella Dallas . . . nah, too much. Stella Houston! That should get it. Think that'd get it, Jesse?*

Sure, I'd said, two weeks gone now, and straightaway Perry was taking this Stella Houston he'd invented on a Western-wear shopping spree which fixed her up with the gaucho hat, a pair of Acme fake snakeskin boots, a couple pairs of off-brand designer-looking jeans, some shiny shirts with yokes and mother-of-pearl–looking snaps on them, and to top it off a fake suede jacket with cloth fringe that hung down about to her knees. He even hauled her into the dentist and bought her a bridge for that missing front tooth. She seemed to fill out the clothes pretty well, even if I couldn't quite get used to the name, and once she'd got them on Perry even went to the trouble of having a new picture shot— Stella Houston strutting her stage gear in front of the group, flashing a big smile with no black gap in it, and the rest of us kind of skulking behind our instruments there in the back.

So now we were hitting the road at last, me caffeine-buzzed but still half asleep, sucking on a Coke and a smoke and half-dreaming while I listened to Neil lay it down. James Culla was asleep, thank God, and Estelle looked like she might be too. Rose-Lee was keeping quiet back there, though she wasn't sleeping. Whenever I checked my rearview mirror I'd see her looking out the window, now and then nibbling on the edge of her thumb in a kind of a lazy way. She was wearing some of Stell's new stage outfit—a pair of the fancy-stitched jeans and a turquoise shirt with the snaps and all, which had ticked Perry off when he saw her get in the car. Though I didn't see the problem with it—she looked as good in that stuff as Stell did.

Chris hauled up alongside us in that yellow Trans Am and

hovered for about half a minute, until he made eye contact—and not so much with me, I realized, as with Rose-Lee there in the back. Then he jerked a thumbs-up, and the Trans Am kind of bunched up its haunches and *swoosh*, it was gone, sweeping around the van ahead of me and vanishing into the sunrise burn on the roadbed. I checked the speedometer; I'd been holding a solid seventy, but Chris left me like I was standing still. He wanted to test this new high-tech fuzzbuster he'd stuck in his car, which was supposed to jam radar along with detecting it. If it worked like it was supposed to he'd get there hours ahead of us, but if it failed he'd likely be a day or so late, and calling for money, as Perry predicted, from whatever small-town speed-trap pokey he managed to land himself into.

Perry had in fact been kind of peevish about the arrangement with the cars. Him and me had even had words about whether I had to pay on the gas for the van (the way Chris was required to do), till I pointed out that even though the van was hauling my bass amp, there was no way it was gonna hold him, me, Allston, all the gear *and* Estelle *and* James Culla *and* Rose Lee . . . and therefore I had a good reason to take the Mustang, not just that I was hooked on new-car smell. This gave Perry a whole other subject to bitch about, but the bottom line was Estelle was not going without James Culla and James Culla was not going without Rose-Lee 'cause none of the rest of us was gonna be available to baby-sit during the gigs. That was a fact any way you sliced it, so Perry had to just back off. The main thing he was really unhappy about was only having Allston to split driving with—it wasn't so much the gas budget that was bugging him.

Anyway I was sort of riding a new-car high still—it was fun taking the Mustang out for a long-distance haul, at least for the first few hours. That Neil Young cassette just kept flipping itself in the deck, and all three passengers were zoned out some way or other, and I myself was maybe enjoying a little highway hypnosis, though not enough to be dangerous.

A couple of hours went by quick enough, then Perry was flashing the trouble light on the van, signaling the lunch break. It was the truck stop where we'd usually eat, just a little before Asheville. Perry, like you might expect, wouldn't eat McDonald's if there was any way around it, and he'd searched out this joint where the food was more or less home-cooked, and pretty decent really. We got a table for the lot of us and ate without saying much.

"Making pretty good time so far," I said as we were ordering the coffee. Perry gave a grunt and that was all. The waitress was clearing off the plates. "Pie?" she asked, but nobody took it. About then James Culla woke and began to fuss, and Estelle hauled up her shirttail and started nursing right there at the table. I could hear the sound of chairs scraping at the tables near us. Home cooking or not, it was the kind of place where they'd notice a nigger, and of course I pretty much looked like a spic, so maybe it was a little too much for Estelle to be showing tit for whatever reason. Anyway it seemed like all these truckers, most of which probably belonged to Posse Comitatus, were starting to give us the hairy eyeball. I have to give Perry credit for not giving a good goddamn about any of this, and Estelle sure didn't look like she did either, but me and Allston somehow made contact without quite looking at each other, and we slid out to gas up the cars, check the oil and clean the glass. When this was done we still had time to smoke us each a cigarette before the rest of them were ready.

Rolling, rolling. My car took the lead this time. We'd made it past Asheville and were looking good when James Culla decided he'd had enough of being in the car. He started in squalling and nothing seemed to make him stop—not bottle or rattle or breast or dollies. I tried him on some different music, but he didn't seem to care for Allman Brothers or Elmore James or Sheryl Crow or Bonnie Raitt. This went on for almost an hour before Estelle told me we had to stop.

As luck would have it there was a rest area coming just ahead, so I pulled off and parked. Estelle dug up an old flannel blanket from somewhere and spread it on a grassy berm and laid James Culla on it. He quieted as soon as she sat down beside him, crawled over to the blanket's edge and started studying the weeds. Rose-Lee sat down next to Estelle and both of them leaned back on their elbows.

Then the van pulled in and stopped behind the Mustang. Perry climbed out and came walking toward me, stiff-legged and creaky from the car seat.

"What the hell?" he said.

"Baby's had enough of it, I guess."

"When did he start calling the shots?" Perry wanted to know.

I shrugged. "You're welcome to have him ride with you if that's how you want it—you think you'd enjoy having him screaming in your ear."

Perry didn't say nothing to that. He scratched the back of his head and squinted at the women on the blanket.

"It ain't like we got to play tonight anyhow," I said.

"We got to set up and sound-check," Perry said.

"Whatever." We looked at each other a minute more and then he got back in the van and pulled out.

After this we were talking torture. James Culla could not resign himself to riding in that car. We made about four more unscheduled stops, but except for that he yelled nonstop. I learned there's something about a baby screaming you really can't get used to—for some important biological reason, I expect. It wasn't that I blamed him really. He'd slept all he could stand to and there was nothing else for him to do. We should have thought of it ahead of time. But it was painful. I kept trying him on different music and finally he seemed to hit a groove listening to Sade; he didn't sleep, but sat quiet finally, eyes shining in the dark. It had been dark for a while by the time we left the interstate for Highway 501, and that last haul seemed awful long with nothing to look at but headlights shining down the dashes on the blacktop. It was past ten o'clock when we finally limped into the motel.

"Message for you," the lady said when I checked in at the desk. She passed me a slip of paper along with the two room keys. Perry's scrawl: *Get on over to the Black Cat and don't waste any more time than you have to.* I balled up the paper and flicked it toward a wastebasket behind the counter.

"He called twicet since," the lady said, worried. "Sump'n about a sound check." She was the biddy type, bouffant hairdo and body like a chicken; she wanted me to do what Perry said.

"He calls again, just tell him I love him," I said.

I went out, key tags hanging from my hand. It wasn't half as cold here as Tennessee, give Perry credit for that, and you could feel the salt on the breeze. Down the rank of motel rooms, Chris's car glowed ochre under an eave light—that'd be our room most likely. Estelle was walking the baby around the parking lot. He was still awake, looking at things. I waved to her and moved the Mustang next to the Trans Am. The women's room was next to ours. I gave Rose-Lee the key to it.

"Might need two of them," she said.

"Right," I told her. "I'll handle it."

Rose-Lee went to hauling their stuff out of the car. I got my bass and my duffel bag, unlocked the room door and popped it open with my hip. Chris had scattered some clothes over both beds, wet towels and shaving cream in the bathroom. Looked like he must have made it straight through without a traffic stop. I set my bass down next to the Strat case; he'd of taken the Les Paul to the sound check. In the bathroom sink a tap was dripping, and I wrapped it with a washrag—I knew otherwise I'd forget later on, and it would keep me awake. I pulled a pint of bourbon out of my bag, poured two fingers in a water glass and knocked it back. Then I found the ice bucket and headed for the office.

Estelle was standing outside their room when I got back, not looking much like she was either coming or going. I handed her the extra key, and she stuck the tag in her jeans pocket, leaving the key itself to hang out on its link of chain.

"How's the baby doing?" I said.

She pointed to the half-open doorway and I leaned past her to look. Rose-Lee and James Culla were both asleep side by side on the bed.

"Finally," I said.

Estelle sniffed. "Smell like ye got a drank hid on ye some-whars."

That first sip of bourbon had fanned out through me, softened the hard-driving edge. I went in the room and fixed two good drinks with the ice I'd picked up and handed one to Estelle where she was standing just outside the door.

"You want some Coke in that or something?"

"Don't need none. Thank ye."

"Want to come in?"

Estelle looked into the room without crossing the doorsill. One of Perry's mildew palaces. We had been cooped up enough all day. I came out and pulled the door to behind me. Estelle drank deep and gave me a smile, working her lip to cover her front teeth, the way she'd do. Then she squinted up at the eave bulb.

"You see a way to shet that light?"

I fumbled around for a minute but I didn't find a switch. "Why don't we go over to the beach?" I said.

There wasn't much traffic on 17, the long flat straightaway down south to Charleston. It was one of your out-of-the-way motels, Perry's specialty. We scuttled across the highway, ice clinking in our glasses, and walked on the opposite shoulder till we came to a break in the pines. A public access parking lot, just a pool of asphalt behind the dunes. It was good dark, no moon, but once we got away from the odd set of headlights drilling down the highway we could begin to see the stars.

Estelle's boot heels slipped on the sand going up; I automatically reached back to help her over the dune. Her hand was hard and dry, callused. She let go of mine quick when we got to the top. No houses on this stretch of the beach—I suppose it must of been parkland. Northways, the lights of the Myrtle Beach strip were a neon burn on the horizon.

"Like to spilt my drink," Stell said, and sipped to prove she hadn't after all. She sat down of a sudden and pulled off her boots, then stood, working her bare toes in the sand. The wind was blowing and I could hear the slap and hush of the waves down on the beach. The calm spreading over me was more than whiskey now.

Estelle walked down the beach to the hard sand. There was enought starlight to pick out the white foam and the water line, and her slim dark shadow moving against it. I wanted to go closer to her but I held myself back. I took my own shoes off and walked the beach in the other direction.

When I headed back, I saw a match flare, Stell lighting a cigarette. The gaucho hat, held by a neck cord, had slipped back on her shoulder, and her hair fanned out in the wind, black and ragged as a crow's wing. The stars behind her head were bright as I'd ever seen them.

"That's something, ain't it?" It sounded different than her regular speaking voice . . . softer, sweeter, like when she sang. It might have been the wind that did that. I wanted to ask if it was the first time she'd seen the ocean, but I decided to keep it to myself.

Next day got off to a sour start, with me catching a ragging from Perry for not having trucked out to the sound check the night before. This happened over the motel breakfast table. Estelle and Rose-Lee dodged out of it, wisely, by discovering they needed to do something for the baby, and Chris and Allston eased out too, but I had to sit there over my cold greasy plate until Perry had finally worn himself out on the subject.

After that it was raining. So much for putt-putt golf or anything like that. We moped around from one room to another. Finally Chris and Perry drove off to town, intending to pick up some CDs that might give us ideas for our own song mix. The girls were watching soaps in their room; Allston found a football game in his. I put on a jacket and a wool hat and walked over to the beach.

It was windy when I crossed the dunes, sea oats practically lying down, and the raindrops were pocking into the sand like the whole beach was being strafed by machine guns. The rain stung my face, till I turned my back to it. There were a couple of surfers sitting their boards out in the rollers, looking sort of glum in their wet suits. I could have gone swimming to get out of the rain, but it was really too cold for it.

The Myrtle Beach Black Cat wasn't really in Myrtle Beach—in fact it was a couple miles south of the hotel, on a little spur off the highway. A cinder-block pillbox, painted puke green, half of it on pilings over a swamp. The mosquitoes would have killed you there in the summer. On the door was a poster with that new picture: STELLA HOUSTON WITH ANYTHING GOES.

"Ambitious," I said to Perry as we went through; I didn't know he'd ordered a poster. It didn't look any worse than the pictures and promos for other loser bands turning yellow underneath it, but I'd swear Estelle flinched when she saw it. Inside, she headed straight to the bar.

Perry leaned to my ear. "Don't let her drink too much," he said.

"Why don't you take care of that, if it's worrying you?" I told him. But I checked anyhow—she just had a beer.

It took me and Chris a whole five minutes to get my bass correct for the sound mix, like I could have told Perry that morning if I'd felt like wasting my breath. I set the ax on the stand and checked the crowd, such as it was—maybe a little better than average for a Black Cat on a Wednesday night. Hump day, what you'd call it here. The place didn't really draw tourists off the Myrtle Beach strip, unless once in a while they had a name band. It was generally locals from the small towns up and down the highway. A few roving bikers, fishermen and boat mechanics, factory guys, high school dropouts with their smokes rolled in their shirt sleeves. Girls with tight jeans and T-shirts cut above the belly button, lacquered over hard with makeup.

Perry was conferring with Estelle over by the edge of the foot-high stage riser. "We're gonna call you up. 'Lonely Avenue,' that's your cue—you'll know the hook to it, right?"

"Cain't miss it," Estelle said. She looked tight-lipped, stiff and uncomfortable in the new clothes. I'd not often seen her nervous but I wondered if she was nervous now. It might have been the clothes, which looked phony when you got too close to them. The new false tooth was more convincing, except she seemed to have taken up the habit of clicking the bridgework with her tongue.

Perry looked at Rose-Lee. "That baby acts up, you're gonna have to take him out of here. Understand? Take him over in the bar. You can get him a drink on me."

Rose-Lee didn't say nothing to that.

"Here's a key to the van if you need somewhere else to go," Perry said. "I mean sit with him, not drive off."

"You intend on buying *me* a drank?" Rose-Lee said.

"You're on the house like the rest of us—I'll tell Phil," Perry said. He winked, though not in a really cheerful way. "Just don't you drop that baby."

We opened with an instrumental shuffle that segued into "One Way Out"—something to make the bikers happy. Then "Southbound." Then "Blue Sky"—Chris opened up the front pickup on the Les Paul and let it go like Duane and Dicky Betts together. A real Allman Brothers jag we had going here, and I also noticed we'd been playing for more than fifteen minutes, what with that long solo. Stell was just waiting in the shadows by the wall—there wasn't no backstage area. The place had a back door behind the riser we were on, but if you went through it you would just fall in the salt marsh.

"Lonely Avenue" was sure to be next, I thought, but Perry called "Sympathy for the Devil" instead. Then "Midnight Rambler." Ladies and gentlemen, the Rolling Stones . . .

I saw he was giving her star treatment—we were gonna play half the whole first set to get built up to *Stella Houston!* This plan had natural drama to it, only I thought Perry ought to have told somebody about it beforehand, especially Estelle, whose face kept lighting up like a traffic signal in the glow of all the cigarettes she was sucking down. Perry called for something else, a Chicago blues I think. Then finally he was ringing out the one-four-three lick that was the signature for Lonely Avenue."

I felt, myself, a little thrill—we actually sounded better than average tonight, and the buildup was working on me too. Allston and I were down in a groove where we could get when things were going specially well, and Chris was putting some nice embroidery around Perry's basic rhythm lick.

"Ladies and gentleman," Perry announced, and then, off-mike, "*Don't make me laugh.*" He leaned to the microphone again. "Stella Houston!"

Estelle stepped on her most recent cigarette and clambered up on the riser like she was trying to get over a barb-wire fence. She tripped on a cable and just about fell on her face (along with unplugging Perry's guitar). But then she got her balance somehow, and shook out her fake suede fringe like a wet bird rearranging its feathers. The song came back around to the top, and Estelle stepped up to the mike and did absolutely nothing at all.

It went on about another four bars before Chris realized he better start playing a lead line, something, anything . . . Perry was glaring at me, for some reason. Estelle was doing this half-ass little dance step, not even specially on the beat, and staring up into the lights with her eyes glazed over and this sick little smile.

Chris finished up his half-a-solo; the tune came around to the top again. Estelle took hold of the mike stand like she expected to get a shock from it or something. She opened her mouth and nothing came out.

My hands were freezing, cramping on the bass; I thought I might throw up myself. Didn't dare look at Perry or Chris now but

I knew they were both purely disgusted. I stole a glance at Allston and saw he was just simmering along like always, not particularly concerned about anything that you could see, which made me feel a little better. I risked another look at Estelle. She had changed, just slightly, relaxed a little; a swing and sway was starting through her hips and shoulders. It was like watching her silhouette on the beach the night before, not quite knowing who she was even, or what she was going to do. Then I realized I was starting to hear something over the monitors (the house P.A. had a couple of half-decent monitors, which was kind of unusual for a Black Cat)—a sort of drone like a didgery-doo or a bagpipe far off in the mountains somewhere. Then it was coming nearer, a sort of rolling *ooooooo*—it must have started off up there where only dogs could hear it, but now it was forming itself into a word, a drawn-out *you* . . . and then, going into the eighth bar, the whole phrase: *You don't gimme nothing but the blues*. Estelle had snatched the mike down from the stand and was just belting it out now, the voice opened up full-bore—

> *I could cry-ahiiiiii* . . .
> *I could die-ahiiiiii* . . .
> *I live on a lonely avenue* . . .
> *A lonely avenue.* . . .

Perry hit a one-note chime on the turn, just for bravado. He was shaking his head with a kind of a grin and looking at me like *Did she pull this stunt on purpose?* and I was looking at him like *What's the difference?* while Allston put a cymbal over the fence. Meanwhile Estelle had started all over on the first verse and people who'd been playing pool in the other room were crowding up around the stage with their sticks still hanging in their hands.

The rest of the gig went good after that—so good that even Perry couldn't find a whole lot to complain about. We were booked at the Black Cat for a three-week run, with Sundays, Mondays and Tuesdays off (and unpaid too, you can believe it). That was before things started snowballing. By Friday night of that first week we'd doubled the crowd we started with and Saturday night was better yet. At the Sunday breakfast table, where me and Allston and Estelle gathered around one o'clock in the afternoon, Perry had this folded square of newspaper by his plate, which he turned over like playing an ace in a card game. Nothing but a giveaway rag for the strip, but there was an arch little paragraph in it that said our Black Cat (which in real life was called Waldo's Terminal) was the place to hit for the hot new chick singer with the tight backup band.

We weren't due to play again till the next Wednesday, and in fact we drove up to the strip that night to blow ourselves to a fried seafood special, but by the time we got back to the hotel, the biddy at the desk was jumping up and down, the phone had rung so many times. Seems that Waldo (who was called Sam Jenkins in real life) had been overrun with people wanting to know where the band was, so that in fact he had promised and advertised to deliver us back there by Tuesday.

So all of a sudden we were working five nights a week—every time the joint unlocked we'd play. They stayed shut altogether on Mondays. This put everybody in a better mood than they might have been otherwise, partly because more money was coming in. Morale went up across the board, and we spent more time than usual practicing—we did need to be putting new songs in the set now that we had more sets to play. Perry always brought along a boom box on these trips, and him and Chris and Estelle would woodshed a while in his room every day: Estelle hitting replay over and over to learn lyrics while Chris doped out the changes, strumming on the unplugged Strat, and Perry wrote down the chords on the backs of old invoices or something he'd scrounged at the office of the motel.

Then almost every afternoon we'd practice with the full group for an hour or so at the Black Cat before they opened, working out intros and endings and crossovers, deciding on when Chris got to solo. It was more work, but more fun too. The gigs themselves were getting a real good feel to them, sort of a buzz. We were changing the clientele of the Black Cat by drawing tourists down from the strip—in fair numbers even though it was off-season—and the shift in the mix meant everybody was getting jostled out of their rut a little. You could feel it when you got on stage, a sort of crackle in the room, and it made for a crowd that gave you something back.

The Black Cat closed for Thanksgiving Day, which meant that we all except Allston and Rose-Lee felt obliged to go out and overeat on turkey and stuff. Friday night we were back in action but it was slow compared to what we'd been pulling, less people and the ones that were there all kind of groggy, like overfed snakes. By Saturday everybody seemed to have got their body chemistry back in order, and the juke was jumping once again.

We were doing a little Hendrix tear at the top of the first set (where we still gave a good long warm-up before Estelle climbed up to join us) when Chris dropped an unrehearsed solo into "Dolly Dagger" and ran with it for about twenty minutes. The whole nine yards including the Elvis pelvic squirm, playing the Strat upside down behind his back in tribute to the Master, Grand Guignol moves out of Alice Cooper and Kiss. Perry came sidling over to me to mutter out the side of his mouth, "You got a bat in your pocket he can bite the head off of?" But Perry wasn't really pissed; things were going too well for that, and anyway the crowd was with it.

I began to understand what it was all about when Chris lifted the Strat up to his face and began picking out the notes of the solo with what looked like about ten inches worth of tongue, all the while maintaining eye contact with a babe pressed up to the front of the riser, who was executing a sort of a white-chick belly dance—I realized I'd seen her in there some time before, because she was fairly noticeable. She was tall and looked a little like Daisy Mae in the funny papers except she had on long pants and high-heel shoes, and her hair was hennaed to a dark cherry shade. She had on a white dress shirt with the tails lashed tight and high over a belly that pretty well cried out *personal trainer*, and it seemed she was trying to get it over to Chris that she knew things to do with this specialized muscle.

Her name was Raquel, or that's what she said when Chris and I bought her a drink during the break. Her friend, the quiet one, was called Annette—though I kind of expected the *-ette* part had been tacked on recently, maybe just for this occasion, by her brassier, louder-mouthed, more confident girlfriend. They both worked for the phone company in Little Rock, and had come over here for a ladies' lost weekend. This in fact was good to know, since bothering the local talent around this area could get you in a fair amount of trouble.

Annette had long and straight blond streaky hair, and high cheekbones on a small head like a cat's. She would have been a bit taller than me if she had held herself straight, but she was sway-backed, curling her shoulders around her plastic cupful of pink frozen daiquiri. She smoked a long Eve cigarette and didn't have a lot to say, though now and then she'd give me a sidelong glance with her almond eyes—appealing in its slightly sulky way. Raquel kept the conversation going for all four of us.

I watched Annette from the stage later on: She was good-looking but carried herself like she was a little ashamed of it. She had on tight blue jeans and a baby-blue T-shirt that said AFTERNOON DELIGHT across her breasts, with colored drips running down from the letters. The clothes worked well to show her off but she wore them like they'd been chosen by somebody else. I watched her submit to dance with a couple of guys who were coming on to the pair of them, without any major enthusiasm but with a kind of languid resigned grace. The hesitant way she moved might have come from shyness or fear, but it seemed to have got more syrupy and seductive by the second break. Who did that remind me of? I imagine she'd got down a good amount of daiquiri by that time and I myself was drinking more than usual, in order to get through my part of the whole routine.

We were saying some stuff to each other now, though I don't remember exactly what. Raquel was still carrying the conversation. A lot later on, as Annette and I were sort of falling out of the car in front of the motel (it had somehow evolved that she and I would use our room while Chris and Raquel drove on to the one the girls had rented on the strip), Raquel leaned close to me, over the car seat. "Be sweet to her," she breathed on me, a fog of perfume and smoke and booze, "she's getting a divorce."

Then we were standing there wobble-kneed and sort of half-holding each other up while we watched the taillights of the Trans Am jounce out of the motel driveway. The door of Estelle's room cracked open then, and I could just see the shadow of one of them looking out through the narrow gap—not enough to tell if it was Stell or Rose-Lee. We had gone to some after-hours joints once the Black Cat closed, and I realized now that we might have woke people up when we rolled in. This was kind of an odd feeling, like somebody waiting up for you, which wasn't an experience I'd ever had too much of. But the door closed almost as quick as it had opened. Annette was sort of slumped into me, her shoulders rounding into mine, and we were trading throbs of animal warmth, which was comforting because the night was misty and chilly and damp, and once we got inside the room it seemed we didn't have to think about anything but that.

I dreamed a grizzly bear was chasing me, and woke up in a sweat. The light somebody'd left on in the bathroom slammed me between the eyes like a sledgehammer. I was scrambled, didn't quite know where I was, and still scared 'cause I could still hear the bear and was half-expecting him to come at me, out of that painful light. But gradually I started putting it together: motel room, Myrtle Beach, daylight creeping round the edge of the closed blind, the AFTERNOON DELIGHT T-shirt wadded on the floor, the knobs of Annette's backbone resting against my arm, and the steady pump of her breathing I felt there. Chris was snoring like gangbusters in the next bed. There's your bear, I told myself.

I wondered what had happened between him and Raquel and what this was going to mean to my day. Ferrying Annette around somewhere through the haze of a mutual hangover, or what? I wondered if the girls would be headed back to Little Rock on Sunday or on Monday.

I sat up and the headache kicked me again. Seemed I might have a long day to come. I remembered seeing the door to Stell's room crack, and I wondered which one of them it had been, and what she'd thought, and how much they would have heard afterward through that thin wall. All of a sudden I had a picture of the motel room like it was a paper cell in a big wasps' nest with me and Chris hemmed between Stell's compartment and Allston's, then Perry's on the other side of Allston's and beyond that more and more people hiving and buzzing and swarming. . . . Annette stirred and mumbled something, her mouth loose and damp on the pillowcase. Her back was long, and her neck long like a swan's. She looked sweet there sleeping, like people do, and I had a warm feeling like I wanted to protect her from something, though all I could really do was cover her up to her neck with the sheet.

It occurred to me that maybe I didn't really want to be doing this type of thing—from the belt up, anyway. Like it was something I just let myself get maneuvered into, path of least resistance, don't you know. I wondered too how often the girls themselves must feel that way. That hopeless syrupy way Annette had moved all through the night didn't really seem so sexy now.

Then all of a sudden I flashed on another girl, the one from Ocean City. I hadn't thought of her once since our last night there. It was like a couple of rolls of the odometer on the highway south had scrubbed her completely out of my mind. I saw her how she'd looked the last time, white shirt and black jeans, hair pulled back tight and her brown eyes wide. Only a stranger I'd seen in a bar. I wondered if she'd thought of me since then, and if she did, was it something that hurt?

I didn't have this kind of idea very often, but it struck me now that I hadn't got very far along with my life . . . whatever it was supposed to be about or get done. And already it seemed like I ought to go back and start over.

5. I FEEL THE SAME

It didn't need to be more than a day's drive from Myrtle Beach to Beaufort—a straight shot almost all the way down Highway 17 through the flat lowland pinewoods—but Perry always had us break the trip in Charleston. I don't know what connection he had to the place; maybe he just liked it. He acted different in Charleston than anywhere else. He would check us into a fancy hotel, the kind where you could get room service and it came with silvery domes over top of the plates. He would take everybody to a big dinner down in the old part of town. It was the one place he didn't whine or holler about money, which was kind of odd, because we sure didn't *make* any money there.

Anyway I'd never objected to that break before Beaufort, and this time around I was even grateful for it, since I was the one driving the women—and James Culla. After the misery of that trip from Tennessee, the thought of another long haul with that baby howling in the back felt like mashing a bruise right on the skin of my brain. But the shot down to Charleston was nothing but a breeze. Old baby slept half the way and was real agreeable for the rest of it. We could even listen to something else besides Sade.

Estelle and Rose-Lee were tripping on the hotel. All the rooms had one of them minibar refrigerators with booze and chocolates and fancy snacks. Perry had said they could take what they wanted and I believe they got goofy on champagne. Anyway when I came to collect them for supper they were both grape-smelling, flushed-up and fizzy and Rose-Lee was jumping on the bed like a teenager.

It was walking distance to the restaurant. We went the long way round, by the Battery, to look at the cannons aimed out over the bay. Perry was talking Civil War history, mostly to the women. Estelle was walking beside Rose-Lee, pushing the baby in a peppermint-stripe stroller. Both of their eyes were twinkling but they were listening like good little schoolgirls. Everybody was on good behavior in Charleston, it seemed. The sun was low and copper-colored over the calm water. There was breeze enough to ruffle your hair, but it was still warm enough for shirtsleeves.

We buttonhooked back to the restaurant and got there just at dark. Inside, it was all white tablecloths and silver. You had oysters, clams, shrimp, all kind of fish cooked plain or fancy. All the waiters were tall black men, with white coats and deep dignified voices.

Estelle and Rose-Lee were a little overawed by the place, I'd imagine. They sat up straight on the edge of their chairs and looked at the heavy leatherbacked menus and then at each other. In an even whisper Allston tipped them off to get the shrimp creole. That was about all he had to say the whole time we were in there. But in fact everybody was pretty subdued; in such a place you were expected to talk low and mind your manners. Even old James Culla didn't raise any commotion. He sat tight in some kind of an antique high chair they hauled out for him, and counted his fingers and looked all around like an owl.

The food was excellent, made you feel on top of the world to eat it. Perry ordered a round of oysters for everybody—they came on their shells in a big bed of ice (but Estelle and Rose-Lee wouldn't touch them). Perry ordered some bottles of quality wine. It was good eating and drinking but not much in the way of conversation. The soft deferential voices of the waiters was just about all you heard. I noticed especially how quiet Allston was, even though nobody else was saying much either and Allston was always quiet anyway. But there was something different about it now. Had he been that way last year? Seemed like I couldn't remember.

Everybody at the other tables felt rich, and by that I mean rich with old Southern money. Excepting of course the couple of parties of black folks who were well dressed and well spoken and you figured well monied too—but you could bet nobody in their family ever fought for the Confederacy. You could also bet, go back twenty years or whatever, no black person could have stepped through the front door of the place. This gave me an idea what kind of cat had got Allston's tongue. I looked from him to Perry and wondered if Perry had just failed to think of this, but that wasn't likely—there wasn't much Perry missed. He must've known and brought us here anyway, for whatever Perry type of a reason. I didn't think he meant it bad, or that Allston necessarily took it that way.

But when we were done dinner, I split with Allston, away from the others. When you went out the door of that restaurant you were facing the little end of a long low building that, we knew from Perry's history lectures, had been the slave market—Before the War. (In Charleston you didn't have to ask which war 'cause there hadn't ever been but one). Allston and I walked down the length of this building, on the other side of the street. Neither one of us had said anything since we got up from the table; we'd just gone off together like two magnets drawing each other along.

Allston's eyes were combing the side of that building. There was nothing remarkable about it. It was just an open-air shed raised on square brick posts. The brick was old and you could see it had been whitewashed at one time. Now, at night, it was dark and empty there, but I figured they still sold something out of it in the daytime—flowers, knickknacks, yuppie groceries. The whole neighborhood was done up in that way, but tastefully, with all the history well preserved. Plenty of people in classy-looking clothes were cruising our side of the street, all good-looking in that way that lets you know they work at it. The shops were closed now, but the cafés had tables out on the street, and music came from the chic little bars.

We went straight up the street past the market till we came to a place with a big plate-glass window overlooking the street: a long airy room with a bar in the center, and behind the bar was a case of crushed ice with bottles of Absolut standing up in it— home-flavored with blueberries, peaches, kiwis, hot peppers, and I don't know what else. Anchovies maybe. There must have been thirty different kinds. Allston and I had still not spoken; it seemed like we already had the same thought. We attempted to taste every one of those vodkas, but I forget if we got there before they threw us out.

From Charleston it was nothing to Beaufort, though it was a world away. Being that it wasn't too near a beach, Beaufort was not a tourist town. The original Black Cat was where we played there— that was the actual name of the place. It was a mile or so to the northwest of town, just near the bridge over the inlet, by a cross-roads called Lobeco. On the other side of the bridge from the bar was that kind of motel that rents you little cabins strung out through the pine woods. A far cry from that plush hotel in Charleston, but like Perry said, we could walk to work.

The Black Cat was another cinder-block box that would have done nice for a prison or an arms depot. Somebody had done a pretty convincing job of painting a cat all across the wall that faced the highway—maybe it was meant for a black panther or jaguar. The painted cat was coiled to pounce and had long claws and red eyes and pointed white teeth. Its open mouth and curling tongue were arranged to frame the door of the place. There was only that one door on the front wall, and no windows anywhere in the building.

By day the joint only looked dismal; even the painted cat seemed shabby, and the building was low and dreary, with the still grey water standing behind it and the flat rows of pines beyond the inlet. At night a row of black-light bulbs shone on the cat and made the teeth and eyes and tongue and claws glow in the dark. The place would be shaking from the sound system too. People had told me they could feel the notes of my bass trembling up through the wheels of their car if they just only tried to drive past the place.

Inside was two rooms, one for the bar and about a dozen pool tables, the other, bigger one for the band. That back room was empty except for the bandstand. No tables, no stools, no nothing. If you weren't dancing you stood there holding your drink in a plastic cup. If you passed out and fell down you were apt to get trampled, for the Black Cat did draw sizable crowds. It was a mixed-up salad of people: you had the locals, plus the military that came up from Parris Island on leave (or AWOL, once in a while) or sometimes from a little airbase that wasn't too far off. Every now and then there might be a few people slumming from the beaches, Hilton Head or Edisto. Any black people you saw were with the military—local black folks kept away. And any biker gang running through that area would not miss a stop at the Black Cat.

It was early afternoon when Estelle first scoped the place, after we'd dropped our bags in the "tourist cabins," as that motel liked to call them. I drove her and Perry across the bridge, just to announce our arrival; we took the car 'cause it was drizzling. Stell studied the Cat for about forty-five seconds through the window of the Mustang, then fired herself up a cigarette.

"Look lak people git kilt in thar," she said.

Perry busted out laughing in the back seat. "It is set up for it, tell the truth," he said. "You could drop bodies in the water right out the back door and if they don't sink, they'll wash down to the ocean."

Stell turned around far enough to blow a lungful of smoke at him. "Go on," she said.

"Sure, where we going?" Perry said. "Who's leading the way?"

But the gig went well there, right from the start. It seemed that Perry had sent some clippings ahead from the Myrtle Beach gig, and the owner of the Beaufort Black Cat, who was a semiretired pool shark name of Luther, had seen fit to do a little advertising on the strength of that. Anyway it was just about always raining around there that time of the year, and what else were you gonna do in Beaufort? Estelle hit her groove right away this time—we didn't see any more wobbling at the beginning like we had in

Myrtle Beach. We pulled a big crowd the first night and it seemed to keep growing. This was good, 'cause we were booked in the place clean through New Year's.

I laid off the ladies from the start of this run. A good idea at any time, because it was hard to know for sure who you were dealing with in that place. The girl who took a shine to you might be free, white and twenty-one, as that old saying goes, but on the other hand she might also be a married woman on a tear, or a rebellious biker chick out to send her old man a message—you didn't know. The soldier boys and the locals were constantly hammering on each other over women, and as a matter of fact people did get killed sometimes, not right on the premises usually, but pursuant to events commencing at the establishment—as you might say if you were writing an indictment.

As well to stay out of it, though that was not what I'd done in the past. Time seemed to hang on my hands a little, the hours we weren't playing. You could only sleep so late, even if the shows did run to two or three in the morning. It seemed to rain a good part of each day—too far south to snow so what it did was rain all winter, and blow bad off the ocean. Rain kept us cooped up in the cabins. I'd brought the Hummingbird along since I had my own car to haul it in, and I'd practice on it a part of each afternoon. Only Chris would beef about that some. We were doing the usual, sharing a cabin, but Chris was getting a little crabby. He hadn't hooked up himself yet here in Beaufort; could be he had got too accustomed to using me as a pilot fish.

I'd carry my box to Allston's room; he didn't care one way or another if I sat there and played. That would leave Chris free to watch the TV—the joint had cable, unbelievably, along with moldy pillows and leaks in the cabin roofs. Or I'd go to Stell's cabin with my guitar, only it didn't figure for her to do sing-alongs like we used to in Nashville 'cause she needed to save her voice for the shows.

What was everybody else doing all day? Allston didn't seem to *need* to do anything, even though it was too wet to work out, outside. He could just put himself into a lizardlike stillness and stay there till it got time to start the gig. Perry tried to teach the women to play bridge, which was pretty funny (Allston was actually good at bridge, though). About once a week Perry and Chris would go to some mall and buy up new records; then we'd have a skull session to add some new songs to the set. That meant Estelle had new lyrics to learn, and the rest of us had some new changes to follow.

From about one to five in the afternoon, we could shoot pool for free at the Black Cat, if Luther hadn't locked the place for one of the money games he still sometimes played. Stell and I got to going there pretty regular, walking over the bridge to the bar, her in that black gaucho hat to keep off the rain. She was a presentable barroom shot, definitely no worse than me, and she looked better than she was because she always shot hard, with a cracking confidence, and her eyes seemed like she knew what she was looking at. I began to watch Luther watching her. Luther was a tall and stringy old dude, with a belly hanging over his belt that didn't hardly go with the rest of him. He had a silver pompadour combed back over a pink spot at the back of his head, and often wore a cowboy hat to cover it. I could see he liked Estelle, in kind of a respectful way, liked to listen to her talk and of course to hear her sing. Luther was pretty country himself, though he'd shot pool all over the world, or so he said, and I believed it. If he wasn't busy at another table, he'd coach Stell a little on her game, which I'd not seen him do with anybody else.

You could rent an aluminum canoe at the motel, so one day I proposed to the women we go alligator gigging. Rose-Lee laughed and Estelle shook her head, but they were bored as I was so they ended up going. We had to take the old baby of course since there wasn't nobody to leave him with. Estelle sat cross-legged on a cushion in the middle and held the baby in her lap. There was no fussing over life jackets like they would have been with some other mama.

We put in just below the bridge and paddled into the little backwaters off the inlet—banks of mud and saw grass, and the pines and some live oaks. Sometimes cypress knees stood up from the black water. It was cloudy but not quite raining and sometimes a pool of sunshine would leak through. We had a six-pack of beer and some juice for the baby and a loaf of bread and a pack of baloney, so after a while we tied up and had a picnic right there in the boat. Never did see any alligators, but there were plenty of frogs and turtles and a few snakes sunning themselves on the low branches. On the mud banks were the tracks of deer and raccoons. White egrets stood in the shadows and once we startled a big blue heron that glided ahead of us, low over the water. On the way back the sunset struck the mist and made us a good half of a rainbow.

A few days later me and Allston took a canoe and went back up in the swamp and got ourselves a half-bushel of crabs. Boiled them up in the motel kitchen—everybody was happy with that.

Then about two weeks into the gig, Chris finally made his connection: a long-legged brunette whose name, no lie, was May-belline, or anyway that's what it said on the ID she flashed at the door of the Black Cat. Luther kept ferocious bouncers, broad as barn doors and pumped up like prime beef. There were usually four of these guys cruising the inside; their main job was to throw fights out of doors (the fights could keep on in the parking lot till they were finished or the cops came). Then there were two more on the door, to collect the cover and stop door-crashers and check IDs. You had to come up with *some* kind of paperwork, but Luther was real liberal about what they'd take.

Maybelline had brown eyes to match the long shiny hair that hung straight down her back, and she wore brown lipstick and nailpolish and a brown suede vest over her yoked Western shirt, and brown Frye boots up to the calves of her tight blue jeans. Her car was maroon, though, a maroon minitruck with a black cap over the bed, and looked like it was brand-spanking new. Maybelline had a friend of course, a shorter, plumper blonde named Jocelyn, who rode shotgun in the minitruck—across from one of the islands, I felt sure.

"Jocelyn likes you," Maybelline told me on Saturday night while I was sitting at the bar on break just before the last set.

"That's nice," I said, and it was nice too—I could scope Jocelyn in the mirror from where I was sitting, half-tanked on Tom Collins and swaying a little as she talked to Chris, looking up sweetly into his face and holding his forearm to help keep her balance. She was fresh and pretty and young and willing . . .

"She *really* likes you," goes Maybelline, and she dropped her hand over my thigh, brown-shining nails digging into the inner seam of my trousers, sort of to accent her point. I couldn't hardly help but respond—and these girls, who apparently didn't belong to any bikers or Marines or Beaufort badasses, were as safe a play as you'd ever find around here. I watched Jocelyn swing her hips in the mirror, and thought about the night, and then past it on through to the morning.

"I know what you're saying," I told Maybelline. "But I really . . ."

Maybelline made her whole brown-tone face into one big question mark.

"I really . . . love my dog."

Her smile congealed and slid off her face, her hand pulled back and she slipped off the stool, leaving a cool empty space there beside. Man, where had I come up with that one? I didn't even have a dog—unless you counted Perry's string of mutts in Tennessee. In my brainless insides I felt a twist and chill of disappointment. I hadn't meant to say that at all—just couldn't think of an end to the sentence. But I had a drink with myself in the mirror and felt pretty good about what I'd done.

"Love your *dog*?" Chris goes the next day, when he finally showed up back at the cabin. Whatever he'd been doing all night seemed to have put him in a lot better humor.

"Jailbait," I said. I hadn't really thought this out loud but it must have always been in the back of my mind. Maybelline looked all grown up, but Jocelyn was a little dubious, and the minitruck struck me as the kind of present a girl like that might get from her daddy, maybe at sweet sixteen: sporty but also safe and practical, with no back seat and a gear stick interrupting the space between the two front buckets.

Chris flumped down on his back on the bed and smiled up at the ceiling.

"ID says she's twenty-two."

"What a nice number," I said. "It's your party. Just let me know when you need the cabin, I can crash with Allston."

"Nah," said Chris, still smiling to himself. "It's cool."

For a week or so, this seemed to be true. Maybelline was turning up every night we played—but by herself now. Jocelyn had quit coming along, and now it would be Chris riding shotgun in that minitruck at the end of the shows. Where they went I had no idea—it was a puzzle since I didn't figure she had her own place, but anyway Chris never came in till midmorning. Nobody objected; Chris was in a good mood, and was playing better than usual. They say love will do that for you, or whatever it was.

For a few nights I felt something like regret—not getting my dip in the old honey pot. For a little while it was hard to sleep, but on the other hand it was nice to wake up without a number-eight hangover and a case of the guilts. I got into a little routine. One Thursday night, after the gig, after I'd drunk one nightcap with Stell and Rose-Lee in their cabin, I had just took off my clothes and was fixing to nod off in front of the late-late movie, when *boom-boom* came on the door—"Police!"

"Okay," I hollered, and grabbed my pants, but they didn't wait. The door splintered open, catching me with one leg in my jeans.

"Freeze!" In they tumbled. "Chris McKendrick?" one said to me. "Where is she?"

I shook my head, tongue-tied.

"Don't move," the first one said again. But after a minute I finished putting on my britches. I didn't think they'd shoot me for that—they didn't even have their guns out actually. The second one tore open the closet, crouched down to look under the bed. . . . I was thinking back the best I could, was there evidence of anything illegal lying where they might be fixing to find it, but no, not really, I had hardly even smoked any weed since we hit

Beaufort, unless maybe a jay was going around at the Black Cat. Still in a situation like that, you wonder, are they gonna hit on a roach I stuck in my watch pocket and forgot about?—whatever, only then I realized they weren't looking at that level, no little stuff, they were only looking places a whole person could hide.

"She ain't in here," the second cop said, coming out of the bathroom with a handful of shower curtain he'd just torn down. "Let's see if this little shit is lying."

That was me he was talking about, evidently. The first cop grabbed onto my wrist and hustled me out through the broken door into the rain. There was the cop car with the blue lights going around on top, and a white Mercedes pulled up behind it. The second cop spotlit me with a monster flashlight.

"This him?"

Jocelyn leaned her head out the passenger window of the Mercedes. "No it ain't," says she. I felt sorry for her; she was crying, and without her makeup and Saturday night duds she didn't hardly look more than fourteen.

"All right, sonny, you got some ID?" the second cop goes.

"My wallet oughta be in there on the dresser," I said, and I made to go get it, but the first cop yanked on my arm, so I just stood there, barefoot on the carpet of wet pine needles and the rain running through my hair. Then the second one came back with my wallet open under his nose; he studied the license and then looked at me.

"Good enough." He folded the wallet and let me have it. The first one turned loose of my arm. I put the wallet in my hip pocket and watched while the second cop went and bent down by the Mercedes. The driver was sucking a cigar while he talked, so the glow of the head lit up the lower part of his face.

"Who is that, anyway?" I said.

"Jew lawyer from Atlanta," said the first cop. "He's the proud father."

I didn't say nothing, but my heart fell. Wouldn't you know it would have to be a lawyer's underage girl Chris had took up with.

"He's retired down to Hilton Head." The first cop turned and spat on the wet pine needles. "Sumbitch cain't be more than fifty —I doubt that old. Got more money than sense, what it looks like."

I went inside and got a shirt and cigarette, then came back out and stood smoking on the concrete steps, under the eave. Lights were coming on in some of the other cabins, which were strung out in a horseshoe pattern through the pine woods; Perry's and Allston's cabins were off to the right, and Stell and Rose-Lee's was to the left of ours. The second cop straightened up from the Merc and walked toward me.

"You do stay with this McKendrick feller, am I right?"

I nodded.

"And that would be his fancy-dan car right there?" Cop jerked his jaw at the Trans Am, which was pulled beside my Mustang by the cabin.

"That's right."

"Well, now where could he have got to, do you think?"

"Don't know," I said. "Last I saw of him was when we finished playing at the bar yonder." I looked at my wrist but there was no watch. "I guess that would have been about one o'clock."

"You didn't see where he went or who with." The cop climbed a couple of steps to where he could breathe all over my face. Foot-long hot dog, I'd say—with onions.

"No I didn't."

"Do you know a girl name of Rachel May Horowitz? Tall, long

brown hair, drives a red truck—she's sixteen but could look older."

I dragged on my cigarette to cover a chuckle—it was a stretch from Rachel May to Maybelline, sure enough. The cop threw his open hand to slap the cigarette out of my mouth, but I just drew my head back and let it go by. The time was past for that kind of thing; too many extra people were watching. Perry had come up behind the white Mercedes, along with the motel manager, and on the other side I could see the silhouette of Stell in her gaucho hat, back-lit by the orange glow of her window, and some people from the other cabins were standing around too.

Perry said something I didn't make out, but the cop made a sharp turn toward him from the steps. Just then here came head-lights curving along the drive and everybody stopped to see who it might be.

It was the maroon minitruck, all right, and out hopped May-belline. I caught a breath, but nobody got out the passenger seat, and when the cops shone a light it was empty.

"Papa, what the hell are you doing here?" goes Maybelline, jamming her little fists on her hips.

Papa climbed out of the Mercedes. He was a little man with a big stomach and a beard, not too much hair on top. "Why don't you try telling me where you been?" he snapped.

"With my girlfriend."

"You're lying, child, I know you're lying—right there's your girlfriend." He aimed his cigar at Jocelyn, still whimpering in the Mercedes. Maybelline shot her a look I thought would melt the chrome right off of the car.

Papa walked in back of the minitruck and opened the cap and the tailgate. The cop shone a light in there, and I thought, no way they got Chris curled up in that truckbed. But Papa cussed, then bent down and pulled at something. Out slid a mattress, no hippie foam pad but an expensive-looking futon with a custom paisley cover.

"Well goddamn," Papa said. He kicked the mattress with his two-hundred-dollar shoes.

Maybelline stamped her Frye boot on the pine needles. "Papa, you are embarrassing me!"

Papa drew in his breath, but before he could get started good, the first cop was at his elbow.

"Sir?"

"*What!*"

"I take it you done found your daughter."

Papa unpuffed considerably. "Yes . . . yes, that's right. I thank both you officers for your help."

The one cop gave a look to the other one, and they both adjusted their caps and hitched up their belts, then climbed in the cop car and drove off. I exhaled and then tossed my cigarette, which had burned right down to my knuckles while all this was going on. Maybelline and her papa were going hammer and tongs now, but it looked like she was giving as good as she got, and it didn't look like there was gonna be no court case coming out of it at least. After a few more minutes, Papa snatched her into the back of the Mercedes and they peeled out of there too, just leaving the minitruck open and the mattress on the ground.

"Reckon they'll send somebody after that later," Perry said.

"Yeah."

Everybody but me and Perry had gone on back wherever they came from. Allston had not stuck his head up at all, though he must have known that something was happening—but Allston liked to keep clear of brushes with the fuzz this far South. Perry and I walked around and heaved the mattress back in the truck and closed it. No sense leaving it to get ruined in the rain.

When we got done, there was Chris standing by the door of his car like he was thinking of doing a bolt after all. He looked kind of sheepish when he saw we were watching him. I figured he'd probably bailed out of Maybelline's truck coming in the driveway, once they'd seen the cop lights in front of the cabin. Like as not he'd observed the whole scene from some hiding place off in the trees.

"How you feel?" said Perry. He walked over to Chris and without breaking his stride he swung low and hooked him in the nuts with his left hand. Chris gasped and bent double.

"Jump on your heels," I said, but it didn't seem like he heard me. After a minute he straightened up and groaned.

"What the hell you do that for?"

"Get some blood flowing into your brain," Perry said. "Listen, sport, if you so much as say *boo* to any woman you don't know her entire pedigree, your equipment is coming right off next time—I got the pruning shears sharp and ready, hear me? That goes for all the rest of this run." And Perry turned on his cowboy boot heel and off he walked.

I guess Chris must have been listening pretty hard, because he didn't seem to be seeking after any more romance for the rest of our gig at the Beaufort Black Cat. Maybe it was what Perry said, or maybe he'd grasped the idea of a statutory rape conviction all by himself—anyway, he kept buckled up tight. When we were off, he would just sleep, or mope around the cabin. He spent a lot of time arranging the mirrors so he could check on how fast that thin spot on the back of his hair was growing. But when we were on, he was still playing better than average, though in a different way from before. His guitar got a hard, angry edge on it, like some pressure was mashing the notes out of him. I said something about this to Perry once, and he smirked and told me, "Must be his bodily fluids backing up on him."

All this while, Christmas was closing in on us, and Christmas was not the happiest season in a place like the Beaufort Black Cat. Luther was cheerful 'cause he was raking in money—we had plenty of people still but they were all in a tricky humor. If your family life was going well, you'd be home hanging stockings and trimming the tree instead of hanging around at the Black Cat. That was about the size of it. It was crunch time down at Parris Island— I never saw so many AWOLs in the place, plus the MPs coming in after them. Then there'd be Hell's Angels coming in threatening to bust up the bar if you didn't play "I Saw Mama Kissing Santa Claus" or something like that. The unattached women were all the more hungry and desperate for love. Everybody wanted something they weren't going to get, so there were a lot more fights than usual, and more drunks passing out on the floor.

The band got moody too, myself included. Everybody kind of turned in on themselves. Christmas had always been a dicey time for me. Daddy would start trying to make up for things then. He'd try hard not to drink, and to make the house nice. We used to put up decorations, make Christmas food. . . . Trouble was, when he did slip off that righteous road he'd land a lot harder than usual.

I didn't have to worry about that now, of course. Daddy was way far off in Tennessee and even if he'd been in the next room he didn't have the power to harm me anymore, supposing he still wanted to, which I didn't much think he did. I wasn't obliged to keep thinking over those bad old days, but I kept brooding; I wondered what Melungeons did for Christmas—the same as everybody else, or some peculiar Melungeon thing? Was there a

Melungeon Santa Claus? and so on. Gloom rolled over me like the daily fog.

All over the Black Cat was the same funk of piss-off and disappointment, heavy and solid as the stale smoke and booze smell that fumed off the floors. But this was something we knew how to suck up and ignite, like a nuclear fuel. Allston and I were tight, as tight as ever we had been, we didn't have to even look at each other, just feel what the other one was doing—together we'd vacuum up that soup of bad-feeling and reprocess it into rhythm. One thing this Black Cat had was power sound, so I knew the swamps were shaking to my bass line, and in spite of the weird head I had, I was happy in a way: my hands were happy, and the parts of me that felt the beat.

What it's all about. We were doing, all of a sudden, not more than four or five songs a set, these endless down-tempo minor-key blues jams. Chris would just play on and on, but without ever getting his phrasing into a rut. I never heard him stay at that level so long; he had got outside himself somehow. I noticed too that it was focused, directed; his playing was being sent to somebody, the way he would send it to some babe on the floor he was trying to fascinate. Only now, if I didn't miss my guess, he was mailing the message to Estelle.

That was different—odd too; it didn't figure. Stell was a good-looking woman—I was aware of that as anybody—but she was quick and sharp and hard-edged, where Chris liked them large and soft and sort of dumb, or if not dumb, then single-minded. Women with babies did not turn him on. Nor was there much for Stell to see in Chris that way. In his heart Chris would have chosen to front some sort of hair band—he would be wearing leopard-skin spandex body suits if Perry had let him, and he did go as far in that direction as the style of the group would allow. Like Perry would say, all his brains were in his fingers—whatever was left over from his dick. There was no intentional harm in the guy, but none of us really took him seriously once he laid down his guitar. You wouldn't think that Stell would either, but now there was this charge between them when we played. Stell stood there humming, eyes half-shut and whites just showing, swaying like an underwater plant through his long solos, which he'd be playing off her phrasing of the verses, and when it came her time to sing again she'd play her lines off of what he'd done, till you couldn't make out the words anymore: there was nothing left but the feeling. Voice and guitar strings hit that pitch together: *Please believe me,* they sang, *I feel the same.* . . .

I didn't exactly know where this was coming from, or why. But like Perry might say, what did it matter so long as the mix was cooking?—and it was.

Three days before Christmas the rain let up and the wind died down, and in the afternoon it turned sunny. Not summer weather, but sort of springlike; you could at least unzip your jacket. In the early afternoon I walked across to the Black Cat and shot pool with myself for a while. Then I got bored, 'cause there was no one around but Luther and there was no point playing him when I would never get a turn to shoot. So I headed back toward the motel.

A gang of bikers was standing on the bridge, and I switched to the other side of the road from them. They wouldn't bother me if they knew I was with the band, but then again it was possible they didn't know that. But when I saw they were hurling big bloody dog bones over the railing, I stopped and called over to them.

"What y'all doing?"

"Chumming for alligators."

I laughed at that, and they did too. The sweet weather had lifted everybody's spirits. On the other side of the bridge, I walked down by the inlet shore a ways. Meat was still splashing down from the parapet. They must have bought out a whole butcher shop, but they weren't attracting any actual alligators. A field day for the crabs down there. It was bright and still, and white egrets were standing in the water.

I cut up through the woods toward the cabins, thinking I might see what Stell and Rose-Lee were up to. There was a fresh pine-tar smell in the woods, and the fallen cones rolling under my feet, beneath the brown needle carpet. I was not quite in sight of their cabin when I heard voices, a man pleading and persuading, a woman rising toward a shrill. Couldn't make out the words, just the tone of it, but it stopped me for a minute to listen.

Smack! came the slap of flesh on flesh, which was a sound I knew too well, then the whine of the door spring, and the door slam. I wondered should I interfere, but feet were beating toward me already, and here came Chris, mad as hell and holding a hand to his jawbone. There was a nice handprint across his cheek—you could make out all four fingers. He blew by like he didn't see me, and of course I didn't say nothing to let him know I was there.

I stood there listening but there was nothing more to hear. But it was plain enough nobody was getting raped or murdered so after a while I picked myself another direction to go. Chris might of been making a play for Rose-Lee—she wouldn't be off the limits Perry'd set, being that she was in the family. Or maybe it was Stell? But that was hard to picture. I didn't know, and maybe, I thought, I didn't want to.

———

But the show that night was awful. Everything went wrong that could. Or maybe not, for Allston and I kept playing solid and Perry was up to his usual. However, Chris's time was shot straight to hell, and Estelle was actually singing off-key half the time, along with fluffing lyrics she'd had cold for a couple of months. The groove was gone—nothing lasts forever, but this was embarrassing. An advantage of the Black Cat circuit was you could really make quite a lot of mistakes without anybody else noticing much, but this was so bad people actually started to walk out. Luther was sticking his head in the door from the bar, rolling that custom pool stick in his hands and frowning. He might not have been the biggest expert on music but he wasn't slow to notice anything that touched his pocketbook.

Perry chewed us all out for about an hour after the show, stamping up and down the riser and bitching like a football coach on a losing streak. The lecture was addressed to the lot of us, including Perry himself, but really intended for Estelle and Chris like we all knew. Chris sulked, which was his way—stuff was piling up on him too hard, with the girl going wrong and now this. Stell was just silent, without being sulky. She'd look Perry straight in the eye, and she didn't say nothing back to him, but it was like somebody that's learned to sit up in church and look awake while their head is one million miles gone to somewhere else. . . .

Next afternoon we rehearsed for three hours and by show time we had a whole new set, spun ninety degrees toward our country rep. All the songs were shorter, brighter, poppier. That night, Chris was playing like himself again, not pumping all that bloody heart into it like he had been, but with the watch-me kind

of flash he normally had, to show what he could do. He was playing to *show Perry* now, but that was good enough, and Stell also was
back on track. She'd developed a pride in her work, I could see, the
kind that would get you through a bad day or week or run—it
went over. Luther could go back to shooting pool, and smile when
he counted the cash box after closing.

Then it was Christmas Eve. The house was thin because you
wouldn't go to a Black Cat on that particular night of the year unless you flat didn't have anywhere else to go, but there were
enough people in that shape to see us through our usual three sets.
Now I saw the reason for taking it country—nice maudlin songs
folks could curl up in the corners and cry over. We did not do
Christmas carols—nobody was about to stand up there and sing
"Silent Night" or whatever—but Jesus kept getting his foot in the
door some way, mostly in these kind of bluegrassy hymns such as
"All My Tears," "Wayfaring Stranger," "By the Mark," "I Am a Pil-
grim." Perry called song after song like that—they must have been
well known to him from his preaching days. I wondered again did
he ever handle snakes at church.

With that, we did have two big weepers from the Dolly Parton
backlist. Stell closed down the second set with "Home for Christmas," and you know it, there wasn't a dry eye in the house, except
maybe out in the pool room of course. The last song of the whole
night was "Hard Candy Christmas," and she did it proud, wrung
every last crying drop out of the thing. My own eyes were pricking
by the time she got through. And even after I had packed up my
bass and headed toward the bar for a closing-time drink, my heart
still felt mushy as a rotten cantaloupe.

There was the usual assortment of people finishing their pool
games and drunks not wanting to go home, the beefcake bouncers

working on them real gentle and reasonable at first, then with a bit more pressure as they began to get impatient. A gang of Luther's after-hours buddies was clustered round the bar, along with a few of the people who worked there. Then the crowd shifted and there on a barstool, drinking Coke from the can and wearing by God a Santa Claus tie, was my daddy.

For one second I felt like I had been shot. Then I was sort of glad to see him.

"Merry Christmas, Jesse," he goes.

"Same to you." I set down my bass and took the stool next to his. The barmaid gave me a bourbon. "What are you doing here?" I asked him.

"Had me some vacation time squirreled up." He grinned and felt himself for a cigarette. "Figured I'd git out of the cold a while—give you a little surprise." He looked at me a little bit crossways. I hadn't known if I trusted that Coke, but now I could see he was clear-eyed and sober.

"You done that, all right," I said. I saw my hand reach out to touch him on the arm, kind of like to make sure he was really there—which he must have been, 'cause next thing you know we were hugging each other.

Daddy had come with a gunnysack full of presents—I mean, an actual burlap bag with the name of a feed company stenciled on it. I don't know where he got this thing; maybe it was saved up in the house somewhere, for he was a bit of a pack rat. He had bought clothes for everybody, which could have seemed strange, but it was his habit to cruise the thrift shops when he wasn't drinking, so I supposed he must be doing it more than ever now. He bought most of his own gear that way, and that was how he used to outfit me for school. It made him a better judge of sizes than you might expect of a man. Anyway he had got Chris some garish Quiana shirts and for me and Perry and Allston some cotton and flannel shirts we might actually wear, plus a denim jacket that fit me pretty well. For the women he had silk blouses, and a couple of fancy Western shirts. It was all picked nicely to suit people's taste. At the bottom of the bag there was stuff for the baby.

I thought back to the year before last—trouble had already been brewing with Melissa, and we spent the day slinking around by ourselves, doing our best to avoid each other and basically just waiting for it to go by. To get through to a normal day without so much riding on it. But this time it was like Daddy showing up had altered the mix just enough to make it better. He distracted everybody from the dust-up between Chris and Estelle and Perry. We could all make like a happy family, at least for that one day. The Black Cat was closed for Christmas, so we were off for the evening. We drove down to Beaufort proper and had a restaurant Christmas special with turkey and the fixings. After that everybody went to bed cheerful, or that's how it seemed.

Come to find out, Daddy had bought himself a week at the same motel. You could get a better deal paying that way—it's how we did it ourselves. So there he was for his winter vacation. I didn't want time to hang on him too heavy, so we went crabbing a couple of times in the canoe, and one time fishing with cane poles, though nothing was biting. He took a ride with me in my car, his head cocked to listen for sounds that only dogs and me- chanics can hear, and then spent about thirty hours tinkering with it till it ran even smoother than before. But other times he'd bug off by himself, hole up in his cabin or drive off who knew where

—he'd driven down from Nashville in his powder-blue pickup truck. Every night he'd go to the shows, standing and watching us part of the time, and otherwise playing pool with people—he wasn't much good but he seemed to enjoy it, and he'd struck up an acquaintance with Luther.

All this was fine, but after a couple of days I did get a little edgy. It just wasn't like him to hold the same course for so long, especially during holiday times—I was braced for some kind of big zigzag. But you know, he really wasn't drinking. Anyway when he came to the bar he kept steady on soft drinks or juice or whatever. I didn't know what he did when he was off by himself, but he never had a smell or a stagger.

The night before New Year's Eve I woke up with kind of a pop, like I'd had a bad dream, but I couldn't remember it. Chris was snoring something awful—that's where all those damn bear dreams kept coming from, I knew. I lay there an hour and still couldn't sleep, so I got up and went out walking, barefoot on the cool pine needles. It was just before dawn, the sky breaking blue above the trees. I saw a light showing in Daddy's cabin so I headed that way. I was thinking if he was up and restless too—we might actually talk or something, who knows?

I went up the steps and was just about to tap on the door when I heard something I wasn't expecting. The window was cracked half open and there was sound coming out. A two-person sound. I bent my ear and heard a woman whimpering and huffing—he was doing the do with somebody in there.

How do you like that? In one way I wanted to break out laughing, but in another it was sort of an embarrassment. Anyway I backed off from there pretty quick. Was he picking up chicks at the bar, or what? I figure it was none of my business. Except, I supposed, I wished him joy. . . .

New Year's Eve was officially party time at the Black Cat—and the last night of our run there, to boot. Luther ran a special where you could buy a whole bottle of Cold Duck for about three bucks, if you were fool enough. The joint was packed, and we turned in a kicking show, if I do say it myself. The third set wound up around twelve-thirty, but being it was a special occasion we were due to play a fourth. I circulated during the break, and had a few more drinks than I really required.

It was hard to move or find anybody in the crowd, and finally I heard Perry on the microphone, calling the band back to the stage. I was just about there, threading my way through all the people, when something tugged on the back of my shirt. When I turned there was my daddy, and it didn't take me a minute to see he was drunk as a skunk, just reeling. "Jesse," he goes, he could barely slur out my name—eyes had that red glow and he leaned in to blow his bourbon up my nose, holding himself up by my shirt collar as he tried to think what he wanted to say.

I twisted loose, and climbed onto the riser. Picked up my bass and checked the tuning. My hands were shaking but I didn't know what I felt. I just wanted to get away from it, go on about my business.

Allston had witnessed this little scene, so he cocked an eyebrow at me from his seat behind the drums.

"He's got a skinful is all," I said.

Allston looked at me like he might say something to that, only just then Perry turned toward us and counted off real quick and we all pounded into the opening riff of "Jumping Jack Flash." Right at that moment, like it was their cue, somebody launched a Cold Duck bottle—it sailed over our heads and shattered against the cinder-block wall behind the stage. All of a sudden about five fights broke out on the floor, or maybe it was just one big riot. Bikers against Marines seemed to be the basic program. When we quit playing you could hear the women holler; some were just roller-coaster screams, but some were real.

I saw my daddy reel back like he'd been hit, and Allston and I dived down in there without hardly glancing at each other. Some soldier boy was blocking my way, but I hooked his leg out from under him and passed over as he tumbled. Allston got to Daddy first and caught him in some kind of lifesaver hold; together we boosted him onto the stage. He tried to get up one time but I gave him a good hard push back down and he seemed willing to lay low after that.

The bouncers weren't trying to break it up—they didn't when it got that big. They just cordoned off the stage and the bar area, to protect the cash and booze and sound system, and waited for the cops to come. This didn't take long because the cops already had the place more or less surrounded, laying for drunk drivers coming out of there. All of which was pretty much routine for the Beaufort Black Cat on New Year's Eve. You didn't expect anybody to get seriously hurt—nothing beyond "treated and released." The Cold Duck special was a bad idea though: bottles were flying all over the place and you had to cover your eyes against the chunks of broken glass.

The cops closed it down pretty quick anyway, so we all headed home a bit earlier than planned. Allston and I hauled Daddy into his cabin with his feet dragging back on the steps, and let him lay facedown on the bed, muttering to himself as we left. I'd had more than enough to drink, so I fell into a heavy dark sleep that lasted till ten or so next morning. By the time I wandered into the motel restaurant, looking for juice to wash down my aspirin, Perry and Allston already had a table.

In a few minutes Daddy drifted in too, blear-eyed and shaky, hands trembling as he fired his first cigarette. The odd thing was he wouldn't stop apologizing, though nobody could quite figure out what for. Perry and Allston were looking at each other—he hadn't done anything to us, after all. Then I realized he didn't know that. Blackout drunk—he had no idea what he might have done.

In the end I walked him out to his truck. He was hell-bent on driving back to Nashville that day, and had already loaded up.

"I'm sorry Jesse," he said one more time. "I never intended to do thataway—missed too many meetings is all."

"Nothing to be sorry for that I can see," I said. "Are you fit to drive? It's a long haul for one day."

"I still got a day or so coming to me," he said. "I can break the trip if I need to, stop over at a motel."

"If you say so. Drive careful, will you?"

"Hey, Jesse?"

"What?"

"I'm sorry about all this, you know."

"Will you quit saying that?" I said. "You didn't do nothing."

"Yes I did too."

"No you didn't," I said. "All right, I admit you got knee-walking drunk, but nobody saw you do any worse. New Year's Eve, anyway—it was a party. Ain't nobody holding anything against you."

He looked at me for a minute, sort of dog-eyed. I noticed there was getting to be some grey in his hair, though it was still full and bushy. "All right then," he said.

We shook hands, and I touched his shoulder as he climbed into the truck. He was holding a straight line when he pulled onto the highway so I figured he would make it all right. What was I supposed to think of it all? I felt a little funny, letting him go like that, but we were pulling out ourselves the next day anyway.

6. BLUE

The Miami Black Cat was a place in a strip mall, and technically it wasn't even Miami, but some town with another name that had been swallowed up by the sprawl pooling up from the south. Even Perry couldn't claim personality for the hotel we stayed at here. It was just cheap . . . a medium-rise building in an iffy location that had been handed off between different chains for ten years it seemed like—anyway there was a different sign on the joint every time we came there. But it was always the same old place, maybe a little moldier from year to year. The restaurant downstairs had evolved into a wino bar and if you came in real late (which we usually did) or left real early (which we almost never did) you'd be stepping over street people passed out in the lobby. Outdoors was a four-lane stop-and-start stretch of road that looked like it went on forever, lined on both sides with low buildings painted those pale Miami colors, or maybe the paint was just faded in the sun. It was hot when you went outside, you worked up a sweat if you had to hump gear in the daytime, but the nights were cool enough, and pleasant. You had to drive to get to the beach, but like Perry said, we could walk to work.

So first thing after we checked in, me and Perry and Chris and Allston went over to unload the amps and drums. The women weren't doing no heavy lifting and in fact I'd loaned Estelle the Mustang to drive so they could bug out with the baby for a couple of hours. At the motel the air-conditioning smelled of mildew, and there was no way to get a window open anywhere. The Black Cat, whose real name was the Silver Spoonful, was just on the next block, in a building set back from the street behind a parking lot, in between a hairdresser and an all-night Cuban diner. We had driven the van, because of the gear.

Miguel, the owner, was just unlocking as we got there. The place didn't open till four o'clock—they didn't do lunch business. Miguel sent out some busboys to help us unload, both of them Haitians who didn't speak English, but some smooth, sweet-sounding language of their own. They were part of the restaurant in the front room of the place, where they served frozen steak and seafood till about nine o'clock. Behind that you went through some other doors to a huge barn of a room in the back of the building larger than looked possible if you were outside in front, and that was where the bandstand was.

So we set everything up and Perry went to fidgeting with the P.A., which wasn't as good as the one in Beaufort, trying to get a mix that would compensate for the tin roof and the concrete floor. They dumped sawdust on the floor at night, and swept it out and replaced it the next day (or so), but like Perry said, it wasn't hardly enough sawdust to really help the sound. But finally he got it as good as it was going to get, and we went and ate a little something at the Cuban place, and then Estelle came over, dressed and ready for the gig.

That first night we drew a medium crowd, and through the rest of the week it stayed medium, picking up just a little heat on the weekend. We weren't going on a roll like we had in South Carolina; that was obvious after the first couple of nights. Partly this was because there was a lot more other stuff to do in Miami than there was in Beaufort. Partly it was the time of year—not the best for partying. Christmas was done with, left the locals feeling poor, and it was too early for all Florida to fill up with college kids on break.

We drew decent, but no better. Even though the owner was Spanish, the clientele was mostly Conchs, this being the local term for rednecks. They'd start drifting in around nine o'clock, just as the dinner business was tailing off. The people who ate at the Silver Spoonful were altogether a different bunch—mostly retired honkies with plaid pants and funny-colored shoes, and they would clear out before we started playing. By nine-thirty the restaurant was empty except for the bar, with the Conchs milling around in their tight jeans and tattoos. We played Wednesday through Saturday, ten to two. By eleven the big room was as full as it would get, maybe half-full, with a few people dancing but most just trailing around through the sawdust, sloshing their beer and making their connections—going about their usual business with us as the background track. You could purchase coke in this place if that happened to be what you wanted. Some of our Conch clientele ran smuggling boats back and forth from the islands, and I guess old Miguel might have had a hand in it too—at the least the name he'd picked for the place suggested it.

We didn't want to go messing with that. Perry was set against cocaine—he said it was bad for musicianship. (Whereas heroin could be a good musician's drug, according to the Perry way of knowledge, though probably not worth the consequences for most people.) Still and all, after the first few nights I began to feel like we needed a jolt of *something*. The fact was, we didn't really sound all that good. The room was a problem—between the tin roof and the concrete floor, the *brang* factor was something serious. Then the crowd itself was lame—we couldn't get them up and rolling with us no matter what we did. They weren't hostile, but they weren't that interested either—they weren't going to give you anything back.

Then there were little jinx-type happenings, the first of which was that James Culla got sick. One of those nasty baby colds, that started with a fever. Stell blamed the motel air-conditioning, the baby going in and out from hot to cold. She lost a few nights' sleep looking after him and then of course she got sick herself, a thick, sticky cold that played hell with her voice. She was a trouper about it, I got to admit. She never really complained and she sung hard as she could, but no amount of cough drops and hot tea and honey and whiskey could put her quite back where she needed to be.

That was the first week. Sunday morning I woke up earlier than I would have thought possible, in time enough for church if I'd wanted to go. Three days off—that felt pretty good, but I couldn't go back to sleep. The room smelt funny and Chris was snoring so I dressed and went down, picking my way through the stroked-out homeless in the lobby. It was sunny outside but not too hot yet, and quieter than I'd ever known it. That four-lane strip roared all day and all night, seemed like, but Sunday morning it was dead, and I could even hear some birds.

I went over to that Cuban diner and had an omelette with chorizo and rice and beans. It was great food in that place (way better than what they slung at the Black Cat next door) and dirt-cheap too. So far it was the only thing I was really liking much about this gig. But after I ate I felt contented, just a little sleepy again. I ordered myself a sweet *café con leche* and had almost got one smoke ring to go through another one when the doorbell jangled and Rose-Lee pushed the stroller in.

I waved her over to my table, and she sat down and ordered a diet Coke and a piece of banana creme pie. She ate about half of that, then lit up a Virginia Slim and pushed the pie over to James Culla to paddle around in. Some flies came over to check out this action.

"How's Stell this morning?" I said.

"Sleeping."

"Yeah," I said. "Let her rest up and she'll be back on track come Wednesday."

Rose-Lee gave me her gimlet look, pointed her cigarette at me like it was a gun. She was more het up than I was used to seeing her lately, and I kind of got a mental picture of her booting her Nashville boyfriend out of the house by his tailbone. Not for the first time, I wondered how or if she was getting her jollies on this trip, 'cause nights we were playing she was tied up with the baby. True, if he was sleeping she could park him in the bar and dance a few rounds or let guys buy her drinks. There were always a few who admired her looks, and some would have been drawn to the sharp edge on her too, but I'd never seen her go beyond a light flirtation. That baby carriage might have been a damper. Of course, I didn't know what she wanted. There were good long parts of the day when she was off duty that I didn't know what she was doing, either.

"Somebody needs to tell Chris to lay off," Rose-Lee goes. Still had me in her gunsight, how she looked.

"Huh?" I said. "Has he been hitting on you?" This might have made sense, under all the circumstances. Rose-Lee jammed her cigarette bang in the center of the remains of that pie, so hard she snapped the filter off.

"*Hayull* no, not me," she said. "It's mmmm—Estelle. Yeah. He's been bothering Estelle."

"Unh-hunh," I said, wisely as I could manage. I slouched down in my chair and looked at the glare coming in the plate-glass windows in front, which excused my having on sunglasses.

"Tell me about it," I said. And I called up to the counter for a beer, without knowing for sure if they'd give me one Sunday morning, but there didn't seem to be any blue laws, or at least not in this diner.

"Ain't much to tell," Rose-Lee said. "Well, he give it the first try back there at Beaufort? Fine, you know, but she ain't interested. Second time he come sniffing around she busted him one and thought that'd be the end of it. But now he keeps on, you know, talking trash to her when nobody else cain't hear him? Nasty stuff like you know what I mean? I mean he's bound to know he ain't gitting nowhar by this time. I believe he's just doing it for meanness."

"Okay," I said, though in fact she'd pretty well blackened my morning. "Let me see what I can do."

"Yeah, sure," Rose-Lee goes. "I tell you what—somebody better do something."

I did give it some thought, all through the next week. It even made it a little easier to dope out what generally was going on. When Wednesday came and we played again, I could hear where the rest of the problem was—not just the bad room or Estelle's cold. It was bad mojo between Estelle and Chris, the flip of what they'd had between them on the stage of the Beaufort Black Cat; they were cutting each other now, instead of courting. And I guessed there hadn't ever been a honeymoon.

So Saturday night when the last set was done, I was sitting at the bar sipping my last bourbon, watching the Haitians, in the mirror, as they laid chairs up on tables and started to sweep. Stell dropped onto the stool next to me and clicked her glass against mine.

"Who's that thar?" she goes.

"Who's who?" I said, but then I saw what she was talking about. There were a lot of old promo shots and posters taped to the mirror or stuck in the frame, and sure enough there was one of us, a two-year-old glossy gone yellow and curly, but anyway the gang was all there except in Estelle's place it was Melissa. I had been looking right at it but not really seeing it.

So I told Estelle what her name was, and yeah, she used to sing with us. "Nothing like you do, though," I said.

Stell was kind of chewing her lip, fussing with the cord to her gaucho hat. "Where is she now?" she wanted to know.

"Back in Nashville," I said. "She still sings the bars and all. I hear she gets by pretty well."

Stell seemed to be looking at herself in the mirror now, and she didn't really seem to be listening anymore. After a minute she threw down her drink and shoved her hat on her head and left.

I sat there looking at the damn picture. Melissa was down on one knee in front of the rest of us, holding up an acoustic guitar in one hand (she couldn't hardly play the thing, just used it as a prop). Chris was directly behind her, one hand on her shoulder, underneath her straight iron-colored hair. The photographer had probably suggested this pose, I didn't seem to remember. Melissa was a nice-looking woman, a bit heavyset in a way that went well with her big blues-mama voice, which had a lot more power than precision. It was true that she wasn't as good as Estelle. She had a bit more jaw than would make her pretty but still it was a handsome face. There had been a stage honeymoon between her and Chris, during the six weeks we were playing Key West. He never sounded better and neither did she and they were sleeping together too at the time. I had our room all to myself for better than a month. But then it went sour and they started to fight, stopped speaking to each other at all after that, but started going to Perry separately with complaints about the one upstaging the other one—oh my. Perry put a lid on that somehow, so the band was at least functional on the return loop through the Deep South states to Nashville, which was where Melissa wished us all to the Devil and quit.

And there you go. I swiveled my stool around to face the room, the Haitians with their mops, 'cause I really didn't want to look at that picture no more. I had a cold feeling way down in my gut, and I knew I really didn't want Estelle to leave.

The solution was simple, I saw quick enough. All Chris needed was to hook up with somebody else, get his rocks off—then he'd feel better and stop hassling Estelle and everything would go back like it ought to. I knew the whole stupid situation went back to Beaufort, Maybelline and the fuzz and what Perry had said. But Perry would forget all that if we just started playing better again. Anyway the rules were different at this Black Cat. If you went tom-catting you might stand a chance to get your ass shot by a ticked-off Conch husband, but nobody's daddy was gonna be a lawyer.

To get this to work, we'd have to go back to the hunt-in-pairs thing. Also, I was going to have to start it. I began surveying the talent that showed up at night, disgusted with myself, but at the same time interested. I needed to make a wise and careful choice, because I definitely did not want to get shot myself, or pounded into the pavement with a car jack, or any of the other good stuff on the menu. I don't think I'd ever done anything quite so calculated, and it made me feel sick and excited all at once, like watching some real nasty piece of pornography.

Then one day, I believe the next Monday, something happened strange. I had been up the road a ways, thinking I'd buy some new tapes for the car. I had bought a couple, and was playing the Doc Watson *Memories* collection as I drove back to the motel, not really wanting to go back there but without much of another plan either. Doc was doing "Windy and Warm," a signature tune for him in those days, with the heavy syncopation that marked his playing—he vamped the chords so hard you'd of thought there was a drum set somewhere but there wasn't, just the two acoustic guitars, his son Merle ornamenting the melody. I filled the bass line in, in my head, letting the drive push me down the road. Key of A minor. I always heard that key as a color, reddish brown, the shade of rust, but Doc Watson was blind. Had been born that way, I thought. That title said what a blind man would be feeling—there was nothing in that phrase to see. I thought too how weird it was that since Merle had been dead for about ten years, it was a dead man's fingers finding those notes now, and had Merle been Doc Watson's eyes?

So I was already in sort of a spooky mood. About a block from the motel I stopped for a red light and noticed a pretty woman waiting on the corner, alone, wearing a black and white polka-dot dress which clung to her legs as the wind dragged at the skirt; she had black hair fastened behind her head, but parts of it had come loose to float across her face in that warm breeze. I felt my heart roll, because her figure was like something you understand completely in your dream and yet you know that when you wake you'll lose the meaning of it, and maybe even the memory. I rolled down my window. That woman caught her hair in one hand and looked at me with her dark eyes, and it was Stell.

"Hey," I said. I wanted to say *Hey, good-looking* or *Hey, whatcha doing?* but the only thing that came out was *Hey.* It didn't seem to matter. Stell's eyes cleared as she saw who I was, and she came around the front end of the car in a floaty way like she was dreaming too, and she got in. The light changed, and I started driving. Didn't know where we were headed yet.

"Who's that playing?" Stell said.

I told her who it was, both of them, and told her what I'd been thinking too.

"How'd he die?" Stell goes.

"Turned over a tractor.

She sniffed. "Ain't that the way."

"Some say he might have been high at the time. Perry used to know him a little, he claims—Perry says he was bad to do coke." As I said this I began to wonder how that played into Perry's coke theory and if he thought it had been bad for Merle's musicianship, along with his health.

Stell coughed and sniffled—her cold had got better but was still hanging on. She unfolded her hand and there was a grotty old paper towel for her to blow her nose on.

"I know," I said. "Let's go to the beach—bake the rest of that cold on out of you."

She looked across at me. "I ain't got no swimming suit."

I went another block till I saw the right kind of store, and pulled up to the curb. "Buy one," I said. "We're all making money."

I thought I'd be in for an hour wait, so I was glad I had the new tapes, an old Joni Mitchell and the Gram Parsons I'd been wanting to get, along with the Doc Watson, but she was done in about twenty minutes, coming down the steps from the shop with a little bag rolled up under her arm and the polka-dot skirt whipping round her knees. It was that dress that had made me not know her, I thought, for since the baby was born I'd only seen her wearing jeans.

The Doc Watson tape lasted us all the way to the beach. Stell ran it back a time or two, on "Moody River" and "Columbus Stockade." I thought maybe she was learning lyrics, which wasn't such a bad idea—I could see us doing "Columbus Stockade," anyway.

We paid at the beach gate, drove in and parked. I found an old blanket in the trunk, which Stell gave a bit of a funny look to.

"Better'n getting all sandy, right?" I shrugged and she looked in the other direction. We climbed up a wooden staircase over a dune. The beach wasn't so crowded, it being a weekday, but we walked a ways north anyway, Stell stopping a minute to slip off her shoes, for better footing on the loose sand. We picked a place and I spread the blanket and found some sticks to pin it down, because it was still breezy. Stell reached to undo something behind her back and all at once her dress came off. There she was standing— in her new suit, which obviously she must have put on in the store, just a simple black one-piece with a spaghetti strap around her neck. It didn't look like she needed the strap. She looked good, natural, ageless. The surf was hushing against the sand and the breeze still blowing warm. I must have been staring at her, I guess.

"Do you burn?" I said, when she noticed me looking. She looked kind of puzzled, glancing down at herself; her skin was a dark olive shade like mine.

"I don't know," she said.

"Better not take a chance on it."

There was a little store there by the gate so I walked back and got some sunscreen and a couple of cold drinks. Stell rubbed the lotion on her arms and legs and then looked at me, a bit hesitant, and I took the tube and put some on her back. It gave me a sort of shy thrill to do it. Her back was firm and smooth and already glowing warm from the sun. She dropped her head forward and pulled up her hair so I could put lotion on her neck, and sighed a little as I rubbed it in. I felt a bone shiver: Who was this anyway? This woman who had had a baby, and could sing like that? She didn't have any chicken skin on her anywhere. When she lay back and closed her eyes, her face looked lineless and young as a teen-ager's.

I had on colored boxers good enough to swim in, especially with nobody real close by, so once I got hot that's what I did. I swam against the drift till I was just slightly tired, and then floated on my back, watching the clouds and the gulls and the pelicans and thinking, Perry really has it nailed—always summer, wherever we are, and almost always the coast. When I rolled up in the water, I'd drifted back to where I started, and Stell was wading in the shallows. I waved her to come out, but she wouldn't till I went and got her. I took her hand and led her through the breakers, her skipping and giggling like any girl, till we were chest-deep in the gentler swells. She looked up at me, mischievous, touching her lip with the tip of her tongue. Her eyes were clear green like the water.

"I cain't swim," she goes.

Lord, Lord. I showed her how she could float in salt water, with my hand under the small of her back at first, then nothing once she got the trick of it. Her eyes closed and her hair spread out on the water. She liked it, but I took her in pretty soon, I mean, what if I drowned her?

In the late afternoon we showered and dried out in the sun—neither one of us had thought of a towel. There was a little restaurant where you could get hot dogs and beer, and it tasted good after the sun and salt water. A little past sunset we got back in the car. Neither one of us said much on the drive, but when I pulled up level with the motel, I looked at Stell and she shook her head.

I drove on past. It was dark now. Stell reached down to the seat between us, picked up my new Joni Mitchell tape and unzipped the plastic with her thumbnail. Blue. The sweetness and skill of that voice . . . Stell played the title cut over and over, her head tipped to one side, lips forming the words.

It was solid dark by the time we came to South Beach, down that main drag, which was all lit up with neon. I didn't know my way around here so well, but I knew there were high-end hotels and clubs.

"You want to get out and walk awhile?"

"Sure," Stell said, her voice softer than it usually was—a lot less of that cracker crow-call in it. More like her singing voice . . . We walked up one side of the street and back down the other. After a few minutes she took my arm, like a lady. Our reflection chased us in the windows of the shops and when I peeked over I thought we looked as natural as any other couple. My skin was still tingling from the sun and the salt and I felt polished all over from the wind blowing on me all afternoon.

"Where's the ocean?" Stell said, raising her nose to the breeze. You could smell the salt still, it wouldn't be far.

"Other side of that hotel, I guess."

We were just coming up to a fancy hotel, with a half-circle driveway curved in front of stone steps, and a high stone facade like a cathedral or something. Taxis and limos were letting people off, and there was quite a stream going up the stairs. Somehow we flowed into it, neither of us saying we intended to. The lobby was grand, fancier even than that Charleston hotel, all high ceilings and chandeliers, the help standing around with tuxedos on. We kept on drifting with the group we'd come in with, Stell smiling around carefully in this way she had, her mouth shut to hide the front tooth she lacked. She had quit using the bridge Perry'd bought her, a few weeks into the run—said she couldn't get used to the way it felt on the roof of her mouth. Perry kicked about this a while and then gave up, though he still badgered her to put it in if there was going to be a picture.

I figured we'd come to a bar or a restaurant, but pretty soon we were outside again—a big walled courtyard with a pool and poolhouse and a six-piece band playing danceable jazz-type tunes, and a whole bunch of other people. A waiter walked up with a tray and handed us each a glass of champagne, and Stell thanked him with a bob of her head and that graceful closed-mouth smile.

By this time we'd caught on it must be a private party back here, but nobody seemed to object to our attending it. Stell looked as good as any woman there and the men were all dressed casual as me. There was a lot of fresh sunburn, and tan-lotion smell. Nobody seemed to expect anything of us—they all just kept humming amongst themselves, in what might as well have been a foreign language for all we cared. Smooth gents in white coats kept coming up and asking us to eat another scallop wrapped in bacon, one more shrimp ball pasted on sugarcane, or to please be good enough to drink another glass of champagne.

Then the band was playing something in waltz time and we were dancing—I was I guess waltzing with Stell though I didn't know I had any idea how to waltz. Maybe she was taking care of it, I don't know, not that it seemed like something she'd know much about either. We kept on somehow, among the other couples at first, but then we danced our way deeper into the courtyard on the far side of the pool. The moon hung high above the courtyard wall and through an arched doorway at the end you could see a road-way of moonlight on the water. Stell's dress felt like silk though I don't suppose it really was, and when the song ended and she swam into me it felt like she didn't have anything on under it either. I tasted salt and a trace of sunscreen on her neck, her cheek, and her mouth was warm and a little smoky. Quick rasp and dart of her tongue on mine, then she pulled away and dipped back over my arm, her head dropping back and down and her hair hanging free.

She came up laughing, and put her hand on my back, two fingers in the waistband of my jeans. "Don't get too drunk," she said, with a deep throaty chuckle. In fact, we didn't stay too much longer after that.

When we got in the car I reached to pull her closer but she just took my hand between the two of hers and stayed on her side of the seat. All the way back to the motel she sang—songs I had heard her sing to the baby, and a few of the sweeter ones we did in the shows, and she sang "Blue," which she must have learned on the way down unless she knew it from before. Word for word and note for note, but an octave lower than the record, and her voice richer and fuller too than what I had on tape.

We walked into the motel side by side, not touching or looking at each other, keeping the secret. I saw Chris and Perry were drinking in the bar—they'd probably be there for a while since it wasn't all that late. When we got into the elevator we fell into each other again, kissing harder, mussing up each other's hair. The door opened on our floor and Stell patted herself back into place and we walked down the hall, a pace apart; I wanted to take her right to my room but she stopped at their door and kissed the corner of my mouth and gave me a look that said *Just a minute.* She laid her finger across my lips, then went inside.

I unlocked our room and hung the DO NOT DISTURB sign on the door in case Chris came up earlier than I thought likely (that was our system, when we needed one, simple enough) and lay on the bed, tingling still, waiting for her to come. After a little while I smoked a cigarette, and a little while later I lit another one and found I didn't want it. After forty minutes I went and stood outside her door. Was I going to start scratching and pounding and slobbering?—they'd think it was Chris come to bother them some more. I listened and didn't hear anything at all. After a minute I went back to our room and took the sign down off the door.

I didn't really feel let down or tricked. Damn if I knew what I felt. All the next week she would give me private, liquid smiles, but I never was alone with her. It didn't seem to happen and I didn't want to push it, I didn't want to risk acting like a kid. Those smiles seemed to say that we had been lovers once and were still friends, or had once been lovers and might be again. Lover was the word in my mind; I had known lots of girls, women, but hadn't called them that. Or maybe it was something else in Estelle's smile. It was like we had a pleasant secret between us—except she knew what it was and I didn't.

None of this bothered me like you might think. It opened up this dreamy space in me where the day at the beach and the night of dancing had never got finished, but was only suspended. Because of this, I felt happy and calm.

Chris was getting edgier and edgier though. What was his deal? I thought about this as the week wore on. He kept coming in a lot later than me, and he had a case of sniffles with no cold to go with it. Bound to be running a few quiet silver spoonfuls up his nose. Under the circumstances I had dropped the project of hooking him up with some Conch chick so that left me with not much to do but wonder. Fact was, I didn't really know Chris that well in a way, in spite of us being running buddies on the road the last few years. We talked about the girls we liked, and bands, and what we were gonna play, and that was about it.

If you were Chris, what did you want out of this world? Say he was halfway between my age and Perry's—that would put him something over thirty. He'd been playing around Nashville or on the road for years. He was good enough and connected enough to get session work when he was in town, and he'd toured with at least three bands that almost, almost signed a record deal. Now he was in a band that didn't even *want* a record deal. That much was official. On that subject I could play Perry's riff in my head like a tape: *Don't overreach yourself and you won't fall flat on your face. Get a band gets too ambitious and everybody ends up hating each other.* Perry could quote you the evidence on that part—it seemed like he knew the secret story of every band breakup in the last ten years. *You're working*—he'd say—*and the weather is fine. What more do you want?*

Chris had been more or less playing by these rules, but he still wrote his songs and kept on hoping for something or other, I supposed, that he most likely wasn't going to get. The songs weren't terrible. He worked out of these mail-order books he had on songwriting, which gave them kind of a kitlike quality. You wouldn't listen to one and come off feeling like you knew that guy that wrote it, the way you got to know Neil Young from listening to his stuff, or just about any songwriter, or hell, you even felt like you knew something about Bonnie Raitt just from the covers she picked to play. Chris's lyrics were clever sometimes, but it mostly seemed like they were there to fill space between big long guitar solos. As for that, he had great chops on guitar, but I was coming around slowly to Perry's opinion, that if he went on for too long he got boring.

His singing voice was presentable, though now with Stell in

the band he was demoted to second harmony parts. It had been the same when we had Melissa (that was something to think about right there) but anyway he still had his own mike on the stand. That meant that if he wanted to bad enough, he could grab the wheel.

On Wednesday night that's what he did. We'd just wound down a slow one, "Sweet Old World," and in the little hush that followed, Chris bent close to his mike and goes, "I'd like to play a song I wrote." He shot me a quick look and off he went, chunking a solid walk-down on the E-string—G chord down to D minor. Automatically I was doubling him on the bass, with Allston locking in behind me—what else were we gonna do? Chris's compositions weren't real demanding, and, though he wasn't the first one to play it, that bass riff made for a catchy hook. He tossed back his seventies rock-star hair mane and addressed himself to Mister Microphone:

> Time is a Firebird
> Fast enough for me
> Rolling round the corner
> like relativity . . .
>
> Time is a slingshot,
> Straight at your heart
> You can try to outrun it
> In your old Dodge Dart . . .
>
> Try to think of how I feel,
> My life's an open road
> You can read the map to me,
> if you can break the code . . .

A love song for cars, Perry would say. In fact I guess he had already said it. Perry was ticked, I could see that, but after a few bars
he caught the tune and started thumping his guitar. As for Estelle,
it gave her time to drink a beer, and otherwise I doubt she gave a
damn. I mean, we could spare the guy five minutes, right? I mean,
whatever makes him happy, and here he was grooving away on his
fast guitar solo, then dropping down into a final chorus.

> No one knows what I know
> No one cares where I go
> and no one knows the secrets
> down in my Secret Heart. . . .

Repeat and out, with a tremendous flourish. One song, big
deal. I'd heard lots worse on Top 40 radio. But it was just a bigger
more concentrated dose of Chris than Perry wanted to have to
swallow, so of course there was a regular dogfight later on, down
in that dirtbag bar at the motel. I ducked out before they got
started good and proper, and went to bed early, so that I was asleep
when Chris came in, banging around and swearing under his
breath. When he finally lay down I could practically smell the
burn coming off of him. But the next night we went on and
started the show like usual and nobody said anything about the
night before.

About four songs into the second set, we had just turned in a
rousing version of "Help Me Somebody," Chris fastens his mouth
to the mike again. "Now here's a song I wrote myself." He played a
different one from the night before. And when he was done, he
wasn't. Still on the mike. "Now this song here, I come to write . . ."
And he was off again.

On a closer look I felt like he'd probably had a snort or two of

the silver spoon already. He strung five or six together like that—
ate up the whole rest of the second set before he got to "Secret
Heart," which was the only one in the pack I thought had much to
recommend it. That one would have been his hit if he'd ever been
going to have one.

> If I knew how to say
> what I thought of it all
> I wouldn't have to stand
> so tough and tall
>
> I'd come clean and tell you
> I don't know who I am
> but since I don't do that
> I stay shut like a clam. . . .
>
> You could pry me open
> an ocean would spill out
> Even bigger than
> what we been talking about
>
> No one knows what I know
> No one cares where I go. . . .

And so on. Allston and I kept backing him right through to
the end, though we had our eyes bugging at each other a bit, once
we saw he didn't mean to stop. Still, it was all four-four time with
easy changes, not like he was requiring us to play bossa nova, and
what were we gonna do, walk off? Midway through his second
number, Estelle did leave—she just shrugged and snapped her

mike to the stand and trucked on out of the place altogether. Later on we found her at the Cuban diner, mopping up the last of a plate of garlic shrimp. As for Perry, he stayed on the bandstand, but I've never been so relieved he didn't carry a gun.

He didn't say anything to Chris at the break—nothing at all—he just didn't speak to him. We climbed back up there for the closing set and it was like usual, or maybe a little better than that, because Perry would call interesting combinations of songs if he had a bee up his nose sometimes, and Chris did exactly what he was supposed to all the way, only a little bit better than he sometimes did it.

I cut the next morning and went to the beach by myself. Allston was asleep and although I looked to see if I might catch Estelle alone she wasn't findable and . . . it didn't seem to be the best day to be hanging too close with my band mates anyhow. I stayed away till an hour before the show, and just bypassed the motel to go straight to the Black Cat, but as it happened as I got there all the others were just coming out of the Cuban place—Perry, Estelle, and Allston, but not Chris. When we filed into the club, there was Chris sitting at a center table, behind a plate of lobster shells and steak bones.

"Hey, sit down a minute," Chris says, real friendly and maybe a little nervous, as soon as he scoped Perry. There was room at the table for like four more people, but just one other guy sitting there, with the same bones and shells in front of him, and the dregs of a bottle of wine.

"This is the guy I told you about," Chris was saying. "That A and R man from Atlantic? And you know what—he likes my stuff."

Perry wouldn't even look at this dude. He was staring straight at Chris. "If that's an A and R man, I'm a ringtail baboon," he says. "This dinner's on you, sport, by the way—don't even think about trying to stick it on the band tab."

Chris stood up, shaking all over he was that mad. I didn't want to look at him much so I took a longer glance at the other dude, this supposed A&R man. He had on a white shirt with a black vest, dark hair waved back with some kind of mousse, and a fairly pleasant, hound-dog expression. Right now both his hands were stuck up in the air and he was giving a look that pretty much said, *What can I do? I always get caught.* He didn't seem to be real upset about it.

But Chris was smoking. "You helt me back since we first got together," he said to Perry. "Worse pick I ever made in my life— you just think you know it all, don't you? Scared to see anybody get ahead of *you*—that's all there is to what *you* are."

He was spitting, Chris was, he was so mad, still spluttering as he rounded on Estelle. "And you, go on, darling, sing while you can. Won't be long before your pipes are dried up like your—"

Crash!

I realized it wasn't really as loud as it seemed—not really more than a shallow tinkle. Stell had picked up a water glass and knocked the rim off on the edge of the table—now she held the butt in her hand and the jagged edges aimed at Chris.

"I about had enough of your lip, old son," she said. She set her face and started edging around the table, the busted glass held low and out from her hip. Chris backed in the opposite direction, keeping the table between them. Nobody else had a word to say. All the old plaid-pants couples finishing supper at the other tables laid down their forks to see what was going to happen.

Then the bouncer came cruising over, cocking a weighted club that normally was kept underneath the bar. Since I happened to be standing between him and Stell, I dropped the butt of my palm on the outer bone of his forearm—nothing real noticeable, just a float and a fall. The club sailed off underneath somebody else's table and the bouncer stopped still and stood there, rubbing the feeling back into his fingers and looking at me kind of puzzled.

Allston touched Estelle just lightly, politely, on the elbow. She shook her head like she was pulling up from a dream, put down the broken glass and sat down in the chair where the A&R man had been. I hadn't seen this guy make a move to leave, but he had somehow stopped being there around the time Stell went on the offensive. Now she put her chin in her hand like she was thinking real serious. Chris relaxed some and leaned on a chair-back.

"Y'all gonna play nice now?" the bouncer asked.

"Oh yes," Allston goes, in a calm, chocolate voice. "You won't see any trouble."

The bouncer collected the club and carried it back over to the bar, shaking his head a little bit still. Chris braced off that chair-back and stood up real straight.

"Jesse, Allston . . ." He looked back and forth between us. "Ain't got nothing against either one of you." He pointed a trembly finger at Perry, still looking at the two of us. "One of these days, you gonna realize that son of a bitch ain't God Almighty." Chris dropped his hand and stalked off down the hall toward the back where the music was played.

Then we all fell into chairs around that same table. One of the Haitians came over and quietly disappeared the remains of the surf and turf.

"What the hell," Perry said. "Why don't we all have a drink?"

About that time, Chris came staggering out of the back, a mite overloaded with the Les Paul case in his right hand and his effects box in his left, the Strat case slung over his shoulder along with a spaghetti snarl of cables. He wouldn't look at us, just marched right by, slapped the cases against the door frame—and gone.

The drinks Perry had ordered arrived and everybody started sipping. Didn't seem to lift our spirits much.

"Perry," I said.

"Yeah?"

"What are we gonna do?"

"What about?" Eyebrows raised like he didn't know what I was talking about—too cute.

"We got to start playing in an hour." And all of a sudden I jacked out of my chair and left the bar. But I didn't hurry too much on my way down to the motel because I was pretty sure there was no point. Sure enough, as I got near, the yellow Trans Am came squealing out of the parking lot and bunched itself to go roaring north up the four-lane.

I went on up to the room just the same. Drawers were hanging open, and so was the closet door. Chris had dropped a sock or two, same way he'd forgotten his soap dish, but otherwise he'd cleaned out all his gear.

So I wandered on back up to the Black Cat, feeling a little queasy, to tell the truth. We had about forty minutes to go. The retirees were thinning out and the Conchs were starting to drift in. Perry was sitting at the bar by himself; I didn't see the others.

"You wrap your mind around this situation yet?" I asked him. "Looks to me like we are twisting in the wind."

"Take it easy," Perry said. "It's nothing you hadn't handled before. I'd about had my fill of that sucker anyhow."

"Perry," I said. "*He took his guitars.*"

"Use mine," Perry goes.

"Right," I said. "I can't play that kind of lead on your guitar. The action's not up to it, and neither am I. I mean, think about it."

148

Perry thought. He mashed thumb and forefinger either side of his nose like maybe he was staving off a headache. Right then my left hand jammed me, throbbing at the base of the thumb. I ordered a glass of ice water from the barmaid.

"Hmmm," Perry said. "Well, but Chris always comes back."

"You don't know." I swallowed a couple of aspirins from my pocket bottle and wrapped my hand around the icy glass to numb the pain. Just nerves really, I could see that, but I still felt it throbbing.

"He's gone, man," I told Perry. "Bag and baggage—the rate he peeled out of there he's probably halfway to Nashville already."

"Think so, huh." Perry frowned at the bar mirror; it wasn't really a question.

"Look," I said. "Here's what. We got to break down and buy a guitar. A cheap Strat or a Tele, off the rack—couple of hundred bucks would set us up. Right?"

Perry raised his eyes to the clock above a mirror. "Yeah, but where's a music store?"

"Get the yellow pages," I said. "A pawnshop, even."

"Hey," somebody goes from behind us. "You need a guitar? I got one to sell."

Perry swiveled on his stool and snorted. "Bless my soul, it's the A and R man."

Same guy, sure enough, sitting up at a shelflike table on the far wall of the bar area. He shrugged, then smiled at Perry with that same *I give up* expression. I took a closer look at him now, and noticed a butterfly bandage on his left eyebrow and a scrape along the left side of his jaw. There was a similar scab on the back of his left hand. Kind of injuries you might get from sliding across pavement after somebody threw you out of somewhere by the seat of your pants.

"Really," Perry said. "No lie?"

"Hey, would I lie to you?" The dude goes palms-up, helpless. The hound-dog look. Women would eat that up, I could see. You looked at that face and knew he'd sucked eggs before and would do it again, but in between times he could be *so sweet* to you . . .

"Sure," Perry goes. "Let's have a look."

The dude reached down around his feet and swung a guitar case up on his table. In doing this he knocked over a salt shaker and a basket of pretzels, but it didn't seem to bother him, and he made no move to pick the stuff up. The case was hammered, with splintered wood showing on every knockable edge. There was not but one hinge left on the back, so the top wobbled when he flipped it up. Inside was some kind of an ancient Fender, Fender headstock anyway. Every scrap of finish had been beaten off the body, and the naked grooved wood was partly covered with traces of old decals. The knobs were missing from the pickup switch and the volume control. I didn't quite know what to make of it. When I looked a little longer I saw that the fretboard had more curve to it than was usual on Fenders nowadays. Somehow I had a funny feeling. No one was touching it, it wasn't plugged in, but there was some kind of hum coming off the thing anyway.

I looked at the guy. The hound-dog expression was gone off his face. He looked calm, serious.

"What do you want for it," Perry said, sort of skeptical; he was gearing up to haggle.

The guy shrugged.

"You play?" I asked him.

"Yeah," he said. "Sure, I play." No palms in the air, no hound-dog appeal.

"What kind of stuff do you play?"

"Whatever," he said. "Whatever you want. Whatever I hear."

All of a sudden the hound-dog expression came back. "Hey, bud, you got a cigarette I could borrow?"

I passed him my pack and looked at Perry.

"What do you think?"

"What about?" Perry goes.

"What say we give this guy a try?"

"What, the whole guy? Not just the guitar?" Perry gave me a very phony look of bewilderment. "If you say so, Jesse. You're the doctor." And he got up and headed off for the back hallway.

Dude was looking at me, hound-dog still. "Hey, bud, if I'm on the payroll, uh, could I . . ."

"Sure, be my guest," I said. "Just don't get too drunk."

Already I felt like I'd made a big fat mistake—the guy was con to the core, didn't I know that? But he just looked hound-dog and asked for a beer, and once he had a good belt from it, asked me my name. He told me his name was Willard. Willard Fenton, he said, with a bit of hesitation that made me think he might be making it up. He said that we could call him Will. About this time we discovered that he had accidentally put my cigarettes in the pocket of his vest, but I got them back, and we headed for the bandstand.

Willard found a stray cord and plugged himself in. The actual guitar amps all belonged to Perry, which was a good thing now, or we'd have been stuck beyond redemption. So Willard twiddled a couple of dials, cocked his head to listen, then backed up a bit, and still looking thoughtfully at the amp, played a few notes and a chord or two, a phrase running downscale from the twelfth fret to the fifth. Nothing, really. But Perry stopped what he was doing and did a take, his hands on his hips. Behind the drum set, Allston let one of his rare grins cruise from one ear to the other.

A guy like that, he didn't *have* to play much to let you know what you were dealing with. Five notes, one note, it hardly mat-

151

tered. Perry called this *authority*, but I thought it was his time, the rock-solid time tuning his hands to his head and letting anybody listening know that this one did have the mojo. We opened with a simple twelve-bar blues, nothing special, but when Willard started his solo, Estelle turned around from her mike stand to watch him work and the Conchs left off whatever else they were doing and started crowding up around the edges of the riser. For myself, I felt like I was off on some newly invented drug. The hound-dog expression was erased from Willard's face, nothing left but clear calm concentration. I knew it was temporary, knew he might be a worthless piece of shit and probably was, but as long as he kept playing like that, it didn't matter.

Perry kept on shaking his head. I didn't know if he was happy or worried—probably some mix of the two. Estelle was doing little dance steps to his solos without knowing it, I thought, the polka-dot skirt swirling around her knees.

We closed the first set with "Going Down Slow"—at least, I thought we'd closed it. But Estelle stayed up there, kind of hugging herself into her mike stand as the rest of us were laying down our instruments. Her eyes half-closed in a dreamy way, and there was a hush and then she started singing.

"Blue . . ." She stretched the word over four or five notes, drawing it on and on . . . *"Songs are like tattoos—you know I've been to sea before . . ."*

Perry just scratched his head and climbed down from the stage—she could do that one by herself as far as he was concerned. He couldn't follow it unrehearsed, no more than I could—there were too many odd inflections. I didn't know what had got into her but she did sound wonderful—enough that Miguel or whoever was near the switches shut down all the lights but one white spot that sealed her alone at the microphone.

I looked at Willard in the shadows, studying her with his lips twitching slightly and his eyes fixed like somebody hypnotized. You knew the guy would suck eggs again, but right now there was nothing between him and the music. Estelle was there, wherever she'd gone, and he was right there with her. When he raised his guitar back in his hands, I knew that for once he hadn't been lying—he really could play anything he heard.

7. SWEET LORRAINE

Willard was the name that stuck; in spite of that invitation, nobody ever took to calling him Will. It seemed to take him a little
while to get used to answering to it, but nobody much cared
about that either—I might of been the only one that noticed. Willard never called me anything but "bud" and I could usually get by
with just a "hey" in his direction, because he had taken Chris's slot
in the rooming arrangement as well as in the band lineup, for the
rest of our run in Miami and then the next spot down the line.

Key West was just about as far as you could go in that direction
if you didn't want to get in a boat or start swimming; the recoil
point, as Perry said, the very last dot in that string of islands that
looked like ink blobs God dripped off his pen while he was drawing the southernmost coast of Florida. When you got there, you
knew you had come to the end of something, you were running
up hard against a limit. Everybody who went there felt that too,
which made it a crazy kind of a place.

Willard, I have to say, just fit right into this atmosphere, no
problem. He had evidently spent some time there before, because
he knew all the ins and outs as well or better than the rest of us. He

also seemed to have some preexisting acquaintanceships; some he was eager to take up again (mostly with women) and others (mostly with men) that made him duck his head way down low and cross to the other side of the street.

With the women he was absolutely shameless, but this was, in a way, the heart of his attraction. I'd run into guys like that before, and always marveled at them. I mean it was a long way beyond Chris, who'd certainly done his bit for the love'm-and-leave'm philosophy (often enough with me trailing along or sometimes even leading the way). It was true that Chris and I had got into some kind of weird happenings every once in a while, but normally it was more like you left the one before you started loving the next one, most often with a couple hundred miles of highway in between—you wouldn't be doubling or tripling or quadrupling all in the same day, the way that Willard liked to do.

He had three secrets to his success: one, he never said no to anything; two, he never hesitated to propose anything; three, he had no problem at all telling the most obvious bareface lies, like Babe A could be standing one side of him with her hand in his front pocket and her tongue in his ear, and Willard would keep ahead denying to Babe B, standing right there on the other side of him, that he had any interest in Babe A or had ever even met her. Strangely enough, a lot of these women agreed with each other a whole lot better than you would have been inclined to expect, meaning that sometimes there would be two or three of them up in our room at once, waiting a turn or willing to join in all together. On these occasions I would most likely head down the hall to Allston's room, shift the drum cases off the other bed and crash there, unless maybe I was already asleep, or pretending to be, when Willard came in with the night's entourage. Willard didn't want to turn me out, and usually as I was going out the door he would raise up and call, "Hey, bud, what's your hurry? There's plenty enough to go round." But I didn't take him up on it.

Onstage, though, Willard didn't play to the women he wanted to nail—in that way he was the opposite of Chris. Willard just stood there and played, loose and relaxed but not pumping his hips or wiggling or jumping up and down or doing any showboat tricks at all. Almost nothing would move, except his two hands, and Willard would be kind of staring at his left hand on the fretboard like he was as startled as anyone else at what that clutch of fingers could do. At the end of a solo he would bend his knees slightly and cut the neck of that beat-up guitar toward Estelle, to cue her in for the next verse.

Perry respected that businesslike way Willard went about his actual playing, though otherwise Willard gave him fits for the fact that he was usually a good bit late and often as not being stalked by somebody's outraged boyfriend. When he got up there and started playing, though, you just completely forgot about what a pain in the neck he was otherwise. And of course, that was all he had to do; anytime we took a break there'd be all sorts of women falling down in front of him, all over the joint, any way he turned.

The Key West Black Cat was in reality called the Raging Razorback or something along those lines. A corner place at the lower end of Duvall Street, just a couple blocks from Mallory Square and the port. Two sides of the place were open to the great outdoors, since the weather was always so sweet there, and on the back wall was the stage, a real stage built nearly four feet off the floor, so you needed a set of steps to climb up there. A humongous horsehoe bar came off the wall on the fourth side, with a brass ship's bell hung on a long rope from the high rafters above it. About every hour a red star would come up on the cash register instead of the price, and whoever was trying to pay would get their tab free, and the bartender would clang that bell and send it ringing and swinging all over the place, so that the world would be sure to know. It annoyed Perry when they did this during slow numbers, though I doubt anybody else really noticed it.

It was pandemonium all up and down Duvall Street, night and day. The whole street was wall-to-wall Black Cat type of places (the lower five or six blocks anyway) and every one of them with live music, from the sizable barns like the one we played to the narrowest little slots in the wall. It was like Lower Broad in Nashville before they closed the Ryman and shipped the Opry off to the park—anyway Perry said that's what it was like, when he'd get on a kick about the good old days of Nashville and what had wrecked it all. As for myself I didn't personally know that much about it since the Opry had moved to Opryland before I was born.

But Duvall Street was carnival, nonstop, or at least up till three or four in the morning. We actually had a sort of earlyish gig—start at nine or nine-thirty and wind up around one-thirty in the morning or so. It left you fit to go to the beach in the daytime, which was good.

Our hotel was in Old Town, like the bars, but at the other end of Duvall Street, where it was quieter and you stood a chance to get some sleep at night. Actually it was a block around the corner from the north end of Duvall, opposite the North Beach hotels, which were more expensive and pretty well closed off the ocean view. There was a public access there, where Duvall itself ran off into the water in the form of a long concrete pier, and there was a pocket where you could swim alongside it, but though I sometimes took a dip there in the morning to wake myself up, the water was pretty silty there next to the pier, and I liked the main beach better, in the park on the east side.

Old Town Key West was so small you could walk anywhere if

you weren't in a hurry. I could almost have put my car on blocks, but Allston and I did rent a pair of bikes—it was easy riding around there since the whole island was flat as a pancake. Afternoons, we might coast over to the main beach, a shoal of soft sand in front of a pine woods, lay out in the sun for an hour or so, then swim. It was turquoise water with a very light chop, just cool enough to feel right when you went in from under the sun. In the afternoons we might go over to work out on the wide concrete dock of Mallory Square (when it was empty, before the whole sunset extravaganza started), and then sit at the outside bar of one of the waterfront hotels, drinking beer and eating boiled shrimp till it got time to go to work.

The gig was going well from the start. Willard and Stell clicked real good together, turning in winning combinations every set we played, and if I say it myself we had the best thing going on the whole strip, or at least, I didn't hear any better. Our Black Cat was closed on Wednesday nights, which was a little unusual but did leave us time to go out and see what everybody else was doing. Perry called this checking the competition, but this year the competition was no threat, and everytime we came out of one of those joints I'd see him just smiling to himself like a cat. Oh, we heard some pretty good players in some of those spots; in fact just about everybody working down there could turn in a decent night's worth of music, but we were the band that had the chemistry.

Partly because we were a full band, I think. A lot of the Old Town acts, especially at the smaller places, didn't have a live rhythm section—they'd be getting bass and drums off a sequencer, and maybe a lot of other stuff too. Often enough you'd think you were hearing a ten-piece band—but walk in and what you found was one person singing against a guitar, with everything else, even harmony vocals, coming off a computer disc. Hard to tell too, if you turned your back. There was something spooky about it really, and I felt a little uneasy sometimes if I noticed Perry really studying those systems. But we were packing them in every night at our Black Cat and were settled in for a nice long run.

Estelle really prospered down there. Her voice was as rich and full as I ever had heard it, never heard her sound quite so good. She took on a nice slow olive-shade tan that erased what few lines there had been on her face. And generally she was just more relaxed and at ease with herself. Even the way she walked had changed—no more of the jits and jerks she once had; she'd just kind of flow along, like the black island women we sometimes saw down there.

I'd catch myself looking at her, just watching her move, or watching her loving up her microphone while she sang some heartbreaker from the stage of the Black Cat, and I realized that I had an actual crush on this woman (maybe), regular teenage sugar-sugar foolishness. Maybe with no more sense to it than that either. It was enjoyable in a way, even though I didn't quite know what to do with it. Try as I might, I never could get her alone anymore. Not for more than a minute or two. I didn't want to get caught trying too hard, like I was coming right out and asking for a date, but I did propose this plan or that—going honky-tonking on Wednesday night, or taking in the sunset circus at Mallory Square or driving partway up the string of keys or . . . whatever.

The only thing she let me do was teach her how to swim, but for that James Culla and Rose-Lee went along, and I'd crank up my car to carry them all over there to the main beach. Rose-Lee wasn't much of a swimmer herself—I think she could swim a stroke or two but all she ever did was splash off real quick to cool herself down between long bouts of lying in the sun. Seemed to be all she wanted. But Stell and I would trip out through the knee-high little breakers till we reached green water about up to the chest. I taught her how to do the dead man's float, and from there we moved on through a dog paddle to the frog kick and something that looked sort of like a breaststroke. All the while I was remembering my daddy teaching me to swim, which mostly took place in lakes around Nashville, how gentle and patient he had been during the whole procedure—in fact, he usually *was* that way, so long as he wasn't drinking. This wasn't the most comfortable thing to think about, though, so I would quit and just watch Stell, her face so calm and dreamy as she floated with her eyes closed and her dark hair streaming out in the pale water, and one time I did lean down and kiss her, not really knowing that I would. She came up with her arms around my neck at first, and I thought maybe it would all start happening by itself like at that fancy hotel in Miami, neither of us planning anything about it. But she came to herself and pulled away, smiling pleasantly enough but pointing to the beach—well, James Culla was just sleeping there under an um-brella that kept the sun off of him, and Rose-Lee was flat on her back with her sunglasses on and her Walkman plugged in, so I doubted she'd of noticed anything short of lightning striking be-tween her toes.

But I let it go. It was easy enough for me to let Stell call the steps. She was the Older Woman, obviously, and it had been a while since I messed with one of those. And after all, I didn't know exactly what I wanted.

Things drifted along about that way for maybe as long as three or four weeks. Then Lorraine showed up.

———

I wouldn't, in fact, have said I was restless. Key West was the place for long lazy days—from when I started traveling with Perry it had about been my favorite stop on the winter run, and I liked how long we stayed there too, like a yo-yo hesitating at the end of the string. If the beach got cold you could while away the afternoon shooting pool in any number of cool breezy bars, or coast a bike down under the deep shade of the big trees on Southard Street. Allston and I, a couple of times, went out on boats to fish or snorkel (this was expensive enough you wouldn't do it too often). And if all else failed, you could always draw a good deal of satisfaction by turning on the TV for the evening news and watching winter all over the rest of the country: rain and sleet and snow and ice. Had to come away smiling from that. So if I was restless, I didn't know it, or else I didn't know I knew.

I was getting to play a lot more lead than usual, thanks to the problems Willard seemed to have with showing up on time. It was a rare thing for him to appear in time for the first set, period. Perry had cursed him out six ways from Sunday but I think he knew himself he was wasting his breath. Whatever he might say (and Perry had a cutting tongue) or whatever he might threaten, Willard would just stand there with the hound-dog look, and when Perry got finished, Willard would throw up his hands and lift his eyebrows with a look that said, Are you through now? Are you really through? And if Perry *was* through, then Willard would climb up on the stage and strap on his guitar and in two or three minutes half the crowd would be whooping and the rest would be just staring at him, maybe with a few tears wobbling in their eyes.

So it got to be kind of routine that I would handle the lead for the first set. It worked out pretty well that way, actually—when Willard finally did get there it added a little excitement to the evening, something to kind of build up to. Perry still gave him a pretty good tongue-lashing every time but more and more it was just for form's sake. As for me I was nervous the first couple times when I wasn't expecting it, and my hand would act up to where I had to take a handful of aspirin against it. But once I realized it didn't really amount to a crisis I even got to enjoy myself up there, playing a little more complicated stuff and, tell the truth, getting a touch more in the spotlight too.

So one night, on into March, I guess, for the whole island was beginning to fill up with college kids on spring break, I'd just turned in a presentable version of "Blue Sky" to close the first set. I racked the guitar and climbed down from the stage feeling pretty good about it. That college crowd would just eat up the Allman Brothers, so they were still stomping and whooping, and I was kind of enjoying that as I cut toward the bar to get a drink. Everybody of course had the same idea once the band went on break, so I worked my way in and picked up a glass and just held it over the inside lip of the horsehoe, waiting for Barney the bartender to work his way around and fill it up with bourbon. Then something stroked down my bare right arm, warm and soft and sort of fuzzy. I turned halfway and here was this girl, a stranger, pushed up very close in the press of people behind her.

"Hi!" she goes. "I'm Lorraine." Like we had an appointment or something. I tried to back up a little to get a look at her, quick: thick strawberry hair just grazing her shoulders, a soft terry-cloth top (she'd brushed me with that), a very tiny pair of cutoffs, bare feet with metallic green polish on the toenails.

"Oh," I said. Great line, sport.

She gave a devilish sort of smile, which I liked right away. I caught her eye—her eyes were green with little gold flecks swimming in them, special. She held the glance, like it meant something, and caught her lower lip in her top teeth, then released it with a little *plop!*—soft and red and flushed from the contact. She held her lips slightly parted, so close I could practically feel her breathing. My tongue kind of stuck to the roof of my mouth.

Lorraine reached behind her and dragged up somebody else, a small dark girl with a slightly stunned look.

"This is my girlfriend Sarah," she says. And over her shoulder, "Hey, you guys!"

Girlfriend Sarah didn't say anything at all. Looked over my shoulder with dark, bruised eyes, expression like maybe she was waiting for somebody to hit her. Dressed in serious, committed art-rock style. Black T-shirt, black jeans, silver jewelry (pierced nose and eyebrows and the works) and a really nicely done tattoo of little black panthers following each other in a circle around her left upper arm. *You must be the quiet one,* I thought. Hadn't they got it backwards? Lorraine was the type to go after Chris (though with Willard she'd just have to take a number). I noticed Willard had just come in and was taking his lecture from Perry on the other side of the horseshoe bar, just smiling like the dog he was and really giving most of his attention to a honey-blond girl he was holding hands with—she had her back to me so I couldn't quite place her, but I felt like there was something to place.

"You play a pretty mean guitar," Lorraine was saying. She gave me a studying look.

"Thanks," I said.

"I'd like to play lead that way myself," she said. "You know, I actually do play some."

I took a glance down at the inch-long nails on her left hand. "Slide?" I said. A little sarky.

"Hey, yeah!" she goes. "Like Bonnie Raitt."

Then these two college meats came strolling over—her "guys," it appeared. They weren't football-size meats, actually fairly small, but muscled up in a noticeable way. Both wearing blue caps with Greek letters on them.

"My brother Chuck." Lorraine pocked her knuckles into his arm. "And Rock, my *so-called* boyfriend." She gave him a knuckle rub through his cap. "They're both on the wrestling team at Virginia Tech." She gave a wink my way. "*Greek* wrestling, you know."

What? I grunted something toward the meats anyway, and they grunted something back. Lorraine turned more toward me, kind of shouldering them out of the scene with the same movement.

"Hey, let me buy you a drink."

I didn't answer right away because I was watching Chuck and Rock (really) headed back toward their table, where there were several more guys with the same sort of hat, and a couple more college-type women. Then I noticed my left hand getting heavier because Butch was finally filling up my glass.

"No, let me," I said, and then to Butch, "Get these ladies what they want."

Lorraine and Sarah each took a margarita, up with salt. Lorraine had a pretty good belt out of hers, then tapped a finger on my arm. "So, maybe you could show me some stuff."

"All sorts of stuff I could show you, sugar." My tongue had come unstuck at last. I did a fake take: "Oh, but I guess you mean on *guitar*."

So we went on shooting the breeze like that, through the rest of that break and again the next. She had booked by the time we shut down, though, along with the rest of her crew (funny hats and everything). I might have been surprised at that, but it didn't really break my heart. After all, she was already equipped with a boyfriend *and* a girlfriend—all she lacked was her mother and her hometown preacher and maybe a couple of cops, and she could have presented a person with some serious complications.

Sweet Lorraine. I was already calling her this in my mind. We packed up, and I went home early, which had been my habit. Willard was out, I didn't know where. The thing he liked to do next to sex was gamble, and he had found every crap table and card game in the area, but for all I knew he might have been chasing skirt tonight, or maybe both at the same time. I watched the end of a late movie and then turned out the light, but it was kind of hard to sleep at first. I realized it had been a long time since I'd had my biological needs taken care of—not since Myrtle Beach and— who was she? That was shameful, not to remember her name. Then I was dreaming, and in my dream I was doing the do with Lorraine herself only she kept changing into Stell, or Chris's Maybelline, or Brown-Eyed Sue from Ocean City, or any one of a whole collage of all the women I'd ever known or wanted to know. It got to be too much. Also she kept calling me "Charlie," moaning it: *Oh, Charlie . . . Ooooh, Charlie . . .*

This annoyed me enough that I finally woke up. Daylight was pressing in at the blinds, and the *Ooooh, Charlie* business was actually coming from the next bed, from a woman bucking over Willard. She kept saying it, rocking her head and tossing her hair, till finally she arched all the way backward to rest her elbows on the mattress, nipples and chin point aimed at the cobwebs on the ceiling, mane of black hair hanging down to the sheet, hips still working hard. The *Oh, Charlie* cry was just noise now.

Then she was done, and after a minute or two she came to herself and noticed I was there, and had been. She gave me kind of a dirty look, switching her hair across her face as she climbed down and stumped toward the bathroom. I heard the pipes squeal as the shower started.

Willard inched his back up the wall, rubbed his eyes and grinned at me. Then leaned over and lifted up the sheet and what do you know? There was another one: the honey-blonde I'd seen him squiring at the bar the night before. Very pretty and very young, with a deep brown tan and traces of white lipstick on her sleep-slack mouth. In fact I did know her, at least by sight: she worked at the fancy crêperie around the corner, where sometimes we had breakfast. She was a real French person herself, over here on some kind of working holiday, and I don't think she spoke any English at all beyond what was written on the menu of the joint. It seemed kind of unfair, this scene, like cruelty to animals.

I took a sip of flat beer from a bottle on the nightstand and lit myself a cigarette. "You don't think she's under the legal limit?" I said.

Willard shrugged and did hound-dog. "What, you expect me to throw her back?" Then he frowned and looked sort of concerned for a minute. "Hey, bud, could you spare me a cigarette?"

"You're depraved, you know that? You know what the word 'depraved' means?"

Willard did me some more hound-dog. In the end it was simplest just to give him the damn cigarette. "Try not to make her late for work," I said as I pulled on my shorts and headed for the door. From the hallway I called back, "Who the hell's Charlie?" and went on without waiting for an answer.

Outside, it felt early, not long after sunrise, a thin mist still floating along the street. I crossed over to the North Beach access, waded into the water and dove. White concrete silt boiled up all around me, but I swam on out, a good ways past the end of the pier, then cut parallel to the beach hotels. In the other direction the horizon was hazy and indistinct, sunrise yellows phased into the slate-blue sky. Also there was a bit of an undertow, which made me have to work to get back in. A slow pull against current (I'd drifted out a good deal further than I'd meant to) with the end of the pier as a target. There was a stick figure standing at the end, which resolved into a woman with her hair blowing loose in the morning breeze. Then she seemed to disappear, or the pier blocked my view. I swam around to the steps at the outer end and rested, holding on to the iron railing. When I got ready to climb out, her hand reached down to help me up.

Sweet Lorraine. "Hi!" she said. Like we had an appointment. I'd admit right away she was pleasant to see. She had on a different pair of cutoffs and a plain V-neck T-shirt which showed her to advantage, though without being too ostentatious about it.

"You must be cold," she said, and put her hand on my wet back, kind of preening herself against me for a second, like a cat, then pulling back as if it had been unintentional. "Can I buy you breakfast?"

"Sure," I said, not hesitating much. I had dropped a T-shirt on the beach, furled around a pack of cigarettes, and once I pulled it on I was good to get served most places, being that Key West wasn't hugely formal. We walked up to the corner of Duvall, Lorraine still managing a fair amount of accidental contact.

"That your car?" she said as we passed the Mustang.

I waited a minute to answer that one. She had to have been watching me, it meant; she had to have seen me driving Stell and the baby to the beach, for otherwise I didn't drive in Old Town. Now that was a kind of a peculiar thought.

"Take me for a ride sometime?"

"Sure," I said. She smiled at me, cooler than butter, then

ducked her head and reached for my hand, shy and innocent as a schoolgirl—right. I already suspected she was a witch, but right then she looked fresh and sweet and clean (especially compared to what was going on up in my room), and at the time it seemed to me that I didn't have anything better to do.

So I began to see a good deal of Lorraine, without very much in the way of planning, without having to work at it much at all. In fact it was sort of like being stalked. I was guaranteed to run into her somewhere within an hour of leaving the hotel in the daytime, pretty much no matter where I went, and after that we'd kind of casually stick together for a while. It wasn't obvious just what she wanted, though. I gave her a try on the Hummingbird, just on the wild chance it *was* about playing guitar. She could play some—I give her credit—knew the chords and had some folky licks. I'd been wrong about the nails; they were stick-ons and she only stuck them on at night. Her natural nails were bitten back, and she even had a layer of guitar-player callus on the tips. I showed her some scales, but she wasn't that interested. She seemed mighty uncomfortable being up in the hotel room, kept jumping up and flitting around, getting herself a glass of water or just posing in the bathroom doorway, leaning *way* far out the window, so that her cutoffs strained.

So the guitar-lesson thing was off the menu. She didn't want to be behind closed doors with me much at all, I noticed—it was only out in the open that she would purr and rub against me in that agreeable kittenish style. It clearly wasn't the usual game of bang-the-bass-player-in-the-bar-band. Lorraine only liked to get cozy in some kind of a semipublic place. In a bar or on the beach she would lead the way. Alone in a room, forget about it.

Also, I never saw her at night. I mean, not *see her* see her. If she had spent the afternoon with me she would usually disappear soon after sundown. She might turn up later at the Black Cat but then she'd be with Sarah and Chuck and Rock and the rest of the funny-hat crew. I don't know where the guys went in the daytime. Maybe they were vampires. More likely they were out fishing or something. Anyway they'd all have left every night before the Black Cat closed, Lorraine along with them. I never did quite figure out where they were staying.

Sometimes Sarah would come along on our afternoon adventures. Lorraine would ask, kind of shy and sheepish, if I minded if Sarah came. In fact I had a liking for Sarah, and anyway I wasn't supposed to say no, so we might go bike-riding (Sarah and Lorraine had rented bikes) or to the beach. Once we went out in the glass-bottomed boat to look at the funny fish through the panes in the hull (but it looked like Sarah got fairly seasick). More often we'd pass the afternoon shooting pool. Sarah was a pretty good player, actually not much better than Lorraine but I liked the grim, efficient way she went about it, where Lorraine used it more as a chance to pose and wallow attractively over the table. As it was three of us, we generally played Screw-Your-Buddy, which seemed appropriate later on.

They were an odd couple, in the matter of style. Sarah had that studied rock-chick look: weird piercings connected to each other with chains; black outfits that kept her sweaty in the Key West weather. A touch of Goth, though not all-out in that direction. She made Lorraine look almost wholesome. Lorraine wore no obvious makeup, no jewelry either, and about as little in the way of clothes as would be legal on the street. Cutoffs, always, in faded blue or black or dusty rose denim, with a T-shirt or bikini top or dress shirt with the tails tied up high on her ribs. The cutoffs were a work of art, cunningly worn-out in just the right places, with sizable areas of parallel threads that would separate when she bent and stretched, giving you more interesting glimpses of her plump, tan skin. She liked to leave the top button undone on the cutoffs, though as far as I could tell it wasn't because she needed extra room to breathe.

Lorraine got herself a piercing, just one, somewhere along that string of days we spent together. I discovered it one afternoon while Sarah was circling the pool table, working out her shot. Lorraine and I were sitting on the bench of a dim booth at the back, her finger tips just barely curling into the waistband of my trousers, and whenever Sarah looked the other way, she would lean in and give me a slow deep kiss. What came in my mouth was more than just tongue, and I have to admit this was one time she really got me. She laughed, husky, at my startled face as I pulled away, then ran out her tongue in a red wet curve, just long enough for me to glimpse the gold stud through the tip of it, which held a flake of jade to match her eyes.

"Damn, where'd that come from?" I said, in true surprise, and then, the great piker reaction: "Does it hurt?"

"No pain, no gain," she told me, and drew the stud back into its hiding place. That was a line that came back to me, later on.

But the tongue stud was surely a master touch. It was just Lorraine all over, hidden, phantom, a secret she might share with you or choose to keep sealed away behind her smiling strawberry lips. If you started to think about what she might do with that thing . . . it could keep a person awake at night. Meanwhile, a couple of points were becoming more and more obvious. One was that Lorraine liked an audience, some kind of audience nearby at least, that gave us the chance of being seen or caught. The other thing— she was either an all-out tease or determined to take it incredibly slow. In the beginning I didn't really care which. What with Willard running his degenerate dog piles in his half of the room every other night (that would have been *too* much of an audience for Sweet Lorraine, I thought), I just wasn't in that much of a hurry to get my candidate in the sack. I saw that it puzzled her that I didn't press harder, and I saw that this gave me an advantage.

Now that was a nice way to be thinking—enough to make you give up thinking altogether. It went on that way for a week or ten days, with nothing much changing except that Sarah looked more and more owl-eyed and desperate, like she had a case of worms, or demons. Then one day I bumped into Estelle coming into the hotel and realized I hadn't seen much of her lately, other than at the shows. She had bought a new dress, a blue pastel print that tied at the waist with a cotton sash—something else that made her look younger.

"Busy man," she goes, her eyes snapping.

What was it to her? "Guess so," I said. I remembered that, because I was so taken up with Lorraine, it had been over a week since I'd run Stell and the family to the beach.

"You know," I said. "You're welcome to take the car any time. I'm hardly using it. . . ."

"S'all right," Estelle said. She was still looking at me like that. "We're using the van."

We stood there a minute, until she shrugged and went on inside. It was an odd moment, which left me kind of confused and annoyed. Was it possible I had been trying to make Stell *jealous?* Hell—all this calculation would give you a headache. I kept on walking the same direction I had been and once I turned the corner, what do you know? here was Lorraine coming out of the crêpe place.

"Well hey!" she goes.

Big surprise. I felt a bit moody all of a sudden. "How long does y'all's spring break last for anyhow?" I said. Because the thought had crossed my mind, Coach must be looking for his wrestlers up there at Virginia Tech. It seemed the entire team must be down at Key West in their funny hats, seven or eight of them besides Chuck and Rock (and only three or four women, not enough to go round). I tended to keep clear of them at the Black Cat; they were a mean-eyed bunch.

The question didn't faze Lorraine. "Just about as long as we want it to," she said, and gave me a jokey dig in the ribs. "Hey, wanna take me for a ride?"

That was one thing we hadn't done yet, and I was in the mood for different, so we fired up the Mustang and headed north, windows down and the radio blasting. Lorraine ran her seat way back so she could brace her feet in the frame of the window.

"Kicking stereo you got in this thing," she said. "Hey, mind if we listen to this?"

When I turned she was holding out a cassette. Couldn't quite guess where she pulled it out of; she didn't have a purse, or much room at all in her pockets either. I stuck it in the deck without looking.

Counting Crows. I'd heard a couple of songs on the radio but never given the whole album a listen. It was catchy stuff, that I would say. The tunes were nice and simple (I was automatically working out the charts in my head)—uncomplicated major-key changes mostly, that sounded fancier than they were because the arrangements were nicely done and because the singer moved around the edges of the chord frame in ways you wouldn't quite expect. The voice was an interesting blend of influences—a lot of Springsteen, a little Dylan (in one of the songs he admitted to this), and with certain inflections you almost thought you heard

Mick Jagger. On the real slow ones he developed a sort of whine that reminded me of Neil Young, considerably. . . . I was saying some of this stuff out loud when I noticed that Lorraine looked really bugged for the first time since I'd known her.

"Do you always have to pick it apart?" she goes. "I mean, like, can't you just listen to it?"

Fair question. I realized it was Perry's line of talk that had been coming out of my mouth—like there was some sort of Perry inside of me that kept figuring out how everything was derivative. Was it gonna be that way forever? And Lorraine really seemed to care, like maybe music really did matter to her. There was something else to think about.

I shut up. The car hummed over the ribbon of highway. On either side the blue-green shallows expanded, and between keys it felt like you were driving right on the surface of the water. The wind poured through the windows, and the Crows sang. . . .

> Help me stay awake, I'm falling. . . .
> Asleep in perfect blue buildings
> Beside the green apple sea . . .
> Gonna get me a little oblivion. . . .

Those lyrics and the edgy melody seemed to plug right into my tricky mood somehow. Like the two things brought each other into balance. There'd be some point to writing songs, I thought, if you could write one that did that. Aside from Perry's stand against it, my nearest example of a songwriter was Chris, and—well, maybe I shouldn't be low-rating Chris. "Secret Heart," which was his best effort by a long shot, had maybe come close to touching the feeling he couldn't otherwise name.

Lorraine and I ran north for about an hour, not passing a word between us, though I think we both were contented enough. In fact it was one of my best times with her—no need to talk, and I felt grateful for the music. Finally we stopped at a little crossroads tavern and got a shrimp po' boy with a couple of beers, and ate on a deck overlooking the water, sailboats zipping along and a couple of sport fishermen. I felt detached and dreamy, like I was drifting myself, no sail and no power, not knowing where I'd ground, or caring either. There was a motel that shared the sand-pitted parking lot with the tavern, and on the way out I stopped the car in front of it, where we both had a good view of the red neon VACANCY sign.

"What's this?" Lorraine said when she registered that the car had stopped moving.

"It's a motel." I didn't put any particular spin on it.

Lorraine took her legs down from the window frame and nibbled at the edge of her fingernail. She looked at me with her green eyes dazed, the gold flecks floating, like she was in some kind of a trance. When she spoke she said one word.

"*Anticipation.*"

Somehow that knocked me off the balance point I'd been holding through the whole drive up the keys. My own fault maybe, for pushing the point. I kept my mouth shut and put us back on the road south to Key West. Same roll of asphalt, the same wind blowing backwards, the same tape flipping itself in the deck. I paid more attention to the lyrics this time through. They were well-written songs, intelligent, and they gave you an idea, maybe a false one, of what the guy singing them was like. You heard a kind of passion in them, driven by pain and confusion underneath (I knew Lorraine was attracted to that part of it). The guy went into some complicated love song, which I could hardly understand the plot, but then the chords went into chorus mode and he was singing,

I'm not gonna break . . .
and I'm not gonna worry any more. . . .

It flashed on me that there was a line a lot like that in "Lithium," though that other song put it a good deal more violently, and I remembered how in my dream Cobain had told me how I had to keep it rough, unfinished-sounding, and I remembered the last picture I saw of him, actually just his feet, dead legs stretched out across a carpet. Now there was a guy who'd figured out how to get himself some oblivion, you know it.

The Crows guy was just telling his version of the same story, I thought. All the songs were about love and loneliness. All the songs we did were about that too. What else was there for a song to be about?—but that was Perry's attitude, talking in my head again. There were songs about death, but we didn't do those.

By the time we got back into Old Town, my mood was weirder than Chinese algebra once again. I dropped Lorraine off, somewhere on Duvall Street (she of course had a nice lush kiss for me, now she was getting out of the car) and idled back up to the hotel. I had to overshoot it by about a block to find a parking place, and as I passed the entrance something struck me sort of wrong for a second, like a quick glimpse of a shark fin from the corner of your eye. I parked and started walking back. Willard came out the front of the hotel, saw me and waved. At the same time a guy who had been sitting on the opposite curb got up and started across the street, a very light-skinned black guy with a shaved head and a muscle-bound upper body, wearing a loose guayabera. A little hump of muscle stood up on the back of his neck. I knew what was up before I could have said it but I was too far away to do anything.

"You got it?" the guayabera guy said. He had a trace of an accent I couldn't quite place, though it didn't strike me as Spanish.

Willard did hound-dog, but without his hands. This struck me strange: as soon as he saw the guy coming he jammed both hands way deep in his pants pockets and left them there.

"Guess you don't got it." The guayabera guy sounded kind of sad. Then, whump-whump!—they were fast fluid punches for such a beefy dude; his shoulders and hips sank a little as he threw them. Then he was leaving and Willard was lying on the sidewalk. He still had his hands in his pockets. I asked him why.

Willard groaned. "Bud, not everybody can be Bruce Lee."

"Okay," I said, "but still, I don't get it."

"Just think about it, bud." Willard turned sideways and gagged. "Let me know when you figure it out." He sat partway up, breathed in and turned pale.

Cracked ribs, I figured, from the look on his face. I helped him inside and went and found Allston; together we got Willard up to the room. Allston felt him over and asked a couple questions while I made a fast drugstore run. We taped him up—not a whole lot else to do about it. When he was able to sit up and sip from a beer, Allston asked him, "How much?"

Willard choked and told us. Then we choked. We went back to Allston's room and counted up what we had, and then we started walking across town.

Strangely enough there was a sort of miniature black slum in Old Town, no more than a few blocks' worth, and fairly pleasant, at least to my eyes. The houses were run-down and peeling and overgrown, but the vines on them were bougainvillea and tropical flowers. Good cooking smells came out of most of them, and the chickens wandering around in the street didn't act like they had any serious worries. I had been over there with Allston a time or two to eat, but the place he went to now was new to me. The guayabera guy was sitting out front on a bench seat ripped out of a car.

"I need to see Romain," Allston told him.

The guayabera guy called into the house in some language I couldn't even make out what it was. A woman in a tomato-stained housecoat stuck her head out, and they gabbled back and forth a minute. Then she beckoned to us, and we climbed a couple of wobbly steps into a room with oilcloth-covered tables and a few guys eating gumbo and drinking beer. She led us through the kitchen and then down some concrete steps into a long tin-roofed shed that had just sort of been stuck on the back of the house, it appeared. There was a homemade crap table, not in use, and a few grim-looking fellows playing poker in the back. At a smaller table a little gnarly old black man with a head of snow-white hair was sitting, squinting at a newspaper under the weak light of a bare bulb hanging from its cord.

"We came to pay for Willard."

The old man folded his paper slowly, looked up. "Weelard?"

"Yeah, Willard," Allston said. "The guitar player at the Razorback, you know him."

"Oh, ees *Charlee*. . . ." The old man smiled, slow and wide. His voice was thick and slow like honey, that strange island accent. "Yesss, thee Geetar-mon."

"That's our boy." Allston took the money out his shirt pocket and laid it on the table. "Romain," he said. "Don't let him play here no more."

"Whyee note?" the old man said.

"'Cause he ain't gonna be able to pay when he loses," Allston said. "Not after this."

After that was done with we went and found Perry and explained to him why Willard's salary was going to be paid straight to us for the next several weeks. Perry acted at first like he was going to rare around about it, but then for some reason he just didn't. All he did was scratch his head and say, mostly to Allston, I guess, "Okay, thanks for taking care of it."

What happened to Willard was bad news anyway you sliced it, but it did take my mind off the whole situation with Lorraine. At least Willard's problem was understandable, and had a sort of solution to it. Afterward, things went back more or less to normal, except Willard couldn't play for two or three days—he just was not physically able to hold up a guitar. This left me playing more lead than I really wanted to. I felt like I was repeating myself too much, and so did the crowd at the Black Cat, except for Lorraine, who kept soaking me with compliments and trying to pay for my drinks at the bar. Then Willard did come back, sitting on a stool to play at first, but finally back on his feet again. By the end of the week he even was bringing girls back to the room, though I noticed, no more than one at a time.

I still killed my afternoons with Lorraine, more often than not, maybe with Lorraine and Sarah. Nothing about it really changed. I took to walking home with Stell, after the Black Cat had closed, having a nightcap and the last cigarette at her room. Actually she and Rose-Lee had a little two-room suite, because the kitchenette was useful for the baby. It was on the back side of the ground floor and even had a tiny brick patio, with a couple of spring chairs it was pleasant to sit in on a cool night. And yet it felt a little awkward, me hanging out there after the shows. Maybe I was trying to prove to Stell that in fact I wasn't shacked up with

Lorraine, but . . . she had just been harder and harder to figure, ever since Miami, really. There was a tension rising up between us as we sat out there finishing our last beers, like she wanted me to either do something or leave, almost. There was next to no chance of doing anything because Rose-Lee or the baby was always there, usually both, so every night, I left.

Then one afternoon I was strolling around by my lonesome, sort of wondering why I hadn't happened to run into Lorraine yet. I was on the edge of actually looking for her, when I went into one of the little sidestreet bars where fairly often we would shoot pool. It was usually quiet in there in the afternoon, and it was quiet today except for Sarah, who was sitting there crying in a back booth, humped up with her face down on her folded elbows.

I sat down across from her and tried to get her to look at me, which finally she did, all snuffly and tear-streaked but trying to smile. I felt bad for her, whatever it was—I'd noticed her looking more and more miserable day by day, and really I liked Sarah, who was sort of more my usual type. In the days of Chris I'd of much more likely ended up with her than with anybody like Lorraine. Supposing that she swung my way, at least. I went and got her some napkins from the bar, and I got her a drink (she asked for whiskey instead of the blender concoctions she usually favored) and I lit two cigarettes and passed her one. By then I'd already asked her more than once what was the trouble.

"You don't get it," she said, kind of angry now. "You still hadn't got it—I suppose there's no way." She sniffed and blew her nose on a napkin. "I was in love with her, you know . . . it wasn't just for—damn it, she *makes* you fall in love with her. But you don't get any good out of it. Not me, and especially not you, Jesse—cut her loose, man, I'm telling you. She's no good for you. Cut loose while you can."

"What are you talking about?" I said. "Cut loose of what? The most we've done is make out like a couple of . . . I mean, it hasn't hardly been beyond a French kiss or whatever."

"Yeah, right," Sarah said, and looked out the window with her red-rimmed eyes. "That's how it works, that's how she operates. I am trying to tell you, man. She's . . . it's all tangled up with Rock and that degenerate brother of hers, like—Chuck and Rock are a mean pair of guys but basically it's Lorraine. It's her. I know you won't believe me. Call me a dyke, call me a carpet-muncher, I don't care, but that is one pack of sick puppies."

"I'm not really following you," I said. Because now I was starting to get bewildered, sure enough.

"I guess I can't tell you," Sarah said, looking grim now but a lot more pulled together. She wasn't crying anymore, and with the savage jewelry and the panther tatt she actually looked kind of fierce. "She's worn me out, that's all I can say. I've had it. I'm going back to Virginia."

I stayed with her a few minutes more, seeing if there was anything I could do, if she needed to borrow money or whatever, but she said she didn't. In the end she shook my hand and I went back out onto the sunstruck street.

I found myself passing down under the deep watery shade of the trees overhanging the Hemingway house, hardly aware of where I was going really. I was half-trying to put it together—actually wondering if Sarah had been meaning to tell me anything I didn't already know. Because I already understood that Lorraine was a tease, and an exhibitionist. I knew she was getting a kick out of sneaking around on her boyfriend (which was not at all un-usual)—and her girlfriend too (which, I admit, was a little different). How the brother fit in I couldn't quite figure. I had never quite managed to tell Chuck apart from Rock; there was nothing that really required me to do that, and besides they looked right much alike, especially when they had their stupid hats on, which was just about all the time. And I couldn't see how I stood to get burned. Because if Lorraine was using me, then I was doing the same with her, so everybody was even and nobody was hurt, and probably I could afford to stop thinking about it.

By this time I had drifted down to the bottom of Old Town and was beginning to get caught up in the flow of people heading for the sunset festivities at Mallory Square. I let myself be carried along in that current. Pretty soon I felt a hand slide into my back pocket and though I thought at first it might be a pickpocket, when I caught the wrist it was sweet Lorraine, tightening her arm as she leaned into me, another one of those heavily arranged coincidences. We went on together that way. She was so tied into me it was a little hard to walk.

Mallory Square was nothing but a big long concrete rectangle overlooking the Gulf. Cruise ships would dock there during the day, so tall and massive they blocked out the sun and sky, but in the late afternoon the mooring was always empty and people poured into the space to watch the sun go down: both locals and tourists and the people who preyed on any open gathering. You had people selling food and trinkets and there were clowns and magic acts and guys twisting balloons into hearts and puppy dogs. Also a couple of more hard-core carney types: a sword-swallower and a fire-eater and a guy that would wiggle his way out from a wrapping of about fifty pounds of padlocked chains.

It was this last guy that attracted Lorraine, and she even managed to get us elected as the ones to tie him up with the stuff. It was always somebody from the crowd that did this, though Lorraine played it up to the point that some people probably thought she was a paid assistant. I would just as soon have passed on this assignment, but Lorraine was into it, twisting and yanking the chains as tight as she could, motioning me what links to padlock, tugging again to make sure the locks were solid.

Finally we stepped away from the guy and stood in the curve of the crowd watching him—a semicircle that closed on the edge of the pier. The guy worked with his back to the bay. Lorraine snuggled into me, running one hand between two buttons of my shirt, as he began to struggle with the chains. Lorraine was kissing up and down my neck, letting me feel her tongue stud, giving everybody another sort of sideshow, while the chain guy heaved and flopped in the center. His face turned colors and his arms and shoulders went rubbery and boneless. It wasn't just some hokum trick, but a lot of hard work to fight his way out of all that stuff, and I didn't really find it all that agreeable to watch, but at the same time it was hard to take my eyes off it, even though Lorraine was providing me with considerable distraction. I'd not known her quite so hot and heavy, but of course it was the number of people that turned her on, and how close they were all pressed up around us.

The chains rattled and shook and finally the guy managed to work his head and shoulder under one loop and then he vibrated himself like a wet dog so that the whole business loosened a little, and then he got another loop . . . but it was a long job. When finally the last chain slipped out he stood there grey-faced and exhausted, and there was just the palest ripple of applause, though everybody did put money in the hat. You knew they were basically paying for pain, and he knew they didn't want to meet his eyes now; he sat on the curb, looking down at the money hat, huffing a little and just beginning to get some color back.

But now the sun was almost down, red as a burning sac of blood and perfectly balanced with the rim just touching the horizon. Lorraine led me over to the sword-swallower, who had timed his act to match the sunset. He was a scrawny-looking little guy, actually about my size, and was just then finishing up his preparatory spiel. He took a drink from a bottle of salad oil, and passed the sword around so people could see there was no fakery. The goddamn thing was three feet long, and definitely not rubber. Lorraine reached to touch the edge of the iron, then licked her finger, with a sly smile at me.

The guy took another slug of oil, then turned in profile to the sun, raising the sword high. Lorraine took my hand and pulled me nearer, and when she was to the front of the crowd she smiled again, over her shoulder, and pulled me in tight behind her, wrapping my arms around her belly. The guy was framed in the disc of the sun, just fitting the sword point between his lips. It was a cross-hilted sword like a crusader's. He pushed it in, about six inches. The crowd moaned, and Lorraine breathed out, and pulled me in a little closer, against the back of the famous cutoffs. She began a slow hip roll, not quite what you'd call a grind, and the guy pushed harder on the sword, taking about a foot of it. I could feel Lorraine gasp under my fingers, and the crowd had groaned again. The sun was about a third below the horizon, standing there like a broken egg bleeding, and Lorraine pulled my hand inside the undone button of the cutoffs, covering it with both of hers, still pushing back into me. I felt the drop, that shift of gravity below my belt buckle, like there was no telling how low I'd go. The crowd groaned again and the guy put more thrust on that sword and suddenly he let go the handle. The cross-piece of the hilt was resting on his teeth. His head was tipped far back, to straighten his gullet, you had to suppose. Lorraine twisted her neck up and around and her tongue rose out of her mouth like a snake, the stud tracing a line under my jawbone. The sword-swallower turned in a slow circle, swaying, to show there was no jiggery-pokery. No blade was sticking out of his back, he had taken the whole thing down. Just as the sun went under completely, he pulled the sword out of himself and took a bow.

A big shout went up all across the pier—mostly for the sunset, for the only people who could see the sword-swallower were those crushed right up next to him. Lorraine turned and plastered herself into me, warm and will-lessly heavy. She kissed me deep and straddled my leg so tight I could feel her lower lips through the fabric, fastening a hot suction seal on my thigh. Then her arms let go and she dropped her head and hands backward, a wild dancer's dip. She shuddered, and then her eyes came open, and I saw them focus on someone to the left. People were looking at us, unsurprisingly, and behind a lot of those people, Rock and Chuck were looking too. It seemed they might have been watching us for quite some time. One of them caught my eye and held it. Very slow and deliberate, he took hold of his hat brim and pulled it lower down.

Lorraine detached herself and gave me a cooler, more distant kiss. "*See you,*" she hissed. Then, with a swing of her hips and one more liquid look over her shoulder, she was gone.

I was out of there too, on my own and in another direction. It was noticeably a whole lot darker after the sun went down, and nobody ever hung around; the crowd was thinning fast. I moved through what was left of it pretty quick, zigzagging and passing people. Since I didn't want to keep obviously looking back I couldn't have said for absolute sure that nobody was following.

At that night's gig I was distracted, enough that sometimes I almost lost the beat. Allston was giving me looks of puzzlement, and Perry went so far as to ask me, during the first break, if anything was the matter, or if I was sick—but I didn't really know what to tell him, supposing I had wanted to tell him anything at all. Lorraine didn't turn up all night, and neither did the wrestling team, and I was just as happy that they didn't.

Willard must have thought I was pining, though, for he came up to me after the last set and said, "You know, bud, you're wasting your effort—that redheaded piece is *never* gonna come across."

"I wouldn't call her an absolute redhead," I told him.

"Close enough for rock and roll," goes Willard, and laid a hand on my shoulder. I got a taste of his whiskey breath. "Now listen, why don't you just come along with me?"

I might not have done this if I hadn't been fairly disoriented already, but as it was, I didn't really feel like limping back to the hotel alone. Since he got his ribs busted Willard had been concentrating most of his attention on one girl, a stripper whose name, professionally at least, was Angelique. She danced in a pink-painted cinder-block bunker that to the best of my knowledge was the only real strip bar in Key West. It was just a few blocks from the Black Cat and it was where Willard was intending to go.

Due to Willard's special relationship with one of the stars, they didn't charge us fifteen dollars a beer and the girls didn't try to make us buy them any so-called champagne cocktails. After about ten minutes though, I still wished I hadn't come in there. The place was mostly empty, except for one sizable gang of guys that reminded me of the wrestling team though it wasn't actually them: frat-boy beef, drunk off their heads and hooting and hollering at this girl who was down writhing around on the floor in front of them. The seats and tables were all raked downward so the floor where the girls danced was a kind of pit in the middle.

But finally this first girl wriggled off the stage, and there was a taped drumroll and Angelique herself burst on, doing a pole dance to the tune of "Billy Jean." Willard was nudging, making sure I appreciated all her charms, and the frat boys were whooping and holding out money, and the mutant-mouse voice of Michael Jackson kept squeaking away. Well, Angelique did have a wonderful body, and I guess I had never seen anybody do a better pole dance, but somehow I just wasn't in the mood to get into it.

When the song ended, two more girls dropped onto the stage to the tune of something else, and Angelique swung through some kind of dressing room and came back over to us, now wearing a Frederick's type of transparent negligée over her G-string and pasties, with a ruff of fake fur floating over the floor. She sat on Willard's knee, giggling while he showed her off like a proud daddy, at the same time making a game of harvesting a few of the bills the frat boys had managed to stick up under her straps here and there. She had a friend with her, whose name was supposedly Emmanuelle, a little silver-blond girl in a similar outfit as Angelique. Emmanuelle didn't seem to require any champagne cocktail but she did want to sit in my lap, and her eyes were so cold I knew she was working. Of course she was working, what else could it be? It was what I hated about a strip joint; the girls' eyes were like the eyes of snakes, still and frosty, no matter what they did with their bodies. Except for Angelique's, because she was sincerely stuck on Willard. His hound-dog mojo had done it again. I knew Willard meant well (ever since Allston and I had bailed him out of the gambling den he'd been trying to find ways to show his appreciation), but I was out of the mood. So I claimed I was tired and split, leaving half my beer undrunk.

A week or so before, I guess, I'd asked Willard why he liked to hang around the strip bar. The stripper girlfriend concept gave me no problem, but that didn't mean you had to spend time in her place of employment, and Willard didn't fit the profile of the lonely guy who can't get laid. I expected hound-dog for my answer, but instead Willard got this long-distance look in his eyes and started talking to me about this place in Detroit called Eight Mile Road, which was lined with strip joints on one side and respectable restaurants on the other—a sort of urban-suburban frontier. Willard had a high school girlfriend who'd graduated into a dancing job there, and going to visit her in that place had made some impression on him he couldn't seem to perfectly describe—not a hundred percent pleasant nor unpleasant either (I got from the way he talked around it) but enough to keep him coming back for more of whatever it was. This was what I was thinking about, walking the waterfront after I left—how that was the one conversation I'd so far had with Willard that didn't feel like it had any lies or tall tales mixed into it. And on the back of my eyeballs I seemed to see Angelique dancing still, but in silence now—no "Billy Jean"—or maybe to some different kind of music.

By the time I wandered back to the spot on Duvall where I'd chained my bike, most of the bars were closing down. I rode up easy toward North Beach, no sound but the breeze and the sprockets clicking. When I turned the corner toward the hotel, they were waiting for me, right beside my car.

It wasn't the entire wrestling team, but five or six of them anyway, most definitely including Chuck and Rock. A couple of them were holding pale, new-looking baseball bats, except Chuck, or maybe it was Rock, who had a two-foot-long heavy-duty screwdriver. That bothered me more than the bats, somehow. The minute he saw me, he leaned in and slid the screwdriver into the grille and popped out the chrome mustang there. It made a little tick when it hit the asphalt, just the smallest sound, and that was the cue—the guys with bats started swinging at the glass on the car, while the rest of the pack dented in the doors with kicks and tore off little tearable things like the antenna and the rest of the grill-work.

I could have ridden on past, I guess—most likely they'd never have caught me on the bike. But instead I dismounted and chained up the bike in the usual spot, not in any kind of a hurry. Then I just strolled over toward them, real slow, with as much of the John Wayne walk as I could manage at my height. They all stopped wailing on the car, and stood there waiting for me.

"I don't know what you're all worked up about," I said. "I didn't even fuck her yet."

Chuck, or maybe it was Rock, let his screwdriver fall out of his hands and clatter on the pavement as he came toward me. Maybe it should have been reassuring, that he wasn't planning to use his weapon, but to me it looked like he was taking it more personal, wanting to rip me apart with his bare hands.

While I stood there watching him wind up a punch, a couple of things became clearer to me, like that my Sweet Lorraine, if she wasn't actually observing this scene from under some bush, was definitely getting off on it, wherever she might be waiting it out (like Sarah had been trying to let me know), and that when it was over she would offer herself entirely up to the fastest, meanest, survivingest animal left standing. That could have been me, but it wasn't gonna—though the punch was so slow and awkward getting itself organized, I had all the time in the world to dodge, to leave the area altogether, to take the guy's arm off at the shoulder if I wanted to.

Instead I just stood there and let it hit me. So long since I'd been hit like that!—it felt like a homecoming, bittersweet. They all moved in on me at once, getting in each other's way, but still not doing so bad for themselves, given that I wasn't putting up any real resistance. Reflex kept pulling my head back from the wild haymakers, but I took a few more solid body shots, then all of a sudden I was on the pavement, curled up like I used to do on the kitchen linoleum when I was small, hands cupped over my ears and head to cover a little from the stampede of kicks, voices cursing me—these guys didn't know I was a Melungeon though. *Spic sonofabitch*, I seemed to hear. I was up against a wheel of my car, then somehow on my feet, floating light and free as a rag. About then I must have caught one to the head because I saw the ragged floating line of shattered Christmas tree lights, and things stopped making sense, stopped hurting so much. A faraway thought came to me, like it sometimes did in such situations, that I might be dead at the end of it. All the oblivion you can eat. They had other plans than killing me though, and presently my head cleared enough I could tell somebody was spreading my hand on the hood of the car, somebody else picking up a bat again, and the voices swollen with excited cruelty—*Asshole won't be playing no more slick guitar*— I flashed on Willard's hands in his pockets and I realized I better not let this happen.

Easy enough to break the hold since they were not expecting anything this late in the game. I came up with a surge and Chuck or Rock was right in position for me to throw an elbow that probably broke his jaw; anyway he went down fast and hard but right behind him was a punch that hit me solid between the eyes. My head snapped back in a moment of darkness, and I blocked blind, feeling my elbows and the edges of my hands making contact with who knows what. When I could see again I tried to break out of the circle, but it was no go, they kept me walled against the car. It was too late, my head was too fuzzy and I was too banged up to move fast and smooth. One of my knees had twisted somehow and didn't want to hold me up. My mouth was filling with blood from my nose and somebody had the baseball bat cocked over his shoulder. I managed to move in to clip his wrists and make him drop it, but hell somebody else just picked it up—too many of them. I could hardly hold my hands up anymore.

Then all of sudden the batter was out of the picture and in his place a dark whirlwind. I laughed, because I thought it was drumsticks at first, but then I realized it was the nunchucks. Two more of the wrestling team were on the ground then, and the rest of them had run away, and Allston was standing there inspecting the scene, holding the nunchucks loose in his left hand, the free stick dangling by his knee.

"What kept you?" I said. I took a loose tooth out of my mouth and stuck it in my watchpocket for safekeeping.

Allston looked at me, kind of irritated. "Started out I was asleep. When I looked out the window, seemed like you were just standing there letting them pound on you. . . ."

"Low morale," I said.

One of the wrestling team raised up to his hands and knees and started crawling around blind, like maybe he was looking for a contact lens. Allston flipped up the loose stick into cock position in his armpit, then let the nunchucks cruise around his head and shoulders while he considered where and how to strike. Finally he let go a short sharp kick that lifted the guy with a big whoof of air. He settled back down onto the pavement, like a parachute collapsing.

Allston was peering into my face. "Reckon we better get you inside," he said.

"Nah, I'm fine . . . not sleepy. Let's go get a drink."

Allston let out a chop of a laugh but I must have done something to persuade him because next thing I know we were walking across town. A couple of times I had to stop and spit blood in the gutter.

"You got an idea where that's coming from?" Allston said.

"It's nothing," I said. "It's just my nose."

My lights kept going on and off, like there was a bad connection, all during the rest of the walk. Then I was sitting on that car seat in front of that gambling den, inhaling the thick scent of the flowers that overgrew the house. I heard Allston calling for gin.

"Bourbon," I said. "I don't drink white liquor."

The guayabera guy was looking at my face, muttering, in the weird blue light of a bug snapper. The woman came out talking in that strange soft language. I felt a wet cloth pass over my face, stinging and smelling of juniper. It cleared my head, and I realized somebody had given me the bourbon I asked for, so I took a slug. No, it was rum, but it would do.

"How many shots did you take to the head?" Allston said. "You ought not to be drinking."

"Hell," I said. "If I can't take a beating I don't know who can."

I started to laugh, then heard myself crying, jabbering. "Look what a mixed-up mongrel I am. I don't know what I'm doing here, don't know how I *got* here, don't even know what breed I am—what am I anyway?"

"Well now," Allston said. "You're welcome to try being a nigger some time—there'll be somebody to let you know what you are every day of your life."

He didn't mean it to hurt, I saw. He meant for me to stop and think. So I did that, for a few minutes. I pictured Allston keeping quiet, always keeping to himself, quiet and calm and polite on the road, all those roads we drove through the Deep South from one cracker joint to another where half the time he'd be the only black face.

"Thanks," I said. "That hits the spot." I laughed again, but it wasn't hysterical now.

Allston and I walked on back to the hotel. Somebody had scraped the wrestlers up off the pavement, or anyway they weren't there anymore. There was no sign if the cops had been there or not. Basically it was pretty quiet. We went upstairs, and Allston asked if I'd be all right, and I said I would be, and we went our opposite ways down the hall. But when I got in front of my door I thought I could hear old Angelique sighing and moaning on the other side of it, and really I wasn't ready for that, so I went back down and out and around the back, to Stell's little brick patio. It was not quite dawn, just a little blue light. I stood outside the screen door, not really wanting to rouse anybody, not really knowing what to do; my mind was a clean, relaxing blank. Then the screen slid aside and Stell was there, sleepy-eyed and blinking, in a loose white T-shirt. In the blue light her face had a look of sad beauty, and she must have got a fair look at me too, for she gasped and said, "Jesse, my God, what happened to you?"

"Walked into a door," I said. I took a step over the sill. She put a light finger on my swollen cheekbone, and her mouth opened in this small dismayed circle, but then I was kissing her, holding her; her breasts seemed to swell into me as her hands locked hard across my spine, and together we melted down to the carpet, which was deep and soft enough. It had been such a long, long night, but now it was ending where it was supposed to—we had always been heading for this, sweet taste of her lips mingling with the blood from mine, the deep warmth opening to let me in.

"Jesse," she said.

"Stell. I'm here."

"Jesse. We cain't do this."

"Yes we can."

"That baby in there. . . ."

"He's asleep."

"Jesse. . . ."

"Don't talk."

"He's your brother."

When I got through puking in the kitchenette sink, I turned on the tap to wash it all down, and once it was clean I kept on standing there, letting the cold water pulse on my wrist. Stell's bridge with the lone false tooth was standing there in a glass of water. I stood there staring at the thing, like somehow it should have answered all my questions.

Finally I felt strong enough to turn around. Stell was sitting up on the edge of the couch, sucking on a cigarette. There was enough daylight now to let me see she looked nervous and jittery, which was understandable, I guess.

"Jesse," she said. "It ain't what you think."

"What is it, then? What is it I think?"

Stell dropped her head and looked at the floor. "I don't hardly know where to start."

"Anywhere," I said. My stomach rolled over again as I thought about it, but there was nothing left in me to come up. "What should I call you? Why did you leave?"

Stell jumped to her feet, scattering sparks when her cigarette brushed a chairback. "No!" she hissed, whispering not to wake anybody, though it still banged on my ears like a shout. "It ain't— Jesse, listen, you done got it backwards."

I propped myself against the counter, gold dots swirling in front of my eyes. "Estelle," I said, "would you please make some sense?"

She sat down. "All right. Let's take Rose-Lee. She ain't my sister. She's my darter."

"You trying to tell me she's kin to me too?"

"No! All I'm trying to tell you, I'm a good deal older than what you might thank . . . even if I did get started early." Stell smiled, kind of rueful out the screen door. "Yeah—well, I never should have got us stuck in that lie, but they was times it just seemed easier. . . ."

She switched back her hair and looked up at me. "I met your daddy when we moved in across the alley, that's all. You know one thing just led to another. He told me some of what was between you, Jesse, but I don't know nothing about your momma. No more does he. No more does anybody, I reckon."

I sat down, then kind of slumped against the couch back. Stell put her hand real light on my knee.

"Jesse . . . I didn't go to upset you. But a body runs up against a limit sometime. I doubt we could have kept it dark forever nohow."

"No," I said. "It's all right, I guess. I'm just . . . *real tired*."

"I'd say you got the right to be," Stell told me. She stood up, and then I felt her actually lifting my legs up from the floor and laying them on the couch. When cool air came across the soles of my feet I knew she must have been taking my shoes off. A couple minutes later I felt a sheet settle over me, and maybe she grazed my forehead with a kiss, only I might have dreamed that part, because I was asleep for a long deep time.

8. ROOM FULL OF TEARS

The windshield had to be fixed on the Mustang, because really you couldn't drive without that, but I didn't replace the rest of the glass. Would have been expensive, all that work, and money was a little tight, what with us covering Willard's debts and all, and besides I was suffering from low motivation. I closed up the window frames with clear plastic and duct tape, rigged up a coat hanger for an antenna. That would do for the time being—not a lot of joyriding was taking place anyhow. Or maybe I thought the car would just regenerate if I left it alone for long enough. Heal its own damage like I was healing mine.

I was lucky, as Allston pointed out, to have come out of it no worse off than I did. Still had all my teeth but one, and no broken bones. I'd have been shot for a good while if I was a horn player, for my mouth was that swollen, it was like having a pair of lemons for lips, and seemed like my nose was going to come back a little crookeder than it had been before. Nothing serious. Nothing to do with my hands, that was the main thing. I did pee blood for a few days, from kicks I must have took to my kidneys while I was on the ground. But that cleared up on its own, before I had to see a doctor. The rest was just bruises, but impressive ones, great flowering bruises bleeding into each other in sickly kinds of sunset shades, all over my belly and chest and my face and cheeks, like somebody had pelted me with fistfuls of paint. The bruises would stiffen up while I slept, which made it hard to get up out of bed. Hot soaks helped, once I'd limped to the tub. A hot tub was not a hard thing to find in Key West. And Allston made me get a hot-water bottle and nurse the worst bruises with it an hour a day—the ones he said were hematomas. He had opportunity to make sure I did this because I had toted my duffel bag down to his room and was officially staying there all the time.

I didn't miss any time off work. Didn't need to, didn't want to, didn't do it. I had always been able to get up after a beat-down and go out and do what I was supposed to, be it school or summer job, whatever. Funny thing to be proud of but there you are. I was up there from the start of the first set to the end of the last one, laying out as solid a bass line as ever I had. The only difference to the gig was that Willard took to showing up on time every night, so I didn't have to cover any lead for him, but could stay back with my bass in the shadows, while my lips deflated and the bruises faded on my face, putting out my share of the rhythm track and staring out over that barnful of people. Now and then my eye would pause on some good-looking strawberry blonde, but it was never my Sweet Lorraine. She and the wrestling team must have mushed on out of there pretty quick after the fight, or anyway I didn't see a one of them again.

I wasn't looking for any replacements. Nothing moved me to go off on some other love jones—no thank you. Anyway I was sort of socially impaired, in a way I remembered from old times, dragging around with all that damage showing, or even with damage that didn't show. Everybody I knew was real ginger with me, kind of exceptionally considerate: Perry fussing like a nervous uncle, Willard making that extra effort to be on time for every show. Estelle had, I guess, more than one reason to be a little shy of me right then, but what she mostly sent my way was a kind of nurse-like kindness. Even Rose-Lee seemed to go out of her way to be agreeable, which was sort of disturbing since usually she didn't take much trouble to be all that nice to anybody. In the end it was easiest to hang out with Allston, because he didn't treat me like somebody something awful had happened to, but more like somebody who had done something stupid, and that, in the long run, was easier to take.

As for people I didn't know but might have fell in with, on the street or at the beach or in the Black Cat between sets, well, I could always see them registering me as someone who had been hurt. If you haven't been torn up that way yourself and you run up against somebody who has been, there's a set of reactions you really can't help. Like you may feel some sympathy, maybe a lot, but at the same time you don't really want that person bringing his blood trail that close to where you are yourself—you don't want to be there when the predators come back.

It had been a long time, so I thought I had maybe forgotten all this, but now it appeared I had just not been thinking about it.

There would always be people who actually were drawn to your wounds more than to you. I had been through a round or several of that, back in the bad old days—a couple of fairly disturbed chicks in my class at high school, a couple or three of the first Older Women. In a way all these people were sharks themselves, even though they were hurting too somewhere—sharks will eat each other as fast as anything, once they all start bleeding in the water.

Nice way to be thinking, I could admit that, but that was the track my thoughts ran on, those nights I stood beside the drum set, my head dropped low to watch my fingers walking the fretboard of the bass, and listening to Estelle work the rim of the stage, whipping her mike cord and belting it out. She'd be singing, and I'd be thinking, *What else would the blues be for?* Package up all the pain and blood you can scrape together and serve it to the rest of the sharks in the tank . . .

Daytimes I'd lay up in the room by myself most likely. Allston pestered me a little to get out, stretch, swim, get my blood moving. Circulation, Allston said, that's what heals. I knew he was right but I didn't much care. I stayed in, scrunched at the head of the bed, leaning on a pair of pillows jammed against the wall, the Hummingbird straddling my raised knee. Doodling, noodling, my mind a wet blank. I didn't think about Sweet Lorraine. The image that kept coming up in my head was Angelique working around that pole, with Willard watching her, only it was Willard in his salad days, and the place was Eight Mile Road. Words ran around in my head like roaches, and a chord progression built pressure under my hand. Power chords marching straight up the neck: A C D F and the turnaround to the bottom and up we go again. No surprise if it was heavy on bass, and slow, at the start, as a dinosaur lumbering.

> She appears as if at the edge
> of a screen, her brown hair black
> in this light, her legs moving the way
> she wants you to want them to move. . . .

I was gonna write a song if I didn't watch out. What would Perry say?

And then the Key West run was finished, and we collected the last of our pay, and Perry unfolded his Southern States map, with the northbound Black Cats all circled in red ballpoint ink, at Fort Myers, and Gulf Shores, and Tuscaloosa, and Auburn. We'd be making our way through the great state of Alabama, staying one good jump ahead of real heat, and get back into the Nashville along with the birds coming back.

Stell and Rose-Lee and the baby rode along with me. They'd traveled in worse-wrecked cars than mine before, I figured, and there was no room for them anywhere else. We had time to catch the touching goodbye scene going on between Willard and Angelique over by the van while we were loading up; it seemed to have a lot to do with how much they were going to miss each other, and even more with how much Angelique was going to miss some amount of money that Willard hadn't managed to pay her back yet.

"This is too damn sad to watch," Rose-Lee snapped, and she kicked the back of my seat. So I cranked it and pulled out—I had a marked copy of the map, and anyhow I knew where we were going. Once we hit the main road and got some speed up, the wind came through those empty window frames and plastered back our hair in kind of an agreeable way, a sweet-smelling breeze that was thick with salt.

"On the road again," Stell said, looking toward me with half a smile. And that was the last thing anybody said for about the next hundred miles.

We covered a good deal of ground with music, but when the tape ran out I didn't change it. The other three people had gone on the nod, and the chord progression running around in my head was enough to keep me busy for a while, with a few new words rolling over it.

> . . . it's hard to see the woman you love
> dance naked in a room full of men
> And come up to your table
> and ask for a light, and the light
> in her eyes is still the same,
> Only her job has changed. . . .

My fingers were just itching to play some hot snarly lead line over this thing, and the whole scene unreeled in my head like a movie. None of it had anything to do with me, either. That was the good thing about it. Except it somehow covered the feeling I'd had walking into that beat-down. At the end it should double the tempo and the lead would be like being whipped with a bike chain.

It was one- or two-week runs at the next string of Black Cats, with short easy hauls from one to the next. With every layover I was getting in better shape physically: you couldn't see much wrong with my face anymore, and the bruises on my body had shrunk down to little invisible lumps like pebbles or severed thumbs under the skin—they didn't hurt anymore at all, though Allston kept after me to melt them down with the hot-water bottle. By the time we made it to Tuscaloosa, new people I didn't know from before had stopped treating me any way weird at all, and I even noticed I was getting the interested eyeball from a few stray women here and there, though I didn't feel like following it up.

I kept to myself, almost altogether, just me and the Hummingbird, perched on the edge of the motel-room bathtub, with the door shut tight to seal in sound and get that fast hard reverb off the tiles. I'm no singer, never wanted to be, but bathroom sound

made my own voice bearable, at least for this kind of a talking
blues:

> . . . *she changes*
> *into clothes*
> *and we cross the street*
> *to a quieter place where we can talk*
> *and the talk turns to me*
> *and what I'm doing*
> *that makes me think I'm better than her.* . . .

Funny thing but it didn't seem to be about Willard anymore.
Not even that picture of young Willard I'd made up in my head. It
was like the scene the song was laying out had grown its own people to live inside it. Like, for the time being, I didn't need more
company than them.

Finally we'd finished our last Alabama date, loaded out from the
last Black Cat, and started motoring up the road to Tennessee.
Pretty soon we weren't seeing any more kudzu, had left the last
red-dirt gully behind. Nobody had much to say in the Mustang;
James Culla was sleeping, and I played the radio, but low enough
the wind pouring through the broken windows washed almost all
of the sound away. That breeze seemed cooler as we got nearer to
Nashville, but it was spring coolness, and the dogwoods were already beginning to bloom.

The van pulled off on the south side of town, headed straight
out to Perry's farm, but I kept on going straight since I needed to
drop Stell and her tribe off in East Nashville. No more than a five-
hour haul that day, but we'd got a late enough start that it was up

in the afternoon by the time I saw the Nashville skyline. I was taking it a little fast, swooping up and down the ramps and enjoying how tight the car held the curves (there was nothing but body damage; it ran as well as ever it had). But by the time I dropped off onto Woodland Street, I felt a spooky tremble in my stomach. I don't know, maybe because I was not in the habit of coming straight into this neighborhood after a road trip. I shut off the radio and drove slow and easy enough to hear kids calling in the back streets, the click of bike sprockets and the bounce of a ball. The rest of them were asleep in the car and didn't stir till I pulled up in the alley, cut the motor and set the parking brake.

"Where we at?" Stell rubbed the back of her head over the car seat, opened up one sleep-clogged eye.

"Home, madam," I said with the snootiest accent I could fake, then gave her a grin, climbed out and slapped my door shut. That roused Rose-Lee, who opened the back door and stretched one leg toward the broken asphalt.

Greg was sitting on their back steps, sucking on a quart of Schlitz Malt Liquor. Supposedly he'd been looking after the house while the ladies were gone. He just threw up a hand when he saw me, but when Rose-Lee climbed out of the car, blinking and rubbing at the car-seat print on her cheek, he got up and came shambling toward her.

"Hey baby . . ." He worked a finger into her back waistband, pulled her hips tight into his. "Miss me?" He handed me the quart so he'd have free use of his other hand. I wiped off the rim and took a quick swallow. Greg and Rose-Lee nuzzled a minute, then she broke away and walked up into the house.

Estelle was out of the car by this time. She set her hands on her hips and arched her back for a bone-popping stretch, then looked around that scrappy back yard, squinting in the red afternoon light. She leaned in the back window to check on the baby, who was still asleep. When she raised up, Greg was hailing her with the quart.

"Cut the dust," he said. "Y'all have a good trip?"

Stell gave that bottle a look that might have cracked it. She was going to say something, but Rose-Lee came blazing out of the back door.

"Aw baby," Greg said.

"Get in here, you son of a bitch, and clean all this crap out of this house!" said Rose-Lee. On her way back inside Rose-Lee banged the door so hard the second floor windows jumped in the frames. In two seconds she had popped out again. "And I mean now!"

Greg and I went up the steps together. She had left the door hanging open this time, and we could hear her crashing around upstairs.

"Aw, man . . ." Greg was looking for a clear place to set down the quart, but there wasn't anywhere obvious. "It ain't that bad." He pushed back some hair and looked at me. "Is it?"

"Oh no," I told him. "Ain't no dead fish laying around or anything like that."

Greg crouched down, setting the bottle on the floor, and started rooting under the sink for garbage bags. He'd be all right if he found a few, I figured. Most of the mess could be raked up pretty quick. The kitchen and front room were littered with cans and cups and takeout containers, and there were a few chicken bones scattered here and there. A funk of stale smoke and spilt beer—pretty much your standard Black Cat smell. I opened up a window or two. Rose-Lee came down the stairs and dumped a load of grotty sheets all over Greg.

"You can hump your skinny ass to the laundromat too," she said. "Once you get done sweeping up in here."

"Aw, baby," Greg goes.

"I guess I'll let you all be together," I said, and I ducked out the kitchen door, the car key ready in my hand. Stell had got the baby out and was holding him to her shoulder, swaying and crooning and trying to convince him not to wake up all the way. I walked around them and got the kid seat out, then opened up the trunk. Give them credit for being light packers. Two trips and I'd be on my way to the country. But as I came back for the second load, I saw Daddy had stepped out his back door and was standing there in the alley.

"Welcome back."

Stell said hey. I said hey. Daddy looked down at his hands like he was expecting to find something in them that wasn't there: bouquet of flowers, car tools, a jug of whiskey maybe, I don't know. His hands were empty, hanging slack. As he crossed the alley I saw he was trying not show how he was noticing the damage to the Mustang. It was a bit early for him to be home from work; I wondered if Stell might have called him. I stayed at the head of the steps where I was. Habit of keeping a clear distance. Behind me, indoors, I could hear Rose-Lee shrilling at Greg, and him answering, low, and not very often.

Daddy put his hand on James Culla's back, rubbed his hair and remarked how it had grown. It looked like he wanted to take him from her. Yeah, I thought, Stell must have called.

"I don't need him woke up," Stell said, but her tone was gentle. "Just let me see if I can get him down, okay?" As she walked toward the steps I came down so as to get out of her way. This left me alone in the yard with Daddy, once she had gone inside, but he was paying more attention to the car, walking around it with his lips pursed up, scratching the back of his head. I knew he'd be trying to match all those dents to an accident and not be having very

much success. He looked smaller, like he always did when I hadn't
seen him in a while, yet I didn't think he was old enough to actually be shrinking.

"What happened?" he said, looking at me across the battered
hood. I realized I had meant to make him ask.

"Pack of guys jumped me," I said. "Beat hell out of me and the
car both."

His eyes cut away and he started pacing around the car again.
"What would that have been about?" he said, not looking my way.

"Woman trouble." I found a cigarette from my top pocket.
Daddy nodded, kept on inspecting the car. In the house I heard the
baby wail, then pipe down pretty quick. Stell would be nursing
him, lying across the bed.

Daddy touched the seal on the new windshield. "Well, they
done all right with this," he said. "Need you four new windows,
the back glass, an aerial—don't know how long it'll take to find
the grille ornament. . . ."

"I got that," I said. "Saved that much." Holding the cigarette
unlit in my lips, I went and found the chrome horse in the glove
compartment and handed it to him. Daddy glanced at it, started
polishing it with his shirttail, not watching what he was doing. He
was studying me now: damage inspection. In the old days I'd
thought it was a toss-up, pretty much, whether he was worried
how bad I was hurt or if there was enough showing to set off a social worker. His eyes dropped. I walked around in back of the car
and took the last two bags from the open trunk.

"I can get those for you," Daddy said.

"All right." I set the bags down on the ground. Daddy gave me
back the grille ornament, then took out a Bic and lit my cigarette
for me. I blew smoke and took a backward step. Close as his hand
had been to my face . . .

"I believe I'd just as soon handle this one here," he said. "I think I got most of what we need and what I don't I'll borrow . . . make it simpler around the shop."

"It's a job of work," I said.

"You're right about that much." Daddy clicked his tongue, a finger running over a dent, his eyes raising back to mine. "You want to help, I could use it."

It was coming on dark by the time I got back out to Perry's, no more of the sunset left than a reddish stain leaking through the grass. I followed the trail the van had broke, mashing down the tall hay and hogweed, parked the Mustang beside it and climbed out. As I was hauling my bass out of the trunk the whole dog pack came storming out from under the house, but when they saw who it was they quit barking and just came over to nose me. I set down the bass case and opened my hands to let them lick my fingers. When I went back to unloading the trunk I noticed the sound of metal banging under the walnut tree to the south of the house.

It was Willard over by that tree, rooting in the guts of an old Karmann Ghia. His hands were grease-stained up past the wrists, so he could have passed for a regular mechanic.

"Didn't know you worked on cars," I said.

Willard straightened up out of the engine, pulled his hound-dog face. "Just do what I have to," he told me. "Perry told me I could drive it if I got it to run," he said.

"That's the rule around here." I figured he must be staying.

"Too dark to see anything right now, though." Willard dropped the hood and walked back up to the Mustang with me. He offered to help with the Hummingbird case, then looked at his hands and thought better of it.

Perry came out to the head of the porch steps, framed like a statue in the yellow light of the doorway behind him, and raised one hand with the palm flat out.

"Blessed is he who comes in the name of the Lord," he declared, then giggled.

"Been in the loco weed already," I said. Perry snickered again and went back in the house. Willard turned to look at me.

"Don't worry about it," I said. "He's just high."

Willard had taken a room upstairs, across the hall from the one I used. He slept in a sleeping bag Perry had loaned him, for it was still pretty chilly at night, and spent his days fiddling with that car. Apart from him being there it was like any other off-time. The first few days we didn't play at all, nobody hardly even felt like listening to music. Exhaustion was just seeping out of my bones. I would sleep in late, take an afternoon nap, and basically never be more than about half-awake at any time.

Outside, Mr. Abel the farmer had started his spring plowing in the truck garden, turning round and round on his tractor, runnels of dark earth furrowing up behind the plow. The ponies had run half-wild through the winter and were so frisky they were hard to catch. I went up into the woods on foot, skirting the pond and heading deeper into the trees. The first new leaves were breaking from the buds, and here and there the rows of winter-dark trunks would be broken by a flare of redbud bloom or the bone-white flowers of the dogwoods. On the far side of the hill the pot plants were looking pretty healthy too, just beginning to come in. Not far from there I scared up some deer, a doe and two spotted fawns, themselves so logy with spring fever they hardly bothered to run from me. I shadowed them through the brush for fifteen minutes, and they would just barely hold their distance, stopping and turning to look back at me, letting me come a little closer. But then a helicopter dropped in low over the treetops—you could hardly see it through the branches but of course the racket spooked the deer; their tails shot up and they were gone.

It was warm enough now to where you could play guitar outdoors without your fingers stiffening up. If Perry was in the house that's what I did. I'd find myself a seat in one of his accidental junkyards, lay out chords and mutter words. "Eight Mile" was just about down by this time, the words and the basic tune anyway, and I had a couple of other things going, both of them variations on the blues. Just the kind of thing Perry would play, but I sure didn't want Perry to catch me at it. Couldn't exactly say what I was afraid of, and maybe it was no more than the sharp side of his tongue.

You didn't have to be all that far off to be out of earshot, and sometimes Perry would stroll out on the porch and take a good long look at me, shading his eyes. I used to stop playing when he did that, or switch to somebody else's song, till I realized there was no way he could hear me. When I wandered back into the house I found myself waiting for him to make some crack. *You posing for an album cover out there or what?* But he never did. I guess he didn't need to. I had my inner Perry right there on the job.

Come Saturday morning I hopped in the Mustang and rode into town. Daddy came out back before I'd even shut the engine. I'd imagined he might be waiting for me. He offered me a coffee but I said no.

"Might as well get at it, then," he said. And we started pulling the front fenders off the car. I'd never been much to work on cars myself—knew where the gas and oil went, but not much more. But I could handle the tools well enough, and follow directions, and soon enough we were in a groove with it. He kept a bench set up under a tin-roofed lean-to set up in his stamp-size back yard, and we laid the left front fender across it and he went to pounding out the dents. After about ten minutes of clanging, one of the neighbors staggered out to the cable spool at the alley's edge and shaded his eyes to look at us. I guess we weren't helping his hangover any. After a minute he went back inside, then came out again a little bit later, cradling a tallboy and a pack of Newports.

Didn't seem to take more than a half-hour for Daddy to have worked up a sweat, though the chill had not quite worn off the morning. He straightened up and grinned at me, wiping his face with the back of one hand and letting the hammer swing free in the other.

"None of your little tinfoil cars," he said. "That's *Dee*-troit iron, what we got here." And he hitched up his shoulders and went back to work.

There was an art to it, I could see that; you had to learn what you were doing, and after a while he started showing me. After a while we could spell each other, one hammering dents out while the other rested and blew. I got into it to where I didn't notice the time passing, till a while after noon when Estelle came out and studied our work, twisting her shirttail up in her hands.

"I got some sandwiches," she said finally. "If y'all are hongry."

Daddy looked at me, and I looked at Stell.

"Guess we could take a break," he said. So we went in her house and ate.

I got Allston to drive me back to the country that night, and came back next afternoon in one of Perry's junkers. Wasn't no point in getting there sooner because Daddy, no lie, was going to church. I didn't know which church that might be, though it was hard to picture him at any. But he was already out there working in the lean-to by the time I hove in, around one o'clock on Sunday afternoon. We put in a decent afternoon on the car, and round the time it was starting to get dark, Estelle walked across the alley to call us in to supper.

In a couple more days Perry got started playing the stereo and issuing his running record reviews, and when Willard passed a guitar he was apt to pick it up and finger out a line or two of something, not bothering to plug it in. We weren't into any kind of jamming just yet. But one day when Perry was out somewhere, I dredged an old four-track recorder out of one of his electronic burial mounds. Two of the channels were still operational, once I had cleaned the heads and the pots, and I didn't figure anybody would miss the thing if I snuck it off to my room upstairs, where headphones gave me plenty of privacy to work out leads against a rhythm guitar track. A time-killer, I'd say, if anyone asked. All I was doing was fooling around. . . .

By the middle of the week I felt restless enough to drive in to see what Allston had been doing with himself. But I hadn't told him I was coming, and he was just stepping out with a girl when I got there, a nice-looking one he introduced as Jahmaya. Nobody I'd seen or heard of before. She had a sweet dark-sugar face, framed in long glossy hair done in tight corn rows, bundled together with gold wire. Her eyes lit up when she talked to Allston, who was tapping out beats on his trouser legs, smiling at her. It seemed pretty plain I should leave them alone, so when they went one way I went the other. I looked back just once to see them walking down the block, their hands swinging not quite close enough to touch. I felt blue looking at them somehow, not knowing why. No use dwelling on it.

Next thing I knew I was strolling past Showbud, slowing down to check the guitars in the window. The first one I noticed was a sunburst Les Paul that looked almost exactly like the one I'd sold when I switched to bass. This interested me enough to go inside. I was tempted to pick it up and see if it had the same scratches and dings on the back, only I was already feeling this gruesome guilt, as if I had intentionally orphaned the goddamn thing, when after all it was only a guitar.

I turned my back on it, then, and walked further into the store. Sometimes the guitars hanging would seem to shiver when you passed them, like wind was flowing through their strings, to make ghost music. No wind, of course, inside this room. At the end of the row of arch-top Gibsons hung a white Aria, except it wasn't really white, but the natural color of curly maple, pale and satiny. The strings breathed softly when I lifted it down.

I didn't even bother to look at the price tag. Just give me fifteen minutes with this thing . . . I cased the place. George wasn't in view. At the counter was some new guy, with a long nose and a brush cut. If they didn't know me they wouldn't know I wasn't seriously gonna buy the guitar. And even if they did—well, I had bought the Hummingbird. Hadn't I?

I walked to the counter. "Could you let me have a cord for the booth?" I was focusing on the buttons on the dude's flannel shirt because I didn't want to let him catch my eye.

"Should be one in there." Something familiar in his voice, but still I didn't look up. "Need a pick?"

"Thanks, I got one," I said as I made for the booth. A closet-sized space with a glass door, so you wouldn't be tempted to try shoving a guitar down your pants in there, whatever. A blue cord was hanging from a Fender Twin. I plugged it in and punched the clean channel. The pale guitar molded to my hand like they had known each other forever.

What? I had a pick in my watch pocket but I didn't bother taking it out. I stroked an A minor seventh chord, jazz voicing, feeling the sadness steam up in the close space. The chords moved like breathing, it was that easy; I was massaging them, sort of, with the meat of my thumb. And my left thumb was coming up over the top of the neck to fret the low E-string, until I felt the pull in the tendon, not yet real pain, and realized that was a bad idea.

I went to string, following the words in my head with thumb and forefinger, notes bending in long syrupy elisions:

> Well I had my fun . . .
> If I don't get well no more. . . .

It was the guitar bringing out all those shades, like it was playing itself and only needed my touch to set it free. What an awful sad song it was, though. No hope in it whatsoever. I finished it and sat there in the quiet. For some reason a picture popped up in my head—that girl in Ocean City, Brown-Eyed Sue. All the brown-eyed–girl songs that would suit her ran through my head one after another. I shaped a few chords on the neck, but I didn't sound them. I was never gonna see her again, and that was a fact. So what would have been the point?

The booth was starting to seem too small, and I wanted something to break that silence. What I could play was "Eight Mile." In some kind of a crooked way it seemed to cover my situation. I played through the progression a time or two, then started just talking the words.

> She appears
> As if at the edge of a screen.
> Her brown hair black in this light
> Her legs moving the way
> She wants you to want them to move . . .

Yeah, right. That just about covered it. But it was actually making me feel better to sing it. The booth seemed the safest place I could possibly hide in. Perry couldn't hear me. No one could. I let my throat open up a little more as I went along:

> . . . the talk turns to me
> and what I'm doing
> that makes me think I'm better than her.
> I'm not, and I know it,
> but she won't be convinced.
> There's nothing I can say
> that will sway her the way she sways
> on stage, and nothing
> Can make me look away. . . .

Then I popped the foot switch to the overdrive channel and doubled the time. I'd practiced enough on the four-track that I had all the corners down, and with distortion the sound was dense enough I didn't miss the rhythm. I must have played forty bars of that solo before I was ready to quit. Lord, what a sweet guitar it was. When it was done I let it ring, a tight rebound in the narrow space behind the glass. Then I shut down the amp and stood up, lifting the guitar clear of my body, careful not to scrape the back against my belt buckle. I saw that flannel shirt angling toward me as I came out of the booth.

"Nice ax," he goes, that familiar voice. "Get almost all of that Les Paul tone, but not hardly any of that Les Paul weight."

"Good God—Chris," I said, looking him in the face for the first time. "I didn't know you."

"Yeah," Chris said. "I guess I sort of suspected that."

"Well, hell," I said, feeling a flush come up under my skin— but that haircut made him damn near unrecognizable, changed the whole shape and balance of his head, plus which the clothes were nothing like Chris's old glamorama wardrobe. "You know I was just . . ."

"Just trying to make it to the booth with that guitar." Chris gave me a grin. "You can stop in any time—well, I work Monday-Wednesday-Friday."

"That's a handsome offer," I said, and then kind of got stuck.

"Hell, we ought to get together. You were smoking in there just now."

"What?" I said, surprised for real.

Chris jerked his head at a pair of cans lying on the counter.

"Sneaky," I said. "Very sneaky."

"Take it as a compliment," Chris said. "Normally speaking, nobody listens. It's just like a way to be sure nobody tries to play 'Stairway to Heaven' in there."

I managed a grin at that old gag, but I was still a little spooked. Most perfect privacy I thought I ever had, and they could have had me piped out on the radio.

"Where'd you pick up that last one you did?" Chris said. "The one about the stripper."

I didn't say anything but something in my face must have given it away.

"Damn, Jesse," Chris said. "Did you write it?"

"Yeah," I said. "Yeah, I guess I did."

"What's Perry gonna think about that?" Chris said, and for a second I saw a shadow of that ugly look in his face I remembered, for instance, from that last bad scene in Miami. But then it was gone.

"Like I give a big rat's ass what Perry thinks." He looked off toward the ranks of guitars hanging on the wall. "Jesse, I'm sorry I cut out like I did—I mean for doing it to you, and Allston. Perry can stick it wherever he wants to—"

"Sure," I said. "I can carry him that message, if you want."

"I don't guess so." Christ tried a laugh but it didn't quite work. "You still staying out there?"

"Yep."

Chris turned off toward the guitars again. "You see Estelle?"

"Once in a while."

"Yeah," Chris said, and then called out, "Aaron, would you cover the counter a minute?" He looked at me. "Come on in the back."

It turned out that Chris had changed his whole game plan, along with his look. He'd more or less quit playing out at all, was taking the sound-engineering course at Belmont College, playing the odd session, teaching guitar lessons in one of the closet-size rooms in the back of Showbud. That's where we went to sit and talk, a room so close our knees were nearly touching. I'd had my first lessons there myself, back when, and not with Chris of course.

"What are you planning to do with that song?" he said, when we'd caught up on all this news. "You gonna start picking up a few vocals?"

"No," I said. I was sure of that much.

"You don't feature Estelle doing it, do you?"

"I don't know," I said. The truth was I hadn't thought about anybody doing it—hadn't got anywhere near that far. "She's crossed over some guy songs before now."

"Yeah, but this would be hanging a big sign right around her neck, wouldn't it? 'Hi! I'm a lesbian!'" Again, the mean shadow passed over his face. "Okay, sorry. I know better'n that. I acted like a bastard to her and I know that too," he said. "I wish—well, my mind was messed up. That's as much as I can say on it, I guess. I think maybe I was just set on blowing myself out of there any way I could do it. Been under Perry's thumb a little too long."

"The coke didn't help, I reckon."

"No," Chris said. The bare bulb that swung above us made dark holes of his eyes. "It didn't." He leaned forward, nudging me partway aside, and started scrabbling through a stack of chord charts on top of an amp. Lesson stuff, it looked like, scrawled on looseleaf notebook paper.

"Here," he said, and handed me two sheets folded longways together. "You can take that to Stell for me if you're willing."

"What is it," I said, but I had already unfolded the papers. More looseleaf, words written out by hand and the chords scrawled up above them.

> *Big dark cloud*
> *Small white sun*
> *Through the window*
> *morning comes*

Now I lay me
Now I don't
Make me sleep
Don't say I won't. . . .

"Red Dreams" was the title written up at the top. That grabbed me, for some reason, right off the bat. Chris had turned his face toward the door hinges and was talking kind of fast.

"It's a song. Look, Jesse, I'm not gonna send her flowers or anything. I'm not gonna mail off any apologies. I won't even say I wrote this for her, but it's one she could do easy enough. Easier than your stripper song, more than likely. I think she'd do well by it. It's hers if she wants it and no strings attached. Oh, if you all end up making a record, I wrote this one, that's all."

"Chris," I said. "Nobody's thinking about making a record."

"You mean Perry's not thinking about making a record." One more time the mean look melted off his face almost as fast as it appeared there. "Look, you don't necessarily have to play it this way but there's one little figure right at the beginning—goes like this." He snapped on the amp beside him and twisted into the corner to hoist his guitar.

Perry was playing Steve Reich so loud that night I could practically hear it from the interstate ramp. *Music for Eighteen Musicians.* The porch floor was trembling like a drumhead when I came across toward the door. Inside it was dark but for one yellow lamp and all the little lights on the stereo console, and there was a heavy funk of dope. And the loud dense music everywhere, with its imperceptible shifts of phase, like staring at the threads of a Persian carpet, or walls of Arabic calligraphy you couldn't understand. I could see the cob pipe jutting out of the shadow of Perry's jaw. He pulled it out and offered it to me as I came through the door.

"Pass," I said. "You think you might back off on the volume just a bit?"

"Snakes don't actually hear so well," Perry said. "It's more like they *feel* sounds, did you know that? At the ends of their rib bones is where they feel it."

I was having some trouble processing this statement, until Perry reached down toward the edge of the small pool of lamp-light and picked up what I had taken to be maybe a pile of dirty socks—only now it began to lash and whip from side to side with its own life. A yard-long snake with a red and black pattern, lean and mean and lively from the winter; it must have just lately crawled out of the cave. I jumped a couple of feet back, not able to help myself.

"Is that as much a copperhead as what it looks like?" I said.

"Well, you don't know but what it might be a common water snake." Perry dandled the snake from its middle, unfolding a foot or so toward his face—scaly head and the tongue searching. "The difference is in the pupil of the eye." His voice rose to small-hall volume. "With God's harmless *water snake*, the pupil is round and innocent as the ebony head of a pin. In the *copperhead*, God's poison adder, the pupil is ogive, wicked as a diamond."

"You already told me that," I said, but that wasn't any hindrance to Perry; he was willing to tell you a thing more than once.

"Come and see." Perry stood up and waved the snake in my direction.

I shook my head, and sidled toward the the kitchen door. Perry didn't seem too bothered. His eyes weren't even tracking me; he seemed to have some kind of invisible audience over there by the porch door. I wondered if he might have got into some magic mushrooms, which would sometimes come up wild on manure piles round the place in the spring. The snake rebalanced on the palm of his open hand, and curved out a length of itself like a question mark.

"*God* knows the difference of all his creatures." Perry's voice had picked up so much resonance and force, the music dropped away behind it, like a wallpaper pattern off in the background. "Heaven is here—it ain't on Pluto! No scripture says that heaven is found in the universe's cold night! No, the souls of the saved are with us here. And the *damned* as well, yes, Hell is here too, *right* here where we make it. . . ."

But by then I had made it into the kitchen, and once the door had closed behind me I couldn't hear his sermon half so well. I filleted a couple of hot dogs and fried them up and ate them on toast for my supper. Perry was still going on in a low rumble—I couldn't make out the words. I washed out the skillet and carried a cold beer up the back stairs. Willard stepped out of his room when he heard me in the hall, puffing a reefer the size of a small cigar.

"Hey bud, that old boy is pretty far out there tonight, don't you think?"

I nodded. "He gets that way sometimes, when he hasn't got enough to do."

"He's keeping busy enough for me," Willard said. "You better get a taste of this doobie."

Why not? I wouldn't be getting to sleep for a long time anyway, what with the noise and excitement and all. I took a deep hit, then coughed most of it out.

"Man, this is kind of green, wouldn't you say? You never got this from Perry's stash."

Willard giggled and waved me into his room. He had a sack of green dope about the size of a pillowcase, and he appeared to be midway in the process of rolling it all up into fat blunts like the one he was smoking.

"What the hell?"

"It grows out there in the woods, buddy boy."

"Willard," I said, "if you think that stuff is growing wild, you might have another think coming."

"You worry too much," Willard said, giving off a cloudy doped smile. "Hey, you think that snake is poison?"

"Don't know," I said. "You got to look in the eyeballs a whole lot closer than I care to."

"I been told about that," Willard said. "You think it's apt to crawl up here tonight?"

"That I doubt," I said. "They like it warm, and it's warmer downstairs."

Willard still looked a little uneasy. "You could always stuff a towel under your door," I told him.

But Willard didn't go for the towel idea. Or maybe he figured there was safety in numbers, I don't know. Anyway, the next night he nudged my door open and caught me hacking on my songs. It was almost like he already knew what I was up to, though it didn't seem likely he would have heard me, towel or no. There wasn't anything to hear except for pick click. I'd brought up an old Squire Tele from downstairs so I could plug straight into the four-track, and I was just listening to myself on headphones.

"Whatcha working on?" Willard goes. He offered me his big green-dope spliff, and I waved it away.

"What, me work?" I said. But I was busted!—stone-cold

busted, sitting there trying to write a song. Willard reached and snagged the notebook I'd been scribbling lyrics in and settled himself as comfortably as he could on the wood floor. What the hell. I pulled off the phones and tossed them his way.

"Slide me that ashtray, would you, bud?"

I did it, and Willard laid down his spliff and scooted a little nearer to the mattress so the headphone cord would reach. My left hand gave me a little jolt, nerves talking back to me, I'm sure, but I managed to keep on playing what I had been—a slow clean lead line over that jazz-voiced progression, one four one four one . . . Willard was nodding to the bass line (count on me for that much at least) and running his finger down the ruled lines of my paper.

> I could have been a man
> Coming home for love and soup,
> Could have been a bird
> Flying high above this stoop
> Could have been a figure
> in a bright-colored painting
> Stopping by a river
> to watch the the sky complaining. . . .

That's where the words ran out, but the music went on, with a cute change, if I said it myself, to four-minor-seven in place of the four, then back to the root and so on. Then I choked and had to stop, and I reached down to shut off the tape for good measure. It was too much having to have somebody as good as Willard be sitting there, just him and me, him giving his whole attention to me trying to play lead. But then it occurred to me that Willard was so stoned on that green weed that he shouldn't be any more threatening an ear than the crowd in your typical Black Cat. Even if I couldn't quite convince myself of this notion, it looked like I was in too far to get back.

"So?" I said.

Willard delivered his classic egg-dripping smile.

"Would you play that?"

Willard seemed to be thinking it over. "Yeah," he said finally. "I don't see why not." And here came his hand reaching out for the Tele.

I snagged the Hummingbird, which was propped on the wall, and started swinging through the tune from the top. Willard tossed me back the phones, so I could hear what he was doing. I mean he didn't even seem to need to hear himself, but I was sold on what came to my ears from the Tele's pickup—what a *real* guitarist might do with this tune. And Willard was getting that semi-surprised smile he'd sometimes wear on stage, like he was just amazed and amused at all the neat little tricks his fingers were doing.

So I relaxed and just followed his groove, and when I took a rest, in the bit I intended to be a cappella for the singer, Willard just carried what I'd imagined for the voice part right on through.

I . . .

I . . .

I . . .

I know it's too late . . .

And with that *too late* the rhythm guitar glided back in on the four-seven minor, back to the root, then the five chord finally, first time in the whole song, resolve on the root, and a quick six-five turnaround. Been done before, only not in that order, and I still thought it was pretty slick, except I didn't have any words over that part, which should have finished out the chorus.

So there we were. I stopped, being I'd made it to the end, but Willard kept on doodling for a minute. Till I pulled the head-phones off. The spliff had gone out in the ashtray. Willard laid the Tele string-down on his knees and picked it up to relight it.

"Yeah," he said once he got his draw. "I could see playing that."

"I'm stuck for words on the chorus," I admitted. "I need two lines there and I don't got'm."

Willard gave me palms-up hound-dog, reefer hanging out of his doggy-dog smile. Then he pulled the joint out of his face and looked serious, for him.

"Who're you writing it for, that's the question," he said. "Get that one answered, you'll know what to say."

Saturday morning I got woke up by a sound something like fire-crackers going off underwater. When I went to the window to check it out I saw the Karmann Ghia was blowing smoke rings, shuddering and popping underneath the walnut tree. I went downstairs. Perry was nowhere in sight; either he'd got up early to go out snake hunting or God knows what, or else he was still asleep—except it was late, near ten o'clock. I'd slept later than I meant to myself.

Willard was winding up a shave at the kitchen sink, combing his hair back slick with water and checking himself in the piece of broken mirror propped between the faucets and the windowsill.

"See you got her running," I said. "Congratulations." Somebody had made coffee. I poured myself a cup from the stove-top percolator and sat down at the kitchen table. Willard grinned at me in the mirror, smoothed his hair back one more time.

"Oh yeah." He hitched up a pillowcase that had been leaning against his ankles. Whatever was in it shifted, like a loose bundle of little sticks.

"Willard," I said. "Tell me you're not planning to sell that stuff in town."

"Oh no. Just going to a party."

"At ten in the morning?"

Willard did hound-dog. "You're welcome to come along."

"Thanks anyway." Seemed I was saying that a lot these days. But I did walk out on the porch with Willard. The dogs came out from under the house too, to watch him leave, the Karmann Ghia bucking and snorting down to the road. The dogs didn't make any fuss or commotion—they were used to Willard now—just watched quietly till the car turned out of sight behind the fencerow, and then went back up under the porch.

Daddy had already put in an hour or so on the Mustang by the time I got there. I said I was sorry for being late, and he told me it didn't matter.

"Got that glass come in this week," he said, nodding toward some sheets of cardboard propped against the back wall of the house. I went to check it out and found four windows and the rear windscreen.

"Might get'm in today," Daddy said, "we keep at it."

We worked steady through that afternoon, stopping now and then for a smoke and a Coke, not bothering to break for lunch.

The neighbors grouped up around the cable spool, nursing their beers and admiring our efforts. Now and then one of them called out a word of encouragement.

At the height of the afternoon it got warm enough we were sweating in our shirt sleeves. But by evening the chill had crept back into the air. We got all the glass installed before we quit—in fact there was not a whole lot left to do but paint. I helped Daddy pull the tarp over the car and tie it down. He took a step back and glanced across the alley. There was no sign of life at Estelle's house and I realized I hadn't seen anything stirring over there all day.

Daddy looked at me and then at his own kitchen door and then at some neutral space in between. "You want to come in for a minute?" he said.

I didn't intend to be pulling his chain; it was more like I just couldn't seem to come up with any sort of response. I stood there doing nothing at all until he'd given up, I guess, and started moving for the kitchen door, alone. Then I fell in behind him and followed him indoors.

Indoors, shadows and sunset stain lipping over the sills. He pulled the light cord and went to the sink. The room seemed smaller, walls closing in, as he stood there lathering his arms with the orange soap, and I felt a choking in my chest, like my breath would not come right.

I walked into the front room. The same couch and rockers, the low table pocked with cigarette burns. The same pictures were on the walls, and the old mirror in the dark walnut frame. In the front window the sunlight broke in rainbow colors on the cracks that spread from a tiny hole I'd put there with a BB pistol, quite a while ago. It was the hour giving me the weirds. Round sunset I'd have been home from school for a couple of hours, and if he was back by this time it would be all right most likely, but if he wasn't back by now the odds would be rising he'd be drunk when he did come in. . . .

I shook my head, walked up the stairs. The corners snatched at me like traps, the places I'd been cornered. My old bedroom was bare, anonymous, the bed made tight underneath an Army blanket, tack holes and scraps of tape on the stripped walls. I pulled open the top dresser drawer and found the kind of sad neglected stuff you might expect: a tube of BBs rusted together, loose guitar strings, a spiral notebook, a Case knife with the tip of the blade broke off, and a half-crushed harmonica. In the next drawer down were some old songbooks on top of the posters he must have taken down from the walls: Rolling Stones, Clapton, and (much as I'd rather not admit it) the Blues Brothers in their stupid hats and sunglasses.

What had I been thinking? I had not been inside these walls since I had first moved out. Not one time since then would I cross the doorsill. Now I stood in the upstairs hallway. I could hear the water shut off in the kitchen sink, the refrigerator door and then a cabinet. Then nothing but the tick of the clock beyond his bedroom door. When I used to lay up on the bed in my room, licking my wounds, I'd listen to that tick across the hall and know that when he next came in he'd come with gentleness, arnica and iodine to treat the bruises and scrapes. He did the nursing with such a calm patience, it was hard even for me to believe he'd done the damage too. Good cop, bad cop, devil or saint; I never would know which was going to show up, and right there, I suppose, was the problem, at least from my point of view.

I turned. It was getting good dark now—darkness flashed from the mirror. In that spasm of no-light I saw something strange. Stell, or a woman like her, turning her face away from me behind a heavy pane of glass, curved like a car window, and the glass was running down with rainwater. At the same time the phrase jumped up in my head, woman's but not like Stell's—it was torn and ragged like Janis Joplin, the crying voice. *Room full of tears*, it said, and I could hear the music, though I couldn't name it then. The feeling was outside of me, sealed in the glass, and I felt like my blood was all full of some really strong drug, so that anything could happen to me and it still wouldn't hurt.

A full pint of bourbon was sitting on the kitchen table when I went down. I must have done a take when I saw it, for Daddy was quick to say, "That's for you, if you want some." He was sitting at the far end of the table from the bottle, working on one more can of Coke.

"Thoughtful of you." I went to the sink and washed my hands with the same slow attention he'd given to his. Then I got a glass from the cupboard and came back to the bottle. Jack Black—the state seal on the cap was unbroken till I twisted it off. I poured myself a pretty good shot and sat down. Daddy was looking at me, a gimlet eye.

"I done you all kinds of harm, in my drinking days," he said. "I'm bound to tell you, I know what I did, and I'm sorry for it. Not that I reckon it helps all that much."

"Sounds like some kind of step in your program."

"You could say that. You're supposed to get back to everybody you hurt and admit what all you did to them."

"Well," I said. "Tell them to give you a gold star."

His eyes didn't drop. "You could say worse than that and I'd deserve it." He shook one of his short Camels out of the pack and put it in his mouth. I took my first taste of the whiskey. Can't say I really felt proud of myself.

"Shoe's been on the other foot quite a while now," he said.

"You could have taken it out of my hide long since. I've sometimes wondered why you didn't."

"I didn't want to give you the satisfaction," I said.

"All right," he said. "That's got the sound of truth to it." He shot the pack of cigarettes across the table to me. I took one, lit it, slid the pack back.

"It's just another form of meanness," I said. "Nothing to be proud of."

"Is that all there's ever been between us?" There was pain in his face. I had seen it before. It had been a bad sign to see that, back then.

"No," I said. "I'm not saying that."

He lit his cigarette then, finally, and looked off toward the window above the sink.

"I could have given you up," I said. "Ratted you out to the cops and the social services and blown the whole situation up a long time ago. All I'd had to do was pull up my shirt."

Daddy scratched his chin, thinking. "Yeah," he said. "But they say sometimes, kids are afraid to . . . do that. Tell."

"Not me," I said. "Anyway, not all the time."

He nodded. Cigarette forgotten in his hand, smoke rippling up in two parallel plumes. "I figured you waited till you were ready and able to walk out of here on your own two feet." He looked at me straight, till he saw what he wanted to, I guess, and then let his eyes drift back toward the window. "I don't know where you learned how to walk away from a fight," he said. "But you sure as hell didn't get it from me."

"That's not all there was to it," I said. "I figured I was better off here. I'd seen those kids in the foster homes."

"Oh," he said. "I reckon that's a comfort."

I tipped a little more whiskey into my glass. His Adam's apple bobbed with a dry swallow.

"Estelle wanted me to talk to you," he said. "She told me, uh, she told me you had just kind of got the wrong idea about who she was to you and all."

"She did?" I said. "That must have been a real interesting conversation."

"Huh," Daddy said, coloring up a bit. It seemed like he couldn't get any further. I rattled my nails on the glass of the pint.

"Want a drink?"

That quick sulphurous flash of anger made me slide back inside myself, though outwardly there was no need to move.

"Hell yes I want a drink," he said. "I want a drink just about every minute. Don't mean I get to have one though."

"Sorry," I said, and I did feel shame.

"You got the right," he told me, and cleared his throat. "Your mother," he said. "Her name was Marie."

I leaned a little way forward. I remembered, he would rave and curse the name of Marie whenever he went on a tear. When he was sober, not a mention. Never. I learned better than to ask.

"She said her name was Marie Bowlin. I don't know if there was any truth to that. There wasn't a whole lot of truth in what she told. She said she came from the town of Sneedville, but there's no Bowlin ever lived there, I come to find out. So I don't exactly know which part was a lie. Maybe both. I know she lied about her age, must have. She was a barmaid down at Soutter's there when we met, but she couldn't have been more than twenty, probably not even eighteen, I'd doubt. I wasn't no more than twenty myself. She'd run off from somewhere, that was plain."

He drew on his cigarette and flinched, spilling the long ash on the table. The coal had burnt right down to the yellow stains on his fingers while he wasn't paying attention. He stubbed it out and swept the ash into the palm of his hand, then rubbed it into the fabric of his jeans. Straightaway he lit up another one.

"Oh, she was always full of the wildest stories. I knew couldn't half of them been true. But it was like listening to a book. And it didn't matter while the good times were rolling. Well, we weren't together for more than one year, I don't think. She got pregnant in nothing flat but she lied about that too, even to herself, I reckon, till it was four months gone and nothing to do. Didn't stay more'n three or four months after you were born neither. I hate to tell it, Jesse, but she just wasn't interested in no baby."

By this time it was dark outside, so we were sealed into the lit space of the kitchen, its pale green walls and cream-colored cabinets. No clutter like there was at Perry's—he did run a tidy ship always, for a man living on his own. When I looked up toward the window all I could see was our watery reflections, featureless in the black pane.

"Have you got a picture?" I'd always wondered that—and looked, sometimes, when he was out at work.

"Used to," he said, looking away. "I wish I did have one for you now. I tore them up one time is what I did. . . . You want to know what she looked like, just check in the mirror. It's her you favor, near a hunnert percent."

I didn't say anything. It wasn't that my mind was blank. I could see him seeing her whenever he looked at me. There was a kind of logic to it all.

"I tried hunting her," he said. "She hadn't left no more trail than a ghost. Nobody ever heard of her up in Sneedville. I showed her picture around amongst the Melungeons up there. Nobody knew her from Adam's off ox."

"What's a Melungeon?" There was something else I'd always sort of wanted to know. Daddy shrugged.

"You just let me know when you figure it out," he said. "Marie told her tales about it. Melungeons was Arabs brought over here by Sir Francis Drake. They was the lost tribes of Israel, I don't know. Maybe nobody does. They're dark-skinned and come down from the hills round about. Some people despised them because of that—said they were next door to being a nigger. I don't know that Marie really was one—I'd not put it past her to cook up the story to account for her coloring. I couldn't really say where her looks came from—she might have had Spanish blood or gypsy or I don't know what all." He looked toward the blind window. "She was a beautiful woman," he said. "I do know that. We had times . . . It tore me up terrible when she left."

I could tell, I knew, that I didn't want to hear this part but that he was going to have to say it anyway. I took a pull at my glass of bourbon but for once it didn't seem to offer a whole lot in the way of fortification.

"I blamed you, I guess," he said, struggling now to keep looking at me. "Like she would have stayed if not for you. Well, mostly I knew better. She was running with other men already before she went, while I was out at work. But still I thought— I knew it wasn't a child's fault no way. But still. . . ."

He was stuck again. I didn't know how to help, though I wished that I could stop it somehow. Funny, but he had never liked to see anything in needless pain. All of a sudden I remembered a time, a man was beating his dog at the end of the alley. I'd been riding my Big Wheel all through that afternoon, up one end and down the other. Must have been five or six years old, dirty-faced, I could imagine, maybe with a bruise or two. The dog was a brown-and-white-spotted shaggy old thing, yelping under the blows of a busted ax handle. I didn't pay it any mind, but it got to Daddy, who was trying to work in the back yard under his lean-to—must have been a Saturday.

I watched him come stalking up the alley, knew the look on his face well enough, that stiffness in his legs as well, but this time he passed without seeming to see me. He'd woke hungover, been nursing beer all afternoon. *Let that animal be*, he said. Man straightened up slow, leaning on his ax handle. I remember the taste of my fingernail in my mouth, the chewiness of it, while I watched them face off. He was twice Daddy's size, a big beer belly and swollen arms like Pop-eye on the TV.

He's my dog to whup if I feel like it.

That right? says Daddy. *What if I don't feel like listening to him holler?*

What do you aim to do about it? The big man opened himself up a little larger. He was still holding that dog by the collar, and he had the ax handle in his other hand, but he would have been expecting a few more moves in the exchange, a threat or two, maybe a shove. Daddy made a small sidewise movement of his arm, like a girl throwing a baseball, and cracked the big man's ribs with the round end of a ball-peen hammer—the same subtle movement he would use to pop out a dent. The big man sank down on one knee, turning loose of the dog, his breath sighing out of the dark hole in his face, and that was all there was to it.

When I remembered all this I thought that Daddy must have had the hammer up his sleeve—he wore a long-sleeve khaki or plaid shirt that day—and I thought too of something Allston taught me, that it don't finally matter how big or strong you are or even how much training or skill you've got—it's how completely you're committed. But at the time I just bit into another fingernail and thought, *Now what a silly old big fat man, he don't know what I know, about my daddy. . . .*

I never knew what happened to the dog.

"There was times," Daddy was saying now, working to keep his voice even, "I thought, if not for you, my whole life would of turned out different. I'd of been happier, I'd be free. That's when I put my hands on you. Beat you. My own son."

"Why didn't you give me up?" I said. It was the first time this thought had entered my mind.

"Well, you know we hadn't got no family nearer than Chattanooga," he said. "My sister, she had troubles of her own back then. She told me to think about adoption, yeah . . . I don't know. You were all I had." The chair creaked under his slight weight. "Do you wish I had give you up?"

I put my hand on the whiskey bottle and then let it go. There wasn't any help in there for me right now, I didn't think. The question had knocked me off my bearings.

"There ain't no answer to that," I finally said. "I wouldn't be who I am if you had. I wouldn't be who you're talking to."

"All right . . ." Daddy said, like he was waiting for some more, only I didn't have any more. That was it. He spread his hands on the table like he meant to push himself up, but only stayed seated where he was.

"It's late," I said, "I got to get back."

"All right, then," Daddy said. "You better carry that whiskey with you."

"Perry's got plenty," I said. Then, when I realized what he meant, I picked up the pint and shoved it down in my hip pocket. We stood together just outside the doorway, looking at the Mustang under the tarp.

"Might get her done tomorrow," Daddy said.

"Yep," I said. "You fixed her up pretty—better than new."

"The car I can fix," he said, and I felt him studying me, the damage inspection. "The rest I don't know about."

"I'll see you tomorrow," I told him, and I could tell right away from his face that at least that had been the right thing to say.

Still, I felt pretty rickety driving back out to the country, the pint stashed under the seat of the truck, my whole brain jumping like a frog in a jar. It was true, I wouldn't have been who I was, whoever the hell that was supposed to be, but then, but then, but then . . . what?

When I got out to Perry's, there was nobody home. I cracked out the Hummingbird and carried it out on the porch and played every lost and lonely sad song I could think of. When I got done with the standards I started in on Chris's number, the slow gloomy bass line that carried the D chord across to an A sus-4.

> Pills to swallow
> Cure for pain
> Now my pillow
> smells like rain
>
> Don't know how or
> what to say . . .
> Now the sun is
> in the way . . .
>
> Now I lay me
> now I don't

> *Make me sleep*
> *Don't say I won't. . . .*

Damn but Chris had outdone himself on that one. I could just feel the rocky landing from a coke flight in this thing. Popping Valium, if you had any, or trying to drink yourself down far enough to sleep. I hadn't done it all that much but I'd done it often enough to know.

A few dogs slunk out from under the porch and turned in the yard to stare up at me. I had been singing pretty loud, being there was no one to hear it. Dogs was the audience that suited me then. My fingers were stabbing underneath the calluses and my left thumb cramped like it was on fire, but somehow I still wasn't ready to quit. I got off on the one I'd done in front of Willard that night.

> *Could have been a preacher*
> *In a church with a tall white steeple*
> *Could have been a lot of things*
> *To a whole lot of different people . . .*

Walking a B-flat to the D-seven—the change that only dogs can hear. They were all sitting there scratching and looking at me with their tongues hanging out. I damped the strings with the heel of my hand and sang that unaccompanied part as true as I was able.

> *I . . .*
> *I . . .*
> *I know it's too late . . .*

Trying my damndest to sustain on that *late* while I started back in on the D minor seven with the guitar. Then the rest of it came out as easy enough.

> *too late now*
> *to change a thing. . . .*
> *Step me up to that microphone*
> *and let me sing. . . .*

Two-four vamp into the turnaround and ladies and gemmun there you have it. I sat in the silence, listening to the bugs in the grass, hush of a car passing way off down the road. The dogs got bored and wandered off somewhere.

The song was for Estelle, I saw that now. More than "Red Dreams," which much as I liked it amounted to one more song about Chris. But "Too Late" was for everything Estelle wasn't and wasn't gonna be and for whatever she really was. And maybe in some kind of roundabout way, the song was also for me.

It must have been a hell of a party Willard had gone to, because the old Karmann Ghia didn't putt back into the yard until sunup next morning. Perry was already up, nursing coffee on the porch, and I came down because the noise roused me. Willard had a couple of girls with him in the car, shrieking and clutching like they were on a roller coaster, half-falling out of the cockpit. He swept the car in a figure eight through the high grass—lucky he didn't knock the bottom out on a stump—and came to a jolting stop in front of the porch. The girls tumbled out, holding on to each other, giggling and dizzy. Willard started up the steps, but Perry moved to block his way. He spoke in a low stiff tone, hoping the girls wouldn't hear him, I thought.

"Get those bimbos out of here."

Willard did his best to look shocked. "Hey, Perry, those are *sorority girls* right there."

He looked at me, hoping for help, and I stood up to see better over the porch rail. One way or another, they'd had a long night. Their hair was all snarled up from riding in the open car, and their makeup had kind of slewed around to the sides of their faces. One of them did have on a Tri-Delt T-shirt, with the tail of it slashed into ribbons that tossed around her navel.

"Really," Perry was saying. "Well, you just take'm right on back to the sorority."

Willard made a face of disgust and started backpedaling down the stairs. I got up from my chair and went after him as far as the car. That same pillowcase was lying on the floorboards, I noticed, folded flat and empty.

"What the hey, bud?" Willard said. "He ain't half so fussy when we're out on the road."

"He's not in charge of what goes on in a motel room," I said. "You know, like he don't own the motel."

"Well, that could be," Willard said, scratching the back of his head. "Let's go, ladies—change of program!"

But they weren't paying him any mind just then. The brunette had gone down on her hands and knees and the blonde was helping her, holding her head.

"You win them in a card game, or what?" I said.

Willard scratched his head some more. "I wish," he said. "My luck's been running the other way."

I was expected at Daddy's to work on the car, but for a long time I couldn't get myself up to go. By the time I did get there, it was pretty near sundown and I felt flutter-stomached, guilty for missing the work. But I could see from his face he was mainly just relieved I had showed up at all. He was just then cleaning out an airbrush, and the car looked done, a shining glossy black, with a few paint sprays around it in the gravel. He'd fitted the silver horse back on the grille—all the patching so seamlessly done you couldn't see it had ever been broken.

"Man," I said, "looks good as new." For some funny reason it was now for the first time I felt flashes of that bad night with the wrestling team coming back to me.

"Yep," he said. "You can drive her tonight." He was cleaning his hands on a rag. "Might let that paint set till after supper."

For the next little while I helped him tidy up the bench, sorting out the tools he owned and kept at home from what he'd borrowed from the shop. Time that was finished, Estelle came wandering across the alley to call us in to supper. She'd made sweet potatoes, country fried steak, biscuits and gravy and the works. Like usual, nobody talked a whole lot while we ate, though Stell did pass a compliment or two about what a nice job Daddy'd done on the car. When we were done eating, all three of us walked outside to admire it. Daddy raised up the hood and stood gazing down at the engine for a minute or more. He didn't touch anything, and I had no idea what he might have been looking for. Finally he dropped the hood with a hollow slam.

"All set," he told me.

I couldn't think of a lot to say. Daddy whipped out a chamois cloth and gave the silver horse a quick buffing.

"Don't be a stranger," he said, turning from me as he tucked the rag in his back pocket.

I drove and drove around the ring roads of Nashville, changing blues tapes on the stereo. I had the notion I might finally fly loose from the loop and go sailing to some other whole part of the country. What was really holding me here? But the car just kept buzzing around and around like a June bug on a string, until finally I noticed it was low on gas. I took the off-ramp from I-40 to West End, and drove across to Allston's. When I got out of the car my head was ringing from highway noise and I knew from the rubbery feeling in my legs I must have been driving longer than I realized. It had been dark for hours; hell, it was the middle of the night.

"I didn't wake you," I said hopefully when Allston opened the door.

"Nope," he said. "No problem. What's up?"

He was shirtless, but he had his sticks in his hand, and when I saw the drum pad and headphones set up on the table I figured he'd probably been up practicing, which made me feel easier about breaking in on him.

"I'm not interrupting anything."

Allston gave a partial smile and cocked the drumsticks against his hip. "Nobody here but the two of us," he said. "What's eating you?"

"What's a Melungeon?" I said. "I really would like an answer to that one. If you're a Melungeon, what does that mean?"

"Now why am I supposed to know?" Allston said.

I sat down on the sofa and covered my eyes.

"We can handle that," Allston said in the kind of a gentle voice you might use to talk to a crazy person. "Library opens at ten in the morning."

I put my feet up on the sofa arm and was out just like that. It seemed like not more than ten minutes before Allston was knocking a drumstick on the sole of my shoe, like a cop rousting a bum from a park bench. We ate some cereal and headed for the library, where we pulled out the "M" volumes of two or three encyclopedias and even found some little books on the subject. Come to find out that nobody knew what a Melungeon was really, though people had different crazy ideas.

Some had claimed that they were Phoenician sailors, shipwrecked in America back before Jesus was born. Some said they descended from the lost colony at Roanoke. There was the story, like Daddy said Marie had claimed, that they came from a lost tribe of Israel, though how they were supposed to have landed up here I couldn't figure. One theory claimed they were Portuguese pirates, another that they were Spaniards who'd come into the country with De Soto. The one I liked for being the nuttiest was that they were a gang of Welshmen who had somehow discovered America all on their own and never let anybody else know about it.

Everybody more or less seemed to agree that a Melungeon wasn't either an Indian or an African. The name had been put on them by French trappers; it came from a French word meaning "all mixed up." The Melungeons weren't ever thought to be white (except, it seemed, by some of the Indians) even though they spoke English amongst themselves and were Christian. When the white settlers did begin to come, they ran the Melungeons out of the bottomland, up onto the ridges of East Tennessee. It was then that a Melungeon got more or less described by law as a special, mysterious kind of a nigger, who couldn't testify in court nor vote nor hold an office. During the Civil War the Melungeons got partly back for that by turning into bushwhackers who preyed on both sides. Nowadays you might still find them living in Hancock and Claiborne or Hawkins County, in places with names like Vardy and Sneedville and Newman's Ridge.

My ears pricked up when Allston mentioned Sneedville. "That's where he said she claimed to come from," I said.

Allston slid his book toward me, one finger pinning down a point on a map. "Right there," he said. "We ought to make that in about four hours."

In fact it ended up closer to five, because once we got past Knoxville we fumbled up a time or two and had to backtrack and ask the way. Sneedville, when we finally found it, didn't seem so remarkable really. Just a small town tucked in a mountain cove. It wasn't like being in a foreign country or anything like that. They had gas stations and a dimestore and a scattering of little diners and cafés, plus also a courthouse and a jail because it was the seat of Hancock County. Allston and I walked up and down.

"You get the feeling they're looking at us?" I said.

"I get the feeling they might be looking at me."

He was right, I realized; regular black people were kind of scarce in this part of the state. As for Melungeons, well, every now and then somebody sort of dark-complected would pass by on the sidewalk but anywhere else I doubt I'd have noticed them. There wasn't anybody I'd have taken for my twin. If any of these people were actual Melungeons they didn't seem all that excited and bothered about it. What was I going to do? Start grabbing hold of people and asking, *Hey, are you a Melungeon? Hey, do I look like another one to you?*

It was ridiculous. "Let's get out of here," I said.

Allston looked at me. "Satisfied?"

I don't know whether I could have said that, but anyway I was ready to leave. We left at the exact right time to get all snarled up with rush hour in Knoxville. By the time we made it past that, it was nighttime, and neither one of us really felt like driving in the dark, so we just pulled off at some motel or other, I don't even remember which chain it was. It might have been anywhere in the country: same food in the restaurant, the same TV. But in the middle of the night I woke sitting straight up in the bed, sweating and shivering a little from a dream I'd had but couldn't remember, only a long stretch of smooth green grass in a mountain cove like the one where Sneedville was, and a winged shadow passing over it.

Out beyond the motel window I could hear the traffic passing on the highway; it never altogether stopped at any hour of the night. Like listening to a river. I had looked in the phone book there at Sneedville, which wasn't any fatter than a good-size monthly magazine. There wasn't any Bowlin listed. Closest you came was one Boylan and two Bowmans. I did notice there were a few of what the books and encyclopedias had called "Melungeon names" but really they were about the same as anybody else's: Collins, Brigman, Grant, Gibson. . . . None of it really connected to me, I understood, watching the processions of headlights bloom and fade on the fuzzy white curtain, not who I had grown to be. I thought how Daddy must have made the same trip way back when and come back empty as I had. I was connected to him, and to Perry and Allston, and to Stell now too, I guessed. Also it appeared I had a baby half-brother. That was all, but it was more than what some people had.

From the next bed Allston spoke out of the dark. "Go back to sleep," he told me. So that's what I did.

We got back to Nashville late in the morning and I drafted Allston to help me shuttle Perry's truck back to the farm. Daddy of course was out to work, and if anybody was home at Stell's they took no notice of us passing through. At Perry's we parked the truck in the row of wrecks, then dribbled away most of the afternoon listening to some of that record collection. I drove Allston back to town before the traffic got too heavy. It felt good driving the Mustang all fixed up, somehow like having a new car twice. Pretty soon I found myself over in East Nashville, just like the car had followed its nose.

His car was there but Daddy was not. Anyway he didn't answer a knock, though a light was on in the kitchen, just the bare bulb hanging from its cord, same as it always had. I'd used to do my homework under that bulb, what part of it I ever bothered to do. Now I stood outside the door, looking into that clean bare space. It must have been a lonely life for him there for a stretch, since he would have about had to give up his drinking buddies when he gave up drinking, I'd suppose. A stroke of luck too when he hooked up with Estelle. Maybe they didn't make such an odd couple, or I might not have thought so if he wasn't my father. I could see how he might look better than all right to her, a quiet sober man with a skill and a job. I thought of his life without me in it, which seemed fair to do since I had taken myself out.

I could have gone around front and rung the doorbell, but then I thought he might be sleeping. So I just headed back toward the car, but then, when I looked up and saw the lit square of Estelle's kitchen window across the alley, I knew, of course, where he would be.

They were just laying plates on the table when I scratched on the door, and James Culla was already strapped into his high chair. Macaroni and cheese, smoked sausage and spinach—all just heated up from the freezer, but what the hell, it was a weeknight. Daddy opened the door, natural as if he lived there, which for some reason made me feel shy and awkward and left me dithering on the sill.

"Draw up a chair," Stell called to me over his shoulder. Her hair was tied back, and her face and the red-checked shirt she wore were a little moist from the warmth of the kitchen.

"I don't guess . . ." I muttered, ". . . you all weren't expecting me."

"They's plenty," Stell said. "Anyway Rose-Lee was gone to eat but now she went somewhar with Greg." When I didn't answer, she said, a bit short now, "Well suit yourself, but come in or go out one—close off that draft."

I didn't see anything for it then so I shuffled inside and shut the door behind me. Estelle nodded, lips pursed, like she was thinking about something else. I helped my plate from the stove and sat down. For a second I thought maybe we were all gonna pray, but instead everybody just pitched in eating, not saying a whole lot, like usual. James Culla was doing modern art all over his face with cheese sauce, gazing across the table at me with his big round brown eyes. His hands were sailing all around with him not minding them, which is how he came to overset his glass of milk.

Daddy made that quick turn toward him that I knew, and his hand moved—but all it did was catch the milk glass and set it right. Daddy started dabbing his napkin at the spill. James Culla was just burbling right along without a break. He hadn't even flinched. I saw he had no reason to. Estelle got a dishrag and mopped up the spill and then she got James Culla some more, not quite so full of a glass this time, and sat down to her place again with a little sigh, though not a terribly unhappy one. We all went back to eating, not saying much, until I dropped my fork to my plate with a clash that made everybody look up at me.

"What is going on here?" I said. "What is this, Mom and Pop and the two kids? Does anybody want to tell me what the hell kind of game we're all playing here?"

Estelle looked like she had swallowed a fish bone. James Culla didn't look any different than usual; he didn't have any idea what I was talking about, being that he hadn't yet learned how to talk. I watched Daddy's eyebrows go up and start to wrinkle as he tried to figure out what he might say.

"I don't know, Jesse," he finally told me. "I reckon none of us really know. We're just all trying to make it one day at a time. Like they say do, down at that goddamn AA."

Nobody said anything back to that. There was this electrical silence for just a few seconds, with all of us sneaking looks at each other. Like a card game gone wrong and everybody wondering which one of the others would be first to draw a pistol or break for the door. I don't really know who was the first to start laughing, but it was a long time before we could stop.

9. SEVEN SONGS
INSIDE YOUR HEAD

Somehow that trip to Melungeon country snuck its way into the song I was working on. That whole notion of going off to some strange place to look for you didn't quite know what.

> *Well I found my way to town*
> *I think it was last week*
> *Well I found my way to town*
> *I think it was last week*
> *I went down the road*
> *I went down the creek. . . .*

Twelve-bar blues with no special tricks. I was working a one-four-three riff it kept coming back to. Talking blues like what the old-timers would do—you could nigh about make it up as you went along.

> *The water was deep*
> *the water was cold*

> the water was deep
> the water was cold
> Whoa-I drifted to sleep
> inside the fold. . . .

I won't claim this was Shakespeare, but the riff was solid—enough that it would keep on beating even after I stopped playing it. Running up the road toward North Nashville, tape deck silent, no sound but rush of the tires and the air parting around the nose of the car, the riff would still be cycling between the bones at the base of my head. Sometimes new words would flower like that too, without my hardly having to think of them at all.

> I went to the place
> where dreams are composed
> I went to the place
> where dreams are composed
> I found four potted plants
> and a murder of crows. . . .

What the . . . ? But on that note I parked the car in the alley back of Daddy's house, knowing full well he wasn't there since it was a weekday and well before quitting time, liking the idea of him seeing it when he came home, all sleek and shiny and waxed to a high gloss, just exactly like nobody had ever trashed it at all.

Guys at the cable spool toasted me with their malt liquor tall-boys. I waved and boosted the Hummingbird case out of the trunk. Stell wasn't expecting me but she was there anyway, and old James Culla was pulling some nap time, as I'd thought likely at this time of day. I'd brought along my own six-pack to help loosen her pipes, though what I could have used myself was a drink of whiskey.

We did a couple of our old standards to warm up. Then, round the time she'd cracked her second can of beer, I dealt the first card I'd run up my sleeve, sliding the "Red Dreams" lyrics, which I'd printed out in neat square letters, across the table toward her. Her eyebrows went up as she reached for the sheet, but she didn't say anything, not right away. I played the opening figure the way Chris had showed me, and talked her through the first verse and chorus and the first time through the bridge. She was tracing the lines with a bit-down fingernail, and once I'd gone two times around, she came in as pretty as you please.

> Someone's here
> they've got a key
> my room's as red
> as anarchy . . .

> Now I lay me,
> Now I don't
> Make me sleep
> don't say I won't

Such a sweetness her voice found in it somehow, a sweet sadness I hadn't known was there. Her whole delivery was gentle in a way it rarely was, except if she was singing to the baby.

> Mind distracted
> Body tense

now it all makes
bright red sense . . .

Brand-new day
or so it seems
I drift off to
bright red dreams . . .

"Huh," she said, when she got done. "Kinda folky, ain't it . . . reckon it could go country too." She drummed her fingers on the lyric sheet and looked across the kitchen table at me. "Whar'd you come by this'n?"

"Chris."

"Chris. You don't mean it."

"Well, yeah I do," I said. "It's one of his."

"He never wrote it."

"Told me he did." I saw my hands palm-up in the air—I was doing hound-dog good as Willard for a second there, but then the guitar tilted off my knee and I had to catch it quick before it fell. She lit herself a cigarette and drew in slow, then hummed a snatch of the melody as the smoke curled out her nose.

"Old boy outdone hisself on this'n, didn't he?"

"Guess I'd have to agree with you there," I said.

"Now what are we supposed to do with this thing?"

"He wants you to sing it is the idea," I told her, kind of rushing my words a little. "Told me he wanted to, like, give you something. Make up for how ugly he acted, in Miami."

Estelle was giving me a real squinty look. "Is that a red-eyed fact."

"What he told me." My hands were dying to do the hound-dog thing some more, but I held them tight and clammy against the guitar. "You're welcome to ask him yourself if you want to."

Estelle snorted out smoke. "Well, where's he at? You got him hid in your hip pocket too?"

I started telling her how I'd stumbled into Chris over at Show-bud, but before I got her caught up on all his news, she sort of re-laxed and waved off the subject. Seemed like her suspicions had died down, anyway. She finished her smoke and we went back to playing.

Couple of songs later I slipped in "Too Late." I'd typed out the words to that one too. She gave me a look when I slid her the paper, but she didn't say anything or ask any questions, and when she sang it she made it sound good. She'd figure Chris wrote that one too, I realized. Maybe that was what I'd planned for her to think.

We all play our best at home in the closet—that was one of Perry's lessons, from around the time we met. *When you try and take it out that closet door is when you might have a problem.* The morning we were supposed to start rehearsing for the run up North, I woke up sweating, with that proverb on my mind. A penny-whistle tune came in at the window, shrill and obnoxious, one short phrase faltering through mistakes and starting over and over again from the top. I wanted to stick my fingers in my ears.

I jacked myself up from the mattress, pulled on some jeans and went out in the hall. Willard's door was swinging open. He hadn't been back the night before, most likely—maybe not for a couple of days. Willard had been sleeping out a good deal of the time, was mostly gone unless the Karmann Ghia failed him, ever since Perry had run off the sorority girls. I thought he was a little shy of me too, maybe because he knew I didn't think it was a wise plan for him to be using that home-grown boo for a calling card, or whatever he was using it for.

I swung through the kitchen and started some coffee, then stepped out barefoot onto the porch. Perry was still tootling away on the penny whistle. One of his notions. He'd picked it up at a music store a few days back, on a run to buy guitar strings—tin whistle and instruction book packaged together at a bargain price. The tunes themselves could have been a lot worse—they were mostly Irish reels and such, pretty listenable. But Perry worked through them painful and slow, going back at each mistake, breaking the lines down into short phrases he would repeat over and over and over, and he seemed to make a special point of starting around dawn.

He raised the whistle to me when I came out, like a glass in a toast, then stuck it back in his choppers again. *Doodle tootle dreedle.* I looked over the field, the tall weeds sprouting over the wrecks. No dogs were in sight. Probably they were all up under the porch with their paws over their ears. I thought of saying that to Perry but it would have just aggravated him. If I asked him why he couldn't play through the whole tune botched a few times till he got it running, instead of working over each bar one at a time, he'd say you had to break it down to get it right (which was true). If I asked if he was crazy enough to think we were going to have a penny-whistle segment in our act next time we ran the Black Cats, I would be in for a lecture on Ian Anderson and Jethro Tull. If I asked him why he was bothering to learn an instrument he didn't have any purpose to know how to play, he would be telling me that it was a good idea to start something from scratch from time to time, and that trying a new instrument might always give you some new ideas about your old one, and that doing something poorly might change how you thought about your ability to do something well, all which might have been true too.

So I didn't say anything. Besides, maybe he was enjoying himself. Though the way his face was screwed up around the mouthpiece, he was making it look like work. I turned my head in the other direction down toward the truck garden, where a couple of the little scrub ponies were grazing beyond the fence corner—I couldn't quite make out from this angle if they were outside that fence or in it. Then Perry pulled the whistle out of his face and spoke.

"Penny for your thoughts."

I just blinked at him. Then a big WAK-WAK-WAK came from the south, and a green Army helicopter was flying high over the house. I craned my head out the corner of the porch and watched it hovering over the crown of the hill for a minute, tilted sideways and holding in the air. Then it dropped to the other side of the hill and out of sight like it was a falling rock. After that it got quieter.

Perry shook his head, irritated. "Wish those sons of bitches would change their flight pattern."

In the afternoon I drove to pick up Estelle. She didn't say much in the car, just smoked and flipped channels on the radio. When I stopped to get green-bottle beer and shrimp for the traditional rehearsal boil-up, she waited in the car. Allston was already there when we got back to Perry's, working around his drumheads with the key, but Willard hadn't shown up yet, and he kept on not showing.

Finally we started without lead guitar. Right away you could tell that something lacked. It wasn't that Allston and I were limping. The rhythm section was tight as you please—I felt the lift of energy that would always come when he and I got back together for the first time after a few weeks' break. It wasn't that Estelle was singing flat. Perry was in an edgy mood, which did have something to do with it. Every time we hit where a guitar solo ought to go, Perry would just break off the song to start beefing about how Willard had skipped out.

"Maybe he's broke down somewhere," I said. It seemed likely enough, with what he had for a car.

Perry snorted. "Shacked up somewhere more like it." He slapped his guitar on the stand and stalked out onto the porch.

We'd been playing about an hour and a half, bits and pieces from songs we'd done over the winter—nothing new. I stood there scratching my shoulder under the instrument strap. Could have told Perry that Willard didn't really *need* to be there for rehearsal. Willard could play the kind of stuff we were doing from a cold start right on stage and still sound like the best musician in the band. It would just have annoyed Perry more to hear it, though.

Stell pushed her hair up on the back of her neck, then let it drop. She stuck an unlit cigarette in a turned-down corner of her mouth and walked outside, standing framed in the doorway to the porch. Beyond her the sky was sinking into darkness. I racked my bass and went into the kitchen, started boiling water for the shrimp. Allston came in and snagged a carton of orange juice from the refrigerator. I reached around him, got myself a beer, and popped the cap off on a drawer handle.

"I don't know," I said to Allston.

"We're stale," he said, pouring a jelly jar half-full of juice. "That's all." He sat down at the kitchen table, sipping.

"I guess so," I said. "Maybe we could use something different in the mix."

"Yeah?" Allston said. "What you got?" He was looking at me pretty sharp, and I had the feeling that he'd seen right through me.

Willard's hammered old Strat had been laid out by either him or Perry on the theory that Willard himself was gonna be here. I switched on his amp and settled in a chair with the guitar. My legs were feeling a little watery, somehow. Perry picked up my bass, automatic.

"D major," I said, and I started the intro figure to "Red Dreams," watching Allston behind the drums, alert and concentrating. I hadn't had time to tell him much but I didn't need to—after eight bars had gone around he feathered in on a cymbal and locked tight to the slow beat.

> *Big dark cloud*
> *Small white sun*
> *Through the window*
> *morning comes. . . .*

Stell was there without a wobble. It's what I'd been rehearsing her for, I realized.

> *Now I lay me,*
> *Now I don't*
> *Make me sleep*
> *don't say I won't . . .*

At about this point Perry got himself comfortable with a simple walking bass, and he turned it up a hair so he was audible. He was looking from Stell to me, curious, interested, no worse than that—it was the listening look he wore for anything that really captured his attention.

When Stell had finished the second chorus I slid naturally into the solo I'd been fooling with on the four-track. With nothing but bass and drum behind it, it sounded a little thin, but I was playing it as well as I could have in the closet really. It was going over.

"Mmmmm," Perry said when the coda was done. "Somehow I don't think I've heard that one before."

"It's a Chris original," I said. What the hell, get it over with. Just jump in.

"Say what?" Perry said. Allston was pumping his bass pedal soft, the pace of a heartbeat more or less. I wasn't sure if he'd started again or if he'd never stopped.

"It's a Chris original—Chris wrote it." Came out a little harder the second time.

"No lie?" Perry said, stroking his jawline. It didn't look like he was gonna catch on fire or explode. "I reckon that's better than average bear, for Chris." He looked from Allston to Stell and then settled on me. Eyebrows up. "So," he said. "Any more surprises?"

Nothing to do with that door but go through it. I kicked into the opening bars of "Too Late." Allston was with it sooner than the first time, and Stell was right there where she should be. We were just going into the bridge when I saw Willard come into the doorframe and stop there, stroking his chin with his fingers while he listened. I cued Allston for a rest with a jerk of my jaw, and Stell went into that a cappella bit with hardly a hitch.

I . . . I . . . I . . .

. . . and I let the D minor chord come swelling up with the cymbal shimmer surrounding it.

I know it's too late . . .
Too late now to change a thing . . .

. . . and now for the five chord that was holding itself back . . .

Step me up to that microphone . . .
And let me sing. . . .

Except there was no more singing to do, till you went back to the top of the verse, so Stell just stepped back from the mike and stood there, her hips adrift in that baby-rocking sway, while I laid the best solo I could down over Perry's bass line. Both my hands were stiffening up since Willard was watching from the doorway, head hung low over a slow-patting foot, and the whole situation was making me nervous anyway. Perry had on his listening look. His concentration was tighter now, honed—I wasn't sure the song would stand up to it. Stell delivered the second verse and chorus and then . . . and then the song just kind of trailed off. It hit me harder than before how that last *let me sing* made for a weak ending when there was nothing to follow.

Perry was thinking. "Be a natural for Bonnie Raitt," he said. "But if she'd ever done it, I think I would have heard it. No?" He hung the bass back on the stand, letting it drop the last couple of inches, so the amp boomed out reverb. I looked toward the doorway but Willard was gone, quiet as a cat and about as sneaky. Willard had got to know Perry pretty well in a short time, I realized. Perry's face had gone piebald with spots of pale white and bright red and streaks of pus-colored yellow over the bone. And Allston was pedaling the bass drum again, *ooomp ooomp ooomp ooomp ooomp* . . .

"We got another *Chris original* here?" Perry did his voice so it filled up the room. *Ooomp ooomp ooomp ooomp ooomp*, the bass drum went on. "I finally get shet of that long-legged pea-brained hair-band retread," Perry continued, "and now I still got his damn *songs* chasing after me! What is this, some goddamn conspiracy?! You set me up, the pack of you!—think you can just set me up!" Perry was really shouting now, his preacher voice turned up high, and prowling the floor like it was a revival stage. *Ooomp ooomp ooomp ooomp ooomp* . . . I had the front end of a headache, beating out Allston's time. All of a sudden Perry wheeled on Allston. "Will you for chrissake *shut up that drum?!*"

And he turned back just as quick and had his mouth open to start hollering at me and Stell some more, when the silence behind him seemed to drag him down. Allston had quit the bass drum but the quiet it left was sort of worse. Nobody ever blew up at Allston. It wasn't like there would be terrible consequences but it just wasn't something you did. I took a quick close look at Allston. He wasn't doing anything and didn't look upset. His face was as empty and still as it would be when he was doing a tai chi form. But somehow I had the notion that without him doing anything or opening his mouth he might have more say over how this shook out than any of the rest of us did.

About half the air seemed to go out of Perry then. He swung through the doorway, and a few seconds later we all heard his boot heels slamming down the steps from the porch.

The water was roiling when I went in the kitchen. I went ahead and dumped in the shrimp even though it didn't seem likely right now that anybody was going to be in a mood to eat them. No seasonings in the pot or anything like that because Perry had the notion they were better plain and pure. You were allowed to use cocktail sauce afterward, or melted butter with lemon. Like Perry had some notion about every damn thing on the planet.

"Pigheaded," Estelle said. She was only picking up my own train of thought, but it bugged me anyway.

"Don't *you* start," I said. It slipped out and I wished right off I could suck it back. But Stell just wilted me with a look and walked out of the room.

The shrimp were turning rosy and floating to the top. I cut off the fire and left them to sit. Allston was there at the kitchen table, doing just exactly nothing. I thought of maybe asking him something, but I knew I wouldn't get any real answer. Allston was fine, nothing eating on him. He was centered and balanced inside of himself, and he wasn't even waiting for the next thing to happen.

No sign of Perry when I crossed the porch, nor Willard either one. Stell was sitting in a rocker, smoking and watching the red sunset colors at the western edge of the field. Higher up the sky, the brightest stars were starting to come out.

I went down the steps and walked through the tall grass, round the corner of the house. It was breezy and I stopped and turned into the wind to light a cigarette, making sure to step on the match when I threw it down. Don't want to start a brush fire, my inner Perry was telling me.

I walked on, behind the house. Last song we played was still going in my head. First time I'd really even heard it at something like band strength.

> I could have been a forest
> or a leaf on its floor . . .

Could have been an ocean
or maybe a screen door. . . .

I could have been this
And I could have been that . . .
Could have been a pair of gloves
and a matching hat. . . .

By damn I did think it was a pretty good song no matter what Perry thought about it. And it was just right for Stell, those verses.

But it's too late now
to change all that
I am what I am
Not no slinky black cat. . . .

The dark was more solid, the tree line at the top of the ridge an inkier black than the rest. Because Perry was wearing a light-color shirt I could see him plain, coming away from the trees. I stepped on my butt and stood there waiting for him to reach me. He dropped a hand on my shoulder and we walked back down toward the house, where Willard had picked up his guitar and was playing some little piece of nothing. He could be doing "Twinkle, Twinkle, Little Star" and somehow you'd still know it was Willard.

I . . . I . . . I . . .

I know it's too late . . .
Too late now to change a thing. . . .
Step me up to that microphone—

Perry's hand was big and hard and warm. He gave a little squeeze and turned me loose.

"Here's how to handle it," he said. "You could use that last line of the chorus to set up solos, you know, like *bring that guitar to the microphone and let it sing*. Nice piece of stage business, really. Introduce the whole band that way. You could close a set with it. You could close shows."

"Oh yeah," I said. "Like . . . *mama don't want no guitar played round here*. Except it would be ours."

Perry gave me a funny look at that and I thought maybe I had blown it. But it was just a second and then he let down.

"Yeah," he said, as we clomped up the porch steps. "It would be."

It had all turned around too easy, I almost thought, while I was draining the water off of the shrimp, but then again, that was sometimes how it went. Everybody would get all pissed off and then, when it was over, we would all play better. Allston was screwed down on his drum stool when I went into the front room. Perry picked up the bass and nodded me toward his L-5.

This amounted to an invitation so I figured I'd make the most of it. I had a lyric sheet in my hip pocket which I guess I must have been saving in case things went well this far. Stell looked a little queer when I gave it to her, because she hadn't seen it before, but it was pretty much a regular twelve-bar blues and she clicked into it quick enough.

> *I didn't know where*
> *my dream would take me*
> *Oh I didn't know where*

my dream would take me
I loosened my grip
handed over my key. . . .

And because Willard was playing the lead line to it, that minor-key bridge was like in my dreams. The song came back to it a second time, after a couple more verses, and this time Stell began to scat along with what Willard was doing, a sort of rolling moan behind the melody. It was one of their moments, I could tell by the hair rising on my arms and the way I heard it all without even knowing what part of it I was playing myself. The idea was that the whole song would resolve into the minor key at the end, with the two solos setting you up for it:

I saw you there
For the first time in years
Oh I saw you there
For the first time in years
You were just sitting there
In a room full of tears

Room full of tears
Room full of fears
Room full of tears
Room full of fears
You were just sitting there
In a room full of tears. . . .

It ended with Allston feathering down a cymbal, and then it was just real quiet, for maybe as long as a minute. You could about hear a dog scratching under the porch.

Then Perry gave the bass strings a slap and sent a brutal rumble rolling all around the room. "You fixing to tell me Chris wrote that?" he said.

"No." I answered him. "That one ain't Chris's." I hadn't planned on saying this part. It felt like somebody else was talking through my mouth. "I wrote it myself." And I caught Stell's eye, dark and turbulent. "For you."

We ran those songs from one Black Cat to the next, all the way up north into New England. Perry never had another word to say about it. I even persuaded him to sing "Eight Mile," after we'd got back into the groove. There'd be an edge on his voice when he introduced that song, and his finger, pointing out who wrote it, looked like the barrel of a gun. But then he'd always sing it well enough to put it over.

I don't know why he didn't put up more resistance. Maybe because I had trapped him like I had. Or because Chris wasn't actually in the band where he might have tried to trade up on this little victory of getting one of his own songs in the mix. Or because Perry had an easier time handling the thought of me writing a half-decent song than Chris. Maybe Perry could see from the beginning that we needed something new to get us rolling, like we'd needed Stell at first, and then Willard.

After the first couple of gigs, he couldn't hardly help but see that it was working. People began to ask for "Too Late," but we always saved it for the end, to close the show. People would call for "Eight Mile" too, and I swear Perry appeared to look forward to that. And of course Willard could fly the closing solo all around those chords like he was a stunt pilot riding a jet plane.

The principle of our northern route, as Perry would generally put it if you asked, was to stay far the hell away from New York City. We strung the Black Cats like beads on a string, across the middle of Virginia, up the Susquehanna River through Pennsylvania, through small towns of upstate New York, west of the Hudson. By the height of summer we'd crossed over into Vermont and come to rest for a long run in a tiny little town called Vergennes, just about a half-an-hour drive from the eastern shore of Lake Champlain.

Perry had rented us a regular summer house on the lake shore, actually a pair of cabins, one perched up on a cliff above the lake, and the other a boathouse right on the water, converted into an extra bedroom. Some blueblood's vacation compound. I don't know how Perry finagled the place—it belonged to some shut-up compartment of his life that had nothing to do with any of us. Last year when we played Vergennes we'd stayed at a motel up the highway, but of course it was better being down on the lake. The neighbors all looked like they had been clipped out of an L.L.Bean catalogue, but their houses were out of sight behind the pine trees, and they never complained about noise or commotion. We kept the commotion level pretty far down, and rehearsed at low volume, late mornings down at the boathouse, the sound cracking back at us from the slate-blue surface of the lake. We didn't need to practice all that much anyway because the sets were good and tight by then.

The Vergennes Black Cat pulled the kind of mixed crowd that was typical of all Vermont in the summer, though our core was local blue-collar, who you could count on for Friday and Saturday night. We drew old grey-beard hippies in holey jeans and Birkenstocks, and college students on summer adventures, and New

Agers who lived up there year-round, plus wandering Deadheads and Pfishophiles and other packs of pilgrims. Down the lake from our cabins was a sizable resort, an old-fashioned yacht-club type of a place, and a few of those people sometimes slipped over to slum the Black Cat, the men dressed down in stiff jeans and polo shirts, their wives Bean-catalogue refugees, homely in an expensive-looking way.

One way or another, the tip jar stayed full and the place was reasonably jumping five nights a week, Tuesday through Saturday. On those slow mornings after the shows it was nice to wake up to the smell of pine tar and the cool fresh air coming off the water. We were living a fairly quiet life out there, except for Willard, who slept out most nights. Vergennes wasn't carpeted with bimbos like Key West and such places, but all the same he had struck up an understanding with a hippie chick who floated around all day and all night in lacy white dresses and bare feet. Chastity was the name she gave out, though it didn't entirely suit her behavior. Perry wouldn't let her spend the night in the cabins, on suspicion she was underage, he claimed, though this struck me as a weak excuse—she looked well up in her twenties to me. Could be Perry thought it would bother the neighbors, or just didn't want another woman tying up the bathroom in the mornings. So Willard shacked up most nights in her vintage VW microbus death trap, parked somewhere on the edge of town.

That way Allston and I were all alone one Sunday morning, two blank lazy days ahead of us, warm boards of the dock rocking under our shoulder blades with the quiet lapping of the lake, staring up at the blue sky, and my mind just as cloudless. Then somehow a piece of a guitar lick leaked into my brain. Around and around it went in there till finally I felt motivated to go and grab the Hummingbird and see if it amounted to anything.

Riff to D, riff to C, riff to G and back to the top. I played this through a couple of times and realized the reason it was starting to sound better was because Allston was slapping out a drumbeat behind it, bare palms on the boards of the dock.

"What you got?" Allston said.

"Don't know," I told him. And I didn't, but it felt like it might turn into something.

We hacked on the thing off and on that afternoon, Allston just brushing on a snare. It gave it more drive and made it a little faster than it might have been if I'd worked it out on my own without a drummer. And as it sometimes had been happening, playing the same line over and over started some scraps of words floating over the chord progression.

> Seven songs inside your head
> Seven sets of words you know . . .

And after that, who knew? I saw I'd close the circle of the chorus by pushing up the scale to the root: B-flat, C and home to the D chord, but I didn't have anything for words. An O sound, I thought. There was that "know" to play off. Allston hung up his brushes and went to work out but I kept right on hacking.

Monday morning I woke up with a piece of a verse like it had come drifting out of my dreams. I picked up the guitar and went back to it. Didn't even bother making coffee—I wanted to stay where I was at, near the place the words were coming from.

> Box of eight-tracks, box of skulls
> The hat you wore last week
> Cigars, cigarettes and cold, cold beer,
> The hole in the bucket leaks . . .

Allston sat up and kicked off the sheet. He was awake. Well, I'd woke him up. Well, he was an early riser.

"Story of our life," he said. A little grumpy maybe. He shook his head till his lips went rubber, pulled on some pants and went outdoors to work out some more. Allston liked to do the Wu form on the floating dock, because the movement of the platform made it more challenging to keep your balance in the stances. I watched him through the boathouse window, still fooling my way into the chorus, what I thought might be a chorus, with no more than a third of my mind.

> *Seven songs inside your head*
> *Seven sets of words you know.*

F chord	I know. . . .
C chord	you know. . . .
G chord	???????????

Then B-flat, C and home to D and you're done. Except the words weren't there. I was still hanging up in the same place when Allston came back in, all aglow from his healthy behavior.

> *Seven songs inside your head*
> *Seven sets of words you know*
> *I know . . .*
> *You know. . . .*

"Anything goes," Allston said. Sang, rather. He just laid it in there. He was standing with his back to me, polishing his lats with a towel—I hadn't even thought he was listening.

Seven songs inside your head
Seven sets of words you know
I know . . .
You know. . . .
Anything goes . . .
You know, you know, you know. . . .

And it locked back onto the opening riff like a magnet slapping itself onto metal. Allston turned toward me.

"Jesse," he said, "it works."

"Yeah," I said, "it does."

And we both sat there looking at each other, not quite believing how neat it had turned out.

"Tell me something," I said, "if you know. How come the band is called Anything Goes?"

Allston swallowed a chuckle and shrugged. "I heard a guy ask Perry that once, a good long time ago," he said. "What Perry told him was, 'It's not Cole Porter.' "

" 'It's not Cole Porter'?" I repeated, just to be sure I got this right. "Now, what the hell is that supposed to mean?"

The weekend rolled around again, and there we were up in the Black Cat on a warm breezy evening, winding up the second set. It had been up-tempo and country-flavored, with enough dancing to lay a tang of sweat and adrenaline in the air of the room. Chastity had been dancing up a storm, sometimes tolerating a local or a Deadhead to wiggle around in her general neighborhood, while she slung her hips and whipped her head of knee-length hair, but really directing most of her charms at Willard on the stand. Chastity didn't wear any underwear of any kind under those loose white shifts of hers, something which became more and more obvious the better she got warmed up. Willard was watching her with his droolingest hound-dog smile. When he broke into the double-tempo solo to "Eight Mile," it propelled Chastity into the best pole dance I ever saw done by somebody with an ankle-length dress on, and no pole.

Bonner, the local police, came in with a breeze that guttered the red candles on the balcony tables and went over to the bar, which was nothing unusual. Bonner was a youngish guy who liked the blues and would stop in often enough, out of uniform like he was now. He didn't take more than a half-second glance at Chastity, though most everybody else had stopped dancing to watch her strut. There was something about the way he whispered to the bartender that struck me for a second. But then I forgot about it, because "Eight Mile" was over, and Chastity was panting and mopping her face, and Perry was clearing his throat by the mike.

"We'll do one more before we break. Got a new one for you." He pointed the gun-barrel finger at me. "You might have seen the name on the poster out front."

Willard and Allston and I all checked each other fast because this hadn't been announced. Perry hadn't mentioned the song since we first played it for him, but what the hell, we knew it. At the bottom of the intro I realized the question of who was going to sing it hadn't been answered yet either, but it was Perry who came in singing, a little throaty at first. When the chorus came around he crooked his finger and brought Stell to the mike, and they did those lines in harmony.

Seven songs inside your head
Seven sets of words you know

> *I know . . .*
> *You know . . .*
> *It's all a pose*
> *You know, you know, you know. . . .*

Sweet. I hadn't thought of that, but clearly somebody had been thinking about it some. Perry stepped out and left Stell with the second verse.

> *Cocaine makes you talk too fast*
> *Liquor slows you down*
> *Everything goes in the trash*
> *Everything goes down. . . .*

> *Seven songs inside your head*
> *Seven sets of words you know*
> *I know . . .*
> *You know . . .*
> *Anything goes—*
> *You know, you know, you know. . . .*

There was a little riffle of clapping amongst people who picked out the band name. Or maybe it was for their favorite drugs, I don't know, but they looked like they were into it. A few people stepped out to shake their booty as Willard hummed into his solo, a leaf or two out of Mick Taylor's book here, watching his own fingers with his usual hound-dog amazement. Some new people were just coming in, beyond the heads of the dancers, at the door by the stairs and at the wider opening that let onto the balcony with the tables. From the resort, was my first thought. They had on the blazers and stiff jeans and polo shirts, but something in their faces didn't quite fit. But the solo had circled back to the top, and Perry pitched in singing again.

> You toss the cards they send you
> Letters that wish you well
> Words spill out, fall on the ground
> You recognize what they spell. . . .

And Estelle stepped in for the last chorus:

> Seven songs inside your head
> Seven sets of words you know
> I know . . .
> You know . . .
> The story's told—
> You know, you know, you know. . . .

It was going so well they did it once more, dropping the "anything goes" tag in this last time to make sure nobody missed it. Then Perry pulled back from the applause to lay his guitar on the rack. "We'll take a short break," he said, and made a beeline for the bar. Everybody had found their seats by then, except for Chastity, who was still rocking around in the sudden quiet, and the yacht-club newcomers hanging in the doorways. Something else about those guys was their shoes—not the usual Topsiders or Rockports or whatever. They all had on black Florsheims. Plus which they seemed to be taking care to keep all the exits covered. My stomach barely had time to drop before one of them caught Bonner's eye and they both started walking toward the bandstand.

"Charles Wilbur?" Florsheim said, the voice effortlessly loud, impersonal. Willard let his Strat fall onto the stand and turned with his best hound-dog smile and shrug. He flipped his hair back with a jerk of his head and held out his wrists for the handcuffs.

In spite of her whole flower-child routine, Chastity *was* over twenty-one—probably over thirty-one if you judged by the corns and bunions on her feet. So it wasn't any morals charge or anything like that. Instead it appeared that Wilbur had been passing bad checks back in Nashville, hanging paper all over town to cover his new gambling debts, or that was the impression Perry had got from talking to somebody down there on the phone. The Florsheim brigade had snaked Willard back to Tennessee faster than we could draw a breath.

Then Chastity called down there on her own account—she must have had a way with her by phone—and drove out to the lake to tell us what she'd learned. She had managed to weasel the name of the public assistance lawyer out of somebody, and what she found from him was that Willard, Wilbur, whoever he was, had done a bit in Florida on a similar check charge; whether he was actually on parole at this point had not come completely clear. Chastity had been crying on her way out to see us, it looked like, and there was mud wedged up between her toes. "I knew he wasn't worth a damn," she sniffed at the end, "but he could be so sweet to me. . . ."

With Willard out of action, we had to switch to our fallback positions, with me on the lead and Perry on bass. I had Willard's Strat to play and . . . nothing was the fault of the guitar. Chastity was no more to be seen—we heard that her microbus had blown its last smoke ring in Vergennes, soon after she'd come out to bring us the word on Willard. Some other regulars fell away too, and we still had three weeks left on the gig. As shaky as this situation was, I still had the feeling that things weren't through going wrong.

Sunday morning I woke up like I had heard a shot, an explosion in my sleep, though I didn't know just what it could have been. Allston was sitting up straight in the bed across the room, like he'd been shocked awake by electricity. It was quiet now, just the water lapping, and kids' voices calling from a dock down the shore. But Allston and I looked at each other, then threw on some clothes and climbed to the main cabin.

The wooden stairs made a couple of zigzags, going up against the dark stones of the cliff, and brought us out into a needle-strewn clearing. It was always dim in the yard between the cabin and the cliff edge, under the big old spruces and firs, and since I had just woken up anyway it took a minute for my eyes to read the scene.

"Where'd they come from?" somebody snapped. I realized he was talking about us. Bonner, who was wearing his uniform this time, started explaining about the boathouse. I took in that the whole place was overrun with state police, looked like at least half a dozen of them, scrambling through the house and tossing stuff out of the van. Perry was standing there in the yard in between a couple of suits, head bowed down to study his bare feet. He'd not had time to get a shirt on either, and his belly hair looked scraggly and gray. I noticed he didn't seem annoyed or irritable or even especially surprised.

"Who's got the keys to that Mustang?" a trooper called toward me and Allston, and when nobody answered right away, "Please yourself—we can break the locks."

I made a move back toward the boathouse steps, but another trooper stopped me with a hard look and a hand floating over his holster.

"Stay where you are," he said. "I think we'll just have a look down there for ourselves."

So for the next little while I didn't move anything but my eyeballs. Bonner was standing a few paces from Perry and the suits, looking kind of hangdog and unhappy about it all. Estelle and Rose-Lee were sitting in white wicker chairs up on the porch, Stell holding James Culla on her knees.

"Doggie," James Culla said, and twisted around toward the door. One of the troopers was coming out of the house with a German shepherd on a chain leash.

"House is clean," the trooper said in the direction of Perry and the suits. He took the dog over to the van, where it started sniffing over the ashtrays and seat covers, without any particular excitement. I began to work on the same worry as last time down in Beaufort—I didn't have any sort of a personal stash, but when had somebody last passed me a joint? Were they gonna find a forgot-about roach in the bottom of a pocket of wadded-up jeans somewhere?

But when the troopers came back from the boathouse all they had was the keys of the Mustang, which had been sitting out on a shelf in plain sight, by my wallet and my change. They opened it up and dug around for a minute or two, then let the dog go over.

"Cars are clean too," the dog handler said finally, looking at the taller suit. "Can't bust'm."

The suit looked down at the dog with a sour expression. "No ham sandwich for you," he said, "you mutt."

The dog sat down, smiling, and hung out a foot or so of tongue. The suit turned to Perry. "That's all right," he said, snapping his fingers. "The Tennessee warrant'll do for you, sport."

A pair of troopers jogged over to handcuff Perry, rougher than necessary, I thought, behind his back. They marched him over to an unmarked sedan and loaded him in the back seat, mashing his head down just to be nasty. Perry's face was blank as concrete—he was down to name, rank and serial number, what it looked like to me. The tall suit climbed in the back beside him and the other one slid behind the wheel. On the back side of the house the troopers' cars started cranking. A siren whooped once and cut off, and then they were all gone.

The rest of that day slid by in a daze, but by nightfall we started making calls to Nashville. Me and Allston took turns calling people who knew Perry, but none of them had heard anything yet. I kept calling Perry's place itself, just to hear the phone ring in the empty house I guess, for Perry'd never bothered with an answering machine.

By the next evening it had occurred to me that if I tried at the right time I might catch Abel the farmer stopping in to feed Perry's dogs. That plan worked on the second try. Abel could tell me the police had been swarming all over the place three days before, complete with helicopters and dope-smelling dogs—they hadn't got anything out of the house, he thought, but they'd cut down a whole mess of marijuana on the far side of the ridge. That was all he knew, and more than he wanted to discuss. As for Perry himself, Abel hadn't seen hide nor hair of him. The cops had tossed Abel's house along with everything else, and he wasn't in a very good humor.

Tuesday evening we all suddenly realized we were still expected at the Black Cat. We rushed over, what was left of us, and turned in one of the lamest shows on record, with me backing Stell on acoustic guitar, and Allston thumping on a tom-tom with his fingers so he wouldn't drown us out. Maybe he should have. There was no way it went over as a trio—not one of us could get the mojo working.

We played one more set for the sake of honor—a short one, since we were all in a hurry to slink out of there. Nobody had a lot to say on the drive back out to the lake. Me and Allston had moved from the boathouse into the room Perry had been using, because the women said they didn't care for being alone up there at night. Allston and the women turned in the minute we got there, but I didn't feel the least bit sleepy, though I couldn't think of much else to do with myself.

I sat downstairs and leafed through a basket of moldy magazines that went back about as far as World War II, as best I could see in the dim light. The cabin wasn't much for wiring—a hundred-watt bulb would be pushing your luck. Rose-Lee complained a certain amount because there wasn't a TV.

I unsnapped the catches on the Hummingbird and carried the guitar out to the porch. My left hand, still aching a little from the tense time I'd put in at the Black Cat, shaped one chord or another on the neck, but I didn't sound the strings. No use in waking anybody up. No use in anything much that I could see right then. I ought to be soaking my hand, maybe, for tomorrow, but I couldn't seem to move myself to do it.

There was a moon, but pretty well hidden by the dense tree-tops joined over the clearing. Through a gap at the cliff edge I could see silver fog rolling over the lake. Goddamn, but we were in a fix. I knew I ought to be thinking, planning, organizing what to do in my mind, but I couldn't seem to turn a corner on the problem. It had been a long time since I'd felt so small and lost. I propped the guitar against the wall, arched my back, covered my navel with my hands, and breathed the way Allston had taught me, trying to bring some balance into my body. Inside the house the phone went off, and I got it before the second ring.

"Jesse?" the dry voice began on the other end. "Thought I'd catch you up on Willard. Wilbur." A low chuckle. "You'll never guess. You know Chastity, the barefoot babe—"

"Perry?" I said. "Where the hell are you?"

"Turns out her name really *is* Chastity," he goes, amused. "She's a trust-fund orphan from the Boston Back Bay. Willard won't be doing no more time."

I let my breath out. "Stand by your man," I said, not singing it quite but drawing the words out to the rhythm of the song.

"Damn straight," Perry said. "Son of a bitch has got better lawyers than I do."

"Where *are* you, man?" I asked again.

"Home," Perry told me. Then he was quiet.

I reached over and pulled the chain on the near-useless lamp. The room filled up with the silvery light of moon and fog. The walls were all bare studs turned brown with age, and decorated with mounted animal heads: deer, a fox, a bobcat. There was even a black-bear pelt on the floor, with the head taxidermied to raise up and snarl at you, the claws coming loose from the dry-rotting skin.

"Don't worry about it," Perry said. "I got me all the lawyers I need." I thought I heard the scrape of him lighting a match. "I might be in for a headache or two, but they won't lock me up, and I'm not going to lose the farm."

"When are you coming back?" I said.

"No time soon," Perry said. "Just at the minute, I can't leave the state."

My left hand stabbed at the base of the thumb.

"We're not doing so hot without you," I said.

"Yeah, well," Perry said. "What you ought to do is go make a tape."

"*What?*" I said. "This can't be Perry talking."

But it was, and he kept on talking right through me. "There's a guy up in Burlington that's got a little studio. Doug Lumera is his name. Allston can find it—he's been there before. Those little low-power stations around there would probably play a few of your songs, if you once get'm recorded."

"Sure, right," I choked—I was having some trouble drawing a breath. "And who're we supposed to get to play this session?" The glass eyes of the animal heads were glittering from all the walls, and my left hand was lit up blue with pain.

"Listen," Perry said. "Here's what you do. You and Allston drive up to Burlington. Run the music stores and the clubs, and hire yourself a bass player."

"Hire a what?" I said. "What we need is lead guitar."

"*You*," Perry said, "are gonna play the lead guitar."

"Perry, I can't." My whole left arm was white-hot by this time. It was like I could see the bones laid out and glowing like they were in an X-ray. "This is not a fill-in you're talking about. People are already walking away. I'm not up to it, Perry—"

Perry, of course, was still talking past me, but I pulled the receiver away from my ear and let it twirl down a foot or two on the kinky cord, till Perry's voice was about the same level as the bugs talking outside in the trees. He was telling about Lumera and his studio and how many tapes we would probably need and where we ought to send them how much in advance—but it didn't matter if I missed some of this because there really was a lot I knew already. For example, I knew that I had been using Perry for a father just about ever since I moved out of my real father's house, and I knew that part of what I felt for Stell was because I never knew my mother, but that the other part was really her, her voice and the music, and I knew that there was nothing really wrong with my left hand and that the pain I felt was fear. The question I couldn't answer yet was whether knowing all this stuff was ever going to do me any good. I brought the receiver back into my head.

"I'm not Willard," I told him. "I'm not even Chris. I don't got that kind of chops."

"No, you don't," Perry said. "But you know what to do."

10. THE FEELING

Doug Lumera was a short bandy-legged fellow, with the remains of his scraggly brown hair tied up with a thong, and a beard so long he would throw the end of it over his shoulder whenever he got up from his stool, to keep from stepping on it, I guess. He wore tire-tread sandals and a blue denim vest, and had a whiskey nose ridged with burst capillaries—the nose and the watery blue eyes were about all you could see of his face since the beard started at the bottom of his eye sockets. Typical Vermont hold-out, hid-out hippie, as Perry would have said, and no doubt had already. He had a little elfin house built into the side of a wooded hill, and on the bottom floor a studio as good as our occasion required, and then some.

Allston had done some sessions work now and then in Nashville, which was more than I could claim, so he knew his way around such places. Allston did most of the talking with Lumera, trading technical lingo and all like that. There wasn't much of the pressure that I had been afraid of, on account of everything was overdubbed so we could redo it as many times as need be, within reason. Allston and I laid down the tracks of bass and drums together, and then I put the rhythm guitar track over that, using the Hummingbird miked for that acoustic tone. I flubbed up a couple of times on the guitar tracks, false starts, wrong notes, but somehow it didn't throw me into a tailspin, and my hand was behaving itself, not hurting me at all.

We had the rhythm tracks down for the first two by noon, so we broke for a while and sent out for beer and hippie sandwiches full of sprouts and avocado and stuff like that, and sat around eating and shooting the breeze, or listening to Allston and Lumera, mostly Lumera telling about stuff he'd engineered twenty and thirty years back, when he worked in New York and California. He'd worked for Zappa and Captain Beefheart, so he claimed, and a whole bunch of other people.

Stell shied, really just like a horse, when Lumera came at her with the big helmetlike headphones, and she was stiff and tight when she first started singing. If we sat in the studio with her she sounded weird anyway because we couldn't hear what she had in the headphones, but even in the booth where we could hear the whole mix, it wasn't a whole lot better. Two or three takes went by without producing anything measurable in the way of improvement. Listening to the playbacks was grim, everybody hanging their head and not wanting to look at each other. I could practically hear the air start hissing out of the balloon. We'd gambled a good deal on this little project, in terms of both money and hope.

"Let's take a break," Allston proposed, and we went out into the yard, Stell and me both firing up cigarettes as soon as we were clear of the house. Lumera had gardens of vegetables and flowers and herbs, not laid out in regular rows but just bursting up in clumps every which way. Stell and I stood there huffing smoke and looking past each other. Allston walked up the slope to the van, which was parked above the house, and came back with a pint of Jack Black. He cut the seal with his pocket knife and spun off the cap.

"Starting early," Stell said to him, which was an understatement because everybody knew Allston didn't drink anything stronger than beer, and not much of that.

"Well," said Allston, "I'm done with my job for the day."

He kissed the rim and passed the bottle to me. I took a good enough belt to be convincing and handed it on. Stell stared at it a minute, then took ahold and bubbled it up. Around it went another time. Mindful I'd still have lead to play, supposing we ever got any vocals, I took a lighter pull than before. But when the bottle came back to Stell she made it go *gloog-gloog*.

Lumera was watching from the glass doors of the studio, half-smiling himself, curious, the swag of his beard looped across his chest like a watch chain. The bottle made the round once more, then Allston took it back and capped it. "Now go on in there," he said to Stell, "and try it with your eyes shut. Don't make any difference where you are."

"Whatever you say, Doc," Stell told him. She gave herself a little secret smile, stepped on her cigarette and went past him into the studio. Lumera reached out and slid the glass door shut behind her, then disappeared into the booth. That left me and Allston outside, watching Stell clamp on her headset, take her position behind the big boxy studio mike. Her eyes slid shut, as Allston had suggested, and maybe she was conjuring up some Black Cat atmosphere: smoke and whiskey smell, the sound of loose talk, whatever she might need to get herself going. Allston backed up a pace or two and sat down on a boulder in the midst of a patch of flowers. The soundproofing was good enough we couldn't hear a thing through the glass, but Stell's expression and the easy swing of her hips as she sang made me begin to feel hopeful.

"Think I might like to hear some of this," I said, but Allston was sticking to his rock. I went around to the other side of the house and down the inside stairway to reach the booth from that direction. The whole small space was booming with her voice, just slamming into the first chorus of "Too Late." Lumera was on the edge of his stool, alert as a fox hovering over a rabbit hole, ears pricked and eyes bright and his fingers light and lively tweaking one dial or another. When she was done, he let himself back down by slow degrees, then looked up at me with a grin and said, "I think you got it."

After that it all went easier, though we were in there the better part of a week. Stell crossed over "Anything Goes" without a wobble, giving it a big blues-mama belt. She took "Secret Heart" across just as well, with a bit of a country twang. That took care of two of the three that Perry used to sing, but like I suspected there hadn't been enough whiskey bottled yet to get Stell to do "Eight Mile." We did a rhythm track for it in case, but never could get the vocal—I figured we could just save what we had for later, for whenever Perry came back.

Once the vocals were wrapped, I brought Willard's Strat in to lay down the fills and a couple of short solos, and by that time I was actually enjoying myself. And next thing you know Lumera hit a button and out came our week of work on a DAT tape no bigger than a matchbox.

We all drove into Burlington to celebrate, Lumera included, all of us giddy from those days of concentration, and the pressure being let off at the end of it, listening to the cassette dub over and over on the Mustang stereo. Lumera steered us to a restaurant where musicians he knew hung out, and got the bartender, a long rawboned, sandy-haired dude name of Joyce, to play the tape for everybody there. This Joyce played bass, as it developed, and by the end of the night we had him signed up.

Lumera gave us a cut rate on a box of fifty dubs, and Allston and I spent the better part of a day sticking labels on tapes, copying a form letter, sticking it all into jiffy packs and scrawling out the addresses: upcoming Black Cats, plus alternative radio and the college stations. Perry had mailed me up the list and he told me I should get Lumera to go over it for an update, but it turned out pretty much on the money. So much so, you'd have thought Perry had done this sort of thing before, which was odd when he'd always declared himself to be dead set against it. But I was too busy, all of a sudden, to spend much time worrying over that. We just shoveled the jiffy packs into the mail and got on with it.

Joyce and Allston clicked solid right from the start—which in fact was a little funny for me. I'd look over my shoulder and see how well Joyce had dropped himself into my slot of the rhythm section and by damn I'd feel a twinge of jealousy almost, for Allston and I had always been a unit, and if Perry was sometimes subbing on bass, well that didn't take it out of the family. But after all it was what we needed, and it mattered more to have that solid backup there than for me to feel like I was irreplaceable on bass and . . . I knew that.

We managed a nice rally and comeback for our last week at the Vergennes Black Cat. Stell was singing at the top of her form, and Joyce and Allston were so dependable, they had me playing a consistent cut above my usual level on lead. When before I'd suffered from finger-stutter through about the first half of every first set, now I could relax and get with it right from the start. They were taxing evenings, with no rhythm guitar in back of me, but the more I saw I could meet the challenge, the more I began to kick back and enjoy it. People were coming back to hear us and the owner started looking cheerful again, and by the time we rolled out of Vergennes we had us a little fire in the tailpipe.

Next stop was Johnson, a good haul further north, in the Green Mountains just shy of the Canadian border. Even in mid-summer it was crisp and cold at night up there, so you needed a sweater to go out and watch the stars. Two weeks at a Black Cat outside of Johnson, then we started down the eastern side of the state: St. Johnsbury, Montpelier, Springfield, Brattleboro.

Estelle just could not get enough of our tape. Like she never had heard her own voice before. Which maybe she hadn't, at least not recorded—they say it sounds different inside your head. She would play the thing over and over and over, long after it had lost its fascination for the rest of us. But there was something innocent in that, so nobody baited or teased her about it. Stell had a hard shell covering most of her, so I guess nobody felt like banging her on it if once she showed a tender spot.

Except Rose-Lee. We were cruising down to Montpelier, I think; anyway we were on the road. I was driving the Mustang and it was a dreamy, warm sunny day, and I was far enough into high-way hypnosis that I didn't even register we were hearing "Red Dreams" one more time. Till Rose-Lee jerked up suddenly, cross from a crick-neck nap in the back seat, with a hair pattern mashed on one side of her face.

"Goddamn, Estelle," she snapped. "Would you *please* shut off that tape already?"

Stell turned and looked over the seat back, her dark eyes round and wide. "It ain't the tape," she said.

"What do you mean it ain't the tape?" Rose-Lee grumbled. "Heard that tape five hunnert times—don't you tell me it ain't the tape."

284

"It ain't the tape," Stell said, a little breathless. "It's the radio."

Right as she said that, they faded the coda and we all heard the smooth, vacant DJ voice: ". . . and that was Stella Houston with Anything Goes, starting tonight at blah-blah-blah . . ." I admit it, I almost ran off the road. Vermont was peppered with little low-power stations like that, most of which didn't carry more than forty miles, but still—*our song on the radio*.

The van overtook us in the right lane, and Stell rolled down her window and hung her head out, her hair sucking and whipping around her face, trying to holler across to them. Allston was behind the wheel, grinning and giving a big thumbs up, so I knew they must have heard it too.

And the house was full, packed to the doors, and even on the weeknights. In all the time I'd traveled with Perry I'd never known anything quite like it. We were hot in a way we'd never been. Estelle, especially, bloomed on the fresh energy. Her eyes were sparkling when she climbed on the stage, and her voice was stronger and richer than ever before. She stayed melodious in the breaks between sets, instead of dropping back into the flat cracker twang that was her ordinary speaking tone. It was like she was actually turning into *Stella Houston*, and not only when she was up there behind the microphone. Stray guys at the shows were attracted to this. Well, she'd always had her share of loose fools, sending her drinks and the like. But now she would actually flirt back, which was not something I had known her to do before. I don't know if she ever brought any of them all the way home, not that it was any of my business if she did. Stell was entitled to whatever fun, I reckoned, and I had plenty else to think about.

I started messing with the first set some, with the idea of playing up Stell in the starring role, now there was nobody for her to share the mike with. We went back to the trick of doing a few before she came out, blues instrumentals mostly. That was good for a bit of a surge when she finally climbed on the stand and let fly. But I felt like it wasn't working quite like it should have. With nobody to sing anything it was hard to get it to really build, plus which there was only so much could be squeezed out of instrumentals with just the one guitar, and nobody better than me to play it.

So one night after we'd run through a couple of standards and come to the point where I'd normally signal out Estelle, I found myself fingering the intro to "Eight Mile" instead. I guess I couldn't have done it if I'd planned it in advance, but Joyce and Allston zeroed in on it easy enough, and when the verse came around it wasn't so tough—I could get away with half-talking the words really, and bending nearer to the melody once I saw nothing terrible was going to happen. In fact the room was changing, but for the better—people were breaking off their conversations and turning toward the stand, and when it came time for the solo I knew I was going to pull it off.

Nothing . . . can make me look away. . . . I was still hearing that last line in my head, when Allston put a period on the solo with a big cymbal crash, and Stell came bounding out from the back like a real serious, heavyweight arrival. Call it a gimmick but at least it worked.

I started doing this pretty regular—"Eight Mile" as item three or four in the first set, and Estelle's cue to come in. The idea was to focus attention on her, but some of it ended up sticking to me. The words of the song accounted for some of that, I guess, along with the guitar strut at the end. I'd already caught on that playing lead got you noticed more by the ladies than standing off in the back with the bass, even if I wasn't half the musician Willard was and didn't play solos with my tongue like Chris would do when he wanted to show somebody something special.

But still there was plenty of good stuff coming my way, and a good deal more of it than usual, or maybe it only seemed like that because I was letting it all go by. Joyce bagged one now and then on the way by, I observed, and welcome to it. As for me, it seemed like I was waiting for something, only I didn't know what.

We made it down to Brattleboro on that same roll, still picking up a little airplay at the bottom end of the FM dial, still packing them pretty good at the local Black Cat. There was a problem with putting ourselves up, because the motel we had planned on folded a week or so before we got there. We spent a couple of nights at the downtown hotel, but that cost too much even though downtown Brattleboro wasn't all that ferociously metropolitan. Finally after some scrambling around I got us set up at a B&B on the highway west of town—a big old country house tucked back in the woods. They had a pond in the back with ducks on it, which I thought would be nice for James Culla, and they slung you a pretty good breakfast too.

So we got settled in, and played the first weekend of the gig, and Monday morning I slept late, because there was nothing to do that day for once, and that night we didn't have to play. It was late morning when I yawned my way downstairs. The house was empty, and out in the back, Stell and Rose-Lee were sunning themselves, sunk low in green Adirondack chairs, while James Culla crawled around on a quilt spread on the grass in front of them. James Culla was watching the ducks on the water, and after a minute he crawled off the edge of the quilt and made for the pond, his fat little body half-hidden in the grass, which didn't appear to have been mowed in quite some time.

Neither of the women seemed to notice his maneuver, which was unusual, for careless as their ways might seem, they never let the child get anywhere near to burning or drowning or doing any serious harm to himself. But maybe Estelle and Rose-Lee had dropped off to sleep at the same time. Stell had stayed late at the bar last night, I remembered, after the rest of us had packed up and left, saying she'd catch a ride later on with somebody in her local fan club.

I skipped down the steps to recapture James Culla before he dunked himself in the duck pond, but before I could get there a slight-built man with greying hair cut in from the side and gathered him up. He looked like he was somewhat accustomed to babies, for the child settled comfortably onto his hip. The man swiveled toward the water, pointing at the ducks that drifted there, then began using the same finger to probe James Culla's creases, checking for ticks, I imagined. I'd known who he was from the start, of course, but still it took me a minute to process that this was my daddy.

"Where'd you come from?" I blurted out, walking over toward them.

He gave an uneasy smile and a shrug that jounced James Culla on his hip. "Home," he said, and then after a minute, "I had a few more vacation days coming."

"Well," I said. "Good to see you." This felt true once I had said it. He got his right hand disengaged from James Culla, and held it out to shake.

"What time you get in?" I asked him.

Another shrug. "Pretty late."

James Culla reached out toward the glint of the chrome pressure gauge in the top pocket of Daddy's khaki shirt. Daddy let him pull it out. We both turned and looked back at the women, slumped in the sun in the deep green chairs. They had on heavy black bug-eye sunglasses, like what Jackie Onassis used to wear. Stell had a floppy straw hat to go with it—you couldn't tell if she was awake or asleep. I wondered how late she'd stayed out last night, and who with and where they finally wound up, and if Daddy would have surprised her with one of her Brattleboro fanciers, blowing in without warning like apparently he had. Then I just sort of shut off that thought.

James Culla was waving his pressure gauge at the pond. "Guck!" he hollered, splattering spit. "G-g-g-guck!"

"Guck is right," Daddy told him. Half a smile. Then James Culla slung the pressure gauge off in the grass somewhere, and Daddy walked over and crouched down to pick it up.

He stayed for a week, and it turned out to be an easygoing time. Most nights he'd only catch the first set at the Black Cat, and then go back and relieve Rose-Lee. That seemed a little odd at first, but Daddy put it out that there was a limit to how long he wanted to hang out in a bar, being he'd given up drinking and all.

The last day of his visit we all went on a picnic—me and Daddy and the women and baby that is, for Allston and Joyce went to an afternoon movie in town. There was a berry patch where you could pay to pick your own, and not far from that a sizable lake with a sandy shore, and a raft moored a hundred yards out, for divers.

We picked a pint or so of raspberries, and left the money in a tin box—it was that trusting kind of a place; there wasn't nobody tending it at all. At the lake we swam, then ate our sandwiches, chasing them with berries and beer. Daddy had brought a bag of Goo Goos up from Nashville, so James Culla got some chocolate smears over the top of the berry stains on his cheeks, and a lesson in how to say "Go get a Goo Goo—it's good!" After that we all went to sleep in the sun.

I woke up before the others, feeling kinky in my joints and a little bit chilled. Clouds had blown up across the whole sky, and everybody had left the lake but us. I walked up and down to shake myself out and then waded into the water, flinching a little as the cold climbed my legs. Then I swam out to the raft and climbed onto it and sat there a while with my legs dangling in, feeling the droplets dry across my back. The boards were still warm from the sunshine earlier, and now the lake was still and flat as a mirror reflecting the grey clouds in the sky.

Daddy sat up on his towel, collected James Culla, who was stirring around, and carried him down into the water. He backed in deep, maybe over his head, and swam a backstroke, holding the baby over his chest, smiling at the froggy swimming motions that James Culla made. They were far enough away from the raft they looked doll-size, but the laughter and splashing sounds came to me clearly, echoing from the surface of the water.

He's not here for me, I thought then, and not for Stell either. He's here for that baby. It seemed stupid not to have seen that before. All he wanted was a second chance. I thought that I wanted him to have it, and I thought that I wanted to have one too.

Estelle was up now, walking into the lake. She was wearing that trim black one-piece she had bought in Florida, and her hair was spread out loose on her back. There was a grace, a dignity, to the way she moved, and she didn't hesitate when the water climbed across her hips, her chest. I didn't know exactly when it was deep enough to float her off her feet, but I did see that she was swimming, the breaststroke, her chin held above the metallic mirror surface of the lake. I thought about that time in Florida, when it seemed I was maybe in love with her myself, when she told me she didn't know how to swim. But she was swimming now, and she looked pretty good at it. She must have been practicing, I thought, on the sly.

Nobody was getting hurt in this thing, I thought then. Unusual as it all might be, there wasn't any damage. That's the idea that came to me while I watched her swim toward the man and boy, a V ripple spreading out behind her, her face calm and steady above the still water.

It ended up we stretched out our run in Brattleboro by about two weeks. The owner brought it up to us—he had room in the schedule for the place, and we were still drawing steady. Of course that one change knocked down all the dominoes, for Perry had us booked tight, and I was forty-eight hours on the phone trying to get them balanced upright again. A good deal of shifting and zigzagging was required but in the end it all worked out except for the one Black Cat boss on the Jersey shore who lost his cool and flat out told me to go to hell and turn on a spit and never come back to bother him no more.

Well, all that meant was we'd be back to the regular program once we made it down to Virginia. And the money would shake out the same, so there was nothing lost—except a contact, Perry would have said, and the chance of any gigs at that Jersey Black Cat in the future. Perry was strong for being reliable, to a higher standard than your average roving bar band. That was what gave you an edge over the others. Perry wouldn't have liked what we done. But then, Perry wasn't around to complain about it.

And the fact was none of us was specially keen to leave Vermont. We'd had good luck there (after the trouble in Vergennes anyway) and the next leg of the trip would be milltown Massachusetts—Black Cats on the wrong side of whatever there was to be on the wrong side of, down at the dark end of the street—our usual venue, as far as that went. There wouldn't be any more Guernsey cows standing around looking like they were ready to squirt out Ben & Jerry's ice cream if only you stuck out your hand for it. On the other hand, you didn't really want to spend a winter in Vermont, with snow ten feet overhead and the cold that wouldn't leave your bones till summer.

Our mojo still seemed to be working pretty well, even in the Black Cats of North Adams and Northampton and places like that. The tape kept getting a little play, down at the bottom end of the dial, and from one town to another that seemed to help our draw. In Northampton some punked-out girl from the local underground rag came out to interview Estelle—wanted to know when there was gonna be an album. She made such a production of it, Stell hardly knew whether to laugh in her face or string her along. But afterward we drove on to the next town and forgot about it.

Our Black Cat of Worcester was an L-shaped roadhouse out on Highway 9 pretty much in the big middle of nowhere. There was a barroom with foosball and pool on the short end of the ell, and a stage and dance hall of sorts on the long one. Big parking lot out the back, which we kept three-quarters full most nights. And everything was business as usual till, after about three days in that place, we had shut down the final set and were filing out. I'd stayed behind talking to somebody on the stand, so I was lagging behind the others when I finally walked into the front bar, hauling Willard's Strat in the battered case. Somebody hailed me from a corner barstool.

"Sounding pretty good up there."

I knew the voice but I couldn't make out the face, which was partly blocked by a low-hanging lamp over the bar, and masked by a fog of cigarette smoke besides. But then he stepped down from the stool and I saw it was Perry. He had on a hat, which had thrown me at first—a canvas porkpie job with a fat plaid band. He took it off when he saw I was puzzled, and crumpled it up in his left hand. He had on dark pants and a suit coat, both with a narrow pinstripe, I saw when I got closer.

"Perry," I said.

He slapped me on the shoulder. "Come on and get a drink."

"You see the rest of them?" I asked him. "They were taking the van."

"Saw them go by," Perry said. "They didn't see me." He waved at the bartender, but the guy had already poured my postshow bourbon on the rocks. I noticed there was a pile of change and crumpled bills on the countertop by Perry's glass and ashtray.

"How come you didn't put yourself on the tab?"

Perry shrugged. "They might not of known me."

I took a closer look at him myself. He had got a haircut, and, it looked like, lost some weight. The dark suit seemed to hang on him, anyway—not that I was used to seeing him in a suit, either. He didn't have a tie or even a collar, just a blue T-shirt under the jacket. His neck was wrinkled, I noticed now, and turtled forward from the shirt collar.

"What in the hell are you talking about?" I said. But he did look different and that was a fact. I had been riding around on his coattails for so long, I hadn't been more than a day or so without seeing him in two or three years. He might have aged some in all that time, and me just finally noticing it now.

"What's with the suit?" I asked him.

Perry glanced down at his pin-striped cuff like he hadn't ex-actly been aware what he had on. "Looks good in court," he said with a smirk. "According to what the lawyers say."

"Oh yeah," I said. "They turn you loose?"

"Well not quite yet, not altogether. They'll have to in the long run though." Perry sent another sour smile toward the mirror be-hind the bottles on the bar. "Ain't got no case."

"You're here, anyhow."

"In a manner of speaking," Perry said, and shook a short Camel from his pack. I didn't quite know what to think about the way he put it. I'd been relieved when I saw him, assuming he was a hundred percent *back*, but the relief itself had felt a little like a let-down.

"Willard's out," Perry told me.

"Home free?" I said. "How'd he swing that?"

"Old Chastity ran around and made good on every last one of those checks he wrote," Perry said. "Nobody's pressing charges."

"There's a good-hearted woman," I said.

"With deep pockets too." Perry looked thoughtful. "Well, it ain't like she was dealing with the DEA."

"I guess Willard'll be wanting his guitar back," I said, feeling a bit uneasy at this thought. I had got very used to playing that Strat.

"No hurry," Perry said.

"He tell you that?"

"Sure—he don't need the meal ticket now." Perry snorted. "Lazy sumbuck, he'd of wanted it more if he *had* landed up in jail, I expect. They went back down to Florida anyway, him and her."

"Really," I said. "Heat's pretty serious down there in the sum-mer, so I been told."

"They ain't gonna be bothered by the heat," Perry said.

"They're planning to purchase a yacht and go sailing around in the cool ocean breezes."

"Oh," I said. "I guess that's one way to stay out of a card game."

Perry laughed, way down in his throat, and stubbed his cigarette out in the ashtray. He reached to his left and riffled a few pages of that music tabloid that came out of Northampton. "So when's the album?" he said, sly.

I felt a flush building up from my collarbones. "Hell, that was just blowing smoke at a reporter," I said. "We hadn't got songs enough for an album no-way."

Perry was studying me pretty serious. "*One* song can make an album, if it's the right song." He shrugged and looked away. "You could fill it out with covers—that's been done."

"Oh man. . . ." Couldn't believe it was Perry telling me this. I shook my head and waved down the bartender.

"Might ought to give it some thought, is all." Perry gave me a nudging grin. "Next fella comes around claiming he's an A and R man might actually be one."

I looked off in the other direction, toward the corner where a gang of college-looking jocks with thick-legged girls in polo shirts were shoving and grunting around the foosball table. I didn't quite like the looks of them—made my winter bruises hurt—though by any rational read they were harmless. Perry, meanwhile, was shuffling the paper. He folded it down quarter-size, to the picture. They had drug us out to some old abandoned mill for a photo shoot. The picture they ran had Estelle looking moodily out over the millstream, wind licking up her hair. She'd stuck in her tooth for this occasion, and you could just see the point of it in her faint smile. The rest of us were rowed off behind her along the bridge rail.

"You ought to try and get some prints of this," Perry said. "Might come in handy later on."

"Perry," I said. "When are you coming back to the band? I mean . . . there's nobody running this show but me, and I'm just drifting around in the dark."

Perry looked at me, hesitating, pale green eyes under the yellowing brows. "I'm not coming back," he said finally, and flagged the bartender for another beer.

"You're not coming back at all? What for?"

"Time for a change," Perry said.

"That's all you got for a reason?"

"I'll tell you," Perry said, picking at the label on his empty bottle. "I was in a band once, had a hit song. What, don't you believe me?"

"You never lied to me yet that I know of," I said. "I'm listening."

"All right then—listen to this." Perry pulled that tin whistle out of his jacket pocket and played a short line once, then again, looking a little impatient the second run-through. It took me a minute to get it because on the album it had been a flanged guitar.

" 'Touch Your Redeemer,' " I said. "Well I'll be damned. The Holy Rolling Seminoles. I pass the quiz?"

"Tell me who they were."

"The Whitehorn brothers. James and Ray."

"Looking good," Perry said. "And you still in diapers when they first came out."

"They still play it on the oldies stations."

"Once in a while," Perry agreed. "Bet you can't name the rest of the lineup."

I stared at the ice cubes melting in my drink. The Whitehorn brothers played drums and guitar—couldn't remember which did which. I tried to picture the album cover—there'd not been but that one first album.

"Neither can anybody else," Perry said. "Yeah. They had a couple of girlfriends singing *doo-wop* in the background and wiggling and banging on tambourines. Bass player was a black dude they called Buffalo Soldier. I had second guitar and harmony vocals. They made me wear war paint when we played out so nobody could see for sure I was a honky. All-Indian band was the angle. Of course they wasn't Seminoles any more than I was—just liked the sound of the name."

"They looked like Indians in the picture," I said. "The Whitehorns did."

"They were three-quarter Apache is what I was told," Perry said. "Started out playing in Austin and came up to Nashville in nineteen eighty-three or -four. There wasn't but one real song on that album, but it was enough to carry it, back then. Live shows they'd mostly just play blues standards, but goddamn they could bring you right out of your seat. That James played all over the guitar—he didn't hardly even need a bass player."

"He was the one got shot, wasn't he," I said, and reached toward Perry's pack of cigarettes, feeling the urge for something a little stronger. Perry nodded the go-ahead.

"Shot stone dead," he told me. "And I was right there watching. Well, I wasn't exactly watching."

"What happened," I said, lighting up.

"Usual story," Perry said. "It had a couple of wrinkles, I guess. James and Ray were half-crazy already by the time I met up with them. They'd come up huffing gasoline and chewing peyote on the rez, and I don't know what else. Time they got to Nashville they were both drunk about twenty-two hours a day and taking all the speed they could lay hands on so they could stay up to keep on drinking. When we first saw folding money from the record they invested a lot of it in coke. Record company had us doing a god-damn stadium tour all over the country. It was bigger halls than we could handle so the shows didn't always go that well, and James and Ray would fight afterwards and tear up the hotel rooms. They would quarrel over women or stealing each other's dope or who had really wrote more of the damn song than the other one. They never could get their heads together to write another song."

Perry pulled on the fresh beer he'd been served and looked at himself in the bar mirror. "So about three-quarters through this tour we were swinging through Texas and the Whitehorns had this big family party with about a hundred cousins and every-body's ex-wife and ex-husband and illegitimate father, whatever. Went all afternoon eating buffalo chili and drinking beer. We were supposed to play that night just for the party but around sundown the hard-core started drinking hard liquor and popping ups. Then pretty soon they all broke out guns and started shooting at each other."

Perry laughed, bitter, and shook his head. "Sort of a family pastime, what I heard later. Normally they were all so whacked they couldn't of hit the broad side of a barn, so nobody expected to really get hurt. Course I wasn't looking for any of this—I thought I'd blundered into a bad Western. There was an old alu-minum johnboat laying in the yard and I dove under that and stayed down till it was over. By the time I crawled out, James was laying there with a twenty-two slug in his brain and the sheriffs had hauled Ray off for manslaughter."

"And the rest is history," I said.

"Right," Perry said. "Read all about it in *Rolling Stone*. There wasn't no band without James in it. Plus Ray pulled about five

years in some badass Texas slammer. The lawyers ate up what was
left of the dough, and there you have it. With a ribbon and bow."

"What did you do?"

"Came back to Tennessee and went on the revival circuit."

"I heard that rumor somewhere."

"Yeah," Perry said. "It's only rock and roll—the audience is a
little bit different, of course."

"Did you really handle snakes?"

"That's God's own truth, boy," Perry said, projecting the
preacher voice from low in his belly. A couple of people turned
from the foosball game to look, and Perry dropped back to his
normal speaking tone. "I tell you what," he said. "I had a pretty
reasonable drug problem myself by the time the Seminoles broke
up. But if you're willing to reach in the tank and pick yourself up
a six-foot rattlesnake, that monkey will hop right off your back
and scramble for the jungle. There's nothing like it, really. Good
hit of snake at a Sunday night service would keep me quiet till the
next weekend."

"You ever get bit?"

"Everybody gets bit," Perry said. "Once bitten, twice shy."

"It doesn't always have to be like that," I said. "Does it?"

"Maybe not," Perry said. He knew I was talking about the
band again. "It's not that I want to rain on your parade. I'm wishing you luck as far as that goes. And you're welcome to stay out on
the farm when you get back, and practice in the house and all, and
you're welcome to any advice I can give you—but just don't cut
me in. I been there once and I'm satisfied."

"Well okay," I said. "I guess I know better than think I can win
an argument with you."

Perry didn't say anything to that, but looked off toward the

mirror behind the bar. I thought about his parable of the copperhead and the watersnake and the lack of a visible difference between them. Which one have I got a hold of now? I wondered, but
for once the question didn't scare me.

"What're you gonna do, though?" I said. "You plan to quit
playing altogether?"

"For a while, maybe. Think I'll lay out and think up a new
trick. At school they used to say I had a short attention span." Perry
stood up and gathered some of his bills from the bar, leaving
enough for a hefty tip.

"Going somewhere?" I asked him.

"Gotta fly back to Nashville at eight in the morning."

"That was quick," I said. "Blink and we miss you."

"Well, I need to get back before the fuzz check on me," Perry
said. "I'm not exactly supposed to be traveling—just wanted to
run up and see if you were handling things." His hand fell on my
shoulder again. "Looks to me like you are."

In the middle of that night I woke up with a jump like somebody
had fired a starter's pistol right in my ear—in reality it was quiet
enough in the room, though, except for Allston's easy breathing.
Allston was too well disciplined to snore. Forty words for fear was the
words in my mind—I didn't know where they had come from. I
was staring at the dead musician's feet and legs like they were
printed on the ceiling, though that was just a memory of something from a magazine, and I knew it was brought on by Perry's
tale about the Seminoles. Just the feet, the legs, stretched across a
ratty-looking carpet. The rest of Kurt Cobain had been unprint-
able, at that point. I couldn't recall if it had been in the actual

photograph or not but in that image I was projecting on the ceiling I could also see the stock of the shotgun he had used, lying about level with his knees. Somehow, instead of being in whatever room it had been, he was laid out under the shadow of tall black trees, on a wide cold blanket of crystal-blue snow.

My head was thumping and my mouth was dry from too much smoking and the extra drinks I'd had with Perry, and it felt like somebody had driven a railroad spike through my left wrist. I got up, softly, and crept toward the crack of light that outlined the bathroom door. There always had to be some kind of nightlight because the rooms were always changing, so you'd end up crashing into things, walking the wrong floor plan in the dark. As it was, I had to pay attention to avoid Allston's drum cases, though he'd stacked them along the wall neat as he could.

The fluorescent glare inside the bathroom was an ugly shock, and my face floating in the mirror looked like it had been raised from the dead. My temples beat a slow bass line, swinging gently in four-four time, but the music wasn't Nirvana. It was Neil Young, from *Sleeps with Angels,* the memorial album for Cobain—second track. I turned on the cold tap and sucked down a couple of aspirin, listening to the chord progression unfold: D minor, G minor seven, then the quick change up from B-flat to C which was the signature, and back to the top. Easy guitar. Like usual with him, it was the texture that made it interesting—the tune and the background tracks were syrupy sweet, and his singing high and shiny like it would sometimes get, but there was an overlay of guitar distortion that gave it a more ragged edge, and on the bridge he'd actually dubbed in the howling of coyotes.

I ran hot water over my left wrist, letting the pain wash down across my palm and out my fingertips—the pain was all illusion anyway, from the scare Perry's story had thrown at me. For some reason I was thinking about my first guitar, the little Yamaha acoustic Daddy got me when I was eleven and smashed against the doorframe of my room about six years later. I'd come too far for him to whip me anymore by then, and it had been a long time since I'd even played the Yamaha. I had already bought my Les Paul, the one I sold later on when I lost my nerve to play it, and Daddy would never have touched that guitar. The strings were rusted on the Yamaha, and smashing it was no more than a gesture, except that I could see, as we looked at each other across the splintered box and the curling strings, that he'd done something truly awful, only not to me this time but to himself. Now I looked at myself in the mirror above the sink and saw the shadow of his face in mine, and thought that maybe that had been his recoil point, the place you have to come back from, or else you don't come back. He went on drinking a couple of years more after I moved out of the house, but instinct told me now that that was where it must have begun, his whole project of making himself into something more like what he wanted to be.

I turned off the hot water and watched the last steamy swirls of it go spiraling down the drain. The Neil Young tune was still going in my head and I considered dropping it into the set, but Estelle wouldn't sing it; the lyrics were sappier than she'd tolerate, though I'd have found it fun to play. *Forty words for fear* . . . Just that phrase and the ghost of a notion. It seemed to me I could hear a big snarling guitar line swelling up behind it. I saw I was going to get another song out of this. It wouldn't be a Neil Young song, but I thought it might be something he'd like.

Say what you will about old Neil, he'd outlived a lot of dead musicians, and when you added it all up, he'd written and played more good material than about all the rest of them put together, and he was still doing it too. So it didn't always have to be one way. For a minute I assumed it was Perry explaining this point, like usual, but then it wasn't Perry's voice in my head—it was mine.

Somewhere in Jersey I bought a B.B. King box set, fifty bucks for four CDs and pretty near fifty years' worth of his career. The photos from the early days all showed him beaming out this big watermelon-eating smile—the fat happy musical darky mask that I guess was pretty much the required disguise for any black musician way back then. Just imagine going through a couple decades of that sort of thing, and then still turning out to be B.B. King— though that wasn't why I'd bought the album. In part it was a backlash against all the Springsteen you got asked to play along the Jersey coast, but mainly I wanted to listen to B.B.'s phrasing, figuring it would be good for me, my limitations. B.B. didn't play such a whole lot of notes usually, but somehow he always sounded stronger, truer, than all the faster, flashier guitarists. I knew there would be lessons in there somewhere. I spent my afternoons breaking down the licks, with the CD jacked through a headphone amp. By the time we got down to Delaware we were playing a fair sampling of B.B. King every show—his few originals plus stuff he'd covered, in his style.

I came to appreciate how tight Perry had timed us to the weather, for with the two-week delay I'd thrown into the schedule, we were seeing our breath the last few days in every town on the slow road south. But in Ocean City we caught up with ourselves, and overtook calm, lazy Indian summer days. Last gig of our summer run, and afterward we'd come surfing into Nashville on that wave of extra attention the tape had bought us, and then . . . I'd probably go see what Chris had been up to, I thought, while we were gone. There might be something more to play and record. Maybe the genuine A&R man Perry had predicted, or maybe not. For once it didn't worry me, not knowing.

It was my birthday, but I didn't tell anybody. I took a day out at the beach and the boardwalk, swimming and sunning myself till my skin just barely tingled. I ate two shrimp cocktails and drank a pint of beer. I was feeling glad enough to be alive, though truth to tell I had a queer hollowed-out feeling too.

When we got cranked up at the Black Cat, the music seemed to pour into that empty space. We were making changes in the set lists that seemed to happen by telepathy, one association feeding into the next like they will do if the mojo's working right. Stell was singing above and outside of herself all night, and I saw that the thing that had happened with her and Chris at their peak was beginning again, only this time I was all the way inside it with her, instead of watching it from out along the edges.

We closed with "Too Late," like we always did now, except that I wasn't quite ready to quit, so as Allston was beginning the close-out cymbal shiver, I signaled him to roll on through and keep going. We came out at the top in the key of D minor, a couple steps up from where we usually play it. I cued Estelle by leaning across into her mike and saying the title "The Thrill Is Gone." She gave me a look but picked it up without any problem, more than a fair amount of enthusiasm really, even when on a whim I dropped in the bridge that *Albert* King had added when he knocked off B.B.'s song as "The Feeling." I had to nudge Stell along through that bit, because she didn't know it, but I whispered the words into her ear during the fills, and she stayed with it. Then we were safely over the bridge and back with B.B.'s lyric, and in the closing solo I lifted those same words up again on the crest of the guitar line: *I I I I I'm free now . . . I'm free from your spell. . . .*

Let it ring. The others packed up and headed out, but I was in no hurry to get back to that motel, even if they were beginning to stack chairs on the back tables of the Black Cat. There were a few other people lingering too, friends of the management free to hang out after hours, but I sat by myself at the corner of the bar, still feeling a pleasant tingle from the sun and the wind and the music.

"Legal at last," I said, as a toast, when the bartender brought my bourbon.

"What's that you say?"

"It's my birthday," I told him. "Twenty-one."

And he gave me a look of real disgust, then started wiping his way down the counter from me with a dishcloth. "You been boozing it up in here for what, how long?" he grumbled. "Ought to cut you off now for a couple of years to make up for it." The guy was actually ticked off, but he wasn't getting to me. Nothing was, but a woman's voice, light and husky, to my left.

"Well—happy birthday."

I swiveled the stool. White shirt, black jeans, pretty much the same as the last time I'd seen her. It was Brown-Eyed Sue, but I realized I didn't want to call her that.

"Susan."

She ducked her head and pressed her lips together. It was odd how clearly I remembered all these little gestures. *Clean* was the main impression she made, and trim in her black and white.

"Didn't think you'd remember," she said. "I wasn't going to come. Then I wasn't going to say anything. But. . . ."

"It's my birthday," I said. "After all."

"Yeah." She tossed back her hair. "Got some new songs, I notice."

"I wrote a few this time around," I said, and looked at her sidelong to see where that might get me.

"That was a good one, the one you sang," she told me, but then her eyes narrowed and slipped away. "The one about the stripper."

But that's not me, I wanted to tell her, that's not who I am in that song, it's just a made-up thing, piece of this and a piece of that. Taste of Sweet Lorraine on my tongue, and blood in my mouth from the beatings I'd taken. I'd buried all that in the song because it was the best way I could think of to get rid of it. Maybe that was what all the songs were for.

There was no way I could tell her all this because I just wasn't going to get enough time. I was near enough to breathe the clean smell of her hair, but I could feel her balance shifting.

"Wait," I said, I hoped not too fast. "I was hoping to see you."

"You what?" Smile like a cat and an arch of her back. "You're seeing me now." But she knew what I meant. She was thinking it over.

"Dinner," I said, "or a movie, go to the beach . . ." Or just about anything but keeling over on top of each other, three-quarters drunk in a mildewed motel room. I could see she was still thinking about it.

"Maybe," she said. The brown eyes cleared. "I guess . . . all right. We could."

"Let's do it tomorrow."

"Oh . . . all right." She smoothed her hair and gave me a smile with no twist in it. "If you're gonna be free."

ABOUT THE AUTHOR

Madison Smartt Bell is the author of twelve previous works of fiction, including *All Souls' Rising*, which was a National Book Award finalist; *Save Me, Joe Louis*; *Dr. Sleep*; *Soldier's Joy*; *Ten Indians*; and *Master of the Crossroads*. He lives in Baltimore, Maryland.